SLAUGHTER MUSIC

Other Foul Play Press books
by the same author

Payback

SLAUGHTER MUSIC

Russell James

A Foul Play Press Book

The Countryman Press, Inc.
Woodstock, Vermont

THIS BOOK IS FOR
PETER DAY AND JANE CONWAY-GORDON

'In whom I trust most,
soonest me deceiveth'

Richard Hill's Commonplace Book of 1530

1

That's the one: that house half-hidden through a tangle of trees and shrubbery behind a wall. Not as difficult as it looks. High brick wall; jagged glass at the top. Looks vicious, doesn't it? That's some wall – it has been there a while. But weather has softened the edges of those broken glass teeth: wind and rain, snow settling. The sharpness has gone. D'you remember how it feels when you pick up a piece of bottle glass from the beach – all the edges worn down? Well, up on top of that old wall there, the glass will be like that. Won't hurt you at all.

Tim Hawk reached down below the dash and switched off the music. He had taken this last mile slowly, waiting to hear the climax of the aria before he cut it to watch the house. A few moments ago, when he crawled round the corner of this respectable lane where Darren lived, the thrilling trumpets had peaked. Tim had braked, closed his eyes to concentrate on the finish. Only then did he move the van gently to his spot, seventy yards from Darren's house. He braked again and cut the engine. Now he wound the window down three inches so he could listen. Breezes among the trees. Night stillness. As his ears absorbed the near silence he began to detect other sounds behind the breeze: an occasional car in the distance; faint music from a distant radio; somebody's dog.

Up here were the leafy suburbs. Even the name of the place – Woodside Park – underlined the leafy image. These houses were owner-occupied, respectable, set independently apart in leafy gardens. Leafy trees and leafy shrubbery planted out in rows. House lights filtering through leafy branches.

People up here expected privacy and security. They expected their houses to be separate from their neighbours, expected the houses arranged so they would not be overlooked. Which suited Hawk. Glancing at his watch, he saw the digits advance to 6.45. He took a breath. When he first picked this time of evening he had worried that it might be too busy; anyone commuting from the City should arrive home around this time. But it hadn't been like that. Hawk had been here twice before and each time the lane was quiet. Last time when he hung around, he noticed that in two of the houses, men slunk home about 7.30. Maybe they had had a drink before they left. That was their affair. But Hawk had made a note of the particular houses: he was a stickler for things like that.

Satisfied that the lane was dead, he switched on the ignition, eased the van forward. After fifty yards he stopped, turned the engine off again, wound the window fully up. Then he slipped the keys out from the ignition, placed them beneath the driver's seat, out of sight. In his pockets they might jingle; under the seat they would be safe. Not that anyone stole cars in Woodside Park. No criminal types around here. Except Darren.

Hawk pulled a tweed cap from his jacket pocket, put it on to obscure his white-blond hair. Then he picked up his canvas gun-bag, stepped out into the lane and paused a moment beside the van. He set down the bag. Useful spot, this: the light from the nearest lamp-post was veiled by a large lime tree. The van was not invisible, but was not conspicuous either. Hawk pushed the door quietly into place, then unhooked the ladder from the side. It was wooden, a single piece, seven feet long. The ladder was heavier than a metal one but was quieter, no clanks. When this wooden ladder banged against something, it would make only a muffled thud. Hawk placed it against the outside of Darren's garden wall. Taking the long canvas bag in his left hand, he ran up the ladder and sat straddled. He shifted his backside, but he couldn't feel the broken glass. Smooth as pebbles on the beach. In a quick, silent movement he pulled the ladder up and flipped it so it leant against the other side. Then he climbed down and waited in the shrubbery. It was damp, dark, silent as midnight. Hawk had been in once before – he knew that the sensors did not reach this far: they cut in somewhere around the edge of Darren's well-cut lawn.

Hawk slung the canvas bag across his shoulder, collected the wooden ladder, carefully picked his way through mud and shrubbery towards the rear. This time he had come equipped. At the side of the house he knew there was another sensor: like the front one, its range also petered out before it reached the shubbery. The infra-red detector scanned an arc across the lawn and gravel paths. Any movement within twenty yards would set it off: just the lights, he assumed, nothing more. No silent, internal alarm. Last time he had come here, Hawk had been crouching in the bushes when a cat had strolled across the lawn, setting off those outdoor lights. The cat paid no more attention than to a notice telling it 'Please Keep off the Grass'. It continued its stately stroll, paused to scratch, disappeared round the back. Hawk had crouched unmoving among the bushes, watching the house. He had seen a curtain twitch – didn't catch the face. He decided then that the lights probably flicked on several times an evening: sometimes a person might look out, sometimes not. The lights were a deterrent, not a guarantee you would be seen. But they posed a risk Hawk could not take.

They had to be dealt with.

He waited two minutes in the dark, until, as expected, the front door opened. He heard voices from the front, heard her calling back to her husband. 'Bye darling. Don't do anything I wouldn't do.'

The burglar lights came on. 'You can count on that.' Darren's voice.

A car door opened. She said, 'I'll be back about half-past nine.'

'Yeah, as usual.' The car door slammed.

All around the house, spotlights illuminated the Darren gardens, colouring the grass stark yellow-green. Hawk watched the windows.

3

She called, 'Bye then. Don't push yourself too hard.'

'Yeah, yeah.'

A second car door opened, then closed.

The lady was a little early tonight, Hawk thought: nearly caught him out. He was already moving forwards through the shrubbery when he heard the engine start. All the time Darren stood watching the car drive away, he and his bodyguard would expect their garden lights to stay on – they were the ones who set them off. It wouldn't occur to them that this could be the very moment someone else might slip inside.

Hawk nipped across the side lawn with his ladder and bag, leant the ladder against the wall, then climbed up. Carefully, he draped his cap across the protruding sensor and climbed down. He heard the front door close. He waited beside the wall, his ladder prominent as a scar in the glaring floodlights, till he heard the creak of Darren's automatic gates swinging slowly shut. He heard them clunk into place.

Hawk waited thirty seconds till the outdoor lights switched off. Around the house, those little sensors were sending their beams out through the dark – except the one above him on the side wall, where it had been decommissioned. Cautiously, Hawk moved away from the wall into the dark. Nothing happened. No lights came on. Confident now, he picked up his bag, removed the ladder from the wall, carried both to the rear extension. The lights stayed off. He slipped into a dark recess beside the bins and began to wait.

Time slowly passed. Last week when Hawk had watched the house from the shrubbery, it had been five minutes before Darren had switched the lights on in the back. His brick-built extension had slit windows about eight feet above head height. Hawk believed he knew what lay behind them, and he assumed Darren would go in again tonight. Twice a week his wife went out to evening classes – art on Tuesday, pottery Thursday – whiling away her leisure time with the middle-class, getting her hands daintily dirty, though she'd be the only one in the class with a bodyguard outside.

4

Through the slit windows from the extension, Hawk saw the interior lights come on. It had to be Darren, Hawk reasoned, not his bodyguard in there.

He continued to wait.

He was glad he had chosen to wear a black rollneck sweater beneath the rainproof jacket, because the night air had grown cold. He flexed his fingers inside black leather gloves. He clenched and unclenched his toes. Eventually he stirred.

From the dark recess Hawk emerged. Silently, he took the short ladder to a spot below one of those slit windows, and gently leant it against the wall. The ladder reached to about a foot below and a foot to the left of that gleaming slit window. Hawk unfastened his canvas bag, brought out his rifle, dropped the bag softly on the ground.

Climbing the wooden ladder, Hawk was as quiet as a squirrel running up a tree. But at the top he found the ladder uncomfortably short. With the upper part of his body unsupported, there was nothing he could hold but the wall. He had the rifle in his left hand and he grasped the brick edge of the window aperture with his right. He felt unstable. His chest pressed against brickwork. This was a slip-up in his planning: he had tried so hard not to make mistakes. Hawk believed that meticulous rehearsal should eliminate things like that.

Slowly he leant across to peer through the high slit window. There he was. From Hawk's high viewpoint he could see the whole interior of the small gymnasium. The far side was clad with wall-bars. There were two exercise machines, a bike, an array of weights in one corner. Darren was in the cradle of the larger exercise machine, wearing a loose white tracksuit. He sat in a padded black vinyl seat, had two chrome handles to heave on, and a rack of weights behind his head. He looked fully occupied. But at the entrance to the gymnasium Hawk noticed another man, fully dressed: Darren's bodyguard.

Hawk moved his head a few inches to the left, back from the bodyguard's line of vision, but still in a position where he could watch Darren fiddling with the machine. Hawk eased his rifle

5

from his left hand to his right. He felt precarious. Balanced on top of the seven-feet ladder, there was no easy way he could hold the rifle with both hands. He couldn't fire it one-handed like a pistol – yet from the position he was in, that might be the only way.

Darren said, 'Don't think you can stand watching me all night.' He was lying on his vinyl squab, addressing his bodyguard at the door.

The man grunted.

'Go put your feet up. We got some peace the next two hours.'

'If you say so, Mr Darren. You don't need me?'

'The fuck for?'

'Right.'

Which was understandable, Hawk thought. Darren wouldn't want to exercise in front of his bodyguard. He wouldn't want to sit straining in his vinyl armchair while the man leant against the door-jamb smoking cigarettes.

As he squirmed carefully to lean his left shoulder against the brickwork, Hawk felt the ladder shift. He paused. There didn't seem any easy way he could get himself positioned with the rifle. If he could just turn a little more and lean over, he might be able to manage . . . but he also might go crashing to the ground. The damn ladder was definitely too short. This part of the job should have been rehearsed properly at home.

From inside the gymnasium Hawk heard weights scraping along the rack, Darren grunting. The slob should be out here wobbling on this ladder, Hawk thought, then he'd lose some weight. He wondered what had happened to that gopher – had he put his feet up or was he on the prowl? If the bodyguard was on duty, he might take a look around. Maybe he only worked from nine to five.

Hawk decided that if he had been sure of his footing on this ladder, he could have taken both men from up there. Smash the window, drop the bodyguard. Take out Darren as he clambered from his chair. But the way things were, he was too restricted in his movement: he'd have to smash the window, get resettled for his first shot, move again to reaim. It could take five seconds. Even without the bodyguard, Darren would have time to jump for it. There was nothing holding him in that chair. He could be off across the floor, out of sight below Hawk's window. To get a shot at him down there, Hawk would have to lean right through, feet off the ladder . . .

Christ, it's cold out here.

When he shivered, the ladder shook beneath his feet. One thing was sure – while there were two men in the gym there was no way to predict what might happen. Hawk wanted this scheme to run to plan.

Maybe this was not such a good idea. Too clever. Maybe a better way would have been to call at the front door, bold as brass – be a charity collector, something like that. All he had to do was take out the bodyguard, there on the step, slip through the house to the gymnasium. Easy. Why had he not chosen the easy way? The house wasn't overlooked, he could pop the bodyguard without a sound: he had a silencer. Oh yes, Hawk remembered now: this was a house where you could not walk to the front door. You had to stand at the front gate and jabber through the entryphone. Great. You do that, seven o'clock at night, and the bodyguard was not going to come traipsing down the path – not in the dark. Maybe Hawk could pretend to make a delivery – pizza perhaps – get the bodyguard to let him in.

What the hell was this, churning through his head? Hawk's mind was racing in the cold. No, *this* was the way to do it, the way he planned: one crack to break the window, one single shot. Neat and precise. Tidy. A quick and clinical way to die. Forget the bodyguard – he was not in the contract.

A hitman had to be meticulous about things like that, Hawk believed. Once again he peeped down through the slit window. Darren was still sweating on his machine. The vinyl squab did not look comfortable for a man to die on – it was like a dentist's chair. Who would want to die on a thing like that? Hawk clenched the rifle in his right hand, breathed out through his teeth.

7

A film of mist settled on the pane of glass. He thought about that glass – wondered how tough it would turn out to be. Darren would hear it break, look up, see the gun . . .

There was no way round that: he would see it coming before he died. If the glass had not been there, Hawk could have waited till Darren heaved on his chrome bar, till he pulled the weights up in the air – then popped him. That way, Darren would not have known a thing. One moment he would be here – the next gone. Finish. Completo. He wouldn't even hear the rack of weights come crashing down.

Hawk ran his fingers along the bottom of the window-frame. It would not ease open. There was no way other than to smash the glass. So it would not be clinical, this death. Darren would hear the window smash; would drop the heavy weights; would try to scramble from the exercise machine, then get a bullet in the chest.

For him, death would not come as a total surprise. The last two seconds of his life, in fact, would seem particularly vivid, though, of course, he wouldn't live to remember them.

Hawk stoops over the basin and rinses his face a second time. The tepid water caresses his skin, leaving him pleasantly alert. The light above his bathroom mirror is the only one on. It has a coral shade – a warm note in the functional beige-tiled bathroom – which concentrates the glow on Hawk's mirror and leaves the rest of the room subdued.

Though it is now a little after eleven o'clock, it will be at least an hour before Hawk goes to bed. His brain is filled with tumbling thoughts. He is completely, satisfyingly, awake.

Earlier, he discarded the warm black outdoor clothes and took a long hot contemplative bath. Now, refreshed, he strolls around his sitting-room, damply naked beneath a burgundy towel bathrobe. The deep red adds a pink flush to the usual pale pallor of his skin. Tim Hawk is medium height, lean build, with pale blue eyes. He is twenty-one years old. At first sight, you might think him a poet or doctor: something about his face suggests he lives

8

on close terms with pain. In that first glance, he might appear delicate – almost pretty – though his pale skin will seem as polished and hard as ivory. He seems self-contained, guarded, even shy – like a favourite child grown up. Which he isn't. Older women want to mother him; younger ones don't try.

He chooses a CD and slips it in the machine. The track that he particularly wants to hear is that second soprano aria from *Alexander's Feast*, 'Darius, great and good'. Hawk finds it stimulating. Its sombre mystery suits his mood.

On his glass-topped table is a bottle of chilled white wine. He pours a glass and carries it with him around the room, nodding his head to the knell-like beat of Handel's dirge.

> Fall'n, fall'n, fall'n, fall'n,
> Fall'n from his high estate
> And welt'ring in his blood.

The violin ostinato sends shivers through the air, and the bass chorus repeats the words.

> Fall'n, fall'n, fall'n, fall'n . . .
> On the bare earth expos'd he lies,
> With not a friend to close his eyes.

Hawk's flat is uncluttered, with a minimal array of dark modern furniture and a single grey long-pile rug upon the floor. The flat is the one place he can relax. Though his long curtains are closed, he is aware of the blue-black darkness beyond the windows, lights across the river, another world. He refills his wineglass, lies down on the black low-slung settee that is more a hammock than a seat, and he listens to the music.

These undisturbed monastic evenings have become a luxury to him. Almost all his life he has felt himself crammed against other people. Sometimes, as a child, he had not even a bedroom of his own: he had to share a small dormitory. And when he did have his own room, they never let him lock his door. Even when fostered, the bedrooms he slept in were not *his* rooms, they were foreign territory, the foster parents' property, their world. The houses, too, were foreign territory, with their own language, laws and smells. Wherever he was placed, the smells were the first thing to strike him, ambushing him at each unfamiliar front door. Family houses smelt differently from Children's Homes: sweet flowery polishes, the last cooked meal. Sometimes the foster parents had cleaned their house especially to welcome him, but the powdery fragrances formed another barrier, wrapping every stick of furniture in a prohibitive protective cloak. Don't sit there, you'll disturb the cushions. Don't rest your fingers on my polished wood.

Before long, those synthetic smells would be replaced by strange odours in odd corners: unfamiliar perfumes, the smell of vegetables. Then, eventually, somebody would make their first furtive defecation. Everyone would pretend they hadn't noticed that unmistakeable smell of shit as it crawled along the corridors. The stench was inescapable in the cramped space of private houses. What made it worse was that everyone knew exactly who had made the smell – there was no anonymity, as in the Home. Hawk dreaded those cloying intimacies of family life: whenever he was assigned to a new house he became constipated for a week.

Now he lives alone. In his small riverside flat he receives few visitors. He owns few possessions – not because he can't afford them but because he does not like to be crowded in. Each piece of furniture Hawk acquires has to be new, unused and clean. There is only one picture on his wall – a reproduction of a gem-bright Renaissance *Madonna* – though he seldom looks at it any more. He prefers to stand at his large window and watch the Thames.

This evening, lying on the low-slung settee, eyes closed, hand drooping to the empty wine glass on the floor, Tim Hawk reviews the last hours with satisfaction. He is a young man setting out on his career: his first killing. Everything is proceeding nicely to his plan. Entering the garden at the same time the wife left for her evening class had foiled the security lights, and his trick with the cap had overcome the sensor. Hawk never normally wore a cap, but he felt that in Darren's street he had to hide his soft blond hair – albino's hair, Raggs called it. Hawk pauses: he had missed Raggs. But the taunt still annoys him, as if the word albino was an insult – an ugly word describing someone whose blood and vigour has been sucked out. Hawk does not see himself like that. His blood flows more vigorously than Darren's, at any rate. But then, he is younger than that old man. Darren looked overweight and slowing down, leading that punk gang of his too long, with other people to do his running: kids like Hawk, maybe, keen beginners, who made sure they got things right. Through the misted slit window of the gymnasium Tim had watched the man sweat as he hauled upon his weights. He had watched that ill-shapen body, those rolls of fat. Darren's thick treacly red blood, already half-congealed, must have had to squeeze its way through his veins. Hawk had stayed motionless on his ladder, studying his quarry, enjoying the exhilaration of watching secretly from the dark. A night breeze had ruffled his hair, and a slight dampness had wet his cheek. Behind him in the garden lay a reassuring silence. The only sounds he could hear were those leaking from the gym: springs creaking, weights thumping to the floor, Darren grunting as he breathed. He had haunches like an ox – too much flesh. Too solid flesh.

Afterwards, when Hawk left, he found his wooden ladder had seemed no heavier than a javelin. He retraced his steps beneath the trees, crossed the wall, rehooked the ladder on the side of his old van. He fired the ignition, left the van with engine ticking, slipped back across the wall beneath the trees. On the side wall of Darren's house, Tim's cap remained hooked over the sensor. Hanging from his cap was a length of string, the ball resting on the ground. Hawk collected the ball, played it out across the lawn, and stood in the shrubbery beyond the sensor's range. He was not certain that this final step would work; it hadn't been rehearsed yet. But when Hawk yanked the string, his cap flopped obediently to the ground and lay inert in the shadows like some small dead animal. Nothing else happened. No lights came on. Exposed to the chill night air, the sensor's infra-red beam resumed its search for any warm-blooded creatures that might cross its path. Hawk gently pulled the string and the cap twitched, as if the small dead animal had come to life. The lights remained off. Hawk pulled again. Jerkily in the darkness, his small dead cap hopped across the lawn.

2

At 9.32, Clive Darren's wife arrives home. The gates, activated by the handset on her dash, swing open, and her car crunches across the gravel. Mrs Darren steps out, sniffs the night air and gazes at the starless sky as if it were a slide from her art class. Rothko, perhaps.

While the driver puts the car away, she lets herself into the house. Quiet. No music playing. She can't hear the TV, so there seems little chance of Darren being in the sitting-room. But she looks anyway. Not there. As she starts down the hall she hears two clinks, a deeper clunk. She walks past the stairs to a room at the side. Again she hears the clunk. Mrs Darren pushes the door open: 'You the only one home?'

The bodyguard in shirtsleeves leans across the snooker table, cue in hand. 'He's still at it.'

She tosses her head. 'Hope it's worth it.'

The bodyguard grins. He fancies Mrs Darren. 'Has to keep himself nice for you – you know, an older man and all.'

She turns away. 'He doesn't do it for me.'

I would, the man thinks.

She leaves before her irritation shows. Playing snooker as if he owns the place. What the hell? The man isn't paid to work twenty-four hours; he is entitled to time off. She just wishes that Darren's minders didn't have to spend so much of it beneath her roof.

She decides to make herself some coffee. When Darren finally does give up he can fix his own. Come to that, perhaps she could make herself a real drink. To hell with coffee, Christ. No, baby, no – don't even think of it. Have coffee. Mrs Darren is proud of the way she has cut down on alcohol. The way she sees it, if she rations the stuff strictly she won't have to quit entirely. Twenty-one units a week. OK, so twenty-one is supposed to be the man's ration, fourteen for women, but Christ, can't she drink it like a man? Outdrink most of them.

Mrs Darren stares at the kettle. Presumably the water *is* getting hot in there? It would be a damn sight quicker to pour a drink. No. She rests her backside on the table. She will stay in this position until that damn slow kettle boils.

All she has to do is keep alcohol in its place – make it part of her life, not the mainstay. She can control it. There's no need to take the cure. Go to some clinic full of holier-than-thou doctors and nurses, hear them lecturing her all day to put it out of her life. Out completely, not a drop. Dry. What, you call that living? Old joke, but still true.

Just look at it like dieting.

Finally the kettle agrees to bring itself to the boil. She pours a mug and stirs sludge around the bottom. Ugh, the taste of it – like drinking mud.

In the next room, the Darrens have a chrome cocktail bar, but one of her rules is not to visit it alone. She can only drink to be sociable. Perhaps she ought to go and drag her husband off that exercise machine, play the wife to him. He should be grateful he still has a wife: she gets out two evenings a week, goes legitimately to evening class, has the opportunity. He never asks her about it. But she doesn't mess with other men. Mind you, for all the attention Darren shows, who could blame her if she did? But she won't allow it; like the drink, she can resist. People would be surprised how strong-willed she can be.

Marriage is a contract, conditions either side. Just because Darren is hardly up to it any more, doesn't mean she should top up her own ration outside. No, she does the opposite – nurtures her man, encourages him along. This last year, he has bought himself the gymnasium to drag his body back to form. Fine, *he*

14

can work on that, and she'll work on his psyche – straighten the wick in his drippy candle. Anyway, here they are, Tuesday night, quarter to ten, they have spent the evening apart, improving themselves. Now it's time to come together again, show the benefit.

She marches down to his gymnasium. She'll call Darren out of there, tell him she is running a hot bath. Darren can sit in the water, wash the sweat off his face while she massages his tired muscles. Starting with his shoulders. Let's hope *all* his muscles aren't too tired, he hasn't used all his energy. Yes, Clive likes it in the bath. She pictures the way he'll sit there, groaning with pleasure. The man loves water, likes it hot. Then she will slip into the tub behind him, continue to massage his fleshy shoulders, watch her man perk up in the water.

Cheerfully she pushes open the gymnasium door. 'Hey Clive!' she calls. 'You got anything left for me?'

Daylight. Bright sunlight. Tim Hawk screwed his eyes tighter against the light. Where was it coming from? He must have left a curtain. Yes, over there. A sheet of sunlight cut through the room on to the bed, unnaturally bright, as if it had gained intensity outside from the shining river, like a sword from the sky stabbing at his eyes.

Tim realised that it was not the light that had wakened him: the phone was warbling. He must have turned the volume control down, because the sound was almost too quiet to waken him. A plastic warble, but insistent. That and the sunlight had sneaked inside his head.

Hawk slid out of bed and padded naked across the floor. He must have left his radio-phone in the other room. By the time he reached it, whoever was there would have rung off. Hawk pulled a face, stretching the muscles in his jaw. He must try not to sound as if he had just climbed out of bed. 'Hello?'

'Ah, good morning, Hawk. I didn't drag you away from something interesting?' The unmistakeable Scottish tones of Leyton Knox.

15

'No.'

'Och, what a shame. The sun shining, birds crapping in the sky. How do you feel about Clive Darren?'

'How should I feel?'

'Enthusiastic. The thing is, Timmy, that we really do want the man dead. Today would be ideal.'

'Consider it done.' Tim enjoyed the pause.

Knox said, 'You can do it?'

'You think I'm not up to it?'

'Och, no one would –'

'Is this official, Leyton?'

'Have I not just said so?'

'Why today?'

'Mr K comes back Friday.'

'This is Wednesday.'

'So you *are* awake, Timmy! Good lad. It's very important that Darren dies before Kazan tries to prevent it. D'ye understand?'

'Think he would?'

'He might try. Can we rely on you for this, Timmy?'

'Consider him dead.'

'Good lad. Good lad.' Knox terminated the call.

Tim returned to his bedroom to get dressed. Yes, Knox could consider Darren dead. Every detail had been rehearsed. For his first job, Hawk had begun planning as soon as he had known Darren might become a target. Careful planning stopped mistakes.

His first task had been to select the place: somewhere the man's behaviour could be predicted. Most places Darren went, his behaviour was not predictable – neither in timing nor in what he did when he was there. And wherever he went he was guarded. He took a lot of care over that. At home he was also guarded, but predictably: he and his guards fell into patterns of behaviour. A man's house was usually the easiest place to kill him.

Hawk's second task was to select the time. Not difficult. With one of Darren's guards occupied twice a week in taking Mrs D

16

to evening class, the time virtually chose itself. Hawk had noted that she and the guard went out 6.30 to 9.30 every Tuesday and Thursday, every week in term-time.

The third task was to prepare an action plan. First, Tim had watched the house. He sat in a car outside. He walked past the gate. Last week, for the first time, he had slipped into their garden. By then he had a fair understanding of how the light sensors worked. On his foray through the garden he had done little more than stalk through shrubbery in the dark, checking access to the house. He had been particularly interested in that rear extension. Part of Darren's predictable pattern seemed to be the way those lights came on about 6.45 every Tuesday and Thursday evening.

Last night had been Hawk's second time in the garden, his first with gun and ladder. He had now rehearsed every step. His action plan was ready and could be implemented any time. Any Tuesday or Thursday.

It would have to be Thursday.

3

'Listen, Hawk, I didn't want to come up here.'

'Life's tough.'

'I'd leave you to it, man. But when Knox says I have to drive you, I drive. I mean, like he's the boss now, right?'

'*Your* boss.'

Calvin snorted. He kept his mournful face aimed dead ahead, staring through the windscreen. It was unfamiliar territory out there. 'Don't push it, Hawk, if you want my advice. Everybody has to take orders.'

'Not me.'

'Oh, listen to the man! We all take orders from somebody, right?'

Tim scowled at the dark suburban gardens passing by. 'You think so?'

'I know so. Listen, I prove it to you: who's sitting beside you in this van?'

Tim sighed. 'You're not so black you're invisible in the dark.'

'What I mean is you didn't want to bring me, but you had to. Why was that?'

'I always fancied you?'

'Come on, you had orders, right? That's my point.'

'Take a left here.'

'I seen the map already, man. Listen, Leyton Knox is not an idiot. He knows there is safety in numbers.'

'What does that mean – are you coming in to help me?'

Cal laughed. 'Not on your sweet life! I am only paid to drive the van.'

'I can drive.'

Cal glanced briefly at Hawk hunched in his seat, looking as he often did, cold and pale. 'Hey, Hawk, ain't you scared on a job like this?'

Tim shrugged.

Cal said, 'I hear this Darren's so nervous he has a bodyguard.'

'You know his name, then?'

'This ain't a mystery tour, man.'

Hawk nodded. Presumably Cal had had to be told, but that would make him an informed witness. Hawk said, 'The bodyguard's out tonight – chauffeur to Darren's missis.'

'Makes it easier, right?'

'There's another bodyguard. And turn left again by those lights.'

'I know the way, I told you.'

'You didn't indicate.'

'Sor – ry.' Cal flicked the switch.

Hawk muttered, 'You always wait till the last moment.'

As he turned the corner, Cal sighed. He decided that Hawk was tense, had tightened up before the action. 'Bodyguards,' he mused. 'More than one, right?'

'Just the two.'

'You sure?'

'I've been watching.'

'Hope you're right.'

'They call it planning, Cal. Preparation. Every move rehearsed.'

'Life ain't like the movies, man. There is no script. We make the whole thing up as we go along.'

'Another left here.'

Cal banged the steering wheel with his palm, then grinned. 'Who's driving this fool van? D'you want me to come to Darren's house, tell you who to shoot?'

'Nope.'

'You *are* going to shoot him, Hawk?'

'Yep.'

'That's a gun in the bag, right?'

'My, what big eyes you have.'

Cal breathed out. 'Well, you are welcome, man. I'll stick to driving cars.'

'You sure that's wise? D'you know how many people die each week, driving cars? Best part of a hundred – every week. But how many hit men do you hear get killed?'

Cal shrugged. 'We'll see which one of us draws an old age pension. This is Darren's street, right?'

'Coming up.'

'Thought I'd save you telling me.' As they turned the corner, Cal made a rapid ticking sound to emphasise that he had switched on the indicator. 'So you don't want my exciting company, right? I can sit outside in the van?'

Tim nodded. He still looked pale. 'You wouldn't like it in there.'

'Too right.'

Cal stopped the van. He would have said 'Good luck', but it seemed out of place. So he asked, 'You got any music in this van, while I wait?'

'Yeah. You wouldn't like that either.'

Cal didn't. He sat in the silent van reading the booklets to Hawk's CDs. What the hell *was* this stuff? Hawk must have nicked it, because no one listened to this from choice. Cal sniffed and picked his nose. He considered sampling one of the CDs, but decided not. God knows what the music was, but he wouldn't like it. He began fiddling with the set to find Capital or Radio One: there must be something he could listen to – though it wouldn't sound much, kept down low. Cal shivered in his seat. For some reason it had just occurred to him that he might be the only black man in the area.

At 6.36 when the security lights came on, Tim Hawk slipped out from the shrubbery, crossed the lawn, and leant his ladder against the wall. While Darren's wife climbed in the waiting car,

20

Hawk ran up the ladder to hang his cap across the sensor. The lights stayed on.

Darren said, 'Same time as usual.'

'That's right.' Wheels began to scrunch across the gravel.

'Have fun.'

'And you.'

'I'll try.'

The car drove away. Gates creaked. The front door slammed. Hawk leant against the floodlit wall and waited until the lights went out. Then he picked up his bag and carried it to the recess where he had waited Tuesday night. He fetched the ladder and rested it against the rear extension wall. He would have to wait another five minutes now, maybe ten.

Tonight the stars seemed brighter in the sky. Less cloud. A soft breeze rustled bare branches in the trees. Hawk decided that while he waited in the recess he would not keep peering at his wristwatch: it only emphasised how slowly the time passed. Instead he let a tune run through his head, concentrated on remembering every bar.

And unburied remain
Inglorious on the plain.

With his mind resonating to the imaginary bass, he did not notice the approaching car. Only when the car stopped in the road outside did he jerk his thoughts back from the Renaissance to today. Where *was* the car – by the gate or alongside Cal? Had Leyton Knox sent someone to check up on them? Had Darren –

The gate creaked open.

Hawk had not heard a bell, but perhaps one had sounded inside the house. The gravel crunched as the car drove in. Lights came on. Hawk pressed deeper into the shadows of his recess, aware that a few feet away from him in the glaring light his ladder stood exposed against the rear extension wall.

He squatted to unfasten his canvas gun-bag.

The engine cut. The car door opened and closed. He heard footsteps on the stones. Then the front door rattled and he heard Darren say, 'You found us, then?'

'No problem.' A female voice, high and clear. 'Shall I leave it here?'

'Why not? It's safe enough.'

'Nice night.'

Hawk listened to her footsteps on the gravel. One pair of feet. He heard her mount the steps, heels clicking, click clack click. He heard the front door close. Not another word. While the floodlight continued to bleach the lawn beyond his recess, Hawk replayed their words of greeting. Some kind of social call, and her first time: Darren had said, you found us then. No names. No indication of why she'd come. Though neither Darren nor the woman had mentioned Mrs Darren: clearly it was not her she had come to see.

The lights went out.

Dirty old goat. Darren knew his wife wouldn't return until 9.30 – thought he'd give himself a change from the exercise machine, try something else. As he had told her on the step, it was safe enough.

Hawk stepped out from the recess and sniffed the air. It smelt fresh. A nice night. He shook his head. Christ, he thought, why did the bastard have to choose tonight? Why couldn't he stick to his normal routine? It wasn't fair – not on Hawk's first job. Well, he might have to abandon his plan, but he could not abandon it. Darren had to go tonight. Leyton had insisted – and as Cal said, he gave the orders. It must be tonight. But how long would that woman stay with Darren in the house? Hawk thought it was a safe bet she'd hang around till nearly half past nine.

'We got two hours,' Darren said. 'Plenty of time. So . . . you wanna drink first, or what?'

'First?' she arched an eyebrow.

'Come *on*. You want one or not?'

Terri smiled. Obviously the gonk did not want her to play the *ingénue*, the sweet amateur swept off her feet. That was fine by her: he could have the main bitch, the charity girl, anything he liked. Though she was happy to waste time on pleasantries if he

22

wanted to. 'I could use a drink,' she said. 'Makes it easier, you know?'

He interrupted the smile that she switched on. 'What, you need a drink before you're down to it? Thought I booked a professional.'

Charming, she thought. Acting tough with his prossie, like he's a bigshot.

'OK,' she said. 'You're in charge, big boy. How d'you want to play it?'

'Nothing kinky,' he said. 'I'm a simple man. We just get right on with it. Straight down the middle – like, you know that joke: tell me, Maxie, what do you like best on a woman, fat legs or thin? Maxie says, neither: I like something in the middle, me – that little something in the middle, that's what I like.'

Terri laughed dutifully, because that's what the gonk wanted. He laughed aggressively, using it as a weapon. So she repeated pleasantly that yes, she could use a drink. She guessed that she was going to *earn* her fee tonight.

'All you do,' Hawk said, leaning through the window of the van, 'is to stay here. Darren's bought a girl home. We have a change of plan.'

'That was her car, right?'

'Yeah. You just stay here in the van. Don't decide you ought to help.'

Cal shook his head. 'No chance of that.'

'Things may take longer than we thought.'

'Right.' Calvin, nodded, shifting his backside on the car-seat. 'How long?'

'Could be two hours.'

'Oh, man. Hey, listen. I'll be honest with you, right? I am not cut out for this. Two hours!' Cal shuddered. 'Look, I am a driver, right. I drive for everyday things, like burglaries, collections, that kind of dodge. Not for killing, man. I mean, Hawk, I know what you're here to do, right? I know what this job is. Hell, even so, man, I did kind of hope that tonight was, well, sussing out, a rehearsal, right?'

23

'I've done the rehearsal.'

'Oh.'

'But you understand what I'm telling you, Cal? I shall have to improvise.'

'Yeah, man. Like this is the live performance, right?'

'Before your very eyes: see Darren die.'

'Oh shit, man.'

'But all you have to do, Cal, is stay here. You don't have a ticket to come inside.'

'No admission, right?'

'Right.'

'But –'

'Do you *want* to come inside?'

'No, but . . .' Calvin swallowed, and said, 'Leyton Knox, you know –'

'What?'

'Said I have to *be* with you, give you cover, that kind of thing.'

'You want to do that?'

'No. I told Leyton: I said I'm just a driver, man. But he said it was time I earned my keep.'

'And you said?'

'Oh, what choice do you think I had, man? I said yes.'

'Fine. And I'm telling you to sit here on your butt and wait till I come back. Now what choice do you have?'

Calvin shrugged. 'I stay sat.'

'Some place, innit?' Darren indicated his cocktail lounge.

'Sure is.' Terri sipped at the over-large glass of whisky. 'Did you do it all yourself?'

'Course not – I got the decorators in.'

'I meant –' Terri glanced again at the chromium cocktail bar, the Japanese wallpaper, the dark oak, the leather stools. 'Did you choose this stuff yourself?'

'Waddyer think – I'm gonna pay some poncey interior designer? Think I'm some kind of faggot?'

My, my, Terri mused, what little secret are *you* trying to conceal? But she knew the correct response. 'Certainly not, Mr Darren. No one could ever call you that.'

'You bet your life on it.' Darren punched a podgy fist in the other palm, threw his head back. 'Are you gonna nurse that drink all night?'

Terri put it down on a side table. 'I bet you're a real hard man, Mr Darren.' That's what the gonk would want to hear.

'You can count on it.'

He took two swaggering paces towards her, then noticed her whisky glass on his side table. 'Hey, don't you leave that there. This place has got to look like no one's been here. Go stick it behind the bar.'

Terri shrugged. This was part of the freak's turn-on, ordering her around. She didn't mind, as long as he didn't try to lay into her with his fists. She wouldn't stand for violence. Behind the cocktail bar was clinically clean – steel sink, bright taps, smooth linoleum floor. She was on the business side of the counter with Darren on the customer's, up to the welts of his shoes in shaggy carpet. As she started out from behind the bar he demanded, 'You leave lipstick on that glass? I don't want no sign you were ever here, understand?'

'Don't you worry, sir,' said Terri, going back to wipe the glass. 'I shan't leave a trace of me behind.'

Hawk stood in the shadows at the rear. What would happen now? It seemed unlikely Darren would use the gym tonight. The girl had been in the house for over quarter of an hour, and she was not collecting for charity. Which room would Darren use?

The disabled sensor allowed him freedom of movement along this side of the house and the rear. The other side of the building and the front were still primed. Inside, Darren presumably had his attention on something more interesting than how the outside lights behaved. But Darren and the floozie were not alone in the house: there was a bodyguard, who might take an occasional glance out here – especially if a floodlight switched on. Hawk prowled along the dark side of the house – right along the side,

25

then around the rear to the far corner. But he could go no further. Even to peep around a corner could set one off.

In the dark areas that he could check, all the windows showed no light. Whatever was happening indoors must be at the front or the other side. Out in this position, Hawk was like a chess piece on the wrong side of the board.

Suddenly a light came on: upstairs side wall, at the front. Master bedroom, bet your life. Light from that upstairs room cast a broad rectangle of pale yellow across the lawn. The rear of the house where Hawk waited remained dark. He ran across the lawn into the shrubbery, from where he could look up into the lit window. He saw Darren close the curtains. Even though the man stood face on at that high window, Hawk made no special effort to hide. From where Darren stood with the light on, everything outside would look black.

Hawk stayed in the shrubbery, watching the house, thinking. It was one thing to pinpoint where Darren was, but another to get inside. The various windows would be locked – though their alarms would be turned off. Houses are at their least protected when occupied. People prime alarms only when they leave, giving possessions more protection than they give themselves. Those windows, he decided, were vulnerable.

After his experience on Tuesday night, balancing outside the gymnasium's high window, Hawk had brought a longer ladder. Though he no longer needed it for its intended purpose, he reckoned it should still get him on to the flat roof of the rear extension. From there, he ought to be able to reach a window on the back wall. Upstairs windows probably were not locked.

'Hey, Terri, whatever your name is – this is what you call a bedroom, right?'

'Oh sure, it's something else. I have to admire your taste, Mr Darren,' which was true enough – she was paid to.

'Fucking fortune, but that's the wife. I make it, she spends it.'

Terri liked the Laura Ashley – ceiling to floor, wall to wall: the flounced lace curtains scalloped across the window. She could do her place like that if she had the money. Terri smiled, undid the top button of her blouse. 'You're married, then?'

Darren tugged at his shirt collar. 'Don't play the chuck with me, girl – you know I'm married. What does a *man* want with a frilly bedroom?'

Terri laughed, appeasing him. 'Or a nice big house in Woodside Park.'

'I'm not good enough for Woodside Park?'

She threw a smile across the duvet, put a hand on her red hair. 'Hey relax, big boy. I bet you can fit anywhere you want.'

He didn't see the innuendo – just said, 'You better believe it,' and frowned at the unruffled bed. 'Right then. Well.'

Seeing doubt behind his eyes, a man uncertain how to start, she changed gear to earn her fee. Coming round the end of the bed, she put on that silly voice she knew they liked: 'You want to give your little girl a cuddle?'

'Yeah – no. No, you get your clothes off. I'll do the shower.' He moved away from her to the *ensuite*.

'Oh, the shower, I love that. It's so sexy, wet and warm.'

'Like your fanny.' Darren reached for the faucet. He was the kind of man you fed him the punchline and he believed he thought of the quip himself. Terri knew him now: she could keep control. Until his damp face reappeared from the cubicle she did not remove a single piece of clothing. She asked softly, 'You want to see a striptease?'

Then she undid a couple of buttons on her blouse. The gonk was watching her, all right, but he shuffled his feet and said, 'We already wasted half an hour.'

'That leaves ninety minutes,' Terri said, slipping off her blouse. 'A lot can happen in ninety minutes.'

Calvin glared at the radio: that's entertainment, right? Politicians arguing, a couple of phone-ins, several middle-of-the-road snore bores and a play about daft old white ladies. Why the hell hadn't Hawk got any decent music in here? Cal flicked through the CDs again. The sleeves sported tiny reproductions of classical paintings – landscapes, minstrels, women in wimples. Those kind of pictures put you right off the music – and made it cold and dull before you even heard it: stockbroker music, would play OK in Finchley. But it couldn't really be that bad – Hawk was not a snob. He was a loner, a bit weird, but basically OK: he wasn't one of those honkies chortling on the radio. His music must be reasonable, right?

Cal tried to convince himself. To be honest – and why not, there was nobody watching him – some of the names on those CDs were not completely unknown. Bach, Handel, Telemann, Purcell. Yeah, Cal had heard of them. Which was it – Bach of a dog or Bach of a tree? Bach of beyond, maybe. Calvin grinned to fight the boredom. Yeah, here's that mother, Handel of the Doors. Telemann what you been doing today. Purcell washes whiter, baby. Trouble is, he thought, even the names I recognise ain't the music I enjoy. Tut, tut – you ain't prejudiced, are you, boy?

All *right* Cal thought, flicking through the CDs. Let's have some education here, a touch of class. All *right*. Anyway, it's only background. Hey, maybe Hawk does that meditation shit – he listens to something serious before sliding out to do a job. It's like church music – stimulating, right? Yeah. You have to remember that this man is learning to be a killer. Yeah. Maybe he needs this stuff to quieten his mind.

Cal grinned into the night beyond his windscreen, then reached into his pocket for something to quieten his own mind: his tin of ganga. Yeah. He rolled one slowly, licking the cigarette paper end to end as if he enjoyed the taste of glue. Then he lit up, closed his eyes, took three long slow drags.

Yeah. Why should he not give one of these disks a try? Yeah. Since they all looked the same to Cal he tried the one already slotted in the machine. Hawk had set it at low volume. Yeah – just as well.

A glorious fanfare of military-sounding trumpets whispered inside the van. Then came the voices. Alone in the darkness, Cal concentrated on the sound. What were they singing? He strained to make out the words: something about revenge. Revenge, revenge, they cried. Somebody cried, anyway. Some mother. He listened more carefully.

> See the Furies arise!
> See the snakes that they rear,
> How they hiss in their hair,
> And the sparkles that flash in their eyes!

Yeah. Music and ganga made Cal intelligent and grave. He tried to imagine himself into the mindset of Tim Hawk. He wondered whether, if he worked at this classical stuff himself, he could ever grow to like it. Maybe it was like smoking – you don't enjoy it at first, but you stick at it, persevere. Yeah. Well, at least they sang in English:

> Behold a ghastly band,
> Each a torch in his hand . . .

Sitting huddled in the driver's seat of the van, Cal blew a cloud of cannabis smoke at the screen.

Hawk is inside the house. He reaches the end of the upstairs hallway, stands with his hands on the bedroom door. Eyes closed, breath suspended, Hawk listens. He tries to visualise the interior of the room. He imagines the chintz and fancy furniture, the puffy bed with two people in it. Perhaps *on* it.

No. Forget it. That isn't where they are.

Hawk can hear a shower running. He stays poised outside the door, listening – waiting for a sound that will tell whether one or both are beneath that shower. In his right hand Hawk carries his short rifle. He holds it upright against his chest, the tip of the barrel against his cheek.

Silently, he pushes the bedroom door. It swings open. No one visible. The room looks moist, a faint cloud of steam. Hawk steps in and shuts the door.

The furniture in the bedroom looks much as he imagined: rose-coloured rather than orange – but the same idea. Lace at

29

the windows, hung like a cinema curtain, bows tied in gathers. A big bed – so smooth it could have been ironed into place. Pictures of pastel pierrots on the wall.

The sounds are clearer now. Punctuating the hiss of that running shower are animal noises of copulation: grunting, gasping, little yelps and slaps of skin. Quietly, quieter than he needs to be, Tim Hawk takes a position opposite the perspex entrance to the shower. Behind the wet frosted glass are the blurred shapes of two naked, heaving bodies. Hawk wonders whether he should wait until Darren apears or whether to take him there. No, do it now, don't let him finish. Let his blood wash down the drain.

Hawk likes to work neatly. He approaches the open perspex doorway, pushes his rifle ahead of him into the steam. He can hear the couple reaching climax. Darren is, anyway: back and buttocks towards the doorway, he pounds the standing whore. Darren jumps at her, thrusting, whimpering. The girl stands motionless, arms clasped round him, ginger hair plastered to her face, eyes aghast at what they see. She stares at Hawk across Darren's shoulder. She lurches backwards against the wall. Darrel stumbles, roaring to stay inside. The girl's arms fall from his back. She tries to say something. He doesn't hear her. Again he shouts, he thumps her against the wall. But now the girl's legs have given way. She crumples, slithering to the floor. The heavy man crashes down on top of her, an incessant stream of water on his rear. 'I'm out, you bastard, you spat me out!'

She tries to writhe away from him through the splashing water. He flounders. He rams his broad hand on her shoulder, pushes her straight, begins to force himself inside her. She sobs into his ear. He shouts what he will do to her, before suddenly he realises. On hands and knees in the threshing water, Darren twists his body round, sees Hawk with the stubby rifle aimed at his dripping chest.

'Stay still.'

'The fuck?'

'This is it,' Hawk says. 'It won't hurt.'

Darren is streaming with water like a cat fresh out the goldfish pond. He shakes his head, and Hawk says, 'The Isle of Dogs. You wouldn't stay away.'

'Oh Christ,' gasps Darren. 'Don't shoot.'

The girl crams her sodden body into the tiled corner of the seething shower.

'You had three warnings.'

'No!'

'Yes.' Hawk puts a single shell through Darren's chest.

Even as the bullet hits him, Darren's mouth falls open to yell for help. When he jolts sideways against the quivering girl he gives a single hollow groan. Maybe he believes that he called somebody's name. Maybe he dies believing that. Hawk says, 'You see, it *didn't* hurt.'

The girl pulls the dead man's body between Hawk's rifle and her own skin. 'Please don't shoot me,' she implores. 'I'm nothing to do with him.' The heavy body slides away from her. Louder than her words is the constant stream of splattering water. She feels submerged in tepid rain. Steam fills the air.

Hawk mutters, 'I'm sorry you had to be here.'

'Not me,' she says. 'Please.' He keeps the rifle aimed at her chest. For the first time, the girl raises her arms to shield her breasts. The young blond man seems insubstantial through the vapour.

'It won't hurt,' he says.

'No!'

'I know you weren't a part of it. Just unlucky, that's all.'

'Why kill me?'

He shakes his head, as if she asked a foolish question. 'A witness.'

'To what?' She sounds desperate. 'I don't know who you are.'

He takes one pace backwards towards the door. 'You saw me.'

'Oh, please! Please let me live. I swear I'll never tell.'

She hears the sound of the rifle cocking as he mumbles, 'I have orders.'

'Not to kill *me*! No! – Just this bastard, not me.'

Hot water hisses. Hawk knows that he should not look into her

31

eyes. He should never hesitate. Something about the look in her frightened eyes reminds him suddenly of Raggs, but he cannot tell why. He doesn't try to remember, but says, 'I have a contract.'

He continues to stare at her, knowing he shouldn't, as she kneels there in the shower. She lets her arms drop, revealing her breasts again. They glisten in the water. Darren's body remains slumped across her thighs. She asks, 'What do I have to do?' She makes her eyes reinforce the message. 'I'll do anything,' she says. 'Whatever you want.'

In the hot shower, Terri feels awfully cold. She wants to stand up, to push Darren's body away from her, but she won't try any move that might make this pale boy fire again.

'Come out and put your clothes on,' he says.

He did not watch her while she dressed. He walked around the rose-coloured bedroom, running a gloved finger along its highly polished surfaces. Suddenly he asked, 'Been here before?'

'No.'

'Been with *him* before?'

'No.' Terri was fastening her buttons. Hawk stood by the smooth pink bed. 'His wife's choice, right?'

'I expect.'

He nodded. 'Gonna have you on her mattress, was he?'

She hesitated. 'Look, I don't care about that gonk. He didn't even pay me.'

'Regular or just this time?'

She had finished dressing. 'I told you – just this once.'

He was watching her, the rifle balanced in his left hand. She couldn't decide whether she should stare back at him or look away. Staring might harass him, looking away might make him doubt. She didn't know what the hell she should do.

He said, 'You were never here. You never saw it. Did anyone know you were coming?'

'No.'

'Think.' A muscle flickered once beneath his right eye, as if perhaps he had just realised that someone might know a thing like that.

'No one.'

'Who arranged this?'

'He did.' Terri inclined her head towards the shower.

'Who drove you here?'

'I came in my own car.'

He nodded, remembering how it was when she arrived. He said, 'I'll take you downstairs. You'll drive away. You won't look back.'

She said, 'Right.'

'Now listen.' He held the pause. 'Do you want to see me again?'

Oh Christ, she thought, which answer does he want? Is he coming on to me or what? She said no, she never wanted to see him again.

In the pause, Terri heard her heart beating. The boy asked, 'What did you touch in here? We'd better wipe the fingerprints.'

At the foot of the stairs she decided that she had better tell him.

'We had a drink,' she said. 'I washed the glasses, but not enough for fingerprints.'

His rifle was no longer pointing at her. He held it loosely, pointing at her feet. 'Which room?'

For about a minute, while she stood at the sink in Darren's kitchen behind the bar, rinsing and wiping both glasses in running water, Hawk leant against a unit behind her, tapping the rifle against his leg.

They were both too close to that running water.

They didn't hear the floor creak, just once, as Darren's bodyguard crossed the cocktail diner, his footsteps deadened in long-pile carpet. They didn't react till his shoes smacked on the lino and his head appeared round the kitchen door.

All three were startled. The guard expected Terri, not this blond kid with a rifle. He whipped his head back from the doorway as that rifle began to rise. Hawk was a long way from the

33

door. He started for it, then stopped: the man could be waiting for him. Hawk motioned for the girl, hands dripping water at the sink. 'Go through that door,' he said.

Her eyes widened. She didn't move.

'Don't worry, he won't shoot you.' Hawk jerked his rifle at her.

Terri blinked, turned towards the door. Her voice tightening, she asked, 'You want me to go in that room ahead of you?' She deliberately spoke loud so the bodyguard would hear. Hawk realised but didn't care. He said, 'Yes.'

'I'll go first then.' She said it clearly.

Two steps inside the cocktail diner she heard Hawk tell her to stop. She did so. Crouching to her left beside the wall was the bodyguard, a pistol in his hand. He had it pointed at the door.

'Look at him,' said Hawk.

She already had. The guard scowled at her, but he kept his pistol aimed behind her at the door.

'Has he got a gun?' Hawk asked. She nodded. 'Go get it.'

Behind her in the kitchen she saw Hawk move quickly toward the door. He and the bodyguard were now separated only by the wall. If it was plasterboard, she thought, either man could shoot straight through and hit the other. But the wall looked solid enough for brick. Though you never know.

She was starting to jabber inside her head. Down on the floor the guard kept his pistol pointing at the doorframe. Hawk had his rifle aimed at her. She licked her lips.

'I told you to take his gun.'

Hawk had drifted away from the dividing wall now, so he could watch Terri when she moved. She took a single step and stopped. What the hell was she to do? Hawk jerked the rifle. As she took a second reluctant step, the crouching guard waved her back with his free hand. Now what? She wondered whether she could ignore both these men, walk away from them into the room, leave them frozen at the doorway, each waiting till the other made a move. Neither man would shoot her, would they? Both knew that if they wasted a shot on *her*, then the other would get *him*. So they wouldn't shoot her. She could walk away. *Couldn't she?* Think about it: the guard didn't care *where* she went so long as she stayed out of his way. He had no quarrel with her – except he thought she was with the blond boy, who had his rifle on her back. He could be regretting he hadn't shot her earlier beside Darren in the shower. It was because of her that he was still trapped inside the house. It was her fault.

She took a breath, stepped across the lino towards the guard. He shot his arm up, palm vertical, pistol concentrated on the door. She forced herself to stare only at the guard, not to let her eyes betray that Hawk had shifted since he last spoke – was now crouching on the floor. From the corner of her eye she saw him nod. She moved forward. That step brought her on to the bodyguard's warning hand. He pushed at her. She grabbed his arm. He tried to punch at her, his gun wavering on the door. Terri grabbed at his hair, saw his pistol swing towards her, shouted, 'No!'

Hawk came ankle-height round the doorframe like a swordfish with his gun. Terri heard an explosion – the guard's pistol – heard nothing from the rifle. She scrambled for the handgun. She toppled the guard to the lino floor. She wrenched the pistol from his hand. She fell against the wall.

Then Terri saw the blood on the bodyguard's shirt. He lay writhing on his back, the bloodstain spreading. The blond boy crouched with his rifle aimed at her heart. He said, 'Drop the gun.'

Terri flung it to the ground. She slumped against the wall. 'Kick it to me.'

As she did so she realised that the blond boy still did not trust her. Jesus Christ. He took the pistol, flicked the safety, slipped it in his pocket and stood up. He motioned *her* to stand as well. At her feet the bodyguard was still moving. The whole of his stomach was stained with red. While they watched, he let out a low sustained 'Aah', and opened his eyes. He was trying to say something. Terri felt a thud of air, saw the guard jerk and then lie still. The blond boy stood with his rifle tilted downwards like a hunter after the kill. That thick chamber around his gun barrel, she realised, must be a silencer. That's why she hadn't heard it fire.

'I had to,' he said. 'I didn't get him properly with the first.'

She frowned at him. He seemed to be apologising. The boy said, '*He* wasn't in the contract either.'

It was as if he were waiting for Terri to say something, to absolve him, perhaps. She knew about men and guilt. She said, 'Don't blame yourself. It's like when you hit an animal with your car, and you only injure it. You have to go back and put it out of its agony.'

'It shouldn't hurt though,' he muttered. 'That's the beauty of it.'

When Calvin saw the security lights, he sat straighter in his seat. That shouldn't happen, should it, unless something had gone wrong? Calvin hadn't asked Hawk what he should do if the job fucked up – because if the job was fucked, then so was Hawk, and if Hawk was fucked he wouldn't care what Cal did in the car.

But Cal cared. He cared a lot. And one of the things he cared about was how he would know if the job *had* fucked. Were the lights a sign, and if so, of what? Oh shit. With the balls of his nervous fingers, Cal tickled the keys dangling from the ignition. He hoped the engine was not too cold.

The gates swung open and a car drove out. Cal recognised it: the little Renault Clio that had gone in an hour ago. He had seen it come, now he saw it go. So what? That was the car that Hawk had told him about – the one that brought the girl – the one that caused Hawk to change his plan. Presumably he had been hanging around waiting till it finally drove away. The man must be freezing in there, doing nothing this last hour. Cal sniffed. It made him realise that the van still smelt of ganga, so he rolled the window down.

Then Hawk walked out of the gate like he owned the place. He strolled along the lane like he was taking the evening air and, when he reached the open window, he told Cal to drive the car inside.

Terri drove the car north beyond Potter's Bar. Out around Brookman's Park were patches of bare country between commuter villages. It wasn't real country – no remote tangled hedgerows or narrow lanes. There were fallow fields, select developments, golf courses. But to Terri this was country. She came out occasionally on high-ticket jobs. At first she had thought that the country gentlemen would be different, but she found they were much the same in bed.

There was a particular house that Terri was heading towards. It belonged to another of those gonks who liked to screw in the bed he shared with his absent wife. This one's undoubtedly better half had been – where was it? – in hospital at the time. Poor cow. Terri had actually stayed with the man all night. Usually when a client suggested that – said they should *sleep* together, as well as sex – all the man meant was that she should stay till he had fucked himself to sleep, somewhere round three o'clock maybe. Then Terri should slip away so they didn't have to see each other's face when they woke up. Not such a stupid idea, come to that: the state of *her* face first thing after a heavy night. Yes, sliding out of bed in the small hours, hauling off into the empty night, was better than waking up beside a gonk with a hangover. And all that male guilt. Anyway, this particular john – that's right, his wife *was* in hospital – female trouble, he said – he made Terri really stay the night. Took another serving before breakfast. And a golden shower.

The creep lived in one of those big houses – well, big to Terri, and it had big gardens – just near here, along these lanes between Epping Green and Wormley. She remembered how secluded she had thought it, stuck out there. Lonely even. Live in a place like that, you'd have to use the car to get to a shop, the nearest pub, or any place at all.

In the long, straight lane ahead of her, the headlamps revealed a dark line in the grass verge: a narrow ditch. Terri didn't know why some country lanes had ditches running by them – drainage, she supposed, like town streets have gutters to take the rain.

She stopped, switched off, got out of the car. She felt a dampness in the evening breeze. Through her thin cotton blouse the night air chilled her, so she reached back inside the car for her shortie coat. It was kinda dressy for the deserted lane – tarty. Too bad. She felt warmer with it on. Terri paused beside the car, and she listened. She heard nothing but the breeze. In the distance across flat fields she saw a glow of light from some village. There were no car lights. Nothing moving.

She put up the tailgate.

Without the blond boy's help, Terri found it difficult to heave the body out. She dragged it bumpily, like a roll of carpet. When the corpse was half in, half out of the car, bent crumpled at the middle, it felt as if its weight had glued its stomach to the sill. She had to lift his legs separately, heave at the body in a way that might give a lesser girl a hernia. When the carcass did flop out, the man's head cracked against the tarmac.

The blond boy had told her that this was the price to save her life. It wouldn't be the worst thing she had had to do. Christ, it wasn't the worst thing she'd done tonight. When she had been begging the blond boy not to kill her she had said that she'd do anything – and this was easy: of course she'd do it. And once she'd done this for him, she would never hear from him again. That's what he said. Believe me, he had said: she had no choice.

Terri lugged the body off the road, across the damp strip of grass into the narrow ditch. Black water squelched beneath him. She found that the bodyguard's stiffening corpse was broader than the ditch: he lay along, rather than inside it. So Terri stood on him in her high heels. She trod him down into the channel and walked on him till he sank. Eventually, it seemed to Terri that the body would be invisible to anyone driving down the lane – though it was not hidden, by any means. Not to someone on foot, with his eyes open, taking in the scenery. There had to be some fink in this rural area whose job it was to wander out

38

occasionally and clear weeds out of the ditches. Finding this might make his day.

With any luck, that wouldn't happen for a week. Anyway, Terri thought as she restarted the car, that was the blond boy's problem. Her priority now was to get herself twenty miles south, and get back home. She was finished. She had done what she had agreed. As the Clio carried her away, she stared dully along its beam of light in the country lanes. This had been one hell of a lousy night. And she hadn't even been paid.

4

Alexander Stanley Kazan, a burly, thickset man in his early fifties, black hair, skin speckled as if with coal dust, still has trouble with his complexion. He gets blackheads – even boils occasionally. He won't use teenagers' zit cream – prefers lotions, face masks, mud packs, hot flannels in the bath. But nothing works: his skin stays coarse. Only in recent years has he stopped brooding about his looks, accepted that this is how he looks and that at his age it won't change. He still buys the lotions, because he can afford them and he likes the smell. Today he sits on the edge of his seat in the back of the Daimler Princess, just as excited and edgy as if he *was* an acne'd teenager. He winks at Irena. She leans against the cushion, blonde hair fanned across the leather as if she rode in Daimlers all her life. Those dark blue eyes, deep, unblinking, that guileless look, make her seem younger than her twenty-five packed years. She looks innocent as a child. Nothing in her face reveals the harshness of her old life back home: running the decrepit wooden house, feeding chickens, collecting eggs, tilling vegetables, teaching English in the village school.

Al reaches for the car-phone. 'Take a look at this. You never seen one of these, am I right?'

Irena mentally corrects him: you never *saw* one of these, but she doesn't say it, only smiles. It is true that she hasn't seen a radio-phone before: their village had only the one public phone, which Irena hardly used. The village phone did not

40

have press buttons either, come to that, just a dial. But Irena concentrates on the view from the car window.

Al speaks into his phone: 'Hey, it's me, Kazan. The hell is that?'

'Oh, hello, Mr K. This is Dirkin.'

Irena is surprised to hear the man's voice aloud on the speaker. 'Dirkin?'

'Yeah, Vinnie Dirkin, remember?'

'Right.' But he does not look as if he remembers, Irena thinks. She continues gazing through the window. This Mr Dirkin does not sound an important sort of fellow: some kind of peasant.

'Who's around?'

'No one, sir, not at the moment. You know – it's lunchtime.'

'The hell am I running there – the civil service?'

'The other guys slipped out for a takeaway – encilladas and pickles. There's this new tapas bar – Spanish, I think, maybe Mexican. You know it?'

'I don't give a stuff what they are eating, Dirkin. Why ain't they with you?'

Irena considers this a pointless conversation. Through the car window she studies the fine houses, the scattered hotels and shops. There are lots of garages. Naturally, she thinks, with so many cars.

Dirkin is still apologising. 'I'm just looking after the place.'

'Tell them to call me.'

'You see, your flight's awful late, Mr K. Was everything OK?'

'Just have them call.' Al kills the phone, turns to her and grins. 'How d'you like that – lunch?'

'No thank you, I am not hungry.'

He laughs, one little snort. Because Irena seems engrossed in the urban scenery he doesn't try to speak to her, just watches her from behind. He admires her golden hair, where it falls between her shoulderblades. Why is Irena like my car? Because she is my princess. Kazan pulls a face behind her head: what am I doing, making riddles? I ain't *that* glad to be home.

Irena is wondering whether he chose this route especially to

41

impress her: the long wide boulevard lined with houses, the clusters of shops lit up in daylight. So lively, so rich. No wonder so many cars come here.

She asks, 'What is this street called?'

'This? The Great West Road.'

'Do only rich people live here?'

'With all this traffic? You'd need to be deaf with double glazing to live out here.'

'Oh, you joke. These houses are pretty.'

'Seen worse, I suppose. Listen, you wanna see fine houses?'

'Of course.'

'Louis.' Kazan touches the driver's shoulders. 'Skip the South Circular. Take us through the West End.'

'That'll take for ever, Mr K. We're three hours late already.'

'So? Let Irena see the sights.'

Louis drove the Daimler via Chiswick and Hammersmith, along Kensington High Street and the bottom of Hyde Park into Knightsbridge. Occasionally he peeped at the blonde girl in the mirror. She was striking, all right, the artless type: hardly any make-up, odd foreign clothes. Louis could imagine her protesting prettily that 'She couldn't help it if she looked this way' – yeah, make other women spit. She had dark eyebrows, though, for a so-called blonde – could be brunette underneath. Louis sniffed. Well, he'd never know. He'd never see underneath. Despite that fragile look to her face, she was by no means just a slip of a thing; had large gypsy bones – though she wasn't overweight. And that was some bosom – what, size thirty-six D? – that drew the eye. Louis decided he could fancy this one any day.

Another thing: the girl could open those blue eyes of hers wider than a kiddie at the circus. In Kensington High Street, for instance, when she saw the huge department stores and crowds of people, she clapped her hands. Just like that. Mr K sat gazing at her lovingly. Well, he would, Louis thought: a man would rather look at a girl like that than at almost anything. Where did Kazan find her – *how* did he find her – did he pick her up on

42

the plane? Louis shook his head, told himself to keep his eyes on the road ahead. Told himself not to let Kazan catch him ogling his pick-up. The man could kill for that, think it only right. Well, Louis thought, they certainly do not build women like that where I come from. Or, if they do, I never saw one. Or if I saw one she moved away. Christ, just once, that's all I ask. Just once alone with her. You'd have to peel me off.

At Westminster she actually called out the name. 'Your Houses of Parliament! I have a picture at home.' Kazan was grinning at Irena just as childishly as she grinned out the window. '*This* is your home now,' he said. 'London: it's yours.' She grabbed the hand that he'd left dangling on the seat. She found his broad, labourer's hand comfortable to hold.

'Don't do that,' Kazan called. 'Go through the City.'

Louis had positioned the Daimler to cut across Westminster Bridge to the south side of the Thames – the quick way home. Dutifully he signalled left for the Embankment.

The girl sat alert in the back, gawping at the sights like Cinderella at the Ball. Louis was touched. He felt like a gateau that had been too long out the freezer: melting into goo. He had definitely not seen a piece like this before. If Kazan wanted to spin out the journey – turn it into some kind of sightseeing trip – that was fine by Louis. He'd do his sightseeing in the mirror.

He turned the car sharp left, off the Embankment to the Horseguards – where she squealed, as they both hoped she would, at the famous sentries in scarlet tunics. Louis eased into Trafalgar Square – another squeal at Nelson's Column – down the Strand to Fleet Street and the City, then over Tower Bridge.

As they continued the journey eastwards on the south side of the river, the scenery changed. Jamaica Road and Evelyn Street were grimmer, hemmed in by smoke-dark buildings. Irena noticed how the people's clothes grew shabbier, the streets dustier, the buildings plainer, more functional. She also registered with some astonishment how many pedestrians were black. The change in scenery, though, was no great surprise to her: she had

43

heard of urban slums. She felt they were avoiding the heart of the city stews and hurrying past, hoping she wouldn't notice. So she asked, 'Is this where the novels of Charles Dickens were set?'

Al frowned at her. 'Pardon?'

' "London: implaccable November weather" – you know Dickens?'

He nodded vaguely. 'It's October.'

She continued, ' "As much mud in the streets as if the waters had but newly retired from the face of the earth, and it would not be wonderful to meet a megalosaurus, forty feet long or so –" '

'Megalo what?'

' "– waddling like an elephantine lizard up Holborn Hill." '

'This ain't Holborn.'

' "Smoke lowering down from chimneypots, making a soft black drizzle with flakes of soot in it as big as full-grown snow-flakes – gone into mourning, one might imagine, for the death of the sun." ' She beamed at him.

'Dickens,' he said.

'*Bleak House*, the beginning. You have read *Bleak House*?'

'That's a book by Dickens, am I right?'

'Of course.'

'I ain't read that one.'

'Haven't,' she said.

'Come again?'

'You *haven't* read that one.'

'That's what I said. You correcting my English?'

Irena smiled, and patted his broad hand.

He said, 'Whose language is it anyway? Bleeding foreigners,' and laughed.

Quite suddenly, the scenery altered again – began to look prettier. She had noticed how, without warning, the environment could transform: one moment the carriageways throttled with cars, next a green tree-filled park or a boulevard glittering with shops; a rapid succession of small streets, grand squares, rows of trees, concrete walls, the wide river, dark alleys, strange disconcerting switches in level – roads above them, roads below – great warehouses, a railway station, cinemas, department stores. Everywhere she looked in this bewildering huge city there were placards and signs, words and pictures, advertisements faintly familiar from rarely seen magazines. Here the advertisements were alongside the roads – up to forty feet long, coloured, vivid, arresting. Some seemed to have been painted on board, others on illuminated glass. Most exciting to Irena were those that moved – rippling streams of neon, pictures on shifting panels. She saw bright signs in shop windows, strange names on the walls – names of products, of people, of endlessly varied shops. Many seemed meaningless – a glorious waste of resources, electrical profligacy. They shouted 'BT Phone Home!', 'Pure Genius!', 'What Takes Your Breath Away?'. Some of the product names she recognised: Gillette, Coca Cola, McDonalds, American Express. One or two images snagged her attention and stuck before fresh ones crowded in: a hugh painting of rich young people playing on tropical island sands, above the words, 'Wet Saturday in Peckham'. Where was that? A stark black and white photo of a gaunt black woman on an arid plain, with the words, 'Just £10 Will Give Her Back Her Eyes'. Irena noticed an enormous handpainted signboard outside a church – at least, she *assumed* it was a church – it looked like one – yet the sign read: 'Try Our Budget Lunch (Here Every Thursday) Only 50p'. *Was* it a church, or had the building been converted into a restaurant? But why would a restaurant open only one day a week?

Irena even read traffic signs: No Entry, No Parking, Slow, Stop, No Left Turn. She frowned at 'Stop Children'. So many names labelling the buildings, so very many names. How could one remember them? But she must; this was to be *her* country now. She must become a part of it. A few names recurred in different streets: Virgin, Marks & Spencer, Co-Op, Mammoth Sale, The Red Lion, Boots, WHSmith. What could you buy in a shop called Virgin? Why were there no shoes in the one called Boots? How did you pronounce WHSmith?

Now the houses became more spaced: another change of

environment. If such fine houses had existed at home, they would have been used for schools, hospitals, the farm manager's house. But in England, of course, these houses were for everyday wealthy families. She knew the kind of people who lived in such places: old Mr Chuzzlewit, Miss Havisham, Scrooge, Dora Spenlow. She smiled, and nodded at the houses as if she suddenly recognised them. She would have a house like these. The dream was coming true.

'Nearly there,' Al said cheerfully. 'Straight ahead, that's Shooters Hill.'

The shrill sound of a solitary baroque trumpet shivered through the flat, singing with happiness. Tim Hawk sat astride a straight-back dining-chair watching silent TV. He had the sound off, so that while he watched he could listen to a lunchtime concert on Radio Three: *Amadigi*, by Handel, the jubilant sinfonia on Melissa's death. He didn't need to *hear* the lunchtime news, just watch the pictures. Politicians stooped in and out of cars, spoke earnestly to camera. Somewhere abroad had atrocious weather. More fighting in Eastern Europe. Another set of politicians – American, the pictures over-coloured by US TV – scuttled beneath a stormburst of photoflash in the lobby of some administrative palace built at the electorate's expense. Democracy, inaction. Outside in the cold, a commentator explained to uncaring viewers why these politicians were meeting, whether it was to wring their hands over the fighting or to wrangle over trade tariffs. Tim concentrated on the radio: Handel was his god. The TV news returned home with a nonsensical tale about winsome royal children – a cheerful ending before the weather forecast. Tim swung his head in time to the baroque music, barely following the flickering pictures. His eyes had glazed, not quite asleep, in the way a drowsy cat sleeps with its eyes open, just in case. He watched London local news: transport problems, domestic tragedies, more views of the winsome children. When the southeast weather map appeared, Tim touched the remote and turned it off. Handel's crystal music expanded in his head.

46

No mention of last night, no shot of Darren's house, no retrieval of a corpse, nothing at all. Hawk felt flat, almost disappointed. People said losing your virginity was just like that – a big deal you dreamt about for years, and then suddenly, was that it? And how was it for you, Mrs Darren? How did you feel when you came home? How did you react to that empty house? It should not have been too alarming – you were not alone. Perhaps you discussed your husband's absence with your chauffeur. Perhaps you both stood at the chrome cocktail bar considering what might have happened. Perhaps you gave the man a drink.

But it was regretable, Hawk thought, that he had had to kill the bodyguard. Two deaths and a living witness. He frowned – as if the musicians had played a discord. It was important that his first project should go smoothly: no loose ends. The redhead, for example, was a loose end. He should have dealt with her. Why hadn't he? Because taking life was a serious business – a grave business, you might say. Hawk grinned: he felt good today – a professional. Now the bodyguard who died, Hawk reasoned, that was a professional risk. He had pulled a gun and left Hawk no choice. But the girl? Death was not a risk in her profession – or was not *supposed* to be. She had done nothing wrong. She and Hawk were each professionals, both on hand to service Darren. But Hawk was sorry about the bodyguard. The gang boss had been despatched with a single shot, had died instantaneously, while his bodyguard had had to lie on the linoleum, blood seeping from his chest. He had tried to speak. Maybe the girl had been right, maybe if the man had been able to speak he would have asked to be put down. Like an animal, the girl said. A man should not have died like that, conscious of his dying. Execution should be painless. The punishment was not the dying, it was the forfeiture of life.

Handel stopped. People coughed – a live performance. The sound of the shuffling audience rustled in stereo around Hawk's flat. Some of that audience would have gone without lunch to hear the music. They would have a bite later – savour both separate experiences to the full. Hawk wondered about the dinner that was planned for that evening. How would Kazan savour that?

47

5

Irena trailed behind Kazan as he showed her the house. After their long tiring journey, this procession through his beautiful rooms was like the trip she had taken recently with schoolchildren to a museum. The guide had marched them to each display, had paused before each piece, had declaimed each one's merit. She and the weary children had not appreciated their beauty. There were too many lovely things they couldn't touch.

Alexei would be disappointed if she seemed overwhelmed by his wealth. He wanted her to feel at home here. She was determined that she would. In the room that he called a lounge (she thought the proper name was drawing-room, and imagined herself sitting there in the evenings like Ada Clare at her embroidery) she could not get over his soft leather upholstery, the feel of it. Al had swept straight past the sofa, giving her little time to stroke its smooth surface with her fingertips, wondering whether it was for sitting on or was only there for show. He had *glass tables* in that room! Irena had never heard of such things. An extraordinary idea, she thought, a table that could so easily break! Was this commonplace in England, or was Alexei an eccentric – an artist, even – and she had not realised? According to Dickens, the master of the house in England often was eccentric. Irena did not mind if Alex was, except that, in stories, such gentlemen often met with unfortunate ends.

There were carpets in every room, covering every scrap of floor. All the curtains were much longer than the windows – they certainly would keep the draughts out, she thought, when winter came.

'This is the dining-room. Hasn't had a lot of use.'

A room solely for eating in! And yes, another glass table – enormous, with metal chairs. Irena had expected English tables to be made of oak. Suddenly, she giggled. 'I hope you put a cloth on it when we eat.'

'Cloth?'

'On your glass table.' She giggled a second time, her hand up to her mouth. 'Or we will see everybody's knees.'

He was smiling too. If this was what made her giggle, he would try to see the funny side as well. 'So?'

'It will look as if we are eating from our laps, and . . . if anyone scratches a leg or kicks off their shoes, everyone will see.'

He grinned. 'Stops you playing footsie, am I right?'

'Footsie?'

'Yeah, you know, footsie: reaching your foot out under the table and touching someone else's shoe. Sending messages.'

'Oh, Alexei, I shall be happy here.'

He nodded, eyes loving her. 'Let's hope.'

When she saw the kitchen she knew he was a millionaire. At first, the room merely seemed impossibly smart: so many cupboards, the sink set into a work surface. Then Alexei started opening cupboard doors. One revealed a refrigerator, then, most incredibly of all, another cupboard housed a cooker. Fancy hiding an oven behind a cupboard door! He showed her how in the slab of darker work surface above were the hot plates for the stove. 'But they look like drawings,' she said.

Al turned the nobs, made all the rings glow for her. 'Don't worry,' he said. 'You don't have to cook.'

She snorted. 'Of course I will cook for you.'

Irena stared wide-eyed at the various strange machines – this one for washing clothes, this one for washing dishes, this one for drying clothes. Well, they were only mechanical devices: she must learn how to operate them.

She let him lead her into the games room. Why not? If he had a kitched lined with magic cabinets, and another room reserved exclusively for eating, why not a room for playing games in? 'What is snooker?' she asked.

As they climbed the stairs, Irena asked if, locked away in another section of the house, he might have an aged relation?

'What the hell gave you that idea?'

Victorian fiction.

In the October dusk, Tim Hawk stood at the high window of his flat, looking at the river. Across the leaden water lay ripples of setting sunlight. Lamps were coming on, but in the grey daylight their reflections looked feeble on the water. The evening rush-hour had begun, but Hawk, isolated in his flat, was not affected by it. His view was dominated by the Thames.

The warbling sound was from his telephone. He fetched it from the black side table, carried it to his previous position at the window while he spoke.

Leyton Knox: 'You were going to ring me, Timmy.'

'Was I?' Hawk was chirpy.

The Glasgow accent flattened. 'Don't play the fool with me, sonny. Have ye topped him yet?'

'Darren?'

'Who else, man? There hasnae been a word on the news.'

'He's disposed of.'

'Ah. Any problems?'

'There was a bodyguard. I had to take him out.'

'Witnesses?'

'Only the bodyguard.' The prepared lie came easily.

'Good man. Where'd you do it?'

'My business.'

'You're a cocky wee bastard, d'ye know that, Hawk?'

'What matters is I do my job. I do it cleanly. I don't get caught.'

Knox let out a breath. 'Are you gonna be like this with everyone, son, or will ye save it all for me?' He sounded almost plaintive.

'What – d'you think I'm prejudiced, Leyton?'

50

'Away with ye, man. Listen, our friend Kazan is back. His plane arrived an hour or two late, but that'll no stop him getting to the restaurant around 8.30.'

'Is that when his table's booked?'

'The whole bloody restaurant, Timmy, from 8 o'clock. *Le Champignon Sauvage*. But Kazan won't arrive bang on the mark. He never does.'

'8.30?'

'I'd assume so.'

'So the best time for me will be at nine?'

'Aye, he'll certainly have arrived by then. Perhaps you should wait till 9.30, Timmy. Let them enjoy their food.'

'Considerate of you.'

'There's more to me than you've heard, son, as I've told ye before. Now, you're sure you want to go ahead with this?'

'We've been through that. You want to come and watch?'

'I'd love to, son, but duty calls.'

'I bet. Well, I shall give them your apologies.'

'How kind.'

When Al came into the room, Irena was sitting on the end of the bed, gazing at the fitted wardrobe. The sliding door was open, revealing the almost empty rail and shelves. He caught the expression as it slipped from her face. 'What's up?'

'Nothing.' She gave the kind of smile that could knock every question out of his head. 'You feeling homesick?'

'No.' She rose, came towards him, put her hands on his broad shoulders. 'I am content now.'

He tilted his head quizzically. 'Penny for them.'

'I do not understand.'

'A penny for your thoughts. That's an expression we have here.'

'Oh.' She kissed his nose.

'So what do I have to do, Irena, find the penny?'

She laughed. 'I am not so . . . mercenary. But that is the point.'

51

'You lost me.'

Her shoulders drooped. 'There is no way I can say this that does not sound bad.' He frowned. 'But look.' She pointed to the open wardrobe. Three dresses hung from the rail, her linen occupied two shelves. On the floor beside her suitcase were two pairs of shoes. 'My things.'

'Pretty.'

'They are all I have.'

'You got nothing in the chest of drawers?'

She shrugged. 'That is also for me? Oh.' She sat heavily on the bed.

'Irena.' He sat down and pulled her into his breast. 'You're sad because you don't have lots of clothes, is that it?'

'I should not have told you.'

'We can *buy* you clothes. We can fill the whole damn room with them.'

'When I packed my case, I brought everything I had.'

He inhaled the smell of her hair. 'Everything?'

'Well, all the nice things. They look lost in there.'

'Tomorrow,' he said firmly, 'we'll go into town and buy new clothes.'

'But –'

'But nothing. I wanna buy you wonderful clothes. Wanna make you look like a princess.'

'But *those* are my clothes.'

'Let me tell you something, Irena. We are gonna fill that cupboard so full you can hardly close the door.'

She let her head remain against his chest. 'What will happen to the clothes that I brought with me?'

'Well, what you want? The nice ones we'll keep.'

She hesitated. 'And the others?'

He patted her head. 'We'll keep them safe, don't worry. We'll put them away in poly bags.'

'With lavender?'

'Yeah, lavender, why not?'

'Like an old lady's childhood dresses. Oh, I can't explain it to you.'

52

'What?'

'They are not just my clothes. They are . . . everything I have.'

'They're who you are, am I right?'

She looked at him with wet blue eyes. 'You understand, Alexei? They are all my life – my old life.'

'Yeah,' he said slowly. 'I understand.'

'You must be patient with me.'

They stood at the open wardrobe to see the clothes that she had brought. This crochet cardigan was made by Grandma. This blouse was from her father when she went to college. These two day dresses she had sewn herself. Although her shoes were not as beautiful as soft leather ones in England, Irena liked them: they were comfortable, and strong.

'And this?' he asked, fingering a long embroidered linen dress.

'You like it?' She unhooked it from the rail, held it against her body.

'Of course.' What else could he say? Though the dress *was* beautiful, in an old-fashioned way – made her look a princess from a fairytale.

'It was my mother's. She was married in this dress.'

'I know.'

'Did I tell you?'

He kissed her forehead. 'You did. We won't hide this in a poly bag. We'll keep it here in the wardrobe.'

'For a special occasion.'

He paused. 'Special?'

She still held the dress against her body. 'One day you may ask me to wear this dress.' She looked at him with big blue eyes.

He paused. 'Special? How about tonight?'

'Oh.' She seemed surprised, as if that was not what she had wanted him to ask. She rehung it in the wardrobe.

'I mean, it's the best you have. The only party dress.'

'Yes,' she agreed. 'It is my only party dress.'

'And it's too late in the day now to buy something else. The shops are shut.'

53

'Of course,' she agreed again.

'Everyone's gonna be there, seeing you for the first time. You wanna look good.'

'I hope I shall.'

'You better believe it!' He began striding around the room. 'What is this – you fishing for compliments? I tell you, Irena, you're gonna knock their heads off. You could walk in there tonight wrapped in a *sheet* and you'd knock them out.'

'I should think I would!'

He laughed with her. 'You're not worried, are you?'

'Of course.' She smiled at him. 'I am frightened stiff.'

'They're gonna love you.' He paused, his face serious. 'Listen, this will be some evening.'

'I really am frightened, you know.' She sank down again on the bed.

'But you don't have to be frightened, Irena, you're so beautiful.'

She blushed and looked away. Then she asked, 'What will . . .? How will you tell your friends about me tonight?'

He looked suddenly as mischievous as a little boy. 'I'm gonna make a speech.'

'Oh!' Her eyes sparkled.

'You imagine that? I'm gonna tell them exactly who you are, straight away, soon as we arrive. No one gets the wrong idea. Don't you worry, Irena, everyone's gonna know you are my princess.'

'Oh no, Alexei, you cannot say that!'

'I'll tell them what I want. Listen, these people – you've gotta hammer it in their skulls.'

'I will be so embarrassed. Which way will I look?'

He smiled, nodding. 'I got an idea about that as well. Look, when I am saying all this, when I am telling everyone about you, we have to . . . well, spare your blushes, hide your face.'

She stared at him. 'Do you want me to wear a veil?'

He laughed. 'Christ no, where d'you think this is? No – no veils, no masks. What we do, we keep you outside the room when

54

I go in. Then I tell them. I make the speech – just a short one, nothing fancy – explain who you are, how they have gotta behave to you –'

'Alexei!'

'Too right! How they behave.' His face had hardened now – the smile still lying on it, but a deep crease across his forehead. 'These people have to be told, believe me. It's easier if everybody knows where they stand from day one.'

'Now I am embarrassed again.' She sensed the power in him.

'Irena, I know these people. You will be the star of the evening – but like a film star, you got to delay your entrance.'

She shook her head, blushing. 'I am not a star.'

'This is a big night, Irena, so we are gonna start it with a bang. Here's what we do: when we get to the restaurant, we go first of all to the back door, you get out. I have – what's his name, the French guy? – John Jack, that's it. He comes out, whips you in. There's a little room you can wait in at the back.'

'On my own, Alexei? How will I know what to do?'

'You don't do anything. You wait a couple of minutes, I come in the front. I say the words, I call you out, you come in. Simple as that. Spontaneous applause.'

'Applause?'

'Spontaneous, I'll make sure of it.' And he would. 'You'll only be waiting two minutes in that room. Three at the maximum.'

'How will I know . . .'

'What?'

'When to come out. What is my cue?'

'Your cue? What is this, amateur dramatics night? You come when I call your name. "Irena" – that's your cue.'

'If you're sure –'

'I'm always sure, Princess.'

6

Tim Hawk examined his wardrobe. His clothes seemed drab, lifeless. No matter what he spent, how carefully he chose, when he put the pieces together they rarely achieved the right effect. Things bought at different times never went together. They might appear to be the same colour, yet they weren't. Even black, the colour he most favoured, came in different shades: jet, ebony, matt, patent, coal-black, blue-black, brown-black, black that shone with hidden timbres, black that reflected nothing at all. White was as bad: he would buy a shirt, plain and virginal; he'd bring it home, lay it against another from his wardrobe, and he'd discover that one of the two was just a trace off white. It might have pink in it, beige or cream. Why couldn't things be straightforward black or white? Glaring at his clothes, Hawk decided that people nowadays had too much diversity: shops crammed with merchandise, homes filled with junk. Even his own minimalist flat held too many things. In olden days, he thought, people didn't have this endless, confusing choice. They owned just two or three sets of clothes, wore them till they stank or became saturated with mud, then sent them off for the lengthy process of laundry. After the wash a little seamstress checked every item, mended loose stitches and rips, sent them back. Clothes rested comfortably in a half-empty press. In Hawk's favourite era, the Renaissance, choice in clothes was even simpler: peasants – town or country – wore virtually the same clothes every day. The poor washed out their cambric, the rich flung on a fresh cloak.

Hawk selected a pair of ebony black trousers. Of course, if he *had* lived in the seventeenth century he wouldn't have been rich – he'd probably have been a street urchin. Living contemporary with Handel, he might never have heard the music. The only tunes he would have known might have been ballads on chap sheets, folk songs, hymns. Imagine having Handel's superb baroque operas performed fresh and new in the same London he was walking in, yet never hearing them! He smiled to himself: no, he would have heard them, he would have known.

To match the black trousers he chose a black roll-neck pullover in fine textured wool, black lightweight shoes – almost dancing pumps – black socks. He rifled again through his wardrobe. Everything he wore tonight was an avoidance of choice: because he couldn't decide on a colour he took black. Any variation, any sudden splash of gaudy colour, seemed unacceptable. He knew the effect was too sombre. It needed brightening, but he did not know how. Once, young men dangled medallions on chains round their necks. In the Sixties they'd sported a bright flower or some beads. What he should do, he told himself, was buy his clothes as an outfit, an *ensemble*, as a woman did. A woman bought her skirt *with* the blouse and the matching scarf, then she chose appropriate shoes. The whole set would be bought in the same shop or at roughly the same time, so that everything coordinated. Men didn't buy their clothes that way.

Hawk posed before the full-length mirror and reviewed the effect. Sombre. Yes, if he'd been a woman he could have added a brooch – one piece, something striking – to lighten all this black. Or a scarf. What he needed was a splash of colour – perhaps a cloak? He had been born in the wrong age. The only solution was to continue this effect, to exaggerate the black. He reached to a low shelf for a pair of black leather gloves.

He was still checking the mirror when Calvin arrived. The black of Calvin's skin had a greenish tinge – another shade.

'What's up, Cal – you nervous?'

'Oh man.' Cal shook his head.

'Don't worry.'

'Listen Hawk, I don't like this shit, man. I mean, I'm just a driver, right? That's what I do. I take you there, I bring you back. I sit outside in the car.'

'Van.'

'Oh *no*, we ain't going in your van?'

'Easier.'

'Oh shit, I am not a van driver, man, I bought a ace car. We got a Marley outside.' Hawk looked blank. 'Bob Marley and the Wailers – a BMW.'

Hawk's face cleared. 'Well, tonight you drive the Morrison.' It was Cal's turn to look puzzled. 'Van Morrison – the van.'

Cal laughed. 'You got no style, Hawk. What the boys are going to say?'

'Who'd you bring?'

'Clint and Ronnie.'

'Invite them up. We're not leaving for an hour, so we might as well have a drink.'

'Hey, no drinking, man. I get the DTs just thinking about this job.'

'Fetch Clint and Ronnie. They'll cheer you up.'

Cal paused at the door. 'You say we got a hour before we go?'

'About that.'

'You're not going to make us listen to your music, are you, man?'

She felt alone in a foreign country. Al had taken the Daimler Princess, and she was in the back seat of his Rover, driven by Louis, who didn't mind. Shortly before 8 o'clock Al had decided that it was important no one spotted her when they arrived at the restaurant – it would spoil his surprise. Someone would be looking out for the Daimler, waiting for him.

So at 8.30 he and Irena left in separate cars. By then it had been dark for two hours. Shooters Hill lit by lamplight seemed to Irena more impressive than in the day. Not difficult. She didn't like to admit it – hardly to herself, certainly not to him – but she had been disappointed when she first arrived on Shooters

Hill. Compared to some parts of London that they had driven through, the road had seemed ... ordinary, she thought. Only when they had passed its summit, had come down into open land, had turned off along the lane into Oxleas Wood, did she begin to be more impressed. Kazan lived in a two-acre development of just six large modern houses. Their brash, mock-Georgian brickwork, sharply gleaming paint, their overly decorative ironwork, stood out among the woodlands like parked caravans in a field. But more opulent.

This evening, once they had driven down the dark narrow lane on to Shooters Hill, the main road looked empty and clean. House lights glowed across front gardens. She had been inside an English house now: she knew what they were like. Sitting alone in the snug back seat of the Rover, Irena shivered with disbelief: she felt cosseted, as if wearing a mink stole. This was to become her way of life. She watched an 89 bus gliding towards them, glowing like a lantern in the street. It was half full. Among the glum passengers lost in private thought, she saw a group of four black girls, laughing, gesticulating, having a good time, ignored by other passengers. Irena kept the image in her mind after the bus passed by. She wondered who the people were, what sort of homes they were returning to. In London there seemed a great many black people – and one of the passengers, Irena thought, had looked Chinese. Many races seemed to live here. Despite the many books she had read about the English – books by Dickens, Shaw, Ruskin, Priestley – she had not expected this cosmopolitan mix. Was all London like this? All England? All Britain? Perhaps it meant that as a foreigner she herself might not stand out.

In Greenwich, Irena was surprised that many of the shops still had their lights on – in the evening, when they were closed. But then the streets themselves were flooded with bright light – not just the main streets, but the side streets as well. In England, electricity was obviously subsidised. And the people, she thought, watching through the car window, not only were they all races and colours, they were all young. The great majority out this

59

evening seemed to be in their early twenties or teens. Where was everybody else?

In the illuminated streets. Irena found it easier to pick out the inns – the Horse & Groom, the Coach & Horses, the Green Man. Dickens always wrote warmly of English inns – their hospitality, strange bedrooms, mulled ale and huge meals. Irena looked forward to the day when she would visit one.

Louis said, 'We'll go round the back.'

Those were Kazan's instructions. He would drive himself to the front door of *Le Champignon Sauvage* and go in alone. Louis, meanwhile, would escort Irena through the back. They needn't hurry, Louis said when he parked the Rover in the dim little alley. 'No sense rushing out in the cold. You've time to check your make-up.'

Perhaps Louis was hinting that she should. From her small leather handbag – slightly scuffed, but precious to Irena – she took a mirror and scrutinised her face. It seemed perfectly all right to her.

Louis sneaked glances from the front. She was a beautiful kid. That was a lovely dress she was wearing, though perhaps not ideal for a restaurant. Especially if the evening degenerated into the kind of beanfight they sometimes did when Al Kazan had downed some drinks. That embroidered dress looked antique, precious, too fragile. Louis hoped it would not get spoilt.

'Ready?' he asked.

Irena nodded. Louis slipped out of the car, came round quickly to play chauffeur with her door. But she had already opened it – was not used to servants. The evening was chilly, the night air dry as paper. The unlit terrace stood between the two of them and the main road, blocking the sound of traffic, leaving this part of the alley dark and cloistered.

The explosion was a shock.

It seemed to shatter the little alley, a deafening crack that stunned their ears. Louis and Irena staggered, lurched against each other, turned to see what made the noise. There was a smell of cordite, someone laughing. Louis left to run ahead.

She stood gasping, eyes blinking, ears ringing from the blast. She saw Louis running along the alley, heard voices, saw him slow. He shouted, 'You bastards!' Voices were shouting back – were they children? 'Swop your old banger for one of mine!'

She felt confused. She wanted to sit down. Louis faded in the night, then reappeared. 'Little bastards,' he said again.

'What happened?'

He stepped forward, arms crooked as if to hold her, but changed his mind. 'Sodding thunderflash,' he said.

She wanted to ask what he meant, but found that her voice had disappeared. The night air felt paralysingly cold.

'Firework,' he explained. 'Sodding big one. Sodding kids shouldn't be allowed. It isn't even November yet.'

She licked her lips, forced saliva into her mouth. 'I do not understand.'

'Come inside. You'll catch your death.'

Ahead of them, light seeped from the restaurant's kitchen window – the only light in the alley. Louis pushed against the wooden door, held it open for her. As she was about to step inside, they heard the whistle of a rocket, safely distant, and both looked up. Part of its cascade of stars appeared above the roofs. They heard crackling sounds, explosive pops.

Irena slipped past Louis into the heat and bustle of the kitchen. Cooks in stained white aprons, waiters in dark suits, a fat woman at a sink. Urgent voices. Steam, the smells of cooking: garlic, hot oil. A pan sizzled, another steamed. As Louis hurried her along, the staff hardly glanced at her. None seemed surprised that she and Louis – clearly customers – came from the alley into the kitchen. One man only – a suited man, perhaps the manager – murmured in Louis's ear, smiled faintly at Irena. Perhaps he expected them. The man led them through the other door out from the kitchen – a swing door that waiters came rushing through – into an ante-chamber, a short passageway, a rear hallway beside the stairs. Ahead stood a second set of swing doors into the dining-room. Here in the alcove were two chairs and a small table heaped with linen. The manager nodded them to the chairs and disappeared immediately into the dining-room. They could hear laughter, excited voices, clattering plates. A wine cork popped. Someone cheered.

'Shall I wait with you?' Louis asked.

She stood bewildered beside the chairs.

'Are you all right?'

She looked him in the eyes and tried to smile. 'Why did they do that?'

'Kids, you know. Guy Fawkes.' He frowned at her. 'You know about Guy Fawkes Night?' She shook her head. 'You know what a firework is?'

'Yes.'

'Well, they invented fireworks for Guy Fawkes Night. He was a feller tried to blow up the Houses of Parliament. But he didn't manage it – unfortunately.' Louis grinned. 'His friends betrayed him, so he was caught. Anyway, that's why we have fireworks.'

She asked, 'When was this?'

'I don't know: 1066 or something. I was never much at school.'

'I thought the Chinese invented fireworks?'

'Yeah? Well, *we* invented Guy Fawkes Night. November 5th. That's when he tried to do it, see? But now, well, every November 5th we blow *him* up instead. Have a big bonfire, stick a Guy on top, have lots of fireworks.'

'You stick a guy on top?'

'Yeah – no, not a person. A Guy, you know, a model – made of paper and straw, dressed up in a suit.'

'Was he a wicked man?'

'Unlucky, that's all. Almost a sodding hero.'

'Then I do not understand. Why do you burn him?'

Louis sniffed. 'Well, anyway, the thing is, for a couple of weeks before Guy Fawkes Night, kids like to get their hands on fireworks and run around letting them off. Sodding nuisance.'

She sat down. She didn't know why she continued this conversation: it didn't help the ringing in her head. Yet she asked, 'How do children get these awful fireworks?'

'Buy them in the shops.'

She nodded. Of course. Everyone knew that the English were a warlike nation with barbarity and violence beneath their supposedly civilised skin. English fiction was always about cruelty and injustice. English soldiers were feared at war.

Louis pointed to the chair beside her. 'Shall I sit there?'

'No, thank you. I think you should guard our car in the alleyway. The car needs you more than I do, don't you think?'

She thought she had made a joke, but Louis seemed a little hurt. Perhaps she had seemed rude. She said, 'Thank you for your help, Louis. I am all right now. I shall wait here for my cue.'

He frowned. When he tried to hold her gaze, she turned away. He took a breath and said, 'Well, I didn't get an invite, so I suppose I better wait outside in the car.'

His decision was greeted with a roar of approval from inside the restaurant. Kazan had arrived.

He had two men on the door and every table occupied. A week ago he had telephoned the guest list from her village phone: friends, employees, one table for his relatives. Everyone was expected to be there by 8 o'clock, and what Al expected, he got.

Outside the restaurant, Al had left his Daimler against the kerb: fat tyres on yellow line. Now he thrust through the discreet door, his hands raised to shoulder level, palms facing, bestowing blessings on his guests. Through the open doorway a blast of cold air swept past him, bringing a chill into the room. But he paused there, framed against the night like a game-show host on TV. The guests clapped. Al strode the length of the small restaurant, pausing to clasp outstretched hands, heading for the top table set across the room for himself and his family. Six chairs stood along the far side, facing down the restaurant – three sets of two, the central two not taken. Al shoved his way to the table like a prize-fighter through spectators round the ring. He reached his chair, stood behind it, beamed at his people. Again he raised his chunky hands. 'Hey! Hey! You ain't pretending that you missed me? Don't make me laugh!'

* * *

Irena smiled at his reception. In her little ante-chamber she sat alone. Waiters no longer bustled to and fro, they took a break. While guests cheered and banged upon the tables, waiters and staff exchanged jokes in the kitchen, leaving Irena unattended between swing doors. No one had spoken to her. In her curious pretty dress she was like a girl ignored beside the dance floor.

In the dining-room, noise subsided. Background music had been switched off. Irena heard a man welcome him – an awkward voice, sentences unprepared. Sitting on her chair in the hallway beside the stairs, Irena strained to hear what Alexei would say.

'So, what are you all doing here – you out of food at home?' Cheers and banging on the table. 'I'm here for a quiet meal with my family – what's your excuse? Right! Now listen. What've you been doing while I been away? You all behave yourselves? Yeah? What the hell do I pay you for?' Laughter. 'You're supposed to work while I'm away, am I right? Now, is everybody hungry? Then I'll sit down.' Cries of No, get on your feet, we want a speech. 'A speech? You don't want that.' Mixed response, good humoured, loud. 'Jeez, if I'd a known that all you bums would be here, I'd have brought my holiday snaps, shown my slides. Then you'd wish you'd stayed at home! But you're lucky tonight, because I ain't brought them – they ain't developed yet. But if you don't behave yourselves I'll drag you back here next week and *make* you watch them! And I got stacks of them, I promise! Well, I would have, wouldn't I? You would not believe. What a country! I mean, me and my family, as you all know, we come originally from Ukraine. Well, Mum and Dad did.' Al turned to the elderly couple on his right. 'You couldn't get out fast enough, could you, Dad? Nineteen thirty – what? – thirty-six, and you never went back. Hey!' Voice rising, readdressing the audience: 'That tells you something about the place, don't it? All right, we know the reason.' Al turned to acknowledge the second old couple on his left. 'All of us, we had to wait a long time till we could go home. Let's face it, before 'ninety-two we didn't dare

64

to. In the old Soviet Union, you see, they loved Ukrainians so much that if any one of us ever did go back, the Ruskies wouldn't let us out! They thought they had such a wonderful set of countries, no one could ever want to leave. So they didn't *let* you leave: even the trains ran just one way – in! Well, that's all changed now, and we are *glad* about it, am I right? Good riddance to them. Ukraine is part of Europe again!'

They cheered him on. In the ante-room, Irena wondered who he had invited – how many Ukrainians. When he had sneered at their country, she had been shocked. Of course, Ukraine had been impoverished and held back under Soviet rule, but one should not blame Ukrainians for that. Irena wondered how his parents felt to hear their son talk this way in front of all those people. She would soon find out. Soon she would meet them again.

'I tell you,' Al continued, 'when I went out the first time – can you imagine that, the first time in my life that I seen my homeland? – after a week I felt like they could keep it, we did not need that place in Europe. Yeah, I admit it. I mean, no pubs, no decent restaurants, no shops worth looking at, no money, nothing. Listen: it took us a day and a half to get from the airport to their village – a day and a half, across a great empty dried-up country hardly out the nineteenth century.'

Irena shook her head. She had not realised how he felt.

'And yet,' Al said, pausing suddenly for effect, 'and yet I did go back – quickly, after just three months. Why? What could it be about the place that dragged me back for another look?' Irena knew now where he was leading. 'And I bet some of you bums wondered why I stayed out there so long this time – *you* did, didn't you, Dad? At first. You reckoned that if you weren't along to show me where to go, I couldn't handle it. You thought that instead of taking a day and a half to reach the village I'd need a week! Well, I didn't. This time I had the system sussed. I'd worked out that all you need is a pocketful of American dollars – the real paper stuff, you know? Not plastic. And don't be shy about flashing those notes around. This time I got to the village on the same day I landed. Yeah! Not bad, eh? So, I have found my way around, I am starting to like the scenery, and I have this job to do. What did you think: I went back for another holiday? Listen, back here in the smoke, I am a fairly big potato, am I right? But out there in Ukraine I am nothing. I am – what?' A moment's muttering. 'Yeah, that's right, Dad. My father tells me that out in Ukraine I am just a little potato *chip*! A Ukrainian joke. But there is something else: I am also family – my roots are there. I am like their long lost uncle who turns up from abroad. And those people . . . they opened their homes to me . . . Ah, hell, I ain't cut out for speechmaking. Listen, what I am trying to tell you is that I went out there the boss, but I have come back with a new boss of my own.' He paused for effect, but the reaction seemed uncertain, muted. 'Yeah, I have a new boss. And now I would like to introduce you to this new boss of mine. Are you ready for this? OK boss, come on out and meet our people.' Al turned to call for her. 'Irena!' He turned back to his audience. 'Irena, my new boss.'

He hurried from the table, disappeared through the swing doors. He didn't hear his guests turn to each other, whispering, 'Was that Irena or Rita? What's he talking about? A new boss, for Chrissake? Where's he gone?'

He was in the ante-chamber, laughing at Irena, pulling her to her feet. 'They will be *mad* about you.'

'Alexei, I am so nervous. All those people.'

'You're the princess, I told you. Come and see.'

Keeping a firm hold of her hand, Al swept back through the swing doors, led his blushing Irena into the restaurant. 'My new boss, Irena. Ain't she beautiful? Ain't she? Right, settle down everyone. *Quiet*, you people!'

The hubbub ceased. Al still had Irena by one hand, and he raised his other in the air. 'Ladies and gentlemen. Friends.' More quietly: 'Mum and Dad. Everyone. This beautiful young lady standing here beside me is Irena Kazan. Yeah, Kazan. Irena, I am pleased to tell all you people, has done me the honour and . . . is now my wife.'

There was one final moment of silence. Then as Al repeated 'my wife', his parents rose from their chairs, beaming with happiness. Everybody started to clap. The other two Ukrainians rose also, and all six stumbled into a clumsy communal embrace: Al's parents, his cousin Gilda, her husband Uri – now known as Harry – Al himself and his precious Ukrainian bride. Applause grew quickly – raucous enthusiasm hiding astonishment beneath. While the guests clapped and banged the tables, they asked each other which of them had known of this, what did they think? No one had known of it. No one admitted what they thought. Not yet.

Al shouted, 'This is why I went back! I met her last summer, we wrote letters. I had to see her again. It's been a whirlwind romance.'

The cheers swelled, then faded. He said, 'You know what I am like – I do not hang around, am I right? I want every one of you good people to recognise this lady: Mrs Alexander Kazan. If I am the king round here, then she is my princess'

His cousin Gilda whispered urgently in his ear. 'Correction!' Al shouted with a laugh. 'She is my queen – not my princess!'

People laughed. Al laughed with them, both hands raised in the air like a politician who had won another term. But several of the applauding guests picked up on the word that Al had used: they whispered that he'd been right the first time: a princess was what she was, young enough for his daughter.

'Sit down, sit down,' Al shouted. 'Let's have a bit of hush.'

But Al's father, his voice proud and surprisingly strong, stopped him and commanded, 'Everyone raise their glasses. We will drink to my son and his beautiful new bride.'

In the little alley behind *Le Champignon Sauvage*, the van came to a stop. Calvin turned off the engine. For several seconds, none of the four men made any attempt to move. Then Hawk opened the door and sniffed the air.

'A fine night,' he said. 'But getting colder.'

He stepped into the alley's darkness and waited for the others. They clambered out, blowing vapour in the air.

'Keep the noise down,' Hawk said.

Ten yards behind them in the alley was a parked Rover with a misted screen. Louis sat motionless in his seat. He watched the four men walk round to the rear of their van, open its door and reach inside. Louis wondered what the hell was going on. He wondered what the hell he should do about it. He did not make a move.

'Speech! Speech!' somebody shouted. They wanted to hear Irena speak. A woman near the entrance to the restaurant, well away from the Kazan's table, asked her husband quietly whether he thought that the girl *could* speak English.

He whispered back, 'All the Kazans speak English.'

'But they *live* here.'

Al stood at the table, defending Irena from the calls. 'Come on, lads, be fair. She's only just arrived.'

The woman hissed: 'See, she don't speak English.'

Al told them that Irena would be embarrassed. She smiled at his side. Someone began a wolf-whistle, but changed it to a yell: 'Let's hear a word from Al's new boss!'

Even as Al shook his head, he realised that Irena had raised her face to speak. He and his father simultaneously motioned for the noise to cease. They made identical gestures, father and son, unaware of each other's action. But it quelled the noise. Irena licked her lips, smiled at the audience, and said, 'Thank you for your welcome. You make me feel that I am at home.'

The guests relaxed. 'Forgive me if I say only a few words.' They would certainly forgive that. 'Everything is so new to me. Yesterday we were in Ukraine, where I have lived all my life. We had our breakfast in my village, where I have lived *nearly* all my life, then we drove across my country to –' she hesitated for the English name, '– Kiev. I had never been there. We flew in an aeroplane. That is remarkable for me: I had never done that before. This morning we have arrived in London – or near London: Alexei tells me that the name of the town there is Thiefrow.' She heard sniggers, glanced at Al, but he waved her on. 'Then

68

we – that is, my husband and I –' Another snigger, which strangled fast at Kazan's glare. 'My husband took me to his home on the Shooter's Hill, and very soon we did come here. I have not even had time to buy English clothes. I wear this old dress of Ukraine – I apologise if it is not suitable, but it is precious to me.' Irena faltered, glanced down at her linen dress, then continued. 'This was my mother's dress, in Ukraine, who is dead for many years. She was married in it, like me.'

Irena's eyes were wide and liquid. Colour had left her face. She gave a brief smile, then suddenly sat down. A roar of South London approval swelled like a crashing wave, sustained itself for ten long seconds, then as suddenly collapsed.

All the lights had gone out.

7

Blackness. Pools of light. Faces underlit. Several restaurant tables are lit by candles, which now provide the only illumination. Suddenly this discreet and cosy eating house has been transformed into a warm and crowded cave. Shadows. Flickering light.

'We had a powercut?'

'Blown fuse.'

'Who's got a pound for the meter?'

'John Jack!'

A pistol fires – one shot – and women scream.

'No one move!' Hawk shouts. 'Absolutely no one makes a move.'

They cannot see him. Their eyes have adjusted to the gloom, but Hawk is invisible. His voice comes from behind the slightly open swing doors.

'Now sit down.'

Few do. Some press into shadows by the walls. One or two curse being forbidden to bring guns. Their tense faces underlit by candles look part of next week's Hallowe'en.

Hawk yells, 'Listen!'

A moment's pause. Then, through the loudspeakers normally used for background music, comes the deep groan of something that sounds like a cello but is in fact the bowed sound of a baroque viol. 'The fuck is that?' someone mutters. Before anyone can react further, a soprano's wistful voice begins:

When I am laid, am laid in earth . . .

'What the hell?' they are muttering. Nobody recognises Purcell's opera but they catch the funereal feel. On the second line of Dido's Lament, the swing doors push fully open. Four men emerge into the gloom – two white men at the front, two black men at the rear. They come slowly, carrying something.

No trouble, no trouble in my breast . . .

The long box on their shoulders is a coffin. Exclamations, unanswered questions. Hasn't someone got a gun?

Remember me, remember me . . .

Al Kazan regains command. 'What the hell are you doing?' He has to speak loudly to raise his voice above the music.

Remember me, remember me . . .

The pall-bearers squeeze in front of his table.

But a-a-a-a-a-ah, forget my fate . . .

Guests are melting from frozen postures in the dark. Hawk's pale face gleams in the candle-light.

But a-a-a-a-a-ah, forget my fate . . .

Hawk says, 'Some security you have here. We could have been anybody.'

Al watches astonished as the four men solemnly shift the coffin from their shoulders and lay it on his table. The suitability of the baroque lament is becoming clear.

When I am laid, am laid in earth . . .

'What *is* this?' Al demands. Then his expression changes. He leans across the table, peers into Tim Hawk's face. 'Is this a wedding present?'

'Wedding?' Hawk wipes his hands. 'You getting married? No, this –' he indicates the long, closed coffin, '– this is just to welcome you home.'

71

Nobody else in the restaurant dares to speak. Only the soprano continues unconcerned.

> May my wrongs create no trouble,
> No trouble in my breast.

Hawk says, 'This is something you set your heart on.'

Al leans back from the table, stands erect. He glares at the coffin but does not touch it. Irena asks, 'Who are these men, Alexei?'

To Irena, this darkened restaurant seems enchanted, almost soothing. She likes the music, which reminds her of church – as do the dark shadows and pools of candle-light. The four solemn men before the table could be officiating at a ceremony. Each is dressed in black, each has a single red carnation pinned to his breast. Their leader is the pale good-looking one whose hair seems silver-white in the erratic glow of flickering candles. She stares at him: something familiar; something she cannot place yet. What is he doing? She would have thought that this intrusion was an insult to her and Alexei, yet her husband tolerates it, seems mesmerised. She nudges him again.

He says, 'This is a joke, Hawk, am I right?'

'Dead serious,' Hawk says.

Al watches him. Irena is close enough to see uncertainty in his eyes. She knows the other guests will be watching what he does. When he speaks, his voice is quiet, does not carry above the music, 'I hope this ain't something you will regret'.

'Open the box,' Hawk says calmly. He and his companions are half a pace from the table. He seems relaxed – though the others, Irena notices, are tense and stiff. She can sense the threat that hangs in the air. She asks, 'Is it safe to open that?'

For the first time, the blond one looks at her properly. He is young, younger than she, and his eyes are palest blue. She remembers now: a ghost. For a moment the boy seems uncertain how to answer her question about the box, but suddenly he says, 'Allow me.' He grins at them, reaches across the coffin to jerk the lid open.

Al is the only one of his family who does not gasp. Inside is a

72

corpse, a man hard to see in the poor light. But the young man fetches a candle from a nearby table, holds it close to the dead face. Irena sees a fleshy, middle-aged man, whose eyes have not been closed. She looks away from him, stares at the white-haired boy again. Al whispers, 'Jesus.'

'No,' the boy says. 'It's Darren. *He* won't rise a second time.'

Al shakes his head. His father and old Harry lean forward to peer at the coffin's contents, but the three women stay where they are. Others in the restaurant are inching forward. Now that the coffin lid has opened, now that nothing has exploded, tension has evaporated. The guests are curious. Hardly anyone heard what was said: that eerie eighteenth-century soprano smothered their words. People want to look inside the box.

But Al snaps out of the trance that he was in. 'Get that stiff out of here! Christ, this is a celebration, Hawk. The hell you think you're on?'

'Producing evidence.'

Irena is impressed by how unmoved the young man is – like a ghost, indeed. The other three, she notices, look like prisoners awaiting sentence.

'Not funny,' Al says. 'Not clever. Not bright at all. And switch off that blasted music!'

No trouble, no trouble . . .

Hawk turns calmly to his assistants. 'Thanks, lads. Turn the music down as you go out.'

'Turn it *off* !'

Remember me, remember me . . .

As the three men start to slink away, Al shouts, 'Don't you leave that thing here!'

Hawk swings the coffin lid shut. 'I'll have someone fetch a clean tablecloth.'

Hawk feels like an actor entering a party after the first night, his first starring role. Suddenly calm and relaxed, performance over,

the actor strolls nonchalantly into the room, watching everybody's eyes for their verdict. Tonight they look away, leaving
him alone. Calvin had insisted he should drive the corpse away
from there. Clint and Ronnie agreed – they went too.

Hawk's audience had had five minutes to digest the play.
Many wished that they had sneaked close enough to peep inside
the coffin. By now the identity of its occupant had sloshed around
the room like blood on a stone floor – but there was nothing like
seeing for yourself.

Al became gradually reassured that his celebration had not
been soured. Most people thought the interruption had improved it. Three men told him the same joke, saying the corpse
had livened up the evening. Harry quipped that Darren's meal
must have disagreed with him. Only Al's mother seemed disturbed: a corpse at a wedding feast brings bad luck. Her face looked
pinched. She kept dabbing at her eyes. Irena puzzled over
strange English customs and etiquette: gifts at the wedding-table
were to be expected; so were gifts in homage to a leader; news
of an enemy's death was cause for joy. It only seemed odd when
they were combined.

When Hawk reappeared, Irena was among the first to notice
him. Yes, the resemblance was remarkable: he really was like
Sergei. She sat at the Kazan table eating red grapes. Like Hawk,
she regarded his performance as a piece of theatre. She assumed
that the corpse had been genuine, though it hadn't *looked* real: its
face seemed dull, as if sculpted from pastry dough. There had been
no blood: it had not been lifelike. When Irena had first glimpsed
that unlikely corpse it reminded her of what Louis had told her
earlier about the dummy the English made of Guy Fawkes – an
effigy of a man that they would burn. The man in the coffin had
seemed no more real. His pall-bearers had worn costume and put
on a show. Perhaps that was why she saw Hawk as an actor after
the play – wearing black leotard and tights, his face scrubbed
clean. The carnation on his breast was a splash of theatrical blood.
Oh God, she thought, not blood again, not Sergei's blood.

She touched her husband on the arm. 'Your friend has re-

74

turned.' She felt she ought to reassure him that the macabre interlude had not upset her.

'Friend?' Al saw Hawk waiting at the edge of the room.

'Is he your friend or is he your – what is the word? – lieutenant?'

'Hawk?'

'A hawk?'

'That's his name.'

Al pushed back his chair – an ugly scraping noise. When he stood up and crossed to Hawk, she followed. She heard him ask, 'So, is this what you do when I'm away – play practical jokes?'

Hawk smiled.

'You think it was funny to produce him here?'

Hawk's eyes flickered to Irena behind Al's shoulder. He said, 'I didn't realise you had brought your own surprise. Sorry to upset you, Ma'am.'

'I was not upset.'

Al seemed uncomfortable that she was with them. 'I want to speak to Hawk alone. Perhaps Mama would like you to hold her hand.'

'Of course,' she said. 'Old ladies can be as melodramatic as young girls.' She smiled at Hawk. 'Or young men.'

Hawk nodded. He said to Al, 'I missed your speech.'

'But you heard my news?'

'Yes.'

Irena still had not moved, so Al said, 'This is my wife, Irena. Tim Hawk.'

'Congratulations to you both. Really.'

She said, 'Thank you,' nodded to him, then returned to Al's mother. Of course the young man did not recognise her, he was not Sergei.

Al said, 'Good job for you I wasn't cutting our wedding-cake.'

'Why?'

'If I'd been holding a knife, I'd a rammed it in your throat.'

Hawk smiled. 'I said I was sorry. Any other time, you'd have laughed.'

* * *

75

Al was surprised how easily the evening shuddered back into gear. Two reasons, he thought. One, everyone had been waiting to see how he would deal with Hawk – would the boy survive? Two, Irena had calmed his mother – she was laughing now, hugging his little princess, tears shining on her frail old cheeks. When Al returned to his table, his father squeezed his arm. 'I wait now for a grandson,' he said.

His mother leant across to reinforce her husband's line. 'I am so happy, Alex. I always worried that you would marry an English girl. But now we will have Ukrainian grandchildren, praise God.' Mama closed her eyes.

Al said, 'Now you know why you had to wait so long to get me married.'

Gilda said, 'It was worth it,' and Harry laughed. He regarded Al with new respect.

Out among the tables, waiters served roast suckling pig. Noise was up again. Most of the talk was about Al's young bride and Hawk's tasteless wedding-present. People wondered about the Kazan family connections in Ukraine. Someone slyly suggested that Al had been there twenty-odd years ago, that Irena really was his daughter. Maybe he had a brother there, and she was his niece. Most guests didn't buy these bizarre ideas. Just look at them: Al swarthy as a coal merchant, Irena blonde as a Swedish milkmaid. They were never family. No, Al had simply found himself someone fresh, untainted by London smoke. And the girl? She had married an air ticket to the West. The man near the restaurant door gazed at Irena's innocent face and well-stacked body, said it was a shame she had to sacrifice herself. But his wife sniffed, chipped in her opinion: Al would pay a heavier price.

At the high table, Irena was relieved to see that Alexei had mellowed, had now seen the comic side. She asked how Hawk had known he could get away with such audacious behaviour.

'That's the kind of stroke I'd have pulled myself at his age.'

'Really, Alexei?' He shrugged. 'Have you known him long?'

'We go back years, Hawk and I. The boy is . . . like a son to me.'

That stopped her for a moment. It was not the answer she had expected: that Alexei should regard the boy as special. She wondered whether he really did think of himself as a father – and whether he realised that his surrogate son was about the same age as his wife.

Suddenly, perhaps inevitably, Al peered around the restaurant. 'Where *is* the boy?' he asked. 'Where's Hawk?'

Everything was fine in Kazan's world – his guests could tell. He remained at the high table, family alongside – mother getting tearful, Harry getting drunk – young bride on his right, Hawk now squeezed in to his left. Al seemed exuberant. He had just told Hawk that he had forgiven him – said if he ever tried such a stunt again, he would personally lay Hawk and his pall-bearers in the coffin side-by-side. Said he'd have them filleted like anchovies in a tin. He slipped his arm around the boy, told him to drink a lot more wine. Irena noticed that Hawk did not seem embarrassed; perhaps he was used to this display. Yet according to what she had read, Englishmen normally avoided displays of warmth, did not embrace. Alexei, of course, had Ukrainian blood, but Mr Hawk – he seemed archetypically Anglo-Saxon: colourless, unemotional. Yet he accepted her husband's embrace.

Hawk saw her watching. He leant across, repeated his apology: he hadn't known about the wedding.

'Do not worry. Your performance was a surprise, but I was not disturbed.'

He smiled at her with unknowing eyes.

Al, though, had been disturbed, but he did not show it. He was disturbed that his wife had witnessed such a thing, her first night in London. Sure, she would have to face up to what he did, but this had been too sudden. He tried to minimise what had happened: 'You see, Irena, this was a family feud, but it's all finished now. Hawk showed me the body so I would know.'

She gave an absent smile – a princess's smile, he might have called it – as if she thought his tale unlikely, but not worth challenging. Hawk changed the subject. 'Al, I missed your speech earlier. Did you marry in Ukraine, or will you marry here?'

'It is already done,' declared Irena.

Al grinned. 'I might take a second crack. Make the bond double strength, you know?' He put his arm round her waist, drew her to him.

'Well, what do I say? Mr and Mrs Kazan, I hope you'll be –'

'My name is Irena.'

'Oh. Unusual.'

'I am from Ukraine.'

Al seemed anxious to explain. 'You know I got roots out there, Hawk. Irena is related to my family.'

Harry spluttered into his wine: 'Oh, we know about your roots, Al – I bet you'll plant them deep!' He laughed merrily, but alone.

Irena looked at Tim Hawk. 'You will forgive that I am not used to your English sense of humour – your jest with the coffin.' Harry was still chortling to himself.

Al said, 'Yeah, some joke, some joke.'

Hawk held Irena's gaze. 'It was a private joke, you understand? Not one you should talk about with anyone.'

'Oh.' She put a finger to her lips. 'But surely, should we not inform the police – about the body?'

Al intervened. 'You don't wanna do that, Irena. They wouldn't understand.'

'Nor do you understand, Alexei. It is my little joke.'

She smiled, and Al laughed uneasily. Harry frowned, trying hard to concentrate. Hawk said, 'I see you're a tease, Mrs Kazan. Well, I hope you'll both be happy.' He stood up. 'I think this table should be for family. I'm sorry I didn't bring a more suitable gift.' He plucked the red carnation from his breast. 'For the moment this is all I have. Perhaps you'll take it as a token.'

Irena reached out, took the red flower from Tim's hand. Then he was gone.

8

Hawk paid off the cab in Rotherhithe New Road. He watched it go. The driver did an illegal U-turn, shot back up the road towards the tunnel for the north side of the river. Taxi drivers don't like the south: they can't get a fare.

October sunlight tried its best to improve the drabness of the street. It lit the pavement and cast shadows, but it did not warm. Hawk strolled to the corner newsagents to buy an *Evening Standard*, morning edition. News inside would be little different from the dailies: a few hours younger and more local. He skimmed the front page and Stop Press, glanced inside at 2 and 3. Still nothing. He would have ditched it if there had been a waste bin, but the council had given up. Back where Hawk lived – a better area – litter bins came in dinky colours, sponsored: Texaco for a better environment, Coca Cola for a cleaner world. Sponsors, like taxi drivers, didn't travel south of the river.

Hawk cut down a side road to his left. Rotherhithe New Road formed a border, Bermondsey that side, Deptford this. He walked into Strong Scaffolding's Yard. Strong Scaffolding used to be called Strong Erections.

Two men he didn't know were throwing poles into a truck. They nodded as he passed. The metallic crash of each tube of scaffolding rang from the surrounding walls. It was quieter in the office. The Strong site was better equipped than some. Instead of a portacabin it had a small house – a shabby terraced conversion that no one would want to live in again. The ground floor had been knocked into open plan. Hawk went in.

The man behind the desk was Irish before he spoke: curly hair, ruddy cheeks, skin like the head on a pint of Guinness. 'And you'd be Hawk?'

'Have we met?'

'Isn't there a first time for everything? I'm Mulroney.'

'Where do I wait?'

'Well, I wouldn't go up to our executive suite just yet, if I were you. Mr Kazan has not arrived, and besides there's no one to bring you a cup of tea.'

'I don't want tea.'

'Isn't it too early for anything else – especially if you've a hangover after last night?'

Hawk grunted, left for the stairs.

'At least you and he are still talking to each other. That's a miracle, I'd say.'

Hawk paused. 'Why shouldn't we be?'

'Well, Hawk, if you'd brought a coffin to *my* wedding, I'd be most upset. But they tell me I'm old-fashioned.' Mulroney grinned. Hawk wanted to ask who had told him, but he didn't. He climbed the uncarpeted stairs, wondering how far the story had spread.

They had the electric fire on, both bars. The room had once been a bedroom – now it was hard to say what it was. There was a desk and a swivel chair, two armchairs, a settee. Beside the desk was a mini-bar that looked as if it had been lifted from a hotel. On the wall was last year's calendar, opened at October. Mulroney thought the pictures worth a second run.

Al stretched full-length on the settee, feet up on the arm, teacup by his side. Hawk gazed out the window. In the middle of the yard stood Kazan's Daimler, where the pick-up had been. Despite the tat in the builders' yard and the lengths of tubing against the wall, the Daimler did not look out of place. It was fat with class.

Al asked, 'What'll you do with our friend Darren – bury him in that coffin?'

'Isn't there a golf course near you? I could plant him beneath a bunker.'

'In the rough. I hear he liked a bit of rough.'

Hawk smiled, though his mind had flicked elsewhere. He had remembered Darren's redhead, and he wondered what had happened to her. Nothing had come out yet about the bodyguard, presumably she had done her job. 'What do you think – shall I lose him or return the body to his wife?'

'His wife?' Kazan looked as if he had woken from a nap.

'She'll need the body.'

'Why?'

'Insurance won't pay out on a missing person.'

'Her problem.'

'There'll be enquiries till they find it.'

'Yeah, I suppose you're right. Take him up to Birmingham.'

'Birmingham?'

'There's a lot of villains in Birmingham. The Bill finds his body up there, they'll think that was where he was done. Always dump a body where there could be a reason.'

'Birmingham.'

'Well, it fits. Dump a brook like Darren out in the country, and no one falls for it. They come sniffing back in town. But if you dump him up in Birmingham, they just think, hello, why here? They think there has to be a reason. The West Midland Crime Squad will find a reason.'

Hawk nodded. He had told the redhead to lose the bodyguard in the country. Perhaps that had not been wise. 'The cops might not buy Birmingham,' Hawk said. 'Word's out about last night.'

'How d'you mean?' Al lay still.

'Downstairs for example. He knows.'

'Mulroney? One of us.'

'But he wasn't at the restaurant.'

'Ah.' Al was silent for a moment. 'That comes from showing off.'

'If Mulroney knows, how long before the law does?'

'Who'd tell them?'

'Everyone tells somebody. Then that somebody tells someone else. It'll reach them eventually.'

'Don't worry, it'll sound different by then. Though we better confuse them a bit.'

'Birmingham?'

'Something closer. Scrap that idea. What you do is deliver Darren in his box right back to his garden gate. Then the Bill will think that that's where this coffin rumour started.'

'A bit nasty, isn't it – leaving him out with the morning milk?'

'Death *is* nasty.'

'All right,' Hawk muttered. 'I'll take him round tonight.'

'No, use a driver. First, you must not be seen. Second, it ain't your job.'

'I'm responsible.'

'I said get a driver, for Chrissake – that charlie you used last night.' Kazan shifted on the settee. 'Listen, I wanna talk to you. Remember what you said when you marched in there? Some security, you said.'

'I was showing off. I'd already squared the doormen.'

'You're quite an organiser, ain't you? I need a decent organiser on the Isle of Dogs.'

Hawk frowned at him. 'What kind of organiser?'

'To pull the place back in line.'

'Leyton Knox does that.'

'He ain't the management type.'

Hawk's face darkened. He mumbled, 'I'm not either.'

'I've been grooming you, haven't I?'

Hawk sat on the bed to face Kazan. 'People hate you in a job like that.'

Kazan grinned. 'You gotta be unpopular to succeed. You could do some special jobs. Like fucking Steed is fiddling me at Throgmorton. Like a surveyor needs persuading at the Piazza.'

'Piazza?'

'Yeah, Limehouse Piazza – it's a development site I got an interest in. Development, Christ, that goddam Isle of Dogs has run so low on money the Piazza's the only decent one I got left.'

'And you own the surveyor?'

'I have to, don't I? But Knox tells me he's gone wobbly.'

'He can deal with it.'

'Knox is an animal, you know that. This surveyor type wears a tie, works in an office, I can't set Knox on to him. I told you, Knox is not the management type.'

'What do you want me to do?'

Al lay on the settee, hands behind his head, eyes black as currants. 'Ask him if he's insured.'

Hawk shook his head. 'Knox is better at that —'

'I told you I don't like Knox.'

'What's this other business — Throgmorton?'

Al blinked. 'Accountants — can't trust them, can I? Steed shows me a string of numbers, and they don't mean nothing. When I don't understand the numbers, I know he's trying to rip me off.'

'It's no use sending me, Al — I can hardly add up.'

'So what? I'll tell Steed you're my new hitman — scare the shit outa him. You just hang around his office, and he'll leap in line.'

Hawk chewed his lip. 'Any other jobs?'

'Yeah.' Al swung his legs off the settee and stood up. 'I need a bodyguard.' He stretched. Hawk groaned. 'Not for me,' Al said. 'Irena. I could be vulnerable there.'

'Al, I can't be your wife's bodyguard —'

'No, no, but she ought to have protection, didn't she? Could be a target. I mean, think a minute. If you had to bump Irena, how'd you do it?'

'I don't know — a hundred ways. One you didn't guard against.'

Al drew nearer, gripped his arm. 'Look, nothing's guaranteed, I understand that. But . . . I don't want nothing to happen to my princess.'

Hawk nodded. Al would reveal himself to no one else like this.

'So, come on, Hawk, what's your advice?'

Hawk glanced across Al's shoulder to the door. 'If I wanted to get to her, no bodyguard would stop me.' He thought a moment.

'You should make sure there's no one out there who does want to.'

'Oh, thanks. What do I do – pretend I'm Mr Nice?'

'Don't let people see that she's important to you. Number one target for them is what you hold dear.'

Al released Hawk's arm and drifted a pace away. 'Thanks a lot.'

'Strike first,' Hawk said. 'Take out anyone who can harm her, before they think of it.'

Kazan blew out noisily. He was not impressed.

Hawk continued: 'But you're right – a bodyguard would be better than nothing. Maybe you should get her some sort of permanent companion – a lady's maid, you know? One who knows how to handle a gun.'

For his new position in Kazan's empire, Hawk decided that he ought to wear a suit. You had to dress right – he knew that. There was a pale grey number he had bought last spring and only worn three times. There was also a sky-blue shirt that should have teamed with it – but, when Hawk tried it against the grey, it gave his skin a sallow tinge. He chose a white shirt, tried several ties. Dark blue looked best.

Hawk left Bank station, walked via Threadneedle Street to Throgmorton. The office was not in Throgmorton Street itself, but in one of those smart little alleys, a gap between two buildings, Fishkettle Row. There wasn't a scrap of ground here that had not been scrubbed clean, resurfaced, born again in the new religion of property development.

Throgmorton's was etched in the glass of an impressive double door. At the desk inside the lobby sat a man in uniform – from an industrial costumiers, which made him look like a cross between a cop and a railway-porter. He took Hawk's name and handed him a badge. Once in the lift, Hawk unpinned the badge and dropped it in his pocket.

On the second floor the receptionist told Hawk to wait. She asked if he had an appointment and Hawk said no. She asked if he'd like a coffee and he said yes. He took his time drinking it. Then he asked who Steed had with him in his office.

'I'm afraid Mr Steed isn't back yet. He won't be long.'

Hawk glanced at his watch. 2.45. 'Some lunch.'

'Perhaps you should have made an appointment.'

Hawk smiled. 'Can you direct me to the men's room while I wait?'

She told him where it was.

Hawk walked down the corridor, past the men's room and up the stairs. Kazan had told him that Steed's office was on the third. Unfortunately, the office doors did not have names on but it didn't matter, a passing brunette told Hawk which one was Steed's.

The room was empty. Hawk had half-expected to find Steed in there, ignoring the visitor waiting downstairs. Steed had a lovely office, small but elegant. Close to the window stood the clean and tidy desk of a man who was thoroughly organised – or had nothing else to do.

Hawk closed the door.

'Who are you? What are you doing in my office?'

'Hello, Steed.'

'Do I know you?'

'It's 3 o'clock.'

'What the –? You've been going through my things.'

Steed appears absolutely stunned. He is a heavy, black-haired man – looks as if he would be more at home on a grouse moor than in town. He sees a young man sitting at his desk, reading files. The PC has been switched on.

Hawk says, 'Amazing what you find.' He gives no sign that he is bluffing – switches off the PC before Steed can see there is nothing meaningful on the screen.

Steed barks, 'What *is* this?' Curiously, he does not call to have Hawk thrown out.

'An audit,' Hawk replies. It sounds a good line, but Steed knows an auditor when he sees one. His eyes narrow. He reaches

85

for the phone and jabs three digits. Hawk watches as he holds it to his ear. Hawk watches as his face changes. Then Hawk shows Steed how the phone-jack is dangling uselessly on its length of cable. 'We don't want to be disturbed.'

Casually, Hawk rises from the chair, moves round the desk to be between Steed and the door. He tells Steed to sit. Steed splutters, so Hawk repeats what he said. Steed hesitates, then makes to go behind his desk. 'Not there,' says Hawk. 'The other chair.' He does not want Steed in his executive chair, back to the light.

Steed says, 'Now listen —'

'Sit down.'

There is a moment here when Steed could head purposely for the door. Come to that, he could take a crack at Hawk, who is shorter than him. But he doesn't. The moment passes without Steed ever noticing. He sinks slowly on to the chair.

Hawk remains standing. 'You're on the take.'

'What do you mean?' Quite convincingly expressed.

'You have been embezzling my client.' Hawk had checked the exact meaning of the word 'embezzling' before he came: covertly taking money that has been entrusted. It sounded right.

'Which client?'

'Kazan.'

Steed does not seem surprised to hear the name, though he resolutely declares, 'That's a downright lie.'

The two men stare at each other. Steed asks, 'Who are you?'

'My name is Hawk.'

He sees Steed flinch. Kazan has given Steed Hawk's name.

'Why have you come?'

Hawk continues to stare at him. Eventually Steed says, 'It isn't true.'

'What isn't?'

'What you implied.'

'Which was?'

Steed cannot bring himself to use the word. 'Do you want to see the figures?'

'I lied to you. I'm not an auditor.'

Steed gazes unhappily from his chair. 'I know who you are.' Hawk looks quizzical. 'You're his new hitman, aren't you?'

Hawk raises his right hand slowly to his lapel, moves it further to adjust his tie. Steed watches those bony white fingers. He hears Hawk say, 'This is your only warning.'

Steed opens his mouth but decides not to speak.

'Put the money back and we'll say no more about it. You have two weeks.'

From the expression on Steed's face, two weeks will not be enough.

Hawk returns to Limehouse on the Docklands Light Railway. Normally he doesn't use the train — it's unreliable. But the middle of the afternoon, sun shining, a rare outing for the suit — he takes the scenic route. Riding the little train, perched on its elevated track above the streets, gives a different view to what lies below. He can see the back streets replaced by office blocks. He can see terraces gutted, back gardens lost, places where people lived turned into waste land.

Hawk wonders if he should care what Steed has heard of him. 'You're his new hitman,' Steed said. Because Kazan had told him — and it was true. After Hawk's performance in the restaurant, he had a reputation. He remembers the way they all sat watching him: one execution, a little stagecraft, and they marked him as Kazan's gun. The new hitman. Hawk doesn't kid himself — he knows he was already thought of as Al's favourite. But when he made that entrance he took centre-stage in his own right. Through the last hour of the banquet he felt them study him.

Then this morning, at the scaffolding yard, Mulroney already knew the score. So, Hawk sucks his cheeks, and his sharp cheekbones appear china-white, everyone will want to know if Hawk can make the grade, which is nothing new. One thing Hawk has learnt is that the less you say, the stronger you appear. Say nothing, be as hard as ice. When you do have to act — and you always do, there is no escaping it — strike suddenly, unexpectedly, a pure white snake.

Hawk realises that his reputation will not stop here, people will build upon it. They will speculate about whom he has killed; they will credit him with other deaths; anyone who drops will be down to him.

Al Kazan, of course, will be content. Hawk's reputation will increase Al's strength. Today, for instance, Al may not have known exactly what schemes Steed was up to, but he knows that they are over now. Because of Hawk's reputation. Back in that office earlier, he had realised Steed was heavily built – older, but not unfit. There was no reason to think he couldn't handle Hawk, but he didn't try. Did he imagine Hawk had brought a gun into his office? He must have. Just the possibility was enough.

This was how it was going to be: people would back off from confronting him. Hawk shrugs. As a kid, he didn't win all his fights – win some, lose some – but he never took the beatings some boys did. At school and especially in the Home there was always some poor brat who asked for it: the sort who was crammed in a dustbin and rolled downstairs, had his head stuffed regularly down the lavatory, was pissed on, smacked about, set on fire. Someone always took that role. He seemed necessary.

It was never Hawk. Years ago, when he saw what happened to those victims, he developed a theory about beatings. He realised that when someone won a fight – no matter how hard or evenly matched before – once one boy had put the other on the floor, his power became absolute. He could smash the other's face to pulp, kick his kidneys in, do anything. The state someone ended in after a fight did not indicate how badly he had lost – only how far the other went in winning. Hawk knew boys – the out and out, dyed-in-the-wool sadists – who'd make jam of a kid they had floored. They would dance with fancy footwork while they kicked him. It was then that Hawk made up his theory that eventually everyone went down, and that when they did, they got back the same treatment they used to serve out. One day, Hawk believed, each sadistic bastard found it his turn to curl up on the concrete, shivering with pain. Hawk has never kicked an inert victim on the floor, because every kick might one day be delivered back. Hawk isn't afraid of pain and violence – he can cope with that – but he cannot allow himself to be powerless, lying on the ground unable to defend himself, shuddering as each new kick hammers in. He cannot die that way. He will not kill that way.

Hawk leaves the train at Limehouse.

Running lightly down the metal steps, he remembers the day he explained this theory to Peter Raggs. The boys lived for three years in a Children's Home in Peckham, and Hawk looked after him. Raggs was pretty – could have become a victim. But he didn't, partly something in himself, partly because Hawk protected him. Raggs disagreed with young Tim's theory. He pointed out that the Nazis who ran concentration camps had not been gassed to death. Hawk insisted that nevertheless they had lost eventually: Hitler had been burnt in a cellar, Goebbels also had been burnt, Himmler had drunk cyanide. Mussolini was hung from a lamp-post upside down. Tim showed Raggs a photograph of that: Il Duce and his mistress strung side-by-side, her skirt flopped around her head, her fat backside revealed to the evening air. The picture had a morbid fascination for Hawk. He and Raggs looked at it several times, though perhaps the only reason Raggs did was because Tim wanted him to.

Hawk finds it odd now that he still thinks of Raggs. He hasn't seen the boy for years. He understands why Raggs was sceptical about his theory, though Hawk himself has not yet completely discarded it. It's like not walking under ladders; it may be stupid, but there are some things it is safer to avoid.

As he approaches his flat in its block of reconditioned houses, Hawk has to pick his way through piles of building sand and fresh craters in the path. Another street under development. Another project they'll abandon halfway through. Across a doleful doorway someone has hung a banner, *We Used TO LIVE Here.* Hawk sighs. When he reaches his door he glances up at the darkening sky. He feels cold and it looks like rain.

Irena said, 'You are playing with me.'

'No I ain't.'

89

'It is a joke.'

'You taste it, then you'll see.'

Al carried the two plates into the diner, leaving Irena in the kitchen studying the microwave. 'Come on!' he called. 'You don't want it cold.'

She wandered after him, saying, 'It cannot be cooked yet.'

'Is this cooked or am I a Chinaman?'

Standing beside his glass-topped dining-table, she smiled, picked up a fork, and prodded dubiously through the pie-crust. Steam. The crust subsided. 'My goodness!'

'Eat.' Al was already seated, napkin in his collar, first forkful in his mouth. Irena slipped into her seat opposite, eyes sparkling like a naughty child. He watched as she tried her first morsel.

'Oh, it is hot!' She fanned her mouth. 'But I like it. Steak and kidney pudding – it is such an English meal.'

'Pie.'

'Excuse me?'

'Steak and kidney pie, not pudding.'

'Oh.' She took a second mouthful. 'They eat a steak and kidney pudding in *David Copperfield* – from the pudding shop.'

'That's nice.' He liked the way she didn't mind talking with her mouth full – not one of those prissy women. He had noticed that about her in Ukraine.

'Do you have mutton pie sometimes?'

'Mutton? Christ, no. We should've had vegetables with this.'

'Tomorrow I will cook magnificent vegetables.'

They were halfway through their pies. Al asked, 'You sure you're OK with this?'

'It is lovely.'

He beamed. 'Yeah, it's favourite with me as well. Just whack something in the microwave, eat in moments. But then, I've been a bachelor a long, long time.'

She missed his uncharacteristic appeal for sympathy. 'How does it work?'

'The microwave? Well, you choose something from the

90

freezer, whack it in – the stuff heats through in two or three minutes. Lovely job.'

She ate her last piece, ran her finger through the sauce. 'But it was not raw?'

'Ready cooked: just heat it up.'

'You have cooked it beforehand?'

'Buy it cooked.'

'As in the pudding shop?'

They both had empty plates. 'You still hungry?' he asked.

'Oh yes! Let's use your microwave again.'

Al laughed and led her back into the kitchen. 'What do you fancy for a spot of pud?'

'It *is* the pudding shop!'

He opened the door to his fridge-freezer. 'Third drawer down,' he said. 'That's my pudding shop: apple pie, apple and blackberry some sort of strudel, black forest gateau ... How about ice cream?'

'We cannot put ice cream in your microwave.'

'OK. Blackberry and apple pie – how's that?'

She clapped her hands and watched him. As the fruit pie reheated, she stooped to peer through the small glass door. 'It is like eating inside a spaceship – so technological.'

Al couldn't keep his eyes off her. She was like a child released into a toy shop. He thought of all the evenings they would have ahead of them – the homely little suppers, front door closed to the outside world.

'I did see a spaceship earlier,' she said. 'Before the rain started. I was in our bedroom changing my dress, looking at the sky as it grew dark.'

'You didn't close the curtains?'

'I saw an arc of light, then a shower of tiny coloured stars – a firework, of course. Why are they set off before the day?'

'Kids can't wait till Guy Fawkes Night. You left the curtains open?'

'No one was out there, Alexei – it is our garden. The rocket was pretty, but last night behind the restaurant, someone threw a firework at me like a bomb.' She had not mentioned this till now.

'What – close to you? Who threw this?'

'Oh, some children – I don't know.'

'Where the hell was Louis?'

'He chased them off.'

'*After* they threw it? I'll talk to him.'

'Don't be angry, it was not his fault. I think our pie is ready.'

'You could have been hurt, Princess.'

She opened the microwave door. 'I cannot believe it is so quick.' She used a cloth to remove the container on to the work-top. Al tried to help but she brushed him away. As she served slices of hot pie she said, 'It is such easy cooking – wonderful! I will cook for you each night. Why do they not cook like this in restaurants? Last night I saw inside the kitchen of that restaurant and it was not like this. Poof! It was frantic.'

She handed him a plate and spoon. He asked, 'You don't mind eating in the kitchen, standing up?'

'Of course not. Is that not correct in England?'

'It is here.' Al spooned pie into his mouth, then asked, 'You weren't upset about last night?'

'Yes, for a moment – several moments, in fact. It was such a loud firework –'

'No, not that. Hawk's . . . joke with the coffin.'

'Oh, that. It was . . . theatrical.' She remembered how it had been. 'The lights out, the music.'

'But you weren't upset?'

'Why should I be?' The blond boy, she thought, the one like Sergei.

'Well, I wanted last night to be a kinda wedding feast, you know?'

'So the coffin was out of place?'

'You could say that.'

They each ate some more fruit pie. She wanted to press him about Tim Hawk, but it wasn't sensible. Instead she asked, 'Why was that man killed?'

'Killed?'

'He did not die of old age.' This time when she looked at him, Irena seemed older, less naïve. Al placed another piece of pie into his mouth.

She said, 'He was an enemy, I suppose?'

Al grunted.

'I do not mind. I expect that some of the things which you do are not lawful?'

'Well —' Al had that chunk of pie stuck in his throat.

'I am not disturbed by unlawful activities, you know? Not at all. I am from Ukraine!' She laughed. Then, seeing that Al did not laugh with her, she said, 'You are my husband, Alexei. Anything you do is fine by me.'

For ten minutes in the van, neither speaks. Calvin concentrates on his driving, Louis keeps his eyes firmly closed. He holds the bridge of his nose between thumb and forefinger as if he has a headache. Because Louis drives for his living, he is a bad passenger. He is bad with anyone, it isn't Calvin. Cal is not the problem.

What worries both of them is the coffin in the back. Darren has been dead two days. When Tim Hawk explained the job they had to do, he seemed embarrassed. Kazan had insisted, Tim said. He apologised, gave simple instructions, had even joked to hide his unease. Like when Calvin asked, 'Is this the stiff?' and prodded it, but found the corpse was no more rigid than if it was a man tensing his muscles. Calvin had jerked his finger away, and Hawk said, 'He won't be stiff. I stored him in the freezer to keep him fresh. It confuses the police.' Cal and Louis both stared at him, then Hawk laughed — told them that rigor mortis only lasts a day or two before it fades. He said he had been joking about the freezer, but were they hungry? Cal and Louis didn't laugh: you never knew with Hawk.

Cal says, 'Better put your gloves on, Louis. Almost time.'

Calvin already has them on. That coffin in the back has been scrubbed so clean of fingerprints that it could have just come out of the shop. Coffins are always in mint condition. There's no trade in used ones.

Louis pulls his gloves on, peers through the damp windscreen as Cal halts the van. This is the second time they have driven along the lane: once to glide past the gate, checking for surprises in the undergrowth; the second time to bring Darren home. Nothing moves outside. Behind trees and mature hedges, each of the houses can barely be seen save two or three uncurtained windows, carriage lamps at front doors. One house has lamps along its drive. But the Darren house looks sombre – just one light, upstairs. It's as if Mrs Darren knows what happened to her husband, and has dimmed the lights to mourn. But she cannot know what happened yet. He has simply vanished with his bodyguard. Sure, most people, given that, would have police crawling through the place, but the Darrens are unquestionably not most people. Calling the police is not their natural reaction. His wife may fear the worst but she'll wait, someone will be in touch. Though Louis still thinks it odd that she turns those lights down low. If he were her, waiting in an empty house, he would turn every lamp on full.

The two men sit in the silent van for another minute and a half. Louis stretches in his seat. 'I'd better check it out.'

Calvin nods. 'I'm just the driver, right?'

Louis steps into the road. The only sound is damp wind in all those leaves. There is a light drizzle, not a star shines in the sky, and when Louis trudges along the lane he has no excuse for why he is there. But in this weather no one else will be outside. He keeps his ears pricked for a car.

He pauses at Darren's gate.

Seen through the rain, that one light in an upstairs window makes the house look even more forlorn. Perhaps she *is* in mourning. No – a more obvious explanation occurs to him – perhaps she is out. Perhaps she has decided that what's good for the old man is good for her – she has run off without explanation. Out with the boyfriend. Has done it to spite Darren, not knowing that he is dead.

Then Louis sees a shadow in the upstairs window. Just a flicker in the glass. He can't say whether it's a man or woman, can't even say that it is definitely a person at all – but it's a movement, he is sure of that. In another moment to confirm it a light appears in a second room. Somebody is in. Louis continues his solitary wet walk along the tree-lined lane. He passes the side of the Darren garden, walks past the next, then turns and heads back towards the van. When he passes the Darren house it still has two lights on, still looks forlorn.

By the time Louis reaches the van he does not look too chipper himself. Soft rain has flattened his hair, his skin shines with damp, his coat has been splattered with rainwater from the trees. 'Let's get on with it,' he mutters.

He hops a ride while Calvin coasts the van a few feet beyond the gate. They are not carrying that damn heavy coffin twenty yards through the rain. They jump out, run round to the rear, haul the coffin to the ground. Calvin closes the van door. The two men half-carry, half-drag the heavy box till it lies on the tarmac, smack in front of the closed security gate.

Calvin asks if they should ring the bell.

'You are joking.'

'Then how they going to know it's here?'

But Louis is already headed for the shelter of the van.

Rain dribbles down the glass outside the phone kiosk. Louis squints at Hawk's piece of paper and stabs the buttons for the number. Calvin has crowded with him into the box. Up to a minute ago Cal thought this a phone call he should not miss, but now he is not so sure. As they listen to the dial-tone, both men hope it won't be Mrs Darren who answers. Neither of them says this, but it's what they hope.

She says, 'Hello?'

'Oh, Mrs Darren?' Louis's voice sounds strained.

'Who is this?'

'Mrs Darren, your husband has come home. He's waiting at the gate.'

95

Louis thumps the phone down and looks at Calvin. Neither thinks this prank at all funny any more, and they don't bother to hide what it is they do think. Both have the same image in their minds. They see Mrs Darren hurrying down her drive. They see gentle evening rain falling softly on the long wooden coffin outside her gate.

9

The Bermondsey Bodyworks stood below the railway off Tower Bridge Road. It was fairly legitimate. The sign outside, in Rasta red, gold and green, was carefully painted: 'All Types of Body Repairs – Accident, Crash, Insurance. Resprays – Any Make Any Colour. Free Estimates.'

The only job they had in today was a total respray on a Peugeot 405, from white to green, which explained the sharp smell of lacquer in the air. Hawk and Louis were on an errand to ask Zak about Kazan's Rover. Zak was wearing what had once been a fashionable shellsuit, now relegated to work.

'Why she don't like the Roll-me-over?' In the yard sat the Rover, looking confident.

Louis shrugged. 'Mr K says it's vulnerable.'

Zak sniffed. 'It have an alarm, don't it?'

'Two alarms,' said Louis. 'But that's not what he meant.'

'No Stevie going to steal such a sad old car.'

'Stevie?'

'Boy Wonder, you know? They don't want a Rover.'

Louis said, 'I like Rovers – they drive easy.'

'But *you* never had no cred, Louis, eh? No offence, man, but you got to face it.'

Louis was not easily put down. 'That's an expensive car.'

'Right. Same as that other thing your man drive – the one look like he going to a wedding.'

'The Daimler.'

'Yeah, that right. Who he think he is anyhow – Lord Mayor of Greenwich?'

Hawk intervened. 'He isn't worried about the car, Zak – it's the person inside.'

'Him making more enemies?'

'This is *her* car.'

'His wife, yeah. I have not got my head round that amazing idea yet. She younger than him, right?'

'So what?' asked Louis. 'You think he should marry some old lady about fifty-five like he is?'

'She pretty?'

'Red hot.'

Zak started a little tune, 'Pretty girl, oh, pretty girl, oh, pretty girl, don't be a fool.' He turned to Hawk. 'So Mr K want to lock his pretty girl in a box nice and secure, right? Hmm, hmm. Like a diamond in a safe, right?'

'But on public view.'

Zak rubbed his chin while he thought about the problem. 'You already got a radio-phone, and door-locks, and a wheel-lock, and *two* alarms, and a computer-coded radio cassette, *and* the car have etchings on the glass – what more does this man want?'

'Bullet-proofing?' suggested Hawk.

'Heh, heh, heh. You cannot be serious.'

'Why not?'

'Him weighing a ton. We have to rebuild the car.'

'You ever do a job like that?'

'No,' Zak admitted. 'But you want I give a estimate? How about armour-plated doors? Heh, heh, heh.' He was enjoying himself now.

'I don't think you're up to this job.'

'Hey man, none of that shit. I giving you expert advice here. No one want to drive around London in a tank.'

'Except diplomats.'

'They cars doing five miles to the gallon – that what you want?'

'So what do we tell him?'

'Right, this pretty girl is a diamond him put out on public view? So, here's my thinking, him should put her right back *out* of view. We install some shaded glass, nice and black. Then even if she sit in the car bare-ass, no mother can see her, right?'

Louis grinned at the thought of it. Zak noticed. 'Except *you* in your little mirror, hey, Louis? We better put a curtain on it. Heh, heh, heh.'

Louis's imagination had shot above the speed limit. Hawk continued, 'How much would it cost?'

'Excluding the little curtain? Hey, wait a minute, Hawk, be serious, eh? Can you think what a Roll-me-over look like with all that black smoked glass? It make a impact, man. Every mother pay attention to a car like that – it why you have the job done, right? Wherever she go, all the villains and all the filth they going to recognise that car.'

Hawk nodded slowly. 'Make us an estimate anyway.'

Zak reached out and touched Hawk's shoulder. 'Try to persuade Mr K that no car can be made really safe, eh? Anyway, who going to shoot her in the car? Him blow it up, him flatten it with a HGV, him hit her when she get *out* the car. Remember how the man get Reagan and Kennedy? Emphatic, they step outside the car. I tell you, man, it have only one thing that is less reliable than a vehicle.'

Hawk fell for it. 'What's that?'

'A woman! Heh, heh, heh. Specially if she young and pretty – like this pretty girl of he.'

'Thanks for your help, Zak.'

Dirkin on the intercom: 'It's your wife.'

'Here? Send her in.'

'She's on the phone.'

'Then put her through.' A rule he had always stuck to: never give your phone number to a woman. But your wife . . . 'Hello, Irena.'

'Alexei, is that you?'

99

'Who else?' He grinned. When he gave her his office number he should have known she'd have to try it.

'Was that man your secretary?'

'Kind of.'

'I am in trouble.'

'Already?' He laughed. 'In trouble! No, that was a joke, Irena – what kind of trouble?'

'I am in a phone box. I don't know what to do.'

His eyes narrowed. 'How d'ya mean?'

'You will think me stupid.'

He relaxed, nothing serious. 'Now calm down, calm down. Where are you, Princess?'

'I have walked down the shooting hill, with the large park on my left. Now I am outside a big shop.'

'The supermarket?'

'It says Convenience Store. It is not a market.'

'Yeah. What's the problem?'

'You know the money that you gave me?'

'Don't tell me you already spent it?' He laughed.

'Only some – what do you think of me? Oh, it was wonderful in that shop.'

'Which shop?' Christ, she has bought a dozen dresses.

'The Convenience Store. They have so many things. It is everything I dreamed was in the West.'

'You been buying groceries?'

'The steak and kidney pies, the chicken pies, all sorts of wonderful fruit pies. We will have such glorious fun with your little oven.'

'Oh, I see. How many of these pies did you buy?'

'I think twenty – and every one is different! I also have bought some beautiful cabbages for soup. But this is my problem, Alexei. In the shop, you see, they have – what do you say? – baskets on wheels. Now my basket on wheels is full of things to eat, but – oh, you will think me stupid because I do not understand these things – how do I take it home?'

'The trolley?'

100

'That is the word. It is too big to put on a bus – but am I *allowed* to take it home?'

Al looked at the receiver as if it might have been malfunctioning. 'You want to wheel your trolley up Shooters Hill?'

'It does not run smoothly. Perhaps it is faulty.'

'Wait, I'll come and fetch you – ah, Christ, I can't. And Louis has got the Rover. Christ. Listen, take a taxi, will you?'

'A taxi – where do I find one?'

'In the street – they go up and down.'

'A taxi . . .'

'Yeah. You know what a taxi looks like, don't you?'

'Of course. I am not that stupid.'

'They got a little sign lit up on top . . . I better send someone.'

'No, I can manage – oh, what is that noise? Can you hear me, Alexei? Hallo?'

'It's the pips, Irena. You need another coin.'

'Hallo?'

'Irena, put in a coin.'

'Hallo?'

The line cut off. Irena listened intently a little longer, then shrugged and hung up. She took the handset back off the cradle, said 'Hello' to the dialling tone, then decided she must have done something wrong. Irena left the phone box, and for the next five minutes she stood with her supermarket trolley at the kerb, hailing every car with a light on top.

When the phone rang, Hawk and Louis had left the Bermondsey Bodyworks and were driving the Rover across Tower Bridge. Hawk took the handset from his pocket. 'Yes?'

'Och, that's extremely helpful.' Leyton Knox.

'I'm afraid we're not answering the phone just now,' Hawk said. 'Please leave your number and –'

'A humorist as well.'

'I try.'

'You surely don't think someone's listening in?'

'This *is* a radio-phone.'

101

'That's a pity, because I had such an interesting piece of news.'

'Yes?'

'It's for your ears only, of course.'

Louis mouthed, 'Don't mind me,' as Hawk asked, 'Where are you? I'm in the car.'

'Then how about I meet ye in a pub? The Grapes.'

'I can be there in ten minutes.'

'Good. I'll let ye buy me a large Bells.' Knox rang off.

Louis muttered, 'Ten minutes, in *this* traffic?'

'You want double fare?'

Louis chuckled. 'You'd never catch *me* hurrying to meet Leyton Knox.'

'Best not to keep him waiting.'

'He always sounds like a tiger before feeding time. I notice he got *you* to buy the drinks.'

'Surprise.'

'You won't mind if I don't join you?'

'Surprise, surprise.'

On the veranda of The Grapes, half-a-dozen early lunchers were admiring the view and pretending they weren't freezing. Inside was not yet busy. The Grapes, clean and ready for the lunchtime rush, smelt of fish soup from the expensive restaurant upstairs.

Downstairs was Leyton Knox. He sat alone at a small table with two whiskies, two halves of Taylor Walker, and a copy of *The Scotsman*. Since he first arrived in London, Knox had flaunted his Scottishness. The only thing he *didn't* do was wear the kilt – not even for Hogmanay or Burns' Night. But then, Knox would have looked even more bizarre than most men in a kilt – being black.

Leyton Knox was six feet two, lean, loose-limbed, hard as an ancient Scots pine on a winter's night. He was second generation-Scots – his grandparents came from Barbados in the Fifties. His father was doing eight years in Barlinnie for armed robbery, and Leyton had come south only after his dad had advised him that English jails were soft.

102

'You're late, Timmy. Don't tell me you got lost.'

'Traffic.'

'You should walk – it's the only way down here. I bought ye a half and half.' Knox pushed the drinks towards him. 'When you buy *your* round, we'll have crab sandwiches as well.'

Hawk sipped at his Taylor Walker. 'What's your news?'

Knox tilted his head. 'You seem awful edgy to me, son. Delayed reaction?'

'Just hungry.'

Knox nodded. 'You and me don't often have a chat.' Hawk showed no reaction, so Knox asked slyly, 'You're no prejudiced against the Scots, by any chance?'

Hawk smiled. 'And you say *I'm* edgy.'

Knox picked up his whisky, frowned at the niggardly English measure, tossed the whole thing back as if he were a Russian drinking vodka. He paused till the fumes had faded. 'I think you and me should be friends.'

Hawk didn't know how to respond to that, so he muttered a noncommittal 'Yeah'.

Knox grunted. 'Listen Timmy, you and me, we're the hard cases in this organisation now.'

Hawk shrugged.

'Let's cut out the shite, Timmy, OK? I've heard about your new job: I'm to do them over, and you do them in.' Knox chuckled, deep in his throat. 'Is that no the size of it? I thump them, you shoot them. Like a pair of nutcrackers. So we ought to co-operate.'

'For Kazan's sake, or ours?'

There was a glint in Leyton's eye. 'Is that no the same thing?' Hawk remained impassive. 'I hear everyone had a riotous evening,' Knox remarked.

'And I hear that everyone is talking about it.'

'About you and yon coffin, d'ye mean, or Kazan and his wee bride?'

'The coffin. I haven't heard talk about his wife.'

'You wouldn't.'

'Why not?'

'Well, you're awful close to our wee Ally. Awful friendly.'

Casually, Hawk asked, 'And you're not?'

'Not as close as you, Timmy. I didnae get an invite to the party.'

'You were busy.'

'No, no.' Knox shook his head ruefully. '*You* may not be prejudiced – against the Scots, I mean – but for some reason our wee Ally left me out.'

'I'll have a word.'

'No, thanks. Well, what d'ye think of his new wife then – is she as pretty as they say?'

'Oh, she's pretty.'

'Pretty young, as well?'

'Yes.'

'An old man and his fresh young bride: second childhood, you could say.'

'I don't think so.'

'D'ye not? Well, other people will, just the same. Ally could lose some respect.'

'Yours, for instance?'

Knox displayed the dirty pink palms of innocence. 'If we're his nutcrackers, we have to make sure that he's respected.'

'Lots of folk get married, Leyton. Kazan's still the boss.'

'Yes, naturally.' Knox moved his beer glass. 'Has he talked to you, by any chance, about the Limehouse Piazza?'

'He said you thought the surveyor was beginning to shake.'

'Wobble was my word. I suggested I paid the man a visit.'

'He didn't like that.'

'No, laddie. In fact he specifically told me to leave everything to you.'

'Oh.'

'Oh. That's what I thought. He hasn't asked you to *burn* this surveyor, has he, Hawk?'

'No. We need the man alive.'

'Exactly. So what does Kazan imagine *you* can do with him that I cannot?'

'Be more gentle.'

'I can be a perfect gentleman if I want.'

'This surveyor's a straight, Leyton. He couldn't survive one of your calls.'

'Know him, do ye?'

'Listen, Leyton, this Limehouse Piazza means a lot to Mr Kazan. The recession has scuppered the Isle of Dogs – all the money's dried up. This Piazza is about the only place where they're still building.'

'Och, is Ally's little island no longer profitable? What a pity, eh? After he's put so much work into it, too.'

'He wants to hold on to what he has left.'

'And there was I thinking he had ambition. So it's this wee Pritchett who hands out the contracts? I look forward to meeting him.'

Knox did look forward to it, Hawk could tell. 'The thing is, Leyton, these office guys can't take a beating. They can't explain away the bruises.'

'Well, you tell this surveyor laddie from me, Timmy, that one could be on its way to him – unless he co-operates.'

A police car draws to a halt outside Kazan's gate. Two uniformed officers in the front seat glance at each other. The driver grins. 'You want to see if Mr Kazan is in?'

'I'll enjoy that.' As he opens the passenger side-door, the other man asks, 'D'you think they'll let us in?' He steps out.

Irena's voice comes from the rear, 'Perhaps it would be easier if I spoke?'

The cop smiles through the window at her. 'Yes, Ma'am, I think that would be best.'

He helps her out. She says, 'You have been so kind. I can manage to the door.'

'We wouldn't hear of it,' he says.

Five minutes earlier they had stopped beside her in the street, thinking she was waving to them for attention. When they discovered she had mistaken them for a taxi, all three of them had laughed. She was so pretty you could not get mad at her. Good-naturedly, they had explained to this attractive young foreign lady what one did to hail a taxi – though as they explained, cabs were not plentiful down here. Where did she want to go?

A pause. 'Sorry lady, what was that name again?'

It was the driver who suggested it: 'Look, Mrs Kazan, why don't you allow us to drive you home?'

'You couldn't do that.'

'Not normally,' he agreed.

People nearby at the kerbside thought it extraordinary to see two cops remove the blonde lady's shopping from the trolley to their car. Was she a shoplifter, or what? Perhaps they were all on *Candid Camera*. The two cops thought it funny too, though they didn't show it. Mrs Al Kazan. Kazan is married? 'Congratulations,' they said. 'Yes, we have heard of him, we know the name.'

Now at the gate, while Irena has her back to them, while she talks into the entryphone, the two cops have grins on their faces as if they really are on *Candid Camera*, but they wipe them off as she turns round. Behind her, the gates slowly swing open on to the property of Al Kazan.

10

'Hawk, this is not what I call funny. I go away three weeks, I come back and the whole damn place is full of clowns playing practical jokes. First I have *you*, for Chrissake, bringing a stiff to my wedding-party – now I got my wife inviting the cops in for a cup of tea! In the goddam lounge, I ask you, sitting on my settee. Holding teacups – with their little fingers crooked. Grinning like they'd landed me in court. And don't *you* start.'

'What?'

'Grinning.'

Hawk strolled across the office so he could smile out of the window. The view around Surrey Docks was of so-called *bijoux* town houses losing their new-built sheen. Another ten years, he thought, and they'll be like all the other grimy terraces in side streets for miles around. In twenty years they'll be worse. At least Victorian terraces were solidly built.

Hawk asked if the cops had tried to question him.

'What, in my own house – with no reason? Listen, if it wasn't I had Irena sitting there acting as if my teapot was a goddam samovar, I'd have flung those smug shit-heads out in the street – and they knew it. No warrant. In my goddam *lounge*, Hawk.'

'Did they enjoy their tea?'

'That's enough. The bastards loved it, you know? Would not give over. "Lovely house, Mr Kazan, must've cost a fortune. What is it you do for a living, once again?" Christ. "Nice cup of tea, Mrs K. Perhaps we should pop round again sometime, check how you've settled in?" Sniggering in their teacups – I could've murdered them.'

'Can be arranged.'

'Ha, ha,' said Kazan flatly. 'But you see why I'm concerned, Hawk? Christ, they walk in off the street. I need security.'

'You have an entryphone −'

'Huh! Some good it did me. OK, so the pillock gateman knew Irena's voice − but he should have looked. Damn police car up my drive. The thing is, this is a young girl − well, twenty-five − she is not gonna stay inside the house.'

'It's a foreign holiday to her.'

'Yeah. What d'ya mean, holiday? She's here for good. And she needs that bodyguard.'

'She'll have one.'

'She'd better. Another thing: I'm still worried about my car. Goddam radio-alarm, what good is that?'

'You know what Zak said.'

'That bozo? Too big for his goddam boots.'

The intercom buzzed. 'Oh, Mr K. Sorry to . . . er . . . Can you tell Hawk his car's arrived?'

'What car?'

Dirkin said, 'Well, Calvin's bought −'

'Not you.' Al flicked the switch. 'What car?'

Hawk said, 'You want a bodyguard? I've bought a choice of three.'

Al frowned but Hawk continued. 'What you want is someone who can stay with her all the time − who can be trusted in your house. That narrows the field.'

'What, they're gonna steal my cutlery?'

'You have to be careful about sex.'

'Sex?'

'Are you going to want some feller to live with her day and night?'

Al narrowed his eyes. Hawk said, 'So I bought you three women could be suitable for the job. They're tough, they know what they're doing, but because they're female, you know, they won't come on to Irena.'

'You mean they're not dykes?'

'Who knows? *She* isn't.'

Al did not seem keen.

'Well, who *do* you want, Al – a woman or some sexy guy like me?'

Al sneered. 'You – sexy?'

'Look, I've bought you three applicants for interview. Do we see them together?'

'Applicants.' Al pulled a wry face at the word. 'It was *you* discovered them, Hawk. Which one's best?'

'They're all good. That's why they're here.'

Al flicked the intercom. 'Those women out there, Vinnie – send them in.' He raised his eyebrows, shook his head, walked round his desk to flop in his swivel chair. Hawk stayed near the window. When the door opened it admitted Calvin and the three women.

'You applying for this job too?'

Calvin coughed. 'What job's that, Mr K?'

Hawk told him to wait outside.

While Calvin slunk away, Al Kazan remained in his chair studying the three women waiting before his desk. He saw a fit-looking blonde, about twenty-one, looked as if she belonged on a tennis court distracting the opposition. He saw a black girl a little older, who carried weight which wasn't fat. She had a gun-fighter's eyes. He saw a third woman in her thirties, frizzled hair, body built of teak. Was probably a black belt in something unpronounceable.

Suddenly, Al asked, 'What do you girls know about a feller called Charles Dickens?'

When he asked Hawk if *he* had any questions, Hawk said he'd save his for later. The women left the room.

'What's to ask?' Al queried. 'Unless you want to wrestle one on the mat.'

'They'd beat me.'

'Is that how you like it – being dominated? Look, I tell you what – we'll do this the easy way. We got three to choose from:

109

one is too ugly, one is black, and one looks pretty good. So where's the difficulty?'

'This is not a beauty contest, Al.'

'If it was, I'd want my money back. Look, I am not having the ugly one – I couldn't stand her round the house.'

'The black girl?'

'You know me, Hawk, I ain't prejudiced or nothing, but I'd rather have the white one.'

'Why?'

'We gotta live together.'

'Let me run another interview.'

'With who?'

'The two younger ones.'

Al squinted at him. 'You're going for the chocolate, am I right?'

'I want to make sure you get the best.'

Al's face clouded. He exhaled. 'Listen, this business about security – there's another thing.'

'What?' Hawk watched Al pace around the room.

'You know my cousin Gilda, and that drunken husband of hers?'

'Harry.'

'Yeah, Uri, as he once was: Harry.'

'What about him?'

Kazan went behind his desk, reached inside a little drawer, tossed the envelope to Hawk. 'Take a look, but . . . leave out the funny jokes.'

Inside the envelope were half-a-dozen photographs. Revealing. All six shots were from the same angle – through a mirror, maybe, or a little peep-hole in the bedroom wall. The girl in the grainy photos was a blonde – though as two of the pictures showed, she had not been born a blonde. Harry was trying to act the lusty goat, but at his age, without his clothes on, he just looked old.

Hawk squinted at them. 'These were taken at different times – she has different hairstyles.'

110

'Yeah? Glad to see you are looking above her tits. And guess which idiot's been paying rent for that little flat?'

'Cousin Harry?'

'He is *not* my cousin, he's my cousin's husband. And who d'you think was blackmailing the stupid shit? Clive Darren.'

Hawk closed his eyes. Kazan said, 'And you know those little businesses we been losing on the Island – the ones you topped the fucker for? Guess who slid Darren into them?'

'Harry wouldn't –'

'Oh, you'd be surprised, boy, what a little pressure can do.'

'When did you get these pictures?'

Kazan stared at him from deep black eyes. 'As soon as you killed Darren.'

Hawk nodded. 'So now they've sent you these pictures so you'll do the same to Harry. Tit for tat.'

'Yeah – wouldn't *that* be neat?'

Hawk paused. 'What do you want me to do about it, Al?'

Kazan enunciated carefully: 'I want you to help Harry out of his difficulty.'

They were interrupted by the phone: Irena, for Al. He gestured Hawk to stay. Hawk returned to the window and tried not to listen to what Al said.

'Yeah, yeah, about six, that's right. Yeah.' Al's voice was softening for her. 'What d'you mean, the TV? Of course there's more than one channel – use the remote. It's a thing that looks like a calculator. That's it. Look, bring it to the phone and I'll explain it.' Al rolled his eyes at Hawk: the family man, the wife. 'Right? Now, press the little buttons – no, Christ, that's the volume, I can hear that from here. Turn it down. *Down*: that's the arrow to the left. What – you lost the colour? That's because you pressed the wrong button, Irena. Press it up again. Up. Yeah, it's pretty, ain't it, the way the colours fade up and down? Irena, I can hardly hear you – the goddam noise. Press the volume down. What? Another channel? How'd you –? OK, never mind. Look, the *numbers* are the channels, ignore them for now. What are you laughing at? No, of course you're not. You'll get the hang of it, you only just arrived. What? I can't hear – No, that's the volume again, Irena – turn it down. *Down!* Yeah, the arrow on the left.'

He was laughing with her now. For another ten seconds Al chuckled into the phone, shaking his head happily as if she were a new kitten he'd brought home. 'About six,' he confirmed as he gently replaced the phone. He grinned at Hawk benignly.

Hawk said, 'About Harry?'

'Oh yeah,' Al said, the smile fading fast. 'Oh yeah. I want you to deal with it.'

Alone in his flat that evening, Hawk sat with his feet on the low black coffee table, radio-phone in his hand.

'Yes,' he said, 'I'm afraid it does have to be tonight.'

'What'll I say to Gilda?'

'Doesn't seem to have bothered you before.'

Harry sighed. 'About an hour?'

'I'll be there.'

An hour. Hawk glanced at his watch: he had time to kill. Oh, very funny. He scratched his head. When he restarted the CD player, *Semele* filled the room. The music was soothing and clear: it helped him think about the Kazans. Since Al had arrived back with Irena he had been transformed. He doted on the girl, kept talking about her. When he sat in the office he kept glancing at the phone, waiting for it to ring.

> Oh sleep, why dost thou leave me?
> Why thy visionary joys remove?

She *was* pretty, Hawk conceded. She had an electric quality – like a lamp that could be switched on. In repose – the switch turned off – she could be as white and still as an unlit bulb. But at the flick of that secret internal switch she blazed with vitality – hands fluttering around her face, eyes wide and alight. Kazan was a moth around her flame: wings beating frantically till death.

> Oh sleep, again deceive me,
> To my arms restore my wandering love.

112

Hawk could not abase himself like that. Women made niggling demands: where are you going; where have you been; when will you do this for me? He didn't want to compromise – someone dictating the films he went to see, how he furnished his flat, what music he could play. He shuddered. He was better by himself. He did not consider himself an introvert, had never tried to contemplate his psyche, nothing like that. Hawk dealt with what was tangible, what he could see and touch. Recently for instance, in his solitary evenings he had found himself examining the backs of his hands. He had firm, smooth hands, lightly seeded with pale gold hair. On the rare occasions that his smooth skin took a scratch he became fascinated by the healing process. Two weeks ago he had snagged his left hand on a nail, had a small but nasty slash across the back of one finger. The skin was tight there; it stretched when he clenched his fist, so the sides of the cut pulled apart like a fish's mouth. Hawk had not bothered with sticking plaster. He just cleaned it – partly because he believed a wound healed faster in fresh air, but also because he liked to watch.

In this case little happened for three whole days. The cut neither reopened nor seeped blood, but the frequent flexing of his fingers made the fish mouth gape as if it drunk the air. Inside the fish's mouth was as red and shiny as if it still contained fresh blood. Through its tiny aperture Hawk glimpsed inside his body beneath the skin. Throughout those three days his skin showed no sign of regenerating – it seemed certain he would have a tiny scar. He kept the wound clean, tried not to knock it, and by the fourth day he saw that an unobtrusive scab had sealed it from the air. The scab became a healthy mid-red colour – not that angry black-red of one that is unclean or has been disturbed. Occasionally he was tempted to lift it and peep beneath, but he didn't. You shouldn't pick at scabs.

Soon the red faded, as if the hard dried blood had leached its colour into the air. The scab became pink, grew smaller, gained a white crust around its edge. Hawk saw that the wound was not closing from the sides as he had expected but from the ends, as if it was easier to close the narrow tips of the fish's mouth than to seal across the whole divide.

Two days later he removed the loosening scab. The scar, such as it was, now comprised a short brown line entirely surrounded by the thin white crust, like a tiny island in a ring of sea. During the next week, he observed the white crust engulf the thin brown squiggle, before dissolving like dried salt. The dull pink inflammation disappeared, and his new skin seemed indistinguishable from the old. Without any effort or involvement on his part, life renewed.

Later, driving along Croydon Road on his way to Harry's office, Hawk remembered his childhood theory – that there were different thicknesses of skin. Kids from the Children's Home, for instance, compared to straight kids at school, had leather skins two inches thick. Their wounds never bled for long.

Hawk stopped at a red light and waited patiently in the dark.

They came from a tough background in the Home, but life wasn't miserable there. They had a hierarchy, some bullying and, if ever a kid acquired a toy that he liked especially, another was sure to steal or break it. Kids had to live without the softness of family life – though they knew how it was meant to be from stories and television commercials. Mum and Dad at the kitchen table. Kids on the carpet by the fire. Mothers in big warm skirts you could throw your arms around and hug.

Kids grew hard without it. Some like Tim were orphans, but others had parents alive outside. Whatever the reason for their families being carved up, it did not stop those kids feeling homesick when they arrived. Sure, there were some who hated their families, had fought with them. Those ones grew hard, while the ones who wept for hopeless families were taunted for their softness. Eventually they decided that they should stop moping, should stop missing their absent parents, should block them out – stop loving them, in fact. Kids can learn to do that.

The light turned to green, and Hawk glided forward.

Raggs was an exception. When he first arrived he would stand at the gate every evening, crying in the dusk. Every night would be the same. For the first week he was left alone but, when he didn't ease up about it, night after night, they lost patience. Living with a boy who made such a production out of missing his mother reminded others of their own. They didn't want to be reminded.

Peter Raggs was a good-looking boy – pretty almost – sweet-natured compared to most, yet he wasn't bullied. When Raggs was not brooding about his mother he was lively, could crack jokes. But every evening, that cloud came down. Boys started creeping up on him, jumped him at the gate. But what could they do to a boy who smiled at them like a friend?

Hawk talked to him about it. He took Raggs aside one day before the evening sadness fell, and he tried to explain how Peter should cut himself off, should build a fence. You can do that, he told him: it usually takes about two weeks. Who your parents are, Tim elaborated, is just an accident of birth – you don't choose each other. You don't have to love each other. You don't even have to *like* each other. What happens, Tim said, is that one night two people have sex, and *your* egg squeezes through. You don't owe them anything for that. Not *them*, Raggs said, just her. I never knew my dad. Nor me, said Tim.

'Don't you miss her?'

'She's dead.'

Something about the way Tim said that, the way he shrugged and tossed his head, caused Peter Raggs to touch his arm. 'I'm sorry.'

Tim had shrugged again, and declared, 'No, it's easier if she's dead. Then it isn't her fault that I'm in this Home.' They were in Goldsmith Road, near Peckham Hill Street. The sun was high. 'If your parents are alive, then either they're so damned incompetent they can't look after their own kid, or they abandoned you, just like that.'

Raggs glanced away. Tim thought the boy might start crying in Goldsmith Road – but he had to face the facts. Tim knew all there was to know about parents. Sometimes at the Home the

115

slobs would show up out of the blue, would go on about it being everyone's fault except their own: the police, the social services, the landlord – there was always someone they could blame. They would fill their kid's ear with sob stuff, as if he could give a damn. All the kid was interested in was had they come to get him out?

'You have to be self-reliant,' Tim said. 'That's what growing up is about.'

He remembered when Raggs had quoted from John Donne – they were doing him at school: No man is an island.

'Crap. A real man *is* an island – a chunk of rock stuck in the sea. Storms and waves come smashing in – but that rock doesn't change. You have to make yourself like a rock.'

Arguing with Tim Hawk had helped clear the anguish in Peter's mind. He looked on Tim as his special friend. They became inseparable – went everywhere together, helped each other grow. Sometimes they argued so violently that they wouldn't speak for days. But they always made up. They crammed as much love and hate into their relationship as would last most brothers a lifetime.

Hawk stopped the van. Since then he had learnt that relationships did not last. He shook the memories from his brain. When he stepped out into the night and approached the low office building, he saw two rockets soar into the sky, burst with a moment's glory, and then die. Hawk paused there in the dark, but there were no more fireworks.

He heard Harry come into the building, then saw him appear cautiously round the office doorway, unsure whether to switch on more light. He looked as if he had donated two pints of blood. Hawk had set the anglepoise lamp low against the desk, and he sat behind it, face in shadow, one white hand in the pool of light. He asked how Gilda was tonight.

Harry coughed, said she was OK.

'What can we do about this problem, Harry?'

'Darren made me do it. He had these photographs –'

'I know.'

116

Harry edged further into the dimly lit room, hesitated by a chair. 'You've seen them?'

'Yes?'

'How about Al? Has he −?'

'Sit down.'

Harry eased himself on to the chair as if he didn't trust it to bear his weight. Hawk asked, 'Is that a permanent tattoo you have on your backside?'

Harry almost chuckled. 'Oh, God.' He shook his head.

Hawk said, 'Well,' and looked at him. 'What should we do about it?'

Because Hawk was half-obscured behind the desk-lamp, Harry had to squint to make out his face. He procrastinated: 'What does Al say?'

'What do *you* say?'

Harry bowed his head, showed his thinning hair. 'You see, it wasn't only Gilda. I mean, when I saw the photographs, well, when I thought about it, I could have told her, I suppose. We'd have got over it somehow.'

'But you didn't tell her.'

'Well.' Harry didn't speak again for several seconds. They heard a car pass nearby, but apart from the sound of that, the office was absolutely silent. 'We've been married thirty years, you know that? One little mistake. But . . . You know, Hawk, she's Al's cousin. If she'd told him . . . You know how he is.'

'Would she have?'

'Well, Darren would.'

'Not now.'

Harry's eyes shone in the lamplight. 'Christ, when you brought him in that restaurant, Hawk, I didn't know what to think. First thing I thought was, it's over, I'm off the hook. Then I remembered about the rest of them − Joe Morgan . . .'

'Morgan?'

'You know, Darren's hitman. He came to see me.'

Joe Morgan, Hawk thought − better make a note of that man's name.

117

Harry sat staring at the edge of his desk till Hawk asked, 'What did this Morgan want you to do?'

Harry cocked his head to look at him, but instead of answering, he asked, 'What'll happen to me?'

'Have you made a will?'

Harry sagged.

'Seriously,' Hawk persisted. 'Have you left things tidy for Gilda to sort out?'

Another car cruised by outside. 'Hawk, you're not . . . Christ, I've known you for years, Hawk.'

'That's right. Where will Gilda find your will?'

Harry paused. 'She'll know.'

'What about investments, unfinished business?'

Harry closed his eyes. 'My mind's gone blank, I'm sorry.'

Hawk tapped the desk three times with his fingernail. 'Start thinking, Harry. This is an important time.'

'Listen, Hawk, I've always liked you −'

'Don't you want to help yourself?'

'Huh?' Harry opened and closed his mouth, then opened it again. 'How d'you mean − help myself?'

'Harry, how long has Al known you?'

'Well, we're cousins − all my life.'

'No, he and *Gilda* are cousins. He told me that.'

'He − Oh, I don't know. Thirty-five years. Forty.'

'Al has known you forty years, and you're the husband of his cousin. You think he *wants* to kill you, Harry?'

Some kind of hope flickered in Harry's eyes. 'He doesn't?'

'He's angry, Harry. You ever seen him really angry?'

Hope faltered.

'Yet, you know? I think he'd like to help − if he could trust you. Who else did Darren touch?'

'No one.'

'Joe Morgan did it for him?'

'No.'

'Come on, Harry, you were turning deals all over the Island. Who else did they get to?'

118

'People just did what I told them, Hawk. Darren didn't get to anyone directly.'

Suddenly Hawk left his chair. He gave an exasperated sigh. 'That's it – I tried to help you. Let's go.'

'No, Hawk, believe me – there was no one else.'

Hawk was coming round the desk. 'No one else! Al was being stuffed all over the Island.'

'The place is dying on its feet, Hawk.'

As Hawk stood over him, Harry seemed welded to his chair. Then he flinched. Hawk had reached past him, grabbed the lamp, had swung it close against his face. 'I don't need this to see you're lying.'

Harry turned away from the glare. 'People thought I spoke for Al. I can prove it.'

'You have really disappointed me, you know that? I used to like you, Harry. Even when I came over here tonight, I thought, not Harry, not my friend Harry, not Gilda's Harry. There must be some way I can help him.'

'I can prove it to you –'

'You're full of shit.'

'I'll give you all the names – I can write them down.'

Hawk hesitated, out of sight above the glare. 'No. No, it's too late for that. Five minutes ago, maybe. I could've believed you then. But now –'

'Five minutes, Christ!' Harry pushed the lamp aside, clutched at Hawk's pale hand. 'Don't make an issue about five minutes, Hawk.'

The lamp was back across the desk, and Harry still had hold of Tim Hawk's hand. The two men stared at each other in the half-light.

Hawk said, 'Five minutes could be a long time from where you're sitting.'

'Let me write the names.'

Hawk told Harry they should use neutral ground. The one chance to appease Al, he said, was for Harry to make a full

119

confession – not just pleading for forgiveness, but exact details. Be comprehensive rather than contrite. Before they left the office, Hawk let Harry outstay the five minutes writing every detail down: which businesses from which date; how much money when; contact names; how Harry fed the money into Darren; what information he had revealed. At this point, Harry had seemed ready to clam up, so Hawk had to repeat that the only way Harry could cut ice with Al was to make his breast cleaner than a novice monk. Honesty, Al might respect. That and family.

When Harry had dredged up everything he could remember, Hawk had him write down the combinations to the safes. Harry started quibbling again, and Hawk had to explain that it would make Al feel better and help re-establish trust. When finally they had finished, Hawk said it was time to talk to Al. Harry seemed to be shrinking in on himself like a tired balloon, but Hawk clapped him manfully on the arm, said they were past the worst now, and where was Harry's car?

As they drove his blue Volvo up to Catford, the old man seemed a little less depressed. It was late now; there were no stragglers from the pubs, few cars left on the road. Hawk told Harry to drive via Brownhill Road to Hither Green. When he told him to stop, they could hear a goods train shunting in the sidings.

Harry asked if they were getting out.

'Doesn't look as if Al's arrived.'

In the silence of the car, Hawk heard Harry breathing like a sick man. Harry grinned weakly and said, 'I wasn't sure if Al was coming.'

'No?'

'Well.' He gulped another breath. 'You picked a lonely spot.'

'Relax, Harry. It's a shame to waste time worrying.'

'That's all right for you to say.'

'Now, let's make sure you've got your story ready.'

'Right.'

'You've covered every detail?'

'Of course.' Harry glanced almost irritably at him.

'You see, we don't know how much Al knows,' Hawk said. 'If he's had a whisper about something you've not written down, he'll get awful angry. You don't want to blow it at this stage.'

'No.'

'You must give it everything you've got.'

'Yes.' Harry suddenly turned to him, their faces close inside the car. 'You will try to help me, Hawk?'

The boy nodded. 'I'll put in a word for you, don't worry. Now, you're sure there's nothing you've forgotten?'

'Christ, no.'

Hawk patted Harry's arm, gave a little smile. 'OK, Uri, just relax.'

'Uri?'

'That's your real name, isn't it?'

'No one calls me Uri nowadays.'

The two men heard the train starting up again in the night. 'You should always hold on to your identity,' Hawk said. 'So you know who you really are.'

'If you say so.'

'You're more comfortable with your real name.'

The Ukrainian exhaled. 'I don't want to talk about this now.'

'Listen.' Hawk touched his arm. 'Was that the sound of a car door?'

'I didn't hear anything.'

'I think he's out there. Take a look. Can you see someone waiting for you, Uri?'

The old man turned, peered out, began to wind the window down. By the time his head was out in the fresh night air, Hawk had pulled the pistol from his pocket and was pointing it at his back. Harry was about to say that he could see no one out there when the single shell hit him from behind. He never spoke. He just jerked forward as if trying to escape. His head dropped and he sprawled from the window as if he had vomited from the car.

'There,' Hawk said. 'You see? That didn't hurt at all.'

121

11

C lear sky and bright sunlight makes the day pleasantly mild for late October. It is 11.30. Along Threadneedle Street and Old Broad Street, City folk seems less hurried than usual, walking without their coats. Office girls on errands sport autumn fashions. Some wear summer frocks and cardigans. Most of the men out at this time of morning are mere messengers between offices, though they dress as executives and eye the girls. No one is eating yet. Sandwich bars stock their windows, the coffee stall does occasional trade, pavements are not yet littered with food wrappings and paper bags. In Throgmorton Street at this dead time of the morning there is so little traffic that it is possible to drive right along without stopping. The courier on the motorbike is able to turn off into Fishkettle Row with hardly any check to his speed. He leans sideways, lets the bike curve gracefully round the corner. He barely signals.

That immaculate little alley is too narrow to have a car parked in it, but the bike does not take much room. The courier, swathed in bulky riding leathers, face invisible behind smoked-glass vizor, hoists his leg over the saddle and trots through the glass double door of Throgmorton's. In one heavily padded glove he holds a package. He says, 'Special D for a Mr Steed.'

The blue-uniformed guard nods from his chair. He is used to couriers. He says, 'Reception's on the second floor,' and watches the courier wait impatiently for the lift. Always in a hurry, those guys: paid by the piece, that's why. Coast around the streets on their big machines, wait for a warble on their radio, scoot around

122

to some office for a pick-up. Drive the roads as if they own them, carve through traffic, ignore the rules. Bikes can go anywhere. Bikers can do anything. That's how they behave, at any rate, hidden behind that padding and mask like spacemen among the aliens.

The courier takes the lift to the second floor. When the young receptionist holds her hand out for the packet, he says. 'Sorry. Need the man's signature. Special D.'

'Mr Steed may be in a meeting.' The receptionist glances briefly at the centre of his vizor, at the point behind which she assumes she'd find his eyes. 'I'll sign it.'

'It has to be Steed, I'm sorry. Give him a buzz and I'll go up.'

She reaches doubtfully for the phone. 'Mr Steed? There's a package for you. Oh, the man's already on his way.'

Steed's mind is on something else. He is expecting an 11.30 visitor – promising new business, by the sound of it. The courier downstairs won't be about that. Couriers are part of the paraphernalia of communication: anything too urgent for the mail which can't be faxed, phoned or electronically transmitted, goes by bike. A man in a biker's oily shell suit no longer seems incongruous in your office.

The courier closes the office door.

It seems odd because, when the courier walks towards him, he removes his padded gloves. A black man, Steed notices. The courier tosses a package on to the desk, comes behind towards Steed's chair.

'What do you think you're –'

The man punches him in the stomach and Steed folds. As the courier grabs him by the hair, Steed's hands fly up to protect his face. The man kicks him in the balls. Steed groans – a deep wet breathy sound, as if he has blown into a bottle. He begins to retch. When he tries to crawl beneath his desk the man thumps him in the kidneys and drags him out. Steed's guts seem full of lava. Although the next blow cracks a rib, Steed hardly feels it. He tries to struggle but cannot speak. The man in padded

123

leathers has his fingers tangled in Steed's hair, holds Steed's face poised above the sharp corner of the desk. A dark vizor rubs Steed's cheek. 'Shall I ram your face against that corner, son? Like a lemon on a squeezer?'

The accent sounds Scottish, distant and muffled behind the vizor. Steed wants to shake his head but the man has him tightly gripped. Steed is aware that his face is perilously close to the wooden corner of his desk. He closes his eyes.

'Shall I do it?'

It is only when Steed says 'No' that he realises he is crying.

'We wouldnae want tae mark your face now, would we, son? You could never explain your bruises, I understand.'

Steed is not listening. He has his hands on the rim of his desk to protect his face against the threat. He kneels retching and sobbing in the courier's grip.

'Now listen,' the man says. It is like a voice from another room. 'I'll put this in a language ye'll understand. Memo to Mr Steed. Mr Kazan sends his respects and begs to remind you that his account is overdue. If he does not receive payment within forty-eight hours he may be forced to consider stronger action.'

Steed tries to protest that he has already seen Tim Hawk, but his words are unintelligible. 'Are you talking or chewing a brick?' comes the muffled voice. 'Let me acquaint ye with our easy payment system, Mr Steed. This is your first reminder – a gentle appeal to your better nature. The second reminder may bring you permanent facial disfigurement. And Steed, you don't want to *think* about the third.'

Suddenly, the courier pulls Steed backwards, throws him to the floor. His heavy boot clumps down upon Steed's breast. He says, 'Well, who's a lucky boy, then? Not a single mark.' He shifts his boot.

It seems an unnecessary precaution but, before he leaves, Knox takes the lightweight telephone handset and smashes it against the desk. He walks out with the package he brought with him.

* * *

Hawk waited while Al sat staring at his desk. 'You know, now it's done,' Al said, 'I feel quite funny about it.'

'We can't bring him back.'

'That's not what I mean.'

When Al looked up, his face seemed washed of cares, yet he said, 'This is the first trouble I ever had with family. My little Gilda could be hurt.'

'Somone should be with her when she hears.'

'Yeah, and we'll do the funeral really tasteful. We got this undertaker down Forest Hill, he'll do it nicely. You think they found him yet?'

'Couldn't miss. He's near the cemetry in Hither Green. Soon as someone walked past that blue Volvo of his in daylight, they'd have caught a sight of him.'

'Is he in a mess?'

'No, I sat him in the driving seat, like a drunk who stopped for a nap. Christ, Al, I wouldn't make a mess of Harry. I used to like the guy.'

'Yeah, he wasn't bad. I suppose Darren's boys will laugh at this?'

'I doubt it. You see, what I did, I left the rifle that hit Darren under the back seat of the car.'

'What for?'

'A gift for the Old Bill. The gun's nicely hidden but they'll find it. They'll assume Harry wanted it out of sight, and the killer didn't see it. Then they'll find it was the gun that did Darren, so they'll think one of *his* friends did Harry to pay him back.'

Kazan thought about it. 'You mean you fingered my cousin's husband for the strike on Darren?'

'Harry's in the spotlight anyway. The police know he wasn't shot for illegal parking or for playing his radio too loud. This way they can settle the Darren case and Harry's in one hit – blame it on Joe Morgan, maybe.'

Kazan looked up from beneath dark brows. 'Oh, you heard of him?'

'I had to size up the opposition.'

Al grimaced. 'Well, you're using your head at any rate. But it doesn't pay to be too clever with the Bill. They're not always bright enough to follow your reasoning.'

12

There were worse ways to earn a living, it seemed to Louis. He had driven Irena into Blackheath and trailed behind her while she window-shopped. It had now become apparent to Irena that there were no shortages in the West, there was no need to stock up. But one purchase she was determined to make today was a pair of shoes; her old ones from Ukraine were heavy and looked shabby in their new home. In Blackheath that afternoon she discovered four shop windows crammed with shoes. They seemed so elegant. From each window Irena could have chosen at least a dozen pairs, eased them on her feet. Louis suggested they went down to Eltham, where there would be more choice, but Irena was happy here: four shoe shops were quite enough. She compared the contents of their windows, rejected the one which, though more attractive, seemed to have half the stock at twice the price. Finally she plunged into a small boutique that displayed a pair of delicate brown patents with high heels. Irena had been immediately attracted to them but felt they would be too fragile for the street.

Louis decided it was his duty to accompany her inside. Normally he didn't like shoe shops – they bored him. Normally he hated shopping with someone else. But somehow today Louis found that he enjoyed lounging in a chair opposite Irena, watching her wriggle her toes inside her stockings before she tried each pretty shoe. He also liked the way the shop assistant assumed that he and Irena were a couple. Some chance of that.

Outside in the street, she let him carry her carrier bag. Just like a couple again. She kept asking him about the shops and offices, wanted to learn about everything she saw. What was a building society and why were there so many? Why did an estate agent need a shop? Louis showed her the price of houses, let her read the descriptive cards. 'For the price of one of these houses,' she said suddenly, 'I could buy 5,000 pairs of shoes.'

Louis nodded. His maths wasn't up to that.

'Here is a house,' she said, 'for 3,000 pairs of shoes. Here is one for – oh, 8,000 pairs. It is not even a nice house. No.' She shuddered. 'I definitely do not like that one – it is how I imagine Dotheboys Hall, you know? I would much rather have my 8,000 pairs of shoes – even 3,000 pairs. What is the sort of house where *you* live, Louis?'

'I have a flat – you know what that is?'

'Of course. We have many flats in Ukraine. How many pairs of shoes is your flat worth?'

Louis shook his head. 'I don't own it, I rent it.'

He looked almost shamefaced, so she touched his arm. 'Do not most people rent their flat? We cannot all be landlords – especially at these prices! Who has such money?'

Louis edged away from the estate agent's window, which had never interested him anyway, and he drifted further down the street.

'Of course, I have read about your deeds and mortgages,' Irena said. 'But for so much money! I did not realise.'

As they passed an alley, two little children materialised, wheeling a battered pushchair containing an even more battered effigy of a man. The stuffed dummy wore an old coat, ragged blue sweater and dirty slacks. Its face was a plastic mask and it wore striped slippers.

'Penny for the guy, mister.'

Louis shrugged and passed by, but Irena stopped. 'What is this?'

The little girl explained, 'His name's Charlie, what me and my brother made.'

'Charlie?'

128

'He's our Guy Fawkes. Can you give us 50p for some fireworks?'

'Ah, this is your Mr Fawkes. He looks a little sad. You are going to burn him?'

'We haven't got no fireworks,' her brother said, screwing up his eyes. 'Everybody's got to have some fireworks.'

Louis said, 'Get your dad to buy them.'

'Oh, please, missis, be a darling,' the boy pleaded. 'Give us 50p.'

His sister seized the opportunity. Rapidly she chanted, 'If you haven't got fifty, then a pound will do.'

Irena turned to smile at Louis. 'It is charming, yes?'

'If you haven't got a pound, then God bless you.'

Louis said, 'We've got to go.'

The boy rushed round to position himself as squarely before Louis as his sister before Irena. 'Trick or treat then,' he said. 'Trick or treat.'

Ordinarily, Louis would have pushed him aside, but the boy guessed that he wouldn't do that while he was with Irena. His sister prodded her. 'I'd rather have a pound than a treat, missis.'

'Why?'

'Please.'

Louis could see that Irena would fall for it. Three pairs of eyes watched her produce her purse from her handbag. 'One pound for your guy?'

'Yes please, missis.'

Irena produced the coin. 'I give you this and you sell me your guy – is that right?'

'Oh no, missis!'

But Irena was laughing. She bent towards the girl, held out the coin, and as the child plucked it from her hand Irena pulled her close and kissed her forehead. 'Wait,' she whispered. Another pound.

'Thanks, missis.'

Louis gave a snort and turned away. The boy was still before him, feet apart. 'Trick or treat,' he said.

* * *

129

When Al Kazan arrived home he bounded up the stone steps, calling to Irena as he came inside.

'Alexei,' she said.

Coming down the stairs to greet him were *two* women – Irena and that black girl he had interviewed. 'Oh,' he said.

He kissed Irena less warmly than he had intended, one eye on the girl behind her, waiting at the foot of the stairs till they had finished. She said, 'Evening, Mr Kazan. I came straight round as instructed.'

'The hell with that. You start tomorrow.'

She raised her eyebrows. Irena said, 'But she is here already.'

He found a smile for her. 'Look, we're in no hurry, Miss er . . . Take a bit more time to get your things straight. Sort yourself out before you move in.'

'I was already packed.'

She was confident, all right. Fit as an athlete. Looked like a highjumper eyeing up the bar. 'You been living out your suitcase?'

'That's right.' Eyes cool, not unfriendly. He remembered her now from the interview: this was the one with gunfighter eyes. Christ, not now. Hadn't he enough on his plate already – goddam Gilda, crying down the phone?

Irena said, 'She has such a *big* suitcase!' She laughed. 'You see, over there. Shall we give her the pink bedroom at the back?'

'Wait.' Turning to the black piece, 'Hawk sent you?'

'He said to come as soon as I could manage. Said you needed me.'

Al's eyes were dark. The spat with Gilda had lasted a full ten minutes. 'Look, I'm sorry, but I want you to take your suitcase out the door, come back tomorrow – understood?'

She shrugged. Irena said, 'Oh, Alexei.'

'No problem,' the black girl said. 'What time shall I turn up?'

Al looked to Irena, waited for her. She said, 'After you have left for work?'

'Yeah, right.' He thought he had better give the girl another smile. 'Look, no offence. I just had a tiring day, all right? Hawk moved a little faster than I expected.'

130

She nodded. As she walked across to collect her suitcase, Al asked, 'Hey, you do have somewhere to stay tonight? I'll pay a hotel if –'

'No need.'

She swung her big suitcase off the floor as if it were no heavier than a handbag, then paused by their front door. 'Is that it?'

'Yeah. A bad day, all right?'

The girl smiled at Kazan's wife. 'What time?'

'About 10 o'clock?'

'On the pip.'

'I really am sorry –'

'Don't mention it.' She inclined her head. 'I'll start tomorrow.'

After she had closed the door, Irena said, 'Oh, Alexei, you were extremely rude.'

'That goddam Hawk – I knew he'd choose the chocolate.'

'You don't like her?'

'It ain't that. I got some bad news. My cousin Harry – remember him?'

Irena wasn't listening. 'I like her, Alex. We made jokes together like old friends. Please let her stay.'

Kazan threw his hands wide – he would tell her about Harry later. 'Well, that's it. You and Hawk settled it between you. Did he *talk* to you about this?'

'No.'

Al smiled. 'Well, you know how it is with me, Princess, you want something, it's yours.'

He was still standing looking hopeful, his big arms half-open, so she floated closer and let him wrap those arms around her. 'You are good to me, Alexei.'

He nuzzled her blonde hair. 'Forgive me?'

'Of course.'

He kissed her. 'Christ, we gotta have one last night on our own.'

The clear day became a clear night. By 10 o'clock there was a sharp frost, and a cold wind began to blow. Standing at his window looking down across the dark river, Hawk was insulated from the world outside. He had turned the lights off in his room. Moonlight and an extra glow of streetlamps – that orange pall that hangs above a city – soaked through his window and lay like dew on the clean surfaces of his furniture. The lack of colour in the light turned Hawk's pale blond hair to grey. His dark clothes had lost their colour. Only his white face stood out, a second moon reflected in his window above the river. It was Hallowe'en. This was the night when ghosts walked, when witches screamed, when the dead crawled out of their graves. Whatever barriers existed between our world and the next were at their weakest that night. Beyond the city, harvests had been gathered in. Residual stubble, dead wood, unwanted refuse from the summer had been piled into purging bonfires to blaze throughout the night. Once, there had been feasts and games, rituals, ceremonies to purify the land for another year. The Celts made it their New Year's Eve. Hawk approved of that idea: now, New Year's Eve fell at an unremarkable point in the year – part of Christmas, submerged in it. *Tonight* was when the real year ended: harvest in, and the old year's rubbish burnt. Now, in the sharper days of winter, blood would flow more vigorously through the veins. There would be a quicker pace, vitality in the air. Beneath those occasional blankets of silent snow, beneath the more familiar mantle of mist and rain, a new, sturdier life would begin. Years were born in winter, reached adulthood in spring, ripened through summer, and died in a fire of autumn gold. The sequence gave an optimistic shape to each year: a cold birth, warm adulthood, then a glorious, blazing end.

Hawk believed in a structured order. When he saw how people complicated their lives, how they suffocated in emotional and financial difficulties, he could not understand their logic. Their lack of it. Did he lack something himself, or was it a privilege that he was different? Other people allowed themselves to be destroyed by their emotions. Ensnared by love, they became destroyed by it. Ensnared by money, they lived like slaves. He remembered the two years he spent in poverty when he left the Children's Home – he had no National Insurance Card, techni-

132

cally he did not exist – he was desperate. With no money he could have no address; with no address he could have no job; with no job he could have no money. He felt he was running through a maze. But he was sixteen then, had been resourceful all his life. He did not starve. Yes, he understood how poverty became self-perpetuating, made its victims frantic, but he could not understand how the same terrible need for money gripped those people who already had it. Steed, for instance, dressed like a gentleman farmer, spent his days in a luxurious office, no doubt ate in fine restaurants. He earnt a generous commission on the cash he managed for Al Kazan – why did he have to cheat for more? Hawk couldn't understand.

And then, why did Harry make such a fool of himself? One tragic step after another. A spot of sex with some blonde harlot – but so what? As Harry said, he'd been married thirty years. Go back for extra visits – all right. But he failed to realise that while he betrayed his wife, that little blonde tart had set him up. Christ, Harry, didn't you wonder why she liked the lights on and blankets off – an old man like you? And Harry, what did you think, when someone handed you those photographs? Who was it, Hawk wondered, the scruffy blonde? A pair of hard men? A letter through the mail? But why Harry, why for Christ's sake, did you not go to Al Kazan? Couldn't you face a lashing from his tongue? Christ, even if he had beaten you unconscious, you'd be alive. Gilda would have thanked you for doing that.

Hawk shook his head. The world seemed full of simpletons – people who made their lives needlessly complicated. Not him. And not Al: he was a simple man, but not a fool. Not Leyton, come to that; Knox was neither simple nor a fool. He acted simple, but that was just a surface you could not crack.

What was it he had said to Hawk? I do them over, you do them in. Those were their roles now. Hawk the hitman. Christ, in less than a week he'd shot three people. Was that the pattern from now on? Hawk shivered. He wasn't sure he'd be up to this – on top of which, Kazan said he was grooming him, wanted him to reorganise his precious island. He wanted Hawk to be his

133

manager, in charge of everything, in charge of Knox. Hawk sighed and shook his head: no one was in charge of Knox. Earlier that day, for instance, Hawk had been waiting for Kazan in his office when slimeball Steed had rung. Because Steed couldn't talk to Al directly, he had unburdened himself on Hawk, *complained* about Knox attacking him, said it wasn't fair! Hawk had hated it. On the one hand, he'd had to apologise; on the other, to remind Steed of the debt. If that was management, Hawk thought, they could keep it. All afternoon he had tried to contact Knox, but he wasn't in. No one knew when he'd be back. No one knew where he had gone. Hawk knew that he would have to find Leyton and explain that crunching Steed was wrong. Knox, of course, would say he was justified – that his was the way that worked. He might be right. Nevertheless, Hawk would have to tell him he was wrong. Management.

Hawk sighed, misting the window. It must be cold out there. The weather was like the music he was playing, the high countertenor aria *Lascia ch'io pianga* – cold, precise, seemingly lacking in emotion. It didn't suit his mood tonight. It was the simplicity of baroque opera that had claimed Hawk's attention the first time he ever heard it; now he listened to nothing else. The tunes were strong and simple, no orchestral sludge to weigh them down. Hawk was introduced to baroque opera by the housemaster at the Children's Home – Derek Cardew, a soft bumbling man, too ingratiating with the boys, who took the rise out of him incessantly. Cardew shrugged off their teasing, played along with them, hoped to improve their boorish minds. He arranged trips to theatres and concerts, though he only tried ballet once. It was at one of those concerts that Hawk had singled himself out by actually liking the music. Derek seized on him. Tim was the only boy in the Home who seemed open to classical music. He taught him gradually, at a distance as it were, so he didn't smother the tiny flame. What he said was – Hawk could still remember the advice he had followed ever since – when you first play these new records, Tim, don't read the sleeve notes, don't ask yourself what it means, just lie on your bed with the room darkened, let the music bathe your mind. He lent Tim two records, said listen, but don't strain at them – just enjoy.

One of those two records was *Alexander's Feast*.

When Tim heard Handel's fanfares cutting through the darkness in his room, when he heard the voices sing in English so he could understand what they sang, he lay on his narrow bed, damp with sweat. It was as if a door had opened in his teenage brain and a hidden compartment had been revealed. In his dimly lit bedroom he felt his body glowed. Tim tried to imagine those musicians – a hopelessly inaccurate picture because he had no idea which instrument made which sound – but the image was of a dazzling line of heralds, of flags and coloured pennants, of sunlight flashing on brass trumpets.

Through Derek Cardew, Tim discovered music. Cardew continued to lend him records, to talk about what he'd heard. Then one day he took Hawk – just the two of them – to his first baroque concert. The Purcell Rooms: *Acis and Galatea*. Derek admitted afterwards he had been worried that the concert might bore him, for, while the recorded music shimmered with passion, in the Purcell Rooms the singers stood static in evening dress before a middle-aged audience. Tim loved it.

Derek now produced more obscure works from his collection. Tim borrowed others from the library. Some were dull, some didn't work for him, but he became obsessive about the baroque. Later music – more complex – did not excite him; earlier pieces seemed simple or austere. Though Derek tried to widen the boy's range, Tim always returned to his baroque idols, Handel, Telemann, Purcell and Bach.

He and Derek shared the listening experience. The whole essence of music, Derek said, was emotion shared. Hawk never was convinced of this; his passion had developed in darkness and solitude, and to share anything was to dilute it. But he went in the evenings to the housemaster's room and Derek would give him a glass of beer. Listening to music with Derek Cardew *did* dilute the pleasure, Tim found, but it also brought a different sensation, a togetherness.

135

On one of his visits to the room, Derek put a fatherly arm around Tim's shoulder. They were sitting on his settee. The gesture was unexpected, but Tim was learning how to share. Cardew took his stillness as encouragement, or acquiescence at least. He placed his other hand on Tim's thigh and moved in to kiss his face.

Looking back on it years later, Tim felt it had all been rather sad. Cardew was not lecherous. He did not prey on young boys. Tim had no evidence that he went for boys at all in preference to men. He had just misread the boy's reactions. Which were quite typical. When Cardew moved in for his kiss, Tim head-butted him on the nose. It was a mistimed blow – Tim was not positioned – but it immediately drew blood. Tim jumped to his feet, and for half a minute yelled all the things a boy needs to yell to prove that he is male. Then he kicked the CD player. Then he smashed a glass. Then he stomped from the room, leaving Derek Cardew to drip snot and blood on to the floor.

Some time later, far too late, Tim realised that if he'd gone to see Derek privately the next day, they would probably have agreed it had just been an unfortunate mistake. Derek could have lent him more records. Tim could have played them in his room. From time to time, Derek might have gazed at him wistfully, but nothing more.

Instead, Tim had grabbed his things and left the Home. Young people do.

Leyton Knox is way outside his territory. North or south of the river is of no significance to him, being a Scot – but East Finchley is seriously north, vertically up from London on the Northern line. South of the river, people say that on the tube map the Northern line is coloured black because it's the line that takes black people home. It runs through Kennington, Stockwell, Balham, Tooting Bec. Occasionally, Leyton rides north of the river to Archway and Tufnell Park – there are pubs there that he likes. Or he will change at Leicester Square for Arsenal. Beyond Archway, though, is suburbia – no place for Leyton Knox.

But it's where Pritchett lives: East Finchley.

He says, 'You'll get me into trouble,' and tries to smile. Knox does not react. 'With the missis,' Pritchett explains.

The surveyor wears his business shirt open at the neck. He has a V-neck sweater with a neat little logo on the chest, and an upmarket anorak draped round his chair. He tries another grin to see if Knox might respond this time, but he doesn't. One of Kazan's hard men, Pritchett thinks. Knox is the only black man in the pub, not the suburban type. He wears a dark tracksuit with the zip half-open and he lolls in his straight-back chair, staring like a boxer at the weigh-in. He fixes the stare on Pritchett's forehead.

'Nearly closing time,' the man remarks.

Knox does not move.

Pritchett shrugs, picks up his glass and sips from it. He wishes that he had not ordered a full pint; he won't finish it. 'Well,' he says. Knox looks at him. Pritchett asks, 'What did you want to say?'

'Oh, nothing,' Knox says, 'I don't talk much.'

Pritchett sighs. 'Great. My wife wonders who the hell I'm meeting, and you play silly buggers.' He tries the grin again. 'I had to pretend that this was business.'

'It is.'

Pritchett looks away. 'You know what I mean.'

'*Serious* business.'

'What's that supposed to mean?'

'Let's step outside.'

The surveyor's face pales. 'I haven't finished my beer.'

'If you're scared that I'll hit you, son, then you'd better not drink that pint. Don't you think?'

They hold eye-contact for a moment before Pritchett looks away. He mutters, 'I hope you're not going to make trouble.'

Leyton Knox leans across the wooden table. 'I hope *you're* not.'

Pritchett glances anxiously round the bar. Knox says, 'Come on.'

Pritchett blinks. 'Why do you want to go outside?' He leans back in his chair while Knox leans forward.

137

'D'ye prefer to discuss your business in front of your neighbours?'

When Pritchett finally does stand up, his pint of beer is hardly touched. He makes reluctantly for the door. Before Leyton leaves the table he takes a leisurely draft from his glass and licks his lips. Not bad, for English beer.

Being Hallowe'en, the pub has been decorated with macabre masks and witches' hats and, when Pritchett reaches the door, his head brushes against a lantern in the shape of a grinning face. Inside is a small flickering light. The surveyor assumes there is a candle there, then realises that there couldn't be, so close to the door: it wouldn't pass the safety regulations.

Outside in the gardens, scattered lights strung from trees sway erratically in spurts of wind. No one sits at the few tables – it is too cold. Pritchett hurries towards the road, aware of Knox at his heels. 'This'll do,' he hears Knox say.

Pritchett flinches like a cat suddenly awakened. 'Let's go in the street.' But even as he starts forward, Knox's hand has gripped his collar. 'I said this will do.'

Keeping his grip on the surveyor's anorak, Knox walks him across the grass to a table beside the hedge. It is dark there, but they are not invisible. Not quite. 'Sit down.'

The surveyor complains that the seat feels damp.

'Don't try your luck.'

Pritchett eases himself on to the chair as if into a cold bath. His knees have begun to quiver.

Knox does not sit down. 'Do I have to tell you why I'm here?'

Pritchett licks his lips.

Knox looms above him. 'Who's going to win this contract?'

The surveyor is almost too cold to speak. 'Which contract?'

Knox sighs. 'Did ye want to get home in one piece?'

Pritchett is relieved to find he has a choice. 'I can't work miracles,' he says.

'Ye'd better.'

'There's a committee.'

'There'll be a committal for murder if you don't watch it.'

138

Pritchett closes his eyes. 'I'll do my best.' He wishes Knox would sit down.

A group of men emerges from the pub. Eagerly, Pritchett looks towards them, starts from his chair, then thinks better of it. Knox stands motionless beside him, hands at his sides. 'What were ye going to tell this committee – that ye'd been taking bribes from Kazan?'

Pritchett stares at the table. The group of men passes through the garden into the street.

'You know what? I think you really want me to beat the shite out of you here and now. Then when I've finished, you want me to leave you here in the garden so this whole thing can be over. But it won't be like that. If we don't win this contract, son, you won't be beaten up – you'll be dismantled. I'll use a screwdriver to take you apart. I'll toss your head on the Piazza floor and your bollocks on your front step. D'ye think I'm joking?'

Pritchett shakes his threatened head.

Leyton stoops towards him. 'Why are ye giving us this aggravation? Have ye a wee secret I should know?'

For several frozen seconds Pritchett barely moves. Then he says, 'I can't do it.'

'Why not?' Leyton's voice has become a whisper.

'I just can't.'

'You've no been talking to Clive Darren?'

Pritchett's face is blank.

'Joe Morgan?'

Pritchett takes a breath. 'It was them that contacted me.'

'And?'

'The same thing really.'

'The same contract?'

Pritchett stares at the garden table. 'For site management.'

'Does he want any other contracts?'

'It's the only one he can get – like Kazan.'

'Why's that?'

Pritchett's voice is low, as if he isn't interested. 'Oh, site management isn't skilled, and it has a lot of perks. He gets to place the contracts that the architects aren't interested in.'

139

'So he earns good commissions?'

Pritchett looks up at him, dull-eyed. 'As stuff comes in and off the site, yes. Site management is like protection, really.'

'I'd better put you straight, son,' says Leyton. 'The Isle of Dogs belongs to Kazan – everything – it's his territory. You do not deal with someone else.'

Pritchett grunts.

'I'm asking this only once, son. Have ye been taking money from both sides?'

The surveyor sighs. 'I've been *threatened* by both sides.'

'We paid you a deposit, son, which you've already banked. How much did Morgan give ye?'

'Nothing. No money.'

Leyton Knox is as erect in the darkness as a minister in his pulpit. 'But you did accept an occasional present, perhaps?'

The surveyor does not seem to have heard him. Pritchett is so cold now that his whole system is shutting down. He does not even look up when the pub door opens to emit another cluster of laughing men. Knox places a hand upon his shoulder.

'You know what night this is, son? It's Hallowe'en. Down here in England ye think Hallowe'en is about witches and beasties, but where I come from, it's more than that. Witches ride tonight, son, and ghosties walk.' Knox sucks his breath between his teeth: he is enjoying this. 'But this is also a night for looking into the future. There's nae other night like it. And d'ye know something? I can see your future, Mr Pritchett. You are at the devil's crossroads: on one side you have wealth and happiness, on the other . . . Don't take that path.'

Leyton grins across Pritchett's downcast head. He can feel the man trembling. 'Now, you slip away home to bed,' he says. 'And you take a peep at your nice wee wife. Ask yourself which path you should be on.'

Knox tightens his grip on Pritchett's collar and pulls him to his feet. He changes his grip to the white man's jaw and turns the frightened face towards his own. 'You wouldnae let me down, son, would ye?'

140

On the last word of his question, Leyton squeezes Pritchett's jaw. The surveyor yelps.

'I didnae catch that, but I hope ye were saying "No".'

Pritchett nods, his eyes watering. 'Yes.'

'Was that yes or no?'

Pritchett stutters.

'I'll tell ye what you said,' Knox whispers. 'You said you *wouldn't* let me down.'

Pritchett tries to speak, but Knox snarls, 'Go home.' Pritchett leaves.

Knox shakes his head. Pritchett must be quite a somebody in his office, yet what is he? Spineless. A typical bloody sassenach. Their idea of Hallowe'en is to hang paper lanterns in the pub. When Leyton was a lad, he and his friends spent all week before Hallowe'en carving lanterns from raw swedes, eating the parings and chunks of root vegetable as they carved. Tumshie lanterns, they called them: grotesque faces, lumpy cottages, misshapen animals, each with its own wee candle in, each one lit for Hallowe'en. Candlelight glared through the jagged holes, gave a luminous pale orange glow to the fibrous flesh. Every handmade lantern would be displayed at the house: the fiercest in windows to grin at passers-by; others arranged on mantles, stood on tables, hung from lintels or outside from trees. Outside was best. Hallowe'en ought to be spent outside. Leyton remembers the tang of autumn darkness, the smell of woodsmoke from the fires. A great game when he was young was to be part of a gang attacking other bonfires. You'd appear out of the darkness, yelling fiercely, wielding sticks and stones to fight opposing keepers. They would be armed as well. You aimed to break the other's bonfire. You'd scatter the embers across the street, ram your stick into something burning, rush off into the darkness with your stick blazing like a torch. Round his way, the kids said Leyton had an unfair advantage because they couldn't see him in the dark. He was a natural Guiser, they said, didn't have to smear his face with soot.

Those were the days. That was how to celebrate. Now, Hallowe'en in Scotland is almost as tame as here in England. It's something you watch on television – a party in a bright-lit studio, a horror film from the States. The only fun in the open nowadays is a council firework display in the park.

Small private celebrations. At midnight, two kids in the Rochester Way send off a rocket from a milk bottle. One boy squats on the pavement, holding the bottle with both hands, while a bigger boy lights the fuse. The bigger boy steps back smartly but the younger one can not. Earlier they both watched an ad on TV in which a firework blew up in some child's hand. The boy holding the milk bottle shuts his eyes.

Irena watches the rocket as it explodes in the sky. Glowing embers of vivid colours hang like a huge electric fritillary, then float down and disappear. She wonders who has fired it, and why. Such celebrations in her own country are strictly organised and rare. Here in Britain, people buy their own fireworks and release them by themselves. Such extravagance: to have each expensive firework blaze in the sky for a mere five seconds then melt away in the night. Though it isn't really *your* firework. Once you have launched it into the air, the firework displays its brilliance for everybody. That rocket she has just admired was bought with somebody else's money, yet she is able to enjoy it. Is it not more sensible that everyone should contribute to a central fund, so they all share the excitement and the cost? That was the old way, of course, at home when she was young: sensible but dull. Here, you buy fireworks because you want them. You might not make such a grand display, but at least it is your own. When your firework erupts in its brief shower of light, you can say, I made that, it is mine.

Of course, in the West they have it both ways. She corrects herself: *we* have it – I live here now. Close to the dark window she smiles at her reflection in the glass. I live here now. I will always live here. Alexei has told her that on Guy Fawkes Night there will be huge organised celebrations, using collective money from local councils. Thousands of people will gather together to

142

watch a festival of fireworks, followed by a bonfire. That bonfire, Alexei said, might be as tall as a small house. People will bring old furniture for the pile. Fancy that – they just burn it.

She had asked him about Guy Fawkes. Would there be an effigy on every fire?

'Of course,' he said.

'And is he put there by the authorities – your councils?'

'Right on the top.'

'And everybody watches Guy Fawkes burn?'

'It's just a dummy, Princess.'

'But he was a hero of the people, was he not? Yet he is executed each year by the authorities while people watch. Do you not think that the English are strange people, Alexei?'

He grinned at her. 'I am English,' he said.

It must be true. His parents speak Ukrainian to her, but he doesn't. He has the words, but is not comfortable with them. Even in the peak of his passion when they make love, he moans in English. It disappoints her. Once, she had thought that to have a lover whisper to her in English would be irresistibly romantic. Now she finds it is not so. Perhaps it is because Alexei does not say romantic things – he has no poetry. She misses the cadence of her own tongue.

Irena shivers at the window, though even at midnight it is still warm indoors. She is reluctant to return to bed yet, in case she misses another firework. These solitary sudden flares have a poignancy that fascinates her. Partly it is their prettiness, partly the spontaneity they represent. Occasional bursts of light, Irena feels, are more satisfying than organised displays – in the way that a solitary wild orchid in the countryside brings more pleasure than a hectare of formal gardens. A blaze of freedom. But then she remembers the single explosive firework the other night which detonated behind the restaurant. That was another face of freedom.

At the side of the window-sill stands an Orangina bottle. She has washed it out and re-used it to contain one flower, a red carnation. It is the flower that the blond boy gave her in the restaurant – Tim Hawk. She smiles at the effrontery of his macabre joke – to turn the lights out, to present Alexei with the body of his enemy by candle-light. That beautiful music, eerie, like a half-heard voice in a deserted church.

Because Tim Hawk was close to Alexei, he was forgiven for his trick. She noticed the closeness between them later when Tim sat with them after the meal. He was at ease at their table, like Alexei's son – and at the same time, though he could not know it, he was the image of little Sergei ... Hawk was older, of course, as she imagined Sergei would have been if he had lived. Tim Hawk: a strange, beautiful boy. At the dinner he had been dressed entirely in black, with one little splash of red carnation. Which he had given to her.

Irena takes the flower from the vase and she sniffs at it. Whatever fragrance there had been once has now faded, yet the petals still seem fresh. The bloom feels soft against her cheek. She studies the red carnation, remembers how that handsome young man wore it across his heart. Carefully, she replaces the flower in its little bottle. As she returns to Alexei, sleeping in their bed, she decides that it is probably just as well he doesn't know whose flower it once was.

13

I t was not the alarm clock. Hawk opened his eyes but still felt
disoriented. His head was beneath the pillow and his mouth
seemed full of feathers. He felt as if he had been knocked out.

The radio-phone was too far across the carpet. When he leant
out of bed to reach it, he slid gently off the mattress and took the
duvet to the floor.

'The hell is this?'

'Morning, Timmy. Did I interrupt your breakfast?'

'What?'

'Thought I'd catch ye before you raced out to the office.'

'What's the time?'

'Och, don't tell me you've missed the commuter special?'

Hawk clambered to his feet. 'Get to the point, Leyton, will
you?'

'I have two points actually. First, are ye sending a representa-
tive to the inquest?'

'What're you talking about?'

'You do know about the inquest?'

'No.'

'Tut, tut. And wee Ally told me only yesterday that *you* were
in charge of security. Congratulations, by the way.'

'Which inquest, Leyton?'

'Clive Darren, lately deceased. But he would be, wouldn't he,
for his inquest? I thought that since you topped him, you might
want to see justice done.'

'Ha, ha. What's your second point?'

145

'Do you no think somebody should be there?'

'Are you off your head?' Tim had walked into his living-room, where he collapsed into a chair.

'It would be only fitting, son. Everybody knows it was you that killed him.'

'Everybody?'

'Well, the wee birdies chatter, Timmy. Anyway, about my second point: I popped round to Philip Pritchett.'

'Pritchett?'

'Oh, come on, son. I thought you were managing this affair? The surveyor, man.'

Hawk groaned. 'Leyton, you've got to stop making calls on people.'

'Am I to become a hermit?'

'What did you do to him?'

'We had a chat.'

'And?'

'And nothing. He went away home to bed.'

'When was this?'

'Well, at bedtime, Timmy – when d'ye think?'

'You called at Pritchett's house?'

'No, I'm too uncivilised, aren't I? I met him in the pub. Dull place. Nice chat.'

'Christ. I've already had a phone call from Steed.'

'Ah, Steed. To apologise, I hope.'

'Why the hell should he apologise, Leyton? You went to his office – you beat the shit out of him.'

'I gave him one wee poke in the belly – the soft underbelly of capitalism, yes? Anyway, what do you mean, why should he apologise? The man cheated us, didn't he? I think you should re-examine your priorities, my wee lad.'

Over breakfast, Philip Pritchett seemed distracted. His wife knew that he had crept into their front room a little earlier to stand staring out the window. She knew that he had also slipped out of the front door, down the path, and peered along the street. In

146

the bedroom when he got up, the first thing he did was to peep out through the curtains, muttering lamely about the weather.

Last night he had gone out suddenly at half-past ten.

Now he sat at the kitchen table, watching his slice of toast go cold. His tea remained untouched. Vanessa Pritchett took a position opposite her husband, stood with her hands on the backrest of her chair. He didn't notice. She asked, 'What on earth's the matter?'

'Mhm?'

'I said what's the matter?'

He looked up at her, unseeing. 'What? I'm sorry.'

She continued watching him. He pushed back his chair, stood up, turned to leave the table.

'No you don't.'

'Mhm?'

'What's going on?'

His mouth twitched, but there was nothing he could say.

'Who are you looking for, Philip, outside the house?'

It seemed that he had lost the power of speech.

'I assume that you're not waiting for your girlfriend?'

That crack seemed to release a logjam in his mind. 'What do you mean, a girlfriend? What are you talking about?'

'You keep looking out in the street. Don't you?'

'Do I?'

'Yes.'

He stared at his wife for a second as if trying to remember who she was. 'Of course I haven't got a girlfriend.'

'No?'

'No.'

She gazed into his face, trying to pin his attention on what was happening here in their kitchen. 'I was beginning to think you might have an announcement to make.'

'What a ridiculous idea!' She had caught his attention now. He even laughed slightly, a kind of choking sound.

Vanessa came round the table. 'If there's something you should tell me —'

147

'There's nothing.' He moved away from her.

'Nothing I should be afraid of?'

'No.'

'Is there something,' she asked, 'that *you* should be afraid of?'

He shook his head, tried that laugh again, lurched into the hall. 'I'm just preoccupied,' he said.

'Why?'

'God, is that the time? I'll be late.'

She had followed him into the hall. She watched him thrust his arms inside his coat and stumble to the front door. He said, 'I'll see you tonight,' and put his hand on the door-catch.

'Don't I get a kiss?'

He tottered back towards her. 'I'm awfully late. I'm sorry, but you don't always −' they kissed briefly − 'want one, do you?' He ran out through the door.

'Sometimes I need a kiss,' she said as he clattered into the garden, 'for reassurance.'

Kazan crashed into the dining-room, singing, 'Ta-ra-ta-ra'. He had the red carnation in his mouth.

'You are happy?' Irena asked.

With a flourish he removed the flower. 'Natch! The sun is shining.'

'Oh, is that all?' she smiled.

'And I love you,' he said.

She gave him a sidelong look.

'I wanna present you with this flower.'

'Yes?'

'We need a little vase.' He was looking round him. 'What do they call this flower?'

She shook her head. 'I do not know, but in Ukraine −'

'Wear it in a buttonhole −'

'Carnation,' she said, 'if it is for a buttonhole − or gardenia.'

'Carnation, that's the one, like the milk?' She frowned. He said, 'Hey, between us, we'll get this language licked, am I right?'

'But it is your language.'

148

'Thing is, I was never good with flowers.'

She smiled sadly. 'I do not know all their names in English.'

'No. Well.' He gazed at her across the table. 'You speak English better than I do, anyhow.'

'*Anyway*, not anyhow.'

He laughed. 'There you are! Look, what am I gonna do with this stupid flower?'

'I thought you wanted to present it to me?'

'That's right – you want it?' He didn't wait for her reply. 'Hey, I chucked out that stupid bottle that you had this in. You want a proper vase.'

'But it was a pretty bottle – I scrubbed the label off. You should not throw such things away.'

'A bottle, for Chrissake. We got vases, Irena. Could've put one on the table, like in a fancy restaurant. You know – just a single bloom, not a whole bunch of the things.' He tossed the carnation on to the glass table. 'Anyway, let's eat.'

He eyed the bowls of fruit and breakfast cereal. She went in for this kind of stuff, wasn't yet used to English sausages. Meanwhile, Irena was disappointed about the pretty bottle. Al threw so many things away. Sitting at the table with her new husband, Irena found her gaze returning to Tim Hawk's red carnation, lying on the glass surface between them.

14

Hawk did not feel cut out for management. He pitched his voice low on the telephone, 'Time's passing, Mr Steed.'

'You said two weeks, for Christ's sake, Hawk, not two days.'

'We're impatient.'

'*You're* impatient! I told you yesterday –'

'How's your broken rib?'

'Look –'

'Shall I send him round again?'

A pause. 'Leave it with me, OK?'

'I want progress reports.'

'Progress, Christ, what d'you expect in just two days?'

'Progress.'

'What am I supposed to say?'

'That you've put the money back.'

'Oh, come on, Hawk, we agreed two weeks.'

'I've been good to you so far.'

'Good?'

'I called the big man off, Steed, but I still have you in my sights.'

Hawk put the phone down. That hadn't been too difficult.

When he rang Pritchett, he found him harder to get through to. There was a telephonist, then a secretary, then 'Could anyone else help?' Then it was 'We'll see if we can find him, Mr Hawk'.

'What do you want?'

'Good morning, Mr Pritchett, my name's Hawk.'

A pause. 'Kazan told me about you.'

'Then you know why I'm calling.'

'I can guess, but tell me.'

'You sound hard on the phone, Mr Pritchett.'

Slight pause. 'Hard?'

'One of our colleagues dropped round to see you last night.'

Pritchett sighed. Hawk asked, 'Did he make our message clear?'

'He emphasised it.'

'But you're in your office.'

'So?'

'If he had emphasised it, Mr Pritchett, you'd be in hospital.'

'I don't have to take this.'

'Take what, Mr Pritchett? That couple of thousand in banknotes, that weekend in Hamburg? You've been drawing a salary from us.'

'Salary? Do you know what I earn?'

'You mean we're paying peanuts?'

'*Your* words.'

'So far, Mr Pritchett, you have *delivered* peanuts.'

'Well . . . maybe I should give Kazan a refund and call it off.'

'You really *didn't* get the message last night, did you?'

'Things look clearer in daylight.'

'Better be careful in the dark.'

Hawk replaced the phone, and scowled at the receiver as if it might have been laughing at him. That call hadn't gone so well. When Knox said he had seen Pritchett, Hawk had assumed that he had frightened him. He did most people. Yet Pritchett did not seem in any way alarmed. Odd. Another thing, Pritchett said Kazan had given him Hawk's name. Surely the only reason Kazan would do that was as a threat? If Pritchett knew he was being telephoned by Kazan's hitman, how did he manage to stay cool? Was he playing tough behind a telephone or did he have another reason for his confidence?

Hawk put in a call for Leyton Knox, but he was out.

Ten o'clock on the pip was what they'd agreed, but Irena was surprised the girl was so punctual. Kazan and the rest of his

151

companions didn't seem to care about time-keeping. Al left at different times in the mornings, returned at different times at night; if he set a meeting for 10 o'clock it meant any time in the morning; their meal in the restaurant had been booked for 8 yet they didn't leave home until 8.30. Time was something Kazan kicked around.

But the girl was here on time. Irena had been looking forward to her arrival; she found it lonely in the house, and was excited at the thought of having her own maid. After that foolish incident with the police car, Irena no longer ventured out alone – which meant, in effect, that she did not go out. Having her own personal maid would be extraordinary – as in a fairy-story where an unspoilt village girl weds the prince. Irena was also excited that the maid was black; she hadn't known a black girl before. Already she had been fascinated to see so many black people in London streets. She knew that Western countries absorbed black people – in Ukraine she had been taught how they were enslaved – but that knowledge had not permeated the image she had previously held of London: there were few negroes in tales of Dickens.

When the woman arrived at Kazan's door, Irena forgot to act like an employer – she stooped to take the suitcase. 'Oh, it is so heavy, Cecille!'

The girl let Irena drag the case inside. Cecille didn't know what maids were supposed to do either; she was there to be a companion, whatever *that* meant. She said, 'It's everything I have.'

When Irena had bought her own possessions from Ukraine they had weighed half as much as this. She abandoned Cecille's suitcase. 'I thought I was strong!'

Cecille grinned. 'I'll do it. Hey, you're not pregnant, are you?'

'Pregnant?' Irena put her hand to her mouth and laughed.

'Well, you *are* married.'

'But for two weeks!'

'Sorry. Round here, people don't get married *till* they're pregnant, seems to me.'

152

'Really?'

'Oh, I'm just a cynic. What do I call you, by the way – Ma'am, or what?'

'Irena – because I hope we will be friends.'

Cecille nodded, picked up the suitcase as if it had suddenly lost its weight, asked if it would be all right to take it straight upstairs.

As they went up, Cecille began to hum a catchy tune. She asked Irena if her husband was in, then continued with the tune. In the upstairs hall she asked, 'First time in England?'

'Oh, yes. My first time outside Ukraine.'

'Quite a shock, I guess.'

'A little. Here is your bedroom.'

'Nice.' Cecille cast a glance around the room and decided that it *was* nice. 'I'll unpack later.'

'Do you have many beautiful dresses, Cecille?'

The girl looked startled. 'Me?'

Irena shrugged. 'Such a large suitcase.'

'Full of junk, honey. I'm a hoarder.'

'People in England wear lovely clothes.'

Cecille recoiled. 'You are joking, aren't you?'

'No, everyone has . . . so much variety.'

'That's one way to put it. Well, what would you like to do?'

The question had not occurred to Irena. 'Now?'

'Now and for ever, honey.'

'Well . . . I could help you unpack. You could show me your lovely dresses.'

Cecille grinned as she moved away from her suitcase. 'I don't have lovely dresses. I'll do this later.'

Irena realised that Cecille might prefer a little privacy. 'I am sorry. I will leave you on your own.' She began backing from the room.

'No need. Let's get to know each other.'

Irena stepped forward, hoping that she might after all get to see inside that suitcase, to peep at a Western woman's wardrobe. But Cecille said, 'Let's go down and make some coffee.'

* * *

At Strong's Scaffolding, Hawk caught up with Leyton Knox.

'Ah, Timmy, are ye not in mourning?'

'What?'

'There's been a death in the family. Have ye no heard?'

'Oh, Harry, yeah. Look –'

'Have ye spoken to Kazan?'

'Why?'

'He'll be on the warpath about it.'

'Oh, sure, he's really upset. What I want to talk to you about, though –'

'Wait a minute, sonny.' Leyton tapped him on the chest. 'This is one of Kazan's family we're talking about.' He stared into Hawk's face. 'Who does he think topped him?'

'Oh.' Hawk looked uncomfortable. 'Of course, when we find out –'

'I see, Timmy, I see. Well, ye'll have to do much better than that when Old William comes to call.' Knox stepped back from him, digesting what he'd learned.

Hawk said, 'This Pritchett guy –'

'Not that again.' Knox glanced around the empty yard.

'Did you frighten him?'

'Let's see now – he didnae finish his pint.'

'But was he frightened?'

Knox stared at him. 'What are ye driving at?'

'He isn't scared now.'

'Oh, really?'

'Cocky, I'd say.'

A car hooted in the street outside. Leyton frowned. 'Where'd ye get this?'

'I phoned him.'

'And?'

'He didn't seem concerned.'

Leyton's eyes narrowed against the sunlight. 'Did he not?'

'He said something about things looking clearer in daylight.'

'Did he now? I knew I should have thumped him.'

'You're sure you didn't?'

'Och, not at all. You would think the Lord made me from Kleenex.'

'When I spoke to him on the phone, he already knew my name.'

Knox met his eyes. 'So?'

'He should have been frightened.'

Knox did not respond. Hawk said, 'You know what I think? He's got protection.'

'Who from?'

Hawk shrugged. 'Somebody made him a better offer.'

Knox reared up. 'Oh yes? Then I'll make him a *special* offer.'

'Kazan said specifically you shouldn't go near him.'

'I didnae *touch* the man!'

Hawk raised a placatory hand. 'That's what he said.'

'Spell this out to me, will ye? Exactly what did wee Ally say?'

'Just what I told you: tell Leyton he is not to go near that surveyor feller.'

'I see. Anything else?'

'No.'

'Well, fine, thank you. Message understood. And I'm afraid I must be off.' He turned away.

'Hey Leyton, wait a minute. What are you going to do?'

Knox paused at the gate. 'Don't worry, Timmy, I shan't go anywhere near the man. Not if Kazan wouldn't like it.' He disappeared.

'It sure is peaceful here,' said Cecille. 'Don't you find it dull?'

'No, I am privileged.'

Cecille pulled a wry face and took another sip of her coffee. Irena waved a hand at the luxurious kitchen. 'You would not understand, Cecille. In the West, you take all this for granted, but in Ukraine . . .'

'No we don't. This ain't typical, Irena. You're lucky – you found yourself a fine rich husband.'

'He *is* rich, I know.'

Cecille studied her. 'Some contrast, huh?'

'Oh! Impossible to describe. No one in my village lives like this – no one in Ukraine, I think.'

'Your family living?'

'Oh yes, they are proud of me.'

'I bet.'

'My husband – Alexei – is Ukrainian also, you know? His family is.'

'Alexei, huh?'

'And your family?'

'Oh, we're British, honey, through and through.'

'Where were you born?'

'Anerley.'

Irena frowned. She couldn't place it.

'Just below Crystal Palace.'

'Oh, I thought you meant an island in the West Indies. But the Crystal Palace, that is wonderful.'

Cecille shrugged.

'The Crystal Palace was destroyed by fire, was it not? It was a glass temple for your Great Exhibition of 1851.'

'Hey! Right on, Irena, that's good.'

Irena smiled. 'I was a schoolteacher.'

'That's where you get the English?'

Irena nodded. 'I always dreamed that I could come here.'

'Well, you did it, honey. Congratulations.'

The two women looked at each other across the table. Cecille was thinking: that's why you married him. Although she couldn't say it, perhaps she showed it in her eyes. Irena smiled slowly, mischievously, as if she read Cecille's thoughts. 'Yes, I did it. I am here now.'

'You have arrived. Yes, indeed.'

Suddenly they both laughed – just for a moment, then they stopped. Irena held her lower lip between her teeth. Cecille smiled. Both women knew what had not been spoken. Both knew it could not be spoken yet.

Leyton Knox has chosen the Deptford Arms. It wouldn't occur

to him that he has no authority. Neither, curiously enough, would it occur to any of the three men who join him. Each has been told that Hawk is in charge of security, yet when Knox summons them, they come. It seems natural, somehow.

Leyton says, 'Ye must handle this professionally.'

'You bet.'

'With three of you, it'll be a doddle – but that's the danger.'

'How come?'

'Too easy, Vinnie. You could go too far.'

'Kill him, you mean?' asks Clint.

Leyton's eyes move towards him. 'Och, you'd no do that.' A warning.

'No, of course not,' Clint and Ronnie say together.

Clint asks, 'But how far do we . . . you know?'

'I want no broken bones.'

Clint frowns. 'Oh, right.'

Vinnie asks, 'Plenty of stick?'

'Watch my lips,' Leyton says. 'Precision surgery. I'll spell out exactly what I mean.'

'I made a promise,' Irena said.

They were in the garden now. Cider-coloured autumn sunshine slanted across the grass, stretching the shadows.

'You had no choice,' Cecille said. While Irena drifted across the large lawn behind the house, Cecille paced behind her, like a labrador at her heels. 'Every immigrant – and that's what you are, honey – sends money back to the folks at home. How much you sending?'

'It will be every month, one hundred pounds.'

Cecille paused. 'A hundred pounds a month?'

'I promised before I came.'

Cecille glanced at the large house. 'Well, that won't break you.'

Irena caught her tone. 'It is not enough?'

'People here can earn a hundred pounds a day.'

'You do not say so! In Ukraine it would take a week at least.'

157

'It's pocket money to you now.'

'Is it?'

Cecille draped a friendly arm about her shoulder. 'Don't feel bad about it, honey. Happens all the time. My Grandpa when he came here − just like you − he was sending home less money than he spent on smokes and drink. He felt guilty about it, but back home they were grateful. What he sent seemed good money in Grenada.'

'Granada? He came from Spain?'

'Grenada. Caribbean.'

'Oh. You will let me meet your grandparents?'

Cecille paused. 'You wouldn't want to.'

'Cecille, I want to meet many people, to visit places I have read about, to get . . . I am bored in this big house. Do you think that is bad?'

'No.' Cecille chuckled.

'We will go out together?'

'Bet your life. This is a nice house, Irena, but . . .' Cecille looked at the surrounding trees. 'Yeah, I'd get bored. We'll go out this afternoon, right?'

'You promise?'

'I don't have to promise, honey. You're in charge.'

'Don't say that, Cecille. We are friends.'

When they strolled indoors from the garden, Irena seemed to have something on her mind. In the front room she asked Cecille how long she had been working for her husband.

'Since today.'

'Oh!' Irena looked at her, surprised. 'I thought you were − what is the word?'

'A permanent employee? No, I'm a hired hand.'

'I see.' Irena studied her openly. 'What work do you normally do?'

Cecille eased away from the subject. 'You see, what happened was that your husband and Hawk interviewed three of us girls.'

'Mr Hawk − the young blond man?'

'Yeah, he works for your husband, right? They're pretty close.'

158

'Do you know him?'

'Which?' Cecille met her gaze. 'Tim Hawk? Yeah, we go back.'

'Go back?'

Cecille chuckled. 'We've known each other some time – that's what it means.'

Irena raised an eyebrow. 'I see. You are his sweetheart.'

'What? No way, get out of here!'

'Oh, Cecille, you can tell me.'

Cecille shook her head. 'Him and me, we're kinda friends, that's all. Not sweethearts.'

'Friends. Mm-hm. But Mr Hawk chose you.'

'Your husband chose me –'

'Don't you say that!' Irena laughed. 'He sent you out of the house. What did he say? About a chocolate. Mr Hawk wanted –'

'Chocolate?'

Irena stopped. 'Oh, Cecille, I'm sorry, I did not realise what he meant. You will not be angry with me?'

Cecille's face had hardened. 'No, I won't be angry with you.'

Irena placed a hand on Cecille's arm. 'He did not mean to insult you. He was angry with Tim Hawk.'

'For choosing me?'

'Oh.' Irena was distressed. 'I should not have said this. I spoke my thoughts aloud. Please do not be insulted.'

Cecille smiled briefly, without warmth. 'No, don't worry, I'm thick-skinned.'

'We are still friends?' Irena's anxiety showed.

'Sure.'

A sparkle of mischief returned to Irena's eyes. 'You will like me as much as you like Tim Hawk?'

Cecille stepped back, amused. 'Hey, what is this interest in Tim Hawk? Has he got under your skin?'

'What do you mean, under my –'

'You have the hots for him, Irena!' Cecille was laughing now.

'I have not – I do not understand.'

'Oh yes, you do, honey. You understand.'

159

Irena was blushing, couldn't keep the smile from off her face.
'Oh, Irena, you can tell me.'

Irena said, 'There is nothing I should tell.' She looked indignant.
Then they both burst out laughing.

Philip Pritchett steps off the tube at East Finchley and immediately feels the cold. The fine November day has become a chilling starry night. He turns his coat collar up, watches his breath vapourise before his face. In The Causeway, his fellow commuters separate – some heading down to the Great North Road, others up to East End Road. Pritchett is in the second group, walking briskly along the narrow pedestrian passageway toward home. No one says much. The cold night air heightens the sound of shoe leather on dry concrete.

Someone says, 'Oh, Mr Pritchett?'

He pretends he hasn't heard it, tries to stay among the throng. Two men have been walking against the flow. They oppose him. Now they are linking their arms through his, walking him backwards. He calls, 'Help!'

'Don't try that,' one hisses.

People ahead in the narrow walkway turn to see what is happening. Some hesitate. Most hurry on.

'Come on, help me!' Pritchett calls. Everyone ignores the panic in his voice.

The two men holding him are joined by a third – tall, with a ginger crewcut. Pritchett has never met Vinnie Dirkin. Behind Dirkin, all but two of the commuters hurriedly slip away, abandoning Pritchett to his attackers. Dirkin moves in to start it, thinking it will be easy. But he should have noticed those two commuters who didn't slip away.

Because he faces Pritchett, the first he knows of the two behind is when the cosh zaps across his shoulder. Before Clint and Ronnie can turn, they have their heads smacked too – not with old socks filled with coins, but with coshes *made* for smacking. Each weighs about four pounds. Usually the first swing drops the victim, and the second knocks him out.

160

Tonight has to be a little different.

At first, Dirkin gets off lightly. While he crouches in pain on the concrete, Clint and Ronnie take the brunt. The two who jumped them calmly and methodically put the boot in, then each drops on to one knee. As they drop, they slam their coshes. They make this dive twice more. Clint and Ronnie are now unconscious, so they don't feel their bones crack.

Pritchett has slunk a few yards away, and stands isolated. Though he doesn't watch when they turn to Dirkin, he can't avoid listening.

'Take this back to Al Kazan.'

Dirkin screams. Pritchett hears another boot go in to cut down Vinnie's noise.

'Wait. Give him the message first – while he can hear you.'

'Listen carefully, you. This is what you tell him. You tell Kazan to stay out of the Limehouse Piazza. Got that? Tell him if he doesn't, then he'll get double what we do to you.'

Vinnie makes a kind of squealing noise, but another cosh blow stops that. Anaesthetic. Pritchett glances – closes his eyes too late. He should not have looked. The man kneeling beside Dirkin is using a Stanley knife to hack off his ear. Pritchett reels away, wondering why he does not immediately throw up.

'That'll do nicely,' he hears. 'Hey, Mr Pritchett,' the man says. Pritchett forces himself to turn round. 'You can go home now. We've finished for tonight.'

Pritchett nods. There is blood all over Dirkin's face.

'You want us to walk you to your door?'

Pritchett nods again.

'Best not,' the man says. He turns to his companion. 'You hear that?'

'That's handy.'

Pritchett watches as the two men stand up and lope away towards the entrance to the tube station. One calls back to him, 'Don't hang about.'

Below The Causeway a train is entering the station, and Pritchett's two bodyguards, job done, intend to catch it. Realising that the train will disgorge passengers, Pritchett stumbles away to East End Road. He is nearly halfway home before suddenly, without warning, he starts to vomit. He leans against a wall, head in hands, splattering mucus on his shoes. No one notices.

But there is an awful commotion at the station.

15

It would have been easier to meet in Kazan's office. But at this time of night the Blackwall Tunnel was almost empty, there were no delays down Southern Approach, and Hawk's van could slip through the underpass and cut off the deserted Rochester Way. At Kazan's house he was let in the front door by Cecille. In the hallway he asked how she had settled in.

'It's been a busy first night.'

'Has Kazan told you what happened?'

'You must be joking.' She led him down the hall. 'But I heard them shouting.'

'How many?'

'Just the two.' She opened the door to Kazan's study.

'You never knock?' Kazan was slumped behind the desk. Leyton Knox sat by the wall. Gently, Hawk closed the door on Cecille, then asked, 'Anything changed?'

'Whadya think – they're royalty? Think the hospital issues press bulletins?' Kazan bounced upon his chair as he rapped this out. Hawk hadn't seen him so angry since Darren tried to take the Isle of Dogs. He asked who else was coming.

'Who the fuck else do we need? You're the two fouled it up.'

Leyton rolled his eyes.

Kazan had amassed a head of steam. He jumped out of his chair, thumped the desk with his fist, kicked the leg of a fine bookcase. He repeated for Hawk that Vinnie, Ronnie and Clint were detained in hospital. Only Ronnie was conscious. Louis had been up there, but Ronnie couldn't tell much. A doctor had told

Louis that Vinnie had a depressed fracture of the skull, and the hospital were hoping they could sew his ear back. He said Clint, whose ribs had caved in, had internal bleeding. And he said Ronnie shouldn't speak.

Al glared at Hawk. 'I told you to lay off that sodding Pritchett.'

Hawk nodded.

Leyton said, 'Hawk mentioned it.'

'You shut up.'

Knox ignored him. 'And you were right, Timmy. Pritchett did have protection.'

Hawk asked, 'It couldn't have been passers-by?'

'They cut his ear off!' Al yelled. 'They carried clubs.'

Knox said, 'It was a message.'

'Saying what?'

'You tell me,' Kazan snarled. He stomped back and forth behind his desk.

Hawk raised an eyebrow at Leyton Knox, who shrugged. 'I'm sorry, Timmy, I misjudged it. I thought, one man alone, a civilian . . .'

'But I told you.'

'Have you heard his answer?' yelled Kazan.

Leyton gave Hawk a tired smile. 'You said I was to stay away from him. *I* was – not the others.'

Hawk sighed. 'That's childish.'

'Aye.'

Al aimed another blow at the desk. 'You should've known this would happen!'

'Hindsight.'

'Listen, you!' Kazan jabbed his finger like a gun. Leyton sat unmoved. With his finger aimed at Leyton's chest, Al turned to Hawk. 'What's this shit about protection?'

Hawk paused. 'I got a sniff of it when I phoned him. Suddenly he wasn't scared.'

Kazan lowered his gun finger and sneered at Leyton Knox. 'And you thought you had frightened him! Maybe you're not so tough.'

Knox smiled.

164

'Also,' Hawk said, 'Pritchett suggested he should call the whole deal off, give us a refund.'

As Kazan drew breath to reply, Knox said, 'He's been talking with Joe Morgan.'

'What?'

'Pritchett told me they had threatened him.'

'Joe Morgan,' Kazan breathed.

'Well, he has a motive,' said Hawk.

'Right,' Al said. 'That settles it. If he wants a fight . . .' He looked at the other two expectantly.

Hawk said, 'Yes?'

Kazan stared at him.

Hawk said, 'What – if he wants a fight, we give him one?'

'Right.'

Hawk frowned at him. 'I thought Darren was small fry?'

Kazan looked irritable. 'He was, but he got bigger. Two years ago he was nothing. He put a bunch of ratbags together up in Tottenham and tried to move into my Isle of Dogs. I told you that.'

'You told me part of it,' Hawk mumbled.

'What – I have to discuss my plans with you?' Al glared at him. 'You got to stamp these bastards out.'

Hawk asked, 'How many bastards are we talking about?'

Al paused. 'You trying to be funny?'

'I need clear instructions,' Hawk said. They stared at each other. Neither looked away.

So Knox said, 'Joe Morgan's a mean one, right enough. D'ye think he's taken Darren's place?'

'You stay out of it,' snapped Kazan. He leant across his desk. 'Now listen, Hawk, I put you in charge of the Isle of Dogs so you could tell *me* what *you're* gonna do about it. You two clowns got me into this – now get me out.' He stood up. 'You hearing me?' He came round from behind his desk and strutted for the door. 'By the way,' he hinted, 'I liked the way you handled Darren.'

In the hall, Kazan marched before them like a butler leading out the sweeps.

165

'Would you like a drink?'

Irena stood in the doorway to the front sitting-room. She wore her full-length dress with high collar and long lacey sleeves. It was all she had for evenings.

'In my country,' Irena said, 'we never let a guest depart without offering something to help their journey. Perhaps a glass of wine?'

The men paused. Al said, 'They're in a hurry, Irena. They gotta go.'

But Knox said, 'Very nice to meet ye, Mrs Kazan. My name is Leyton Knox.'

'How do you do?'

Knox could sense Kazan twitching at his side, so he said, 'And have you met our friend Tim Hawk?'

'Oh yes, I think so.' She inclined her head. Behind her, in the sitting-room, Cecille chuckled.

'Please won't you accept a drink?'

Leyton cut across Kazan's refusal. 'Thank you, Mrs Kazan. D'ye have a whisky, by any chance?'

Knox had half an eye on Kazan. Kazan had both eyes on Leyton Knox. Neither of them saw that Irena's eyes were on Tim Hawk.

'Follow me,' she said, smiling.

16

Morning: grey, cold and sullen. Driving out of town against the traffic, Hawk watches faces in oncoming cars: grey, cold and sullen. One person to each car. Most of the time, they sit glumly with their cars in neutral, waiting to advance ten yards. Driving north is easier, though not much. At Holloway, Hawk forks left at Archway, uses Highgate and North Hill – then hits the High Street. Now Hawk waits like the southbound drivers: van in neutral, can't make ten yards. He sucks his teeth.

Beside the road is a council notice: 'Grand Fireworks Display In Waterlow Park'. Kids have improved it with their spray-cans. First, somebody blocked out the 'Grand' and the 'D' of 'Display', crossed out 'In Waterlow Park', leaving 'Fireworks Is Play'. Some prig extended that to 'Fireworks Is Playing With Fire'. Someone else made it 'Fireworks Is Playing With Fireworks'. Hawk is so engrossed in these additions that he doesn't notice when the traffic begins to move. He hears a blast from the car behind. He moves. North Hill and Deansway are uncongested, so Hawk has plenty of time to find the address off East End Road.

Vanessa Pritchett does not want breakfast. She will wait until he has gone. She sits at the table with a cold slice of toast and an untasted cup of tea on which the milk has formed a scum. She watches Philip spread butter evenly across a second slice of toast. Normally he eats only one. By concentrating on his butter and marmalade, he does not have to look at her. She is aware of that.

At breakfast yesterday he was unaccountably nervous – peeping out of the window, checking along the street. Nothing was the matter, he said – he was just preoccupied.

He had been preoccupied last night.

At first when he staggered in, she thought that it showed why he had been odd that morning, at breakfast, he had been ill. He came in white-faced, breath pungent with vomit, and let her send him up to bed. But later he had come downstairs in his dressing-gown, saying he was all right now, he wasn't tired. He kept fidgeting while they watched television. Then he left the room. When he returned, he tried to deny he had made a phone call. Then he said it was just something unimportant about work. When she tried to question him further he said he wanted to watch the News. She turned it off. Philip said that they'd been through all of this at breakfast: she was irrational, he had a head-ache, he did not have a girlfriend. No, he had not lost his job. Yes, there was an office drama, but she did not have to worry about it. He would not discuss it.

Now over today's breakfast he still will not discuss it. He is dressed normally for work. Whatever stomach upset he had last night seems to have slipped away completely. He eats breakfast slowly and steadily. Occasionally he glances at his watch as if he is waiting for somebody.

When the gentle knock comes at the door, he jumps to his feet and makes for the hall.

'That was the *back* door,' says Vanessa.

'The back?'

She rises leisurely from her chair, saying she will answer it. He says no, leave it to him. She doesn't. She thinks it curious that someone should come round to the back, this early in the day. When she opens the kitchen door, her husband Philip is right beside her.

'Mrs Pritchett?'

'Oh Christ,' says Pritchett. 'Get out. Shut the door.'

But Hawk has already pushed inside.

'What is it?' she cries.

'Don't worry,' murmurs Hawk. 'I don't mean you any harm.'

Mr and Mrs Pritchett shout at the intruder, who says, 'Tell her to go upstairs.'

'No!' she screams.

'There's nothing to worry about,' says Hawk, locking the kitchen door.

'Who is this man?' she yells. 'Philip?' He seems helpless, as he was last night. 'Do you know this man?'

'Of course he knows me,' says Hawk, slipping the door-key in his pocket. 'We have a little business to discuss.'

'Not here,' the surveyor says.

Vanessa stares at the two men. She feels she should rush to the kitchen drawer and grab a carving knife, or perhaps the telephone. She asks, 'What are you going to do?'

'I won't hurt him,' says Hawk. He turns to Philip Pritchett. 'Sit down.' The man does.

She says, 'Promise?'

Hawk frowns.

'Do you promise?' she asks.

'Promise?'

'That you won't hurt him?'

Hawk smiles.

She licks her lips. 'Should I really go upstairs? Do you want to talk to him in private – is that it?'

'That's it.'

Vanessa glances at her husband, as if he might possibly have an opinion that matters. 'Will you be all right, Philip, if I go upstairs?'

He glances dumbly at her.

'Perhaps I should.'

As if creeping from a room at night, Vanessa eases into the hall, starts towards the closed front door. Hawk sees the telephone. He says, 'Stop.' She pauses. 'I suppose there's an extension in the bedroom?'

'No.'

'Come back here.'

She hesitates. 'No.'

169

Hawk inclines his head. 'Best not to cause trouble.'

Vanessa walks further into the hall. 'Philip,' she says clearly. 'Run outside.'

She is now standing two yards from their front door, her hand inches from the telephone. No one moves. She wonders which is better: to dial 999 will take longer than to get outside. There is another phone next door.

Suddenly she turns and rushes for the front door. She has it open when Hawk arrives. He slams against it, grabs hold of her, drags her back along the hall. She snatches the phone, tries to dial. He pulls the cable from the wall, bundles her back into the kitchen.

Vanessa clutches the useless telephone. Philip Pritchett stays on his chair. Hawk says, 'Sit down.' But when he releases her, Vanessa stands with the phone against her breast like a rock that she could throw.

'Sit down.'

'No.'

'I don't want to hurt you.'

She cannot outface him. She slams the handset on the kitchen table and shouts in her husband's face: 'Who is this man? What on earth is this about?'

Pritchett does not reply. She tells Hawk to leave the house immediately. She shouts but he does not move. Quietly Hawk repeats that it would be better if she sat down – but she screams 'No!' It is only anger that prevents her from breaking down in tears.

Hawk addresses Pritchett. 'You see? I haven't even touched her.'

She says, 'You wouldn't dare!'

'You don't know what I would dare.'

Pritchett keeps glancing at his watch. 'Waiting for your minders? What time are they due?' Pritchett does not answer. 'Must be soon,' Hawk says. 'You usually leave about this time. I've watched you.'

For a moment, Pritchett looks as if he might, finally, rise from his chair – but he doesn't. He meets nobody's eyes. Hawk leans on the kitchen table and says to Pritchett's wife, 'You might just as well sit down while we wait.'

It takes nearly twenty minutes before the Pritchett's front door-bell rings. Twenty long minutes. At one point she had said suddenly, 'That's enough', and had tried to leave the room. But Hawk said 'Don't', quite mildly, and showed her the pistol in his hand. It made her jump. It was the first time that she had seen it. He rubbed the gun against his sleeve as if to polish it, then put it back inside his jacket. She sat down then – not only because her legs had become numb, but because she didn't want him to see that she was frightened. Yet it was *his* face that was white, so extraordinarily white. It still is, she notices.

When the bell does ring, the Pritchetts look at Hawk, who says, 'Come on'. He and Vanessa begin to move but Philip stays where he is. Hawk asks, 'Are you glued to that chair or have you messed your pants?'

She says, 'Come on, Philip', and he stands up.

As they move into the hall, Hawk says, 'Let him in.' He holds the pistol in his hand. 'You do it, Pritchett. Act naturally.' Hawk smiles meaningfully at Vanessa to show that he still does not trust her.

Like an old man in carpet slippers, Pritchett opens the door a crack. He says, 'Come in a moment, won't you?'

A man smiles and steps inside. Immediately, he realises that Hawk is behind the door. Hawk slams it. 'Take it easy.' The man tenses as if to pounce, but sees the gun aimed at his chest. 'Carrying anything?' Hawk asks.

The man stares at him. Beneath his jacket is his four-pound cosh and he does not want to surrender that. 'Nothing.'

'Don't lie to me,' says Hawk. 'I hate being lied to.'

The man stays silent.

'Easy or hard?' Hawk asks. 'Are you carrying anything?'

'No.'

'Hard, then. Turn round, put your hands against the wall. Try to help me keep you alive.'

171

The man does as he is told. He is thinking fast. He decides that the blond boy is not about to shoot him – which means that he'll probably try to whack him about the head. All he has to do, the big man thinks, is to duck and butt him when he comes close. Shouldn't even need the cosh.

'Mrs Pritchett,' Hawk says. 'Move towards the kitchen. Don't go inside. Stay in sight.'

As she parts from her husband beside the door, Vanessa squeezes his arm. It might be the last chance she gets to touch him. Hawk says, 'Everybody wait. It won't be long.'

They are so quiet that all four of them can hear the footsteps on the path, yet the doorbell still makes them flinch. 'Open it,' says Hawk.

The big man at the wall turns his head. This could be his chance. It isn't. He sees his companion pushed indoors by Leyton Knox.

Six people in the hall makes it crowded. Hawk doesn't want Pritchett to rejoin his wife because he'd have to pass between the big man and Hawk's gun. He transfers his aim to the second man with Knox, and says, 'My one claims that he's not carrying.'

'That's all right, then,' says Knox as he moves forward. He rams a blow in the big man's kidneys which shakes the partition wall. He slams another to the big man's face and two pictures topple to the floor. Knox buries a third blow in his guts. Knox clasps his hand around his throat and holds him upright while he searches inside his jacket. Broken glass crunches in the carpet. Knox finds the cosh.

'So you were the sweeties from last night.'

Vanessa Pritchett can take no more. She runs into the kitchen and shakes the outside door. It is locked, and the blond man has the key. She holds her head in her hands. From the hallway, she hears the cosh like a butcher's cleaver hitting meat. She runs to the kitchen sink and turns on the water to drown the sound. Cold water on her face. From the hall she hears a cry. Then the cosh again. Then again. Through the doorway appears her husband. He looks shaky. She rears from the splashing sink, face awash

172

with tears and water – and she flings a plate at him. She throws a second plate. It shatters against the wall. As she grabs a third she sees the blond boy push her husband aside and rush towards her. She breaks the plate on his blond head as he grabs her arm. He drags her across the floor, pushes her against a chair, thrusts her on to it. She struggles. They tumble to the floor and he writhes on top of her, sits astride her, holds her shoulders down. She swears at him. She spits at him. She screams.

Then she relaxes, and he lets her cry.

He stands up.

Philip has not moved from where he stood. He looks like a man who has survived a car crash. Hawk walks past him to look in the hall. Knox is strolling between the bodies and is stamping on them. Blood glistens on his shoes. 'That's enough,' Hawk says. Knox nods, kicks each body one more time. He kneels beside the big man, saying, 'I'll just run through their pockets.' He gazes solemnly at Hawk, as if his thoughts were elsewhere. His eyes are blank.

Hawk returns to Mrs Pritchett, who is now sitting on the floor. 'I'm really sorry,' he says, 'about the mess.' Awkwardly, he puts an arm around her, saying, 'Don't worry about those two men. It's their business, you see. You mustn't worry about them.'

She stares at him.

'It's all finished now, Mrs Pritchett, all done. You've been a very brave girl. Nothing's going to happen to you, no trouble, just as long as your husband does as he's told. That's only fair, isn't it?'

She begins to sob. Hawk kneels with his arm around her. When he looks across the kitchen at her husband, he sees him staring into the hall. 'Oh, my God,' Pritchett moans. 'Don't do that.'

'What's happening?' asks Hawk.

Pritchett's breath comes in short gasps. 'That man out there,' he whimpers. 'He's – he's – breaking their fingers, snapping them one by one.'

* * *

173

Hawk did it the easy way. He backed the van into Pritchett's drive and had Pritchett and Knox help throw the two men in the back. One was conscious now, and moaning. They were both tied up with kitchen string. When Knox tried to return the ball to Vanessa, she would not accept it. Knox rolled the ball in his hands to show it had no blood on it, but she wouldn't change her mind. She was as silent as her husband had been earlier. Pritchett himself was beginning to talk again, but no one listened. Vanessa just wanted everyone out of her house.

Suddenly they were gone. Hawk had tried to reassure her that they were taking her husband to the tube station, that they would not do him harm. But she didn't listen. When the front door slammed, she emerged from the kitchen into the hall. She noticed marks on the wallpaper, broken glass on the carpet, and the little connector that had been ripped off from the phone cable. She heard the van start and drive away.

Vanessa ran lightly upstairs to their bedroom. She tried the phone there, but it was dead. When she checked the cable, she found that its connector too had been torn off. Vanessa sat on the unrumpled bed, looking around the room. One of those men had been in here.

Downstairs again, she picked up pieces of her broken pictures and she carried them carefully to the kitchen. The broken frames and shards of glass went in the trash can, but she kept the pictures, tried to straighten them on the table. They were only prints. Without their frames and board backings they could have been cut from magazines. She held a print in each hand, looked from one familiar image to the other. Then she screwed them up and threw them in the bin.

She fetched the vacuum cleaner.

17

L eyton Knox knew all the phone numbers. He sat beside
Hawk in the office till they had tracked Joe Morgan down.
Not that the man would speak to them himself, of course, they
got a functionary – a woman. She sounded hard. 'Pritchett?' she
repeated. 'What about him?'

'You gave protection.'

'That's right, and put your boys in hospital.'

'We've been back to our friend Pritchett,' Hawk said, 'and
taught your boys a lesson.'

'You'll regret it.'

'Dumped their bodies in Walthamstow.'

'Bodies – you topped them?'

'Not this time.'

She snorted sibilantly down the telephone. 'So you're some
smart-arse tough guy – and you work for Al Kazan?'

'That's right.'

'You wouldn't be the one who killed Darren?'

Hawk hesitated.

She asked, 'What was your name again?'

'Here's the message,' Hawk said. 'You stay out of the Isle of
Dogs. Darren tried it once, and you saw what happened. Tell
Joe Morgan not to make the same mistake.'

'So it *was* you who killed Clive Darren?'

'No one wants a war, Miss – whatever your name is.'

'Darren,' she said. 'Mrs. And what was *your* name?'

Hawk slowly put down the phone. He felt weak, as if he had been awakened in the night.

Knox asked, 'Did I hear that right?'

'Mrs Darren,' Hawk said.

'Well, well,' breathed Knox. 'Back in harness, eh?'

The intercom buzzed. It was Kazan on the loudspeaker phone. Leyton immediately mouthed that he wasn't there.

'You off that phone yet, Hawk? Where've you been?'

Hawk exhaled slowly. 'Out.'

'I told you to call me this morning.'

'This is morning.'

'*You* were supposed to call *me*.'

Leyton grinned and shook his head. Hawk did not smile back. 'What about?'

'Joe Morgan.'

'Taken care of.' Hawk felt numbed, as if he had the 'flu.

'What? Get closer to the speaker – you're echoing.'

Hawk leant forward. 'Leyton and I sorted out Morgan's boys.'

'What's that supposed to mean?'

'We left them in Walthamstow Marshes.'

Leyton laced his fingers and cracked his knuckles. Hawk remembered him doing that in Pritchett's hall.

Al chuckled. 'Walthamstow, that's nice. Right on Morgan's doorstep.'

'We talked to Pritchett, of course.'

'You *have* been busy.'

'He's beginning to see things our way. Though that could change – he's soft as Plasticine, I think.'

'Hey, I don't like the sound of that, Hawk. Are we supposed to sit around and wait?'

'For a little while. Listen, Al, when I phoned Morgan, Mrs Darren picked up the phone.'

'Christ, would you credit it?'

'I wasn't expecting that.'

'Life's full of surprises, son.' Al snorted, distorting harshly on the loudspeaker. 'You didn't tell her you popped her hubby, did you?'

176

'No-o, but she asked.'

'Did she shit? What the hell d'you think she's doing, answering Morgan's phone?'

'She used to be his boss's wife.'

'So who the hell is running that mob now? Christ, it's gotta be Morgan, hasn't it? Where's Knox?'

Hawk glanced at Leyton, who peered around the room. Hawk said, 'He's out. D'you have a message for him?'

'Nah. But you watch him, Hawk. This was all his fault.'

Leyton did not react. Kazan continued, 'Listen. Come over to the house this evening, will you? We'll talk about it then.'

'Sorry, Al, I have to go out.'

'Tonight? Don't tell me you found yourself a girlfriend at last?'

'Just going out.'

'I need to talk to you, Hawk. Come around earlier – for tea, or something.'

'OK.'

When Hawk had switched off the speaker-phone, Knox said, 'Popping round for tea, is it, Timmy? How quaint.'

'You could have had an invite if you'd let him know you were here.'

'No, no, Timmy, Kazan would no invite me to tea. I always said that you and him were awful close.'

When Irena emerged from Harrods she looked as if she had fulfilled a lifelong dream. There were now two green Harrods carriers to add to the three bags they already had. Large items would be delivered.

'Wait,' Irena called. 'Slow down, please, Cecille! These shoes are beautiful but I can hardly walk in them.'

'You should have bought the trainers.'

'They looked ridiculous.'

'Comfortable, though.'

'My old shoes from Ukraine were comfortable.'

Cecille smiled. 'Where next?'

'Oh, home I think. I want to open the parcels and look at these lovely clothes.'

177

'Another taxi then.'

'There are some behind us.' The commissionaire outside Harrods was organising taxis at the kerb.

Cecille scowled. 'We can get our own. There's plenty around.'

'As you like. I cannot believe we spent so much money.'

At the junction of Brompton Road and Knightsbridge, someone touched Irena's arm. She saw a thin, straggly haired woman, about twenty-five, dark-eyed and cold. 'Can yer give us something for a bus-fare, missis? We can't get home.'

Clutching the woman's hand was a grubby toddler, face deadened with exhaustion. His cheeks had an unhealthy redness as if he had grazed them against a wall.

Irena gazed at these two people. 'You have lost your money?'

'Can't get home,' she repeated. 'Lend us something for the bus-fare.'

Cecille said, 'Try someone else.' She whistled shrilly for a passing cab.

'Me kiddy's sick and needs a doctor,' continued the thin woman hurriedly. 'Just 50p will help.'

Irena was reaching for her handbag. 'Leave it,' Cecille snapped. 'Oh hell!' She turned on the thin woman. 'See what you just done? We lost the taxi. How we gonna get a cab with you whimpering by our side? Get lost.'

Irena spoke firmly: 'We must help her, Cecille. She is unfortunate.' She had her purse out.

'She's a smackhead.'

The thin woman leant over Irena's purse as if she wanted to plunge her hand in. 'Course, if you could manage a little more . . . you'd be a very kind lady . . . and my little boy, he keeps being sick . . .' The child stared dully across the road. 'We haven't eaten all day. If you could let us have a fiver?'

'No,' Cecille snapped. She could see that Irena was determined to give something. 'You said 50p. That's what you get.'

Irena was frowning at the English money. The woman realised – took her chance: 'That blue and green one's the fiver. That's

178

it, that one there.' Her bony fingers clawed the air above the purse. Irena began to draw it out.

Cecille stopped her. 'That's a twenty.' Her finger jabbed at the woman's nose. 'Too greedy, you. Now beat it.'

But the thin woman would not leave now. Her fingers met Irena's, fumbling for the note. 'Lord bless yer, lady, you're a saint. May you never have to suffer.' Irena tried to separate the money.

'I'll do it,' Cecille said. But Irena turned away from both of them, taking out the twenty note. The thin woman thrust her shoulder in front of Cecille, kept close to Irena's purse. But she need not have bothered, Irena would not be dissuaded now. The woman did not push her luck too far. 'Lord bless yer, lady, thank you,' she said, scuttling away with her urchin child. No sense wasting time on thanks – don't give your mark enough time to change her mind.

Cecille said, 'She's going to spend your cash on drugs. I guess you wouldn't know about all that.'

Irena's blue eyes were calm. 'We have drugs in Ukraine. Did you not see that little boy?'

Cecille shook her head. 'Twenty pounds! All she asked for was 50p – didn't expect to get even that.'

'Of course. She just wanted me to take out my purse. I know how beggars work.'

'Then why –'

'He was such an unhappy little boy.' Irena's face was full of pity. 'An English boy – fancy that!'

Cecille sighed, stepped off the kerb. She whistled again. 'Taxi!'

As the cab slowed, Irena asked, 'How much will this taxi charge to take us home – twenty pounds?'

It stopped beside them. 'Not as much as that,' Cecille muttered.

Irena smiled. 'What is the better use for my money?'

Vanessa Pritchett stares in the shop window as if she has just seen a bargain. But she hasn't. She hasn't seen anything. Behind the blank screen of her eyes the same sequence of thought keeps repeating, returning, carving a channel in her mind like a river through wet sand. She is borne along by the river – it is carrying her to her fate. Who are these people? What is the reason? When will they come back? There is a fork in the river: she can do nothing or she can do something. If she does nothing, it will not end here. Those men will return to the house, or perhaps Philip will not come home. Vanessa has now realised what happened to him last night: two of those men met him, frightened him, shook him up. That was why he came home white-faced and sick. Today the other pair arrived to make *their* claim. The two sets of men fought over her husband like wild dogs over meat. Where have they gone now? What have they done with Philip? Vanessa remembers how the young blond man squatted beside her on the kitchen floor, his arm around her shoulders as if comforting a friend. He tried to reassure her. *He* did – the man who had burst into their house, had held them prisoner, had carried a gun.

Vanessa stands at the shop window, contemplating this fork in her imaginary river. She looks in the direction of doing nothing. Can she do that, simply wait? Can she float on the river's tide till the next unexpected attack? What about the other fork – to do something, to take action, not to let the current sweep her away? What can she do? To confront Philip will be pointless – he is paralysed with fright and with guilt: Philip's dark tide of guilt is part of this swirling river. What has he done? Some kind of bribery, some shady deal. Her husband is trapped in a pool of corruption, is immersed in it, is floundering, will not strike out for the shore. She could throw him a lifeline, but it wouldn't help. Philip, helpless Philip, would have to reach for it, clutch at it, heave himself clear. He cannot do that. He is flotsam, tossed, buffeted by waves. He will let himself be carried until slowly he submerges and is drowned. There is no lifeline for Philip. His only hope is to be rescued, to be plucked bodily from the water, unresisting, sodden, to surrender to others as he has surrendered before.

180

A middle-aged man's face appears in the window. Behind the glass, he leans forward to peer at her: the shopkeeper. Vanessa shakes her head and hurries on. She knows what she must do.

When she walks into the police station it seems as quiet as in a library. It smells dusty. The man behind the desk looks reassuringly solid and he gives off his own smell of heavy cloth. The words flow easily. 'My husband has been threatened. He was taken away by horrible men.'

18

It was the first time in his life Hawk had had proper afternoon tea. He had drunk the stuff any number of times, but never like this, from the Women's Institute manual. Irena showed that she knew all about English tea – she had read it up, studied the procedure. She knew that the tea should be infused in freshly boiled water – one spoonful per cup, plus one for the pot. She knew to pour tea through a strainer, put a little milk afterwards into each cup, serve tea-cakes and biscuits, warm little scones, crustless triangular sandwiches made with cucumber or jam. She used the best china.

When they sat in the lounge with tea served on side tables, it seemed to Hawk that Kazan was embarrassed at the display. But in fact he'd grown used to it. On Irena's second day she had established this ritual, convinced it was customary and what he would expect. The first time she presented this unexpected tea she looked anxious and proud. Even Al saw what it meant to her. He had sat gravely on their leather settee, had sipped tea more politely than you'd think he could manage, had eaten sandwiches, and scones, found he enjoyed them. Soon he looked forward to this dainty end to each working day. He sent Louis out to buy a cakestand.

Today Al sat in his lounge in a business suit, cup in one hand, saucer in the other, a black armband tight upon one arm. Irena fluttered between them offering refills, while Cecille gulped her tea down and bowed out. Part of the pattern of their behaviour nowadays was that Al would sit on the settee, leaving a space for

182

Irena, but she would choose an armchair to sit upright and correct. Al would have preferred Irena beside him, but he liked to look across at her too. Sitting pert in her armchair with a plate on her knee, she looked achingly pretty. Sometimes he wanted to dash across the room and give her a hug. But he drank tea instead.

Irena was up again with the teapot. As she stooped over the boy who looked like Sergei, she said, 'Alex always speaks well of you.'

Hawk's eyes flickered to his boss. 'Sometimes maybe.'

Irena didn't move from Hawk's chair. 'Oh, more often than that. He told me —'

'That's enough,' Al declared. 'You'll embarrass the boy.'

She caught Tim's gaze. 'Will I?'

'Anyway,' Al said, 'he owes everything to me.'

She said, 'Now it is *you* who will embarrass the boy.'

Al grinned. 'True, though, ain't it, Hawk?'

Tim smiled.

'See, he was on the streets going nowhere,' Al said. 'And I said to him: you got a choice. You can carry on in the same stupid way you are doing — which is all the same to me — or you can work for me permanent, which is also OK.'

'Permanent*ly*,' said Irena. 'So you found him in the street?' She smiled at Hawk. 'A street urchin, perhaps?'

Hawk sipped his tea.

She said, 'Today I also found a street urchin. He was begging. Was Mr Hawk once like that?'

'Tim,' he said.

'Hawk was a beggar all right,' quipped Al, his eyes hard as he laughed. 'No, he did some jobs for me — was one of the few bozos I could trust. Nothing's changed there, Hawk, am I right?'

'You're always right.'

When she moved away, Hawk was glad. With Irena standing over him, he felt tongue-tied, mouth dry. Now he watched from the corner of his eye as she sat down, gracefully, a swish of skirt.

'What work do you do for my husband, Mr — Tim?'

183

'Security.'

'He's in charge of it.'

Irena nodded. 'You protect Alexei?'

'That's right.'

'And keep his warehouse secure?'

Hawk glanced toward Kazan, who asked 'Warehouse?'

She turned to him innocently. 'It is where things are stored.'

Al explained, 'We don't exactly have a warehouse, Princess.'

She turned to Hawk. 'You see? He does not talk to me about his work. When I first came here – I mean here in this house – and I saw all the electrical machines in the kitchen, I thought Alexei must have an electrical shop!'

They both grinned. Al asked. 'What?'

She was still smiling at Tim. 'But still he does not talk about it. He thinks that I don't know.'

Al was feeling cut out. He asked, 'What don't you know?'

'That you are a gangster.'

Al choked on his tea, pushed himself up from his seat. 'Gangster?'

'Is that not the word? I learnt it from TV.'

'I'm a businessman.' An indignant businessman. A splash of tea on his suit.

'Then why did Tim bring that corpse to the restaurant?'

A slight pause. Al glared at Hawk, and said, 'It was a joke, like I told you.'

She said, 'No, I think it was a tribute to the chief.'

Al opened his mouth to reply, took in what she'd said, changed his expression to a grin. 'A tribute?'

'You *are* the chief, aren't you?'

The grin spread further. 'Hey, that's right.'

'Of course.' She beamed across the room at Hawk. 'My husband is an important man, and you are his – what is the word – his prince. No, his accomplice.'

'I like the word prince.'

She giggled. 'But I am princess of the shooting hill.'

Al asked, 'What the hell are you two on about?'

She turned to Hawk: 'Is Alexei in danger?'

'I don't think so,' Hawk said.

'But you must tell me, Tim – if they shot his cousin Uri, will they not come after him?'

Hawk saw Kazan blow irritatedly on his teacup. Irena said, 'I think Alexei will take revenge but doesn't want to tell me.'

'Just leave it,' Kazan said.

She leant forward in her chair. 'You are mourning him, of course. I am so sorry.'

'I must go.' Hawk stood up.

Kazan put down his teacup with a clatter as he rose too. 'Yeah, fine,' he said in obvious relief. 'You told me – you're out with some girl tonight, am I right?'

'No.'

Irena smiled mischievously. 'Oh, what is this? You must tell me about your girl, Tim. Is she pretty?'

'I don't – I'm going to a concert.'

She scoffed. 'A concert – on your own?'

'Yes.'

'He likes music,' Al told her. 'You'd hate it.'

'I love music.'

'Not this. Hawk is weird.'

'Really?' She looked at Hawk, eyes laughing. 'Are you weird?'

'I'm sorry, I must leave now. It was nice to meet you again.'

'Oh, do not be so formal! We will meet many times, I am sure.' She turned to Al. 'Perhaps Mr Hawk could show me round your warehouse one day?'

'I don't have a warehouse. I told you.'

'Your office, then. I want to see where you work.'

'*I* can do that.'

Hawk said goodbye and left the room. Cecille was waiting in the hall. 'How come you're off so soon, Hawk?'

'Going out.'

'Leaving me with the lovebirds?'

'Is that how they are?'

'He chases, she dances. Listen, I don't work evenings. Where you going?'

185

'To a concert – Handel.'

'Oh, man, you're not still into that shit? Hey, what d'you think of Irena?'

'Seems OK.'

'I think she's hot for you, Hawk. Interested?'

'She's Al's wife.'

'That is a politician's answer, honey, evades the point. She's been asking about you – twice.' Cecille laughed. 'You better watch yourself.'

'I do.'

'Young wife to an old husband, you know?'

'They just got married.'

'What, you think she's in love? Shit. She married Kazan for his British passport. Where she comes from, that's a small price to pay.'

Hawk put his hand on the door. 'Make sure nothing happens to her: that's your job.'

Cecille grinned. 'Don't worry. I'll look after her for you.'

After the concert the audience came out into crisp night air, faces tingling, memories ringing with baroque tunes. Bright light from the foyer flooded across river walkways, while hundreds of lights twinkled in the Thames. They had heard Handel's short *Daphne and Apollo*, then the whole of his *Music For The Royal Fireworks*. With only two days now till Guy Fawkes Night, people had brought sparklers and other genteel concert-going fireworks to set off in the dark. Little groups from the audience clustered by the river wall, laughing and chattering, waving pretty fireworks in the night. Some, like Hawk, gazed out across the river, imagining a huge water-borne display of fiery lights, cascading flares, coloured smoke and crackling rockets. Inside, the courtly music had seemed tame – dull even – but, if it had been performed out here in the night, all the fireworks shimmering on flowing water, how might it have seemed? Hawk clasped his palms against the cold. The music had not excited him: *Daphne and Apollo* had, for some reason, been sung in French, and the

186

main orchestral piece had seemed ponderous. The concert, to him, seemed pale and insipid. Not like fireworks at all.

'Tim?' A light, masculine voice. He turned round, surprised.

Peter Raggs stood before him, wearing a dark wool jacket, a white scarf round his neck. Doubt faded from Peter's face. 'It *is* you. So you haven't lost your taste for the baroque?'

Tim gaped at him, but only said, 'I don't change.'

Raggs had. The pretty teenage boy had become a handsome young man. He wore a small moustache, though in the soft evening light his skin looked as if it had never seen a razor. He threw his hands wide and grinned that old boyish grin. 'Well, Tim, what do we say? I always hoped we'd meet again.'

Hawk returned the warm smile. 'And I still think about you.'

'Kindly, I hope?' The smile faltered on Peter's face as if he could doubt it, and for one brief moment Hawk saw the boy at the gate who used to cry for his mother.

'Of course kindly.'

'You never wrote, Tim.' Raggs tilted his head in a way Hawk thought he had forgotten. 'You never even said goodbye.' Raggs parodied a girlish pout. They both laughed.

Hawk felt a sweet sadness creeping over him – the one that sometimes came when he thought of his friend. 'I was in a hurry when I left. But I said goodbye.'

'No, you didn't.' Raggs held his gaze. 'I remember.'

Tim looked away. 'Didn't I?' He tried to recall that hasty morning.

'No,' said Raggs softly. 'You just slipped away.'

'Oh.' Tim did not meet his gaze.

'In fact, you never spoke to me at all since the day that you hit me.'

'Didn't I?' Hawk shrugged. 'Well, kids, you know.'

Raggs tilted his head again. 'I didn't really mind you hitting me, Tim. That wasn't what hurt me.'

'I know.'

They both had troubled eyes, were as unaware of the crowd around them as if alone in the chilly night.

187

Raggs said, 'I'd half-expected it.' He smiled wistfully. 'Dreaded it, perhaps, but . . .'

Tim said, 'We were both hurt.'

'Oh, Christ!' Raggs exclaimed, reaching out to touch Hawk's arm.

The day Hawk had hit Raggs had been less than a fortnight before that final incident with Cardew when Tim had packed and left the Home. For those two unsettled weeks Tim had been irritable and alone, hardly speaking to anybody, and it made him particularly sensitive that final night: Cardew had not had a prayer. All those days leading up to it, Tim had been hurt, embarrassed, unsure what to do – how to react. Cardew had been easy to deal with – no problems there.

Like many groups of teenage boys, those in the Home shared their sexual experiments. They hungered for the same girls, larked with the same few younger boys. Tim had fought one who suggested that was the reason he was attracted to Peter Raggs, though it was not entirely untrue. Once, for instance, Peter and Tim had shared an adolescent fixation on another boy, younger than them – a pert, black-haired twelve-year-old, only in the Home three months. The boy had arrived already alive to the games that boys played under blankets after dark. Tim and Peter were not the only ones to touch him up, to stroke him, to masturbate with him. Rumour was that the boy would go further than that. On one hot, humid occasion – unasked – he had efficiently sucked Tim off. Tim had never talked about it, not even to Raggs, not even when Raggs admitted that the boy had done it to him.

In those days, Tim and Peter shared a small collection of erotic magazines. From time to time, the two boys would disappear to gaze at the contents. Sometimes they would masturbate – not each other, as the dark-haired boy had done – but *beside* each other, to each other. They would make a race of it, see who was first to make it come. They would laugh as the thrill hit, and the sight of their friend coming would help bring the other to his climax. Twice, Peter had suggested that they masturbate each

188

other, but Tim would not do that. They had touched each other's penises, but it hadn't seemed right, not with Raggs. They were friends, not bum-boys. Then one day Raggs went too far. They had been doing it over a photo and Tim had won the race. But this time, Peter had suddenly leant forward, grasped Tim's tingling cock and had slipped it into his mouth. His tongue lapped at Tim's juices.

Tim had hit him in the face.

'When you vanished like that,' Peter said, 'I thought it was because – you know . . .'

'It wasn't.'

Raggs smiled. 'You didn't despise me?'

Lightly, Tim punched his stomach. 'You were still my best friend. That was the trouble – I couldn't deal with it. No, I didn't despise you.'

'You could have *said* – come back – wrote. Oh, no reproaches, eh, Tim?'

Hawk laughed. 'I didn't really think you were gay.'

'But I am.'

Raggs had never looked so handsome, smiling in the night. He watched the cloud fall across Tim's face.

'Even then?' Hawk tried to sound unperturbed.

Peter shrugged, smiling wryly.

'But . . . those magazines we used to read?'

'*You* bought them, Tim. I did try to get turned on by them, but, well, it doesn't take much to give a boy a stiff.' Raggs smiled again. 'Especially when I was doing it with you.' He shrugged. '*Now* do you despise me?'

'No. I didn't realise.' Hawk felt oddly betrayed, but wouldn't show it.

Raggs was watching him. 'You haven't found since that *you* . . .'

'No.'

'Ever tempted?'

'No.' When Raggs glanced away across the river, Tim added, 'It doesn't mean we can't be friends.' He wanted that to be true.

189

Peter smiled, knowing how difficult that could be. 'Well, we could try. Are you here on your own, Tim?'

'Yes.' Hawk noticed that people were now beginning to drift away. A man and his girl walked by the river wall, arms linked, each holding a sparkler in the air.

'You always were a loner, Tim, you don't change. Come and meet a friend – if I can find him.'

Tim hesitated. A friend – Christ, now he *did* feel betrayed.

'Don't worry, he won't be jealous! Anyway, you *must* meet him, I insist.'

Hawk noticed now a slight campness in Peter's tone. He felt uneasy.

'He'll be furious if you don't.'

Raggs drew Tim through the thinning crowd towards a small cluster of well-dressed men, chattering, gesticulating. Quivering between them was the same campness just detectable in Raggs. The men sang out their witticisms, glowed in the dark. Peter merged among them, then touched one on the arm. Hawk froze. He had recognised Derek Cardew before the man turned.

19

Yes, you'd want a little romance in your life, Terri thought.
It was one of those four-storey, grey-faced concrete con-
structions that probably started out as council housing but had
since been sold. Some geraniums on the balconies and a square
of grass regularly cut. Maybe the lift worked. Not that it mattered
to Terri, because the john lived on the ground floor, first on the
left. Another sign that the place had been privatised was the
entryphone, the little namecards in different ink. His was the
newest.

'Mr Johnstone?'

'Yeah, come in.'

The electric grating sound as he released the door. Inside, the
place at least had carpet on the floor but, instead of reassuring
her, it underlined that this was the kind of dump where you
remarked on things like that, where a communal carpet seemed
a luxury. She would have to check he could afford her.

First on the left. When she raised her hand, the door opened
before she could knock. The john who stood there wore suit and
tie as if ready to go out. He was tall, lean and quite good-looking,
for what it mattered. Maybe passing through, a guy who shouldn't
find it hard to get himself laid, shouldn't have to pay for it.

As she walked past him into the flat, Terri thought it possible
they had dealt before – something about his face. The slight
perfume in the room seemed almost feminine. As he closed the
door she turned to study him: dark hair, neatly combed, evening
shadow on his jaw.

191

'We'll use the other room,' he said.

If they *had* met he did not refer to it. He led her across the shabby room into the bedroom that lay beyond. The contrast between his good clothes and the dull furniture made him seem no more at home in the flat than she was: could have been the landlord showing her round. The bed was made but looked uninviting – just the kind of thing a landlord would supply.

Terri gave a little chuckle. 'You want to get straight down to it?'

'That's right.' He was studying her – more an assessment than an appraisal. 'You don't remember me?'

'Oh, you know, I thought I did – it's coming back to me.' She felt herself babbling, and switched on the smile. 'Called me back a second time? That's –'

'Shut up.'

She did. The man wanted to be the master, she knew the type. Standing there in his suit, not cracking his face, giving her the fish eye.

'I've got some questions for you.'

He wasn't the law, she did know that.

'A man called Clive Darren.'

Holy shit.

'You turned a trick for him.'

'Is that right?'

'It's where we met before.'

Terri frowned.

'I arranged it. Remember now?'

She did not remember him, but she had to get her story right. He pointed. 'Don't play games now.'

'No.' She coughed, because her mouth was dry.

'Did you kill him?'

'Kill?' She had to cough again. 'Kill – Mr Darren? I hardly remember the guy.'

'You better.'

He moved towards her – too close – but when she stepped back, her legs rubbed against the bed. The man spoke in a reasonable tone: 'I could knock the shit out of you, of course, or you could be sensible.'

'I'll talk – I'll try to help.'

'No, not try – you *will* help. You'll tell me exactly what happened, won't you?'

'Yes.'

'Well?'

'I screwed him. I was to be paid for it but I never got the money.'

'I know that.'

The bed was pressing against her legs. She wished she could sit on it. The man was ominously close, and he smelt different now.

'Well, after we'd done it, I went home –'

He hit her. Terri sprawled across the bed, raising her hands to protect her face.

'Get up.'

She felt safer on the bed, but in a moment the man had reached down to her and grabbed her by the dress. When he yanked her upright she felt the dress tear. His eyes stayed on her face.

'If you don't talk, I'll kill you.'

She remembered the second door, on the far side of the bed. Where did it go – the bathroom? Would it have a window?

'Were you a part of it?'

'Of what?'

He hit her again and cursed, losing his coolness. Terri tried to slither away from him across the bed but he grabbed the dress again and pulled. As the material parted from her body she threw herself toward the bathroom door, but she couldn't make it. The man knelt across her on the bed, his hand around her throat, looked like a rapist, but was worse.

'You *were* a part of it.'

'No!'

'You set him up, didn't you?'

'No.'

'You let them in.'

193

'No.'

'So you shot the man yourself?'

Terri hesitated, but she had no alternative. 'I saw it happen, but I was not a part of it.'

'No.'

'I wasn't!'

'So far, all you've done is lie to me.' He was still pinning her to the bed – the man immaculate in his suit, Terri bedraggled without her dress. He said, 'Last chance. Tell me exactly how it happened.'

'We were in the shower –'

'Before that – who'd you tell that you were going there?'

'No one.'

'You're lying again.'

'I'm not!'

'So a coincidence. You're in the house with him and what happens – some stranger comes bursting in?'

'That's right.'

His hand tightened around her throat. 'Before I strangle you, I'll smash your face in.'

'It's the truth. We were in the shower.'

'You said that. You and Darren.'

'Yes, and –'

'Had you fucked him by that time?'

'Yes.' She stopped, trying to catch the expression in his eyes. Did he want the details? Was this a turn-on for the gonk? 'We were halfway through doing it.'

'In the shower?'

'Yes.' She moved slightly beneath him, trying to sense any hardness in his pants. 'Both of us were naked.'

'Well, you would be.' He actually grinned at her. He *was* enjoying this.

Terri spoke more slowly, allowing him to picture it. 'Mr Darren said, before we climbed into bed, you know, we should take a shower – he said he liked it wet and warm. So we took our clothes off. And we got in the shower. Together. Naked. And

194

then . . . we soaped each other. You know, like we weren't *washing* each other, we were just greasing our hands with soap so they would slide more easily over each other's bodies.'

Terri held his eyes, felt his grip slackening around her throat. She licked her lips, continued: 'Well, he soaped my tits for me – you know, one by one, seeing how they felt, the weight of them. Tweaked my nipples and . . . well, that kinda turned me on. So I got a blob of white soap lather in my hands – you know, really creamy – and I reached down between his legs and I took his cock really gently in my hand and I began to massage it – as if I was washing it – you know, up and down and squeezing it as if I wanted to squeeze it nice and clean. By this time his cock was really hard – and warm, what with the shower and all –'

'That's enough of that.'

Terri froze. A woman's voice: 'Stick to the story, bitch'.

The woman was behind her in the bathroom. She must have been waiting all this while in the very room where Terri had hoped to escape. As she leant back to squint behind she felt the man release his weight. He said, 'I was letting her tell the story in her own words –'

'Shut up.'

He was standing now. Terri moved to a sitting position. So far, she hadn't seen the woman, and it might be better if she never did. So she watched the suit, who now seemed less frightening.

Behind her, the woman hissed, 'Who killed him, bitch?'

'I don't know. I mean I'd never seen the man before. A kid really, not a man.'

The suit narrowed his eyes at her.

'Well, not a child. About twenty, I guess. Innocent-looking. Blond.'

'A burglar?' he asked.

'No. No, he came in with the gun.'

The suit wanted to reassert his authority, as if the woman in the bathroom did not exist. 'What sort of gun?'

'I don't know. It had a silencer. He came and . . . shot Mr Darren in the shower.'

195

'Did he mean to do that?'

Terri nodded. 'That's what he came for.'

Behind, the woman asked, 'What was his name?'

'I don't know. He –'

'Why didn't he kill you?'

'I . . . At first he was going to shoot me, but I guess he bottled out.'

All three remained silent till the woman asked, 'Did he say why he had come?'

'No – oh yes, something about . . . about the Isle of Dogs job.'

Terri saw the man frown, then heard the woman ask, 'Any idea who he'd have been?'

The man said, 'No.'

Terri realised that the woman had emerged from the bathroom and must be standing beside the bed. But she did not look round. She knew who the woman was but she would not show her that she knew.

The man leant closer. 'You're saying that this kid was a hitman?'

'Yes – though no, he wasn't really a kid – he just seemed that way.'

The woman said, 'We had a chauffeur in the house as well. What happened to him?'

'Shot.'

'Uh huh. And the kid took away both bodies?'

'Yes,' Terri said convincingly.

'And you've no idea . . . who this blond kid was?'

'No.'

All three fell silent again. Terri saw her dress lying crumpled at the edge of the bed, and she almost reached for it. But the suit asked, 'What shall we do with her?'

Terri froze.

'She screwed my husband.'

Oh shit, you cow, now you've *told* me who you are!

'I could cut her face,' the man suggested.

Terri remained motionless between them. They talked flatly,

196

as if deciding whether or not to change the sheets. Mrs Darren said, 'She's a tart. Cut her face and she won't be able to work.'

'Isn't that what you want?'

'It'd be no life for her. No money coming in. Nothing to do all day except plan how she could get revenge. You brought your gun with you?'

'Wouldn't be without it.'

Terri turned now to face Mrs Darren for the first time. 'Please don't. I didn't kill your husband.'

'You screwed him.'

'I could be a witness. I could try to find the blond man.'

'You don't know who he is.' Mrs Darren's eyes were bleak and cold.

'I could *look* for him.'

'So can we.' As she glanced across Terri's shoulder, Mrs Darren looked tired. 'You won't fuck this up?'

'No.'

When Terri turned, she saw that the man had a pistol pointing at her chest, its barrel swollen with a silencer. Again Terri had that urge to pick up her discarded dress, only this time she wanted to clutch it to her like a shield. She felt her fists clench. Her tiny fists.

'I'll find the kid.'

'You won't.'

He pulled the trigger, and for Terri the room crashed silently through red to black.

20

'Well, I'm doing it while I think about it,' Al said.
Oliver nodded. He was a tall balding man who once had had red hair. In fact, he had been proud of it and, even now, at least once an hour, he would find an opportunity to run a comb through what was left. He was the undertaker. He stood with Al, Hawk and Gilda in the front parlour of his premises, gazing at an impressive catalogue of flowers. All the wreaths had discreet prices. Everything in Oliver's catalogue had a price, fair and above board. But when you waded through the unending funeral accessories you lost track of where you had reached, forgot the cumulative total. So, fairly and above board, you increased the bill.

Al had already explained to Oliver that Harry's funeral wouldn't be for at least another week, the police had not released the body. But he emphasised that this would be a prestigious occasion, for Gilda's sake, and for the family. Now he turned to Gilda – she was the only one in sombre clothes apart from Oliver, though Al wore his armband. 'Look, Gilda, I'm leaving the flowers to you, OK? Anything you want. Don't stint yourself.'

Gilda nodded. She still found it hard to talk – her eyes were red and Al found it embarrassing to look at her. Hawk had noticed that. But he had also noticed, to his surprise, that he himself could be in Gilda's presence and still feel nothing. He didn't associate her with Harry. He hardly associated himself with Harry's death: it was Kazan who had ordered that.

'You'll be OK with those flowers?' Kazan asked. 'Remember, only the best will do for Harry.'

198

Gilda nodded, tried to speak, could only manage a little sob. Al patted her arm as she began to cry.

'Perhaps a cup of tea?' suggested Oliver. But Gilda trembled, continued crying, had to be helped on to a chair. She shielded her eyes with a crumpled hankie which looked as if it had been used several times before.

'No tea,' she said. 'Everywhere I go, people offer me tea. They want to drown me in it.'

She sat weeping into her hankie, and Oliver slid a box of tissues on to her lap. 'We can look at the flowers a little later,' he murmured.

While Al stared helplessly around the room, Hawk took care not to catch his eye.

Gilda exclaimed, 'Why did the bastards have to kill him?'

Al rested his hand briefly on her shoulder, but then he raised it, as if she were hot.

'Who could have done such a terrible thing?'

Al cleared his throat. 'I guess the police are doing their best.'

'The police! They are nothing. *You* must find these killers, Al.'

'Yeah, sure,' he mumbled. 'I will. Not a stone, you know, unturned. Listen, Oliver, about these flowers, you put on a good display.'

Oliver nodded. Funerals were for the living, not the gone-before. Al could rely on his professionalism. Al said, 'Gilda, you take your time. I got some business I must get on with.' He turned to Oliver. 'We'll use your parlour in the back.'

Oliver had murmured when they came in that there was an occupied coffin lying in that room. But its presence hadn't seemed to worry the coloured gentleman who arrived earlier, and it certainly didn't stop Mr Kazan.

The back room was not ideal for holding meetings, since it was about twelve feet by ten, and some old guy's six-feet coffin lay waist-high along the centre, soft lit by spotlights. Knox had been waiting about ten minutes, and had closed the lid when he arrived. When Kazan and Hawk came in, Knox was slumped in a

199

wooden chair, tilted against the wall. He wore a dark tracksuit bottom and an orange sweater. That and the rose spotlights made his black skin look purple-brown. He said, 'My condolences for cousin Harry.'

Kazan said, 'This was your fault.'

'*My* fault? Ye think I topped old Harry?'

'I ain't talking about that.'

Hawk saw the teasing glint in Leyton's eyes, but Al wasn't in the mood for jokes. 'I'm talking about goddam Pritchett – and his stupid wife.'

Leyton paused before replying. 'You said, "If he wants a fight, then we'll give him one." *You* said that.'

'That was Joe Morgan, not Pritchett. If you hadn't sent Vinnie and the boys in, none of this would have happened.'

'If, if, if,' Knox said.

Al started round the coffin, but Hawk intervened. 'It was *my* fault. I shouldn't have gone to Pritchett's house.'

Leyton sighed. 'You know what they say, Timmy: there's no point crying about spilt blood.'

Al pointed a stubby finger. 'Don't start cracking stupid jokes. I've had you up to here.' He thumped the coffin.

Knox stared at him, and Hawk said, 'Blame *me*, if you want to blame someone. I should have known how she'd react. She's eating her breakfast when a bunch of heavies invades her house.'

Al stomped across to the rear of the room, pushed the dark curtain aside to reveal a window-frame boarded up with unpainted wood.

Knox said, 'She's ruined her husband's precious career. Did she no think of that?'

Hawk agreed: 'And she's lost us a bloody contract.'

'Morgan's lost it too,' Knox said.

'Sod Morgan!' snapped Kazan. He fixed the curtain and came back to face Leyton across the coffin. 'Half-a-million quid I stand to lose – it *could* be, half-a-million. Christ, this was one of the few decent scams left on the island.' He lurched against the table. 'And think of the scandal, the investigations.'

200

Hawk said, 'You'll have that coffin on the floor.'

'Listen, boy, you understand what you did? GBH inside their house. Her husband fingers you – no, not you, me – he fingers *me*. Because you're all right, ain't you, Hawk? He don't know you from sodding Adam.'

'He does.'

'How?'

'I spoke to him on the phone. He already knew my name.'

'You didn't give him your address?'

Knox said, 'When I spoke to him in the pub –'

Al turned on him. 'I told you to shut it.' He knocked against the coffin again and it shuddered. Knox put out a hand to steady it as Al continued, 'The only thing I wanna hear from you two pillocks is how we dig ourselves out of the shit.'

Hawk said, 'They can't prove it.'

'Come on!' said Al. 'You were both there in her house.'

'They have to find us, Al.'

Knox said, 'Pritchett knows our names, doesn't he?' He took his hand off the coffin. 'You see, Ally, *you're* upset because you lost a deal, but Hawk and me could go inside.'

Al groaned. 'This could stuff me on the island – ruin everything.'

Knox rose to his feet, stretched his arms above his head. He touched the ceiling. 'Where's Pritchett now?'

Al didn't answer. They could guess where Pritchett was, singing his heart out like a choirboy.

Hawk said, 'He won't talk. He'll stick to what we told him.'

Leyton smiled. 'A touching faith.'

Al said, 'They'll break him down.'

It was true, Hawk thought, Pritchett could reveal everybody's name. He knew Knox, he knew Hawk, he knew Kazan and Joe Morgan. He even knew the two bozos who should have protected him. He knew everyone. And once he had blown the gaff on the Piazza, all Al's other deals would start to shake. The Law would probe into that Piazza deal like they were sticking a jemmy into a crack. They'd force the door open, walk inside.

201

Then there were the two bozos up in Walthamstow. Hawk wondered who had found them – Morgan or the Law. The schmucks must be in hospital by now, with name-tags on their wrists and a couple of six-feet policemen, considerate and concerned, sitting by their beds with notebooks on their laps. 'Take your time, son. Tell us exactly how it happened.' One of them might talk – they had nothing else to do. They would not be at their strongest just now.

Pritchett was even more sure to blab. He was the kind of straight who believed that the law was on his side. Even if Pritchett did try to stay schtumm, they would apply pressure, tell him he was in deep enough already, but they'd go easy if he told. Pritchett was a natural for Queen's evidence – a local government officer led astray, a white collar man, the antithesis of a thug. Why shouldn't he co-operate? The hunters were closing in.

Leyton was ahead of him. 'We'll have to silence that man Pritchett.'

'He has police protection.'

'Only while he's at the station,' Leyton said. 'When they let him out we'll top him. It's the only way.'

'He'll have made a statement.'

'Counts for nothing when he's dead.'

Hawk shook his head. 'They'll know we did it. Murdering a key witness? No thanks.'

Leyton stared at him, his mind assessing possibilities. They were each at a corner of the coffin, as if awaiting a missing pall-bearer. Leyton lifted the lid a few inches, peeped inside, and said, 'If this was Poker, Timmy, I'd jack my hand.'

Al protested, 'It ain't that bad.'

'Eight years,' Knox said, closing the lid. 'For what we did yesterday. Add the rest they could throw at us – another four. Timmy and me, you realise, are looking at twelve years in the stir for this alone.' He chuckled mirthlessly across the coffin. 'Well, Ally, here's another fine mess you've landed us in.'

Kazan's voice was very quiet. 'You caused this, Leyton.'

'Leave it,' Hawk snapped. 'We have enough trouble without you two tearing each other apart. There must be some way out.'

Knox exhaled between pursed lips. 'If this house of cards collapses, Timmy, you'll be at the bottom of the heap. Have ye thought of that?'

Hawk nodded.

'It doesnae look good, son. Have ye nowhere ye can run to?'

Kazan stamped his foot. 'That's enough! You two are talking like we already lost.'

'No,' said Knox peaceably, running his finger down the polished pine. 'I'm just anticipating what will happen when the police take Pritchett's statement.'

He is not the only one. Although Vanessa Pritchett is used to living in the house alone, she has never felt as solitary as today. The house seems silent as a cave. She fidgets with the radio but it irritates her. She finds that she is waiting for news bulletins, as if her husband's shame might be broadcast to the world. But it won't be.

Will it?

In this day and a half since her house was desecrated, Vanessa has tidied, retidied, scrubbed every surface clean. The rooms are filled with the fragrance of cleansing sprays. The chairs look as if no one ever sits on them. The kitchen door stays locked.

Curiously, she finds that whenever the doorbell rings she is not afraid to answer it. She feels calm, detached, as if there is nothing more that can happen to her. Last time the bell rang, there was a man on the doorstep who said he was from British Telecom. 'Come to reconnect your phones, love.' She let the stranger in, stood near him while he worked. She even made a cup of tea, watched him drink it in their bedroom. She was not afraid. She had feared that, like a rape victim, she might be terrified of strangers, yet she was not. She wasn't anything.

When he left, she cleaned the cup three times.

It occurs to Vanessa now that she and the house are no longer attached to each other in the way they were before. It is as if she has decided to move out, as if the house is already on the market. *Already.* Not that it might go on the market, but that it already is. The Pritchetts will not stay here. *She* won't. Because after whatever skulduggery her husband has got himself involved in, he won't be allowed to make that choice. The police seem more interested in him than in the villains. They want to know why he was threatened. Vanessa herself has been interviewed twice, but the police must see that she doesn't know anything about it. Maybe she can guess, but she keeps her guesses to herself. Bribery. Corruption. Her husband has taken bribes with both hands. From both sides.

The stupid, stupid man. Vanessa fills a bowl with hot water, pulls on her rubber gloves. She has not cleaned the oven properly for a month. Everywhere else is spotless but not this, the dirtiest job of all. On her knees on the kitchen floor, the bowl of water at her side, she opens the oven door and smiles bleakly at the grime.

Well, Vanessa snorts as she slides out the metal shelves, he deserves what he has coming, without a doubt. He betrayed his employers, he betrayed her, he must take his medicine. What will happen to him? She wonders. Does she care? Does she really, really care? Isn't it odd, that in a few jolting moments, in one sudden lifting of a curtain, everything is transformed? Vanessa finds that she actually doesn't care whether Philip comes out or is put inside. She feels as detached from her husband as from the house. If Philip does go to jail, then she will move, will start again, God knows at what, it doesn't matter. That prospect doesn't worry her a bit. Quite the contrary, in fact. Of course, he *will* come back, Philip's type always does. He'll want her to share his slow disgrace as his case drags painfully through the courts. Stand by her man while he disintegrates.

She wrings out the cloth, enjoying the splash of warm trickling water. Oh yes, she might stay with him – but on her terms. She might and she might not. It will be perfectly simple for her to tell him he is on his own, that he put himself out there. People will understand – she has been wronged. People! What does she care what people think? It is time she looked after number one.

* * *

'Your man can stuff himself, as far as I'm concerned.'

Leyton Knox sat on the edge of Kazan's desk, eating take-away curry with his fingers. He and Hawk had returned to the office in Surrey Docks when Al left to visit his financial advisor.

'Don't we get cutlery?'

'This is Balti, son – you eat it with your fingers.'

'You might in Glasgow.'

'Use your Nan bread to mop it up.'

Hawk frowned at his greasy fingers.

'Like it?' asked Knox.

'I like the *taste*.'

'Using fingers gets you closer to it – like communion.'

Hawk grunted, ate some more, licked his fingers yet again.

'It'll no stain ye, Hawk. It isnae nicotine.'

'This smell will be here for days.'

'Let's hope we're around to smell it. Wee Ally hates the stuff.' Knox wiped the end of his Nan bread round the inside of his aluminium container, dropped the empty in the bin. 'Have you no finished yet?'

'I'm getting there.'

'You're awful finnicky, Hawk, you know? Almost ladylike sometimes.'

Hawk stopped munching. Ladylike made him think of Peter Raggs. What the hell did Leyton mean?

The Scot continued, 'Someone told me that when you blow your nose, Timmy, you refold your hankie on its creases before you put it in your pocket. Is that true?'

'You looking for a fight?'

Knox grinned. 'Och, don't hit me, son, I'm afeared. Aren't you going to finish that Balti?'

Hawk looked at the brown sludge.

'Because if you're not, I'll hide what's left in his bottom drawer.'

'I'll eat it.'

'Aye, you're right, it's past a joke. That man's put us in a lot of trouble.' He watched Hawk chomping through his curry.

205

'Can't even look after his own family. Then he blames *us* for cocking up, eh?'

Hawk dropped the container in Kazan's bin. He wished Leyton hadn't reminded him about Raggs. 'We misinterpreted our instructions.'

'Don't give me that! Maybe he didn't "instruct" me to call on Pritchett in the first place, but I only talked to the man. And for all he complains about yesterday morning, *he* was the one who sent us in.'

'Not specifically.'

'How specific do ye want? He said specifically – your word – that he wanted a fight with Joe Morgan. How were we supposed to put pressure on prat-head Pritchett if we didnae meet with him?'

'We shouldn't have done it at his house.' Hawk sucked curry from beneath his fingernails.

'Don't blame yourself, son, you were only carrying out instructions. I tell ye, Timmy, that man makes too many mistakes, and he cannae fob them off on us.'

There was a buzz on the intercom. Calvin's voice: 'Hey, the boss ain't there, right?'

'Right,' Knox said.

Calvin said, 'The thing is, right, I got his missis here to see him.'

'He's at Throgmorton's – trying to redeem his investments.'

'When's he coming back?'

'God knows.' Knox looked enquiringly at Hawk, who shrugged. Knox said, 'Tell Ally's wife that this is not a convenient time to visit.' He flicked off the switch. To Hawk he said, 'She's as much to blame as anyone.'

'Irena?'

Knox raised a brow at Hawk's use of her first name. 'Well, since he came home with yon child bride of his, he hasnae done anything that's right. He's gone soft on her.'

The buzzer bleeped again. Calvin said, 'Hey Hawk, are you there?'

'Yes.'

'Mrs K says that if *Mr* K's away, then you'll do.'

Hawk closed his eyes. 'What for?'

'You want I ask or I send her in?'

'We're in a meeting. Ask her to wait.' Hawk killed the line.

Knox asked, 'Ally's no bringing his wife into the business?'

Hawk shook his head.

'Joe Morgan brought yon Mrs Darren into his business, didn't he?'

Hawk sniffed, 'Maybe she brought him into hers.'

'Ah, who's in charge, you mean?' Leyton smiled. 'Maybe we ought to find out.' He paused, but Hawk did not react.

Leyton said, 'Well, maybe Mrs Kazan here – yon child-like Irena – wants you to take her out to lunch. I know a good Balti house.'

Hawk groaned.

'It's because of her Joe Morgan's pushing us.'

'What d'you mean?'

'Wee Ally's become a laughing stock. You must have heard the boys talking?'

'Not Joe Morgan's boys. I haven't heard *them* talking.'

Leyton shrugged. Hawk asked, 'How d'you know what his boys say?'

Leyton smiled disarmingly. 'You phoned them yourself yesterday, Hawk.'

'I didn't know you'd phoned them separately.'

Leyton shrugged again.

Hawk asked, 'Or have you met with them?'

'Who, me, Timmy?'

'Yes, you.'

A pause. Leyton tried the smile again, saw it didn't work. 'Christ, we all know who their boys are, son. I expect Vinnie Dirkin went to school with some of them.'

'The ones who did him?'

'Not those, perhaps.'

'Who, then? They were *North* London boys.'

Knox snorted. 'What's that – three miles away? Twenty minutes on the tube.'

'Been up there, have you?'

Knox had recovered his equanimity. 'We don't need papers to cross the river, Timmy.'

The intercom buzzed again. Calvin sounded apologetic: 'Er, Hawk, um, like how long you going to be, man? She's asked about lunch.'

'Give her a magazine.'

'What you think this is, man, the dentist's?'

'Make some coffee.'

'I'm a driver, man, not a chef.'

'Do it.'

Hawk turned to Leyton. 'OK, this chat with the Morgan/ Darren boys – how far did it go?'

Leyton sniffed. 'They've no time for Al Kazan. When it comes to a fight, they think Morgan would tear him up.'

'That's what they say?'

Knox nodded.

'You must have spoken to them recently, Leyton.'

'Listen, Timmy, I don't give a toss about this north of the river, south of the river nonsense, but I do like to be in the winning team. Up to now, Darren would stick to his territory, Kazan to his. But there were always little excursions, you know, to test the water? Well, since Ally came back from his wee holiday he's been like Samson with a haircut. So the boys up north want to flex their muscles.'

Hawk felt a chill in his stomach. Al Kazan had been like a father to him, yet he understood Leyton's drift. No, not father, he thought, but leader of the pack, who holds position by fighting off his challengers. When he ages, the fights get harder. When he falls, he falls alone.

'What's Morgan's plan?'

'Och, I can't tell ye that.'

'So you've joined them?'

'Would I be talking to ye if I had?'

208

Hawk sighed, looked round the office. The walls were scruffy, in need of a coat of paint.

'It does no harm to talk to them, Timmy. When a ship is sinking, you have two choices – go down with it or jump for safety.'

'So you'll jump?'

Knox shrugged. 'It's only the captain who needs go down with his ship.'

'Cut and dried, is it?'

'Let's say I'm considering my position. They would talk to you, if you asked them.'

'Maybe I should.'

'Maybe you should.'

Irena did not want lunch. She did not want a tour around the office. What she did want, she confided to Hawk, was to visit a traditional London inn. He took her to the Ball o'Yarn.

She entered the pub, eyes dancing, looking like a sixteen-year-old at her first X-film. She wriggled on her velour seat as if it were the back row of the cinema. They would have had to shush her in the cinema because she never stopped chattering. She commented on the decor. She told Hawk more than he would ever need to know about the inns of Dickensian London: the Ship, the Bull Hotel, The Green Man, the White Hart and the Six Jolly Fellowship Porters. She had a glass of ale. At the counter Irena noticed a fat, coarse-looking biddy dressed in dirty black, with veins in her face the colour of mouldy raspberries. 'Mrs Gamp,' she whispered. The woman was ordering herself another port and lemon, and Irena watched with unconcealed curiosity. She leant across to whisper again in Hawk's ear, 'Is that really a port and lemon, Tim? I thought it was served hot.'

Hawk bought her a packet of pickled cockles. It sounded the sort of snack Dickens might have had.

'Does Al take you out to pubs?'

'No, he prefers to watch me while I watch television.'

'That's what you do every night?'

'Not every night. Sometimes he does not come home.'

'What then?'

'I watch television with Cecille.'

'Sounds like you watch a lot of it.'

She sighed, turning to him. 'Alexei always comes home eventually. I do not mean that he stays out all night.'

'Well, he wouldn't, so soon married.'

She nudged him, grinning up into his face. 'He and I are not like that. He is no longer young, you know.'

'That bother you?'

'He is good to me.'

'He was good to me, as well.'

Irena studied him in the same open way she had watched the woman at the bar. 'We are in his debt, I think. You and I have that in common.'

'Debt?'

'He said that you owed everything to him.'

'Yeah, win or lose.' He looked in her eyes, perhaps for the first time since they came in. 'So, is that it – d'you think you are in his debt, Irena?'

She gave a strange crooked smile, keeping full eye contact as if they shared a secret. 'I am repaying it.'

'Oh,' he said, picking up his drink.

'Take me for a walk.'

He took her along the sapling-lined path to the ecological park in Little Russia Dock Woodland. 'It's pretty here,' she said. Urban London was lost behind young trees. Weak afternoon sun filtered through autumn leaves on to the path and its black metal benches. Irena took Hawk's hand and walked with loping strides.

'Is this a special park? There are few people.'

'It's mainly for locals.'

'And schoolchildren.' They watched a gang of twelve-year-olds swirl around two teachers on the path.

'They'll be going to the ecology park to look at weeds. There's some kind of study centre there.'

'They should study *that*.' Irena nodded to the small stream

210

beside the path, half-choked with rubbish: boxes, paper bags, gaudy plastic, a railway sleeper, half a pram. She clucked her tongue. 'It is very dirty here.'

'Yeah, try to build somewhere pleasant, and kids wreck it.'

'Why do they not clean it up?'

'You can't find the kids who junk it.'

'Any children – like those who study ecology. They should put their boots on and wade into the stream to clear rubbish out. *That* is ecology – it would teach them more than reading books. In *my* country . . .' She shook her head.

'Tell me.'

'Oh, it is . . . far away.' She wrinkled her brow at him. 'London seems like a hundred different places all in one.'

'It's everything you want.'

'Perhaps. It is very crowded.'

'Some people, you know, never leave it. They're afraid that if they stray beyond the end of a tube line, they'll reach the edge of the world and fall off.'

'It is the same in Ukraine.' The path had become more open here. 'People live in one village all their lives. I know old people who never travelled more than ten miles from the bedroom they were born in.'

'Yet they could walk that in a single morning.'

'How wide is London?'

He squinted into the pale blue sky. 'I don't know. Twenty miles?'

She clutched his elbow. 'So people who are born at Piccadilly Circus are still only ten miles from the edge of their own little world?'

He shrugged, and she reached down to reclaim his hand. He felt uncomfortable about that; her hand was warm, intimate, and to Hawk it wasn't right that they held hands. She was married. To his boss.

She said, 'Alexei is worried.'

'About what?'

'He talks to me in the night.'

211

Hawk removed his hand. Irena asked, 'Is he in danger of a *putsch?*'

'*Putsch?*'

'Don't you know the word? Sometimes I have to explain to Alexei what words mean.'

Street noises were muffled through the trees, and a cold breeze came from the river. 'Does Al believe that – a *putsch?*'

She shrugged. 'I don't know. Poor Harry has been killed, and Alex seems . . . distracted. If there were a *putsch*, who would take over Alexei's gang?'

Hawk did not reply.

She said, 'You are his right-hand man. Would you take over?'

'We'd go down together.'

They walked several steps in silence, then she said, 'So you and I are both tied to Alex?'

'Maybe we're the only ones who are.'

He should not have said that. But when he glanced at her, he saw that she was smiling. She stopped in the middle of the empty path and pointed to her right. 'What is that funny lump?'

He smiled with her. 'Stave Hill.'

'Hill? Is it for children? It is like a pudding.' It was a small man-made mound, with grass, but without trees or flowers.

'You see, they built this park on disused docklands. They made the hill back in the Eighties using earth from a canal in Rotherhithe.'

'Can we climb up?'

'That's why I brought you.'

Mill Hill East was the last station on its branch of the Northern Line. Leyton Knox had a brisk five-minute walk to the cemetery, and he didn't slow till he was inside. He wore a dark coat over his lurid sweater and he moved like a shadow between the graves. He had arrived in time.

Only the small inner circle stood beside the grave. Everyone else, he assumed, had left for the reception and a drink. Leyton stayed about twenty yards away. He didn't pretend that he was visiting another plot, he simply waited, immobile, and watched the service. He could have been a chauffeur waiting for the end.

In the midst of life we are in death . . .

The sky was grey but it would not rain, the breeze autumnal. The woman in shades and dark green coat would be Mrs Darren; the man in the boxy suit and open coat would be Joe Morgan. He was a large bulky man with red face and blond curly hair. He wore square-rimmed, brown-tinted glasses, and stood on the far side of the grave from Leyton Knox. He may have seen him, but he never moved.

Mrs Darren, beside the preacher, gazed into her husband's grave. The preacher's familiar words floated on the breeze.

Though knowest, Lord, the secrets of our hearts . . .

Leyton watched while a little thin man handed Mrs Darren a shining trowel. She held it like a filleting knife in her black-gloved hand. When she raised her gaze, Leyton could have sworn she looked straight at him.

> Suffer us not, at our last hour,
> for any pains of death,
> to fall from thee.

The view across Russia Dock Woodland took in the whole of the ecological park, then continued either side of the gasometer to Saint Paul's Cathedral and Tower Bridge. London glowed in slanted sunlight. Across the river, the London landscape was interrupted by tower blocks. The biggest – the overweening, catastrophic obelisk at Canary Wharf – thrust itself into every view across the city, impossible to avoid. Warning lights flashed on its pinnacle and down its sides, so no passing aircraft might do Londoners a favour and smash it down. Around it, in a haze of blue, sulked the muted cityscape of the Isle of Dogs.

Tim and Irena stood on the paved plateau on Stave Hill and rested against the circular metal rail. 'London is not how I imagined.'

213

'It's industrial out there.'

A damp wind blew across the hillock and buffeted their faces. She tapped his arm. 'I must see more of your country. Is it as beautiful as they say?'

He chuckled. 'I'm a ten-mile man myself.'

'I want to see everything, all England – and Scotland, and Wales.'

'Not Ireland?'

'Surely you are at war in Ireland?'

Hawk laughed. 'Is that what they teach you back home?'

She shrugged. 'I knew a boy once – he was younger than you.' She stopped and gazed at Hawk almost maternally. 'His name was Sergei. All his life he wanted to see America.'

'Perhaps he will.'

'No.' She smiled sadly. 'I shall see it for him.'

'You and Al?'

She did not reply at first. 'Italy and France . . . so many countries I want to see.'

She stood on the artificial hillock like Cortez gazing out across his new world.

'Which country would you do first?' Hawk asked. 'Say you could visit one or two a year.'

She snorted, as if the subject no longer interested her. 'I cannot wait for years. I want to see many places.' She stamped her foot. 'Alexei must take me.'

Hawk looked away. The damp wind tangled at their hair.

She persisted: 'Do you think that he might not?'

'He's a busy man.'

'Pah! He is very rich.' She peeped at Hawk's pale face as he looked out across the city. 'Do you think Alexei is too old for so much travel?'

Hawk was aware of her gaze but did not acknowledge it. 'I said he was too busy, not too old.'

Her hand was on his arm. Her mood seemed sombre now. 'If we come here tomorrow,' she said, 'in the evening, we would see fireworks for your Guy Fawkes Night all across the city. It would be exciting, yes?'

'Out there is just banks and offices.'

'There will be no fireworks?'

'Not here. It's time to go.'

She hesitated, as if reluctant to leave the hilltop, but then, after two steps, she stopped, exclaiming, 'Wait! I have something in my eye.'

Hawk turned, saw her rubbing at one eyelid.

'It is an insect or a piece of dirt. Oh!' Irena pulled a face. 'Please Tim, will you look?'

He came closer, cupped her face in his hands while she blinked at him. Moist blue eyes. Soft blonde hair. White teeth.

'Can you see it, Tim?' Softly, she took his hand and moved it from her cheek, closer to her eye. 'You can look inside.'

As he lifted her eyelid, Irena said, 'I will trust you.' She chuckled. Her fingers stroked the back of his hand and she whispered, 'You must come closer.'

He felt a shiver between his shoulderblades. He could not tell whether Irena had something in her eye or not. 'I can't see anything.'

She seemed to sway forward and their thighs touched. It would be so very easy now to kiss her. He could feel her breath upon his face: she was so close he could hardly focus. Those wet blue eyes, damp with tears. That blonde hair. Then, momentarily, another face seemed to drift across Irena's and replace it, it was only there one moment but it was the face of Peter Raggs.

Hawk stepped back. 'Nothing there,' he said.

'Nothing?'

'Nothing.'

As they came down the concrete steps, the sun slipped lower in the sky and they entered the shadow without talking.

> The grace of our Lord Jesus Christ
> and the love of God
> and the fellowship of the Holy Ghost
> Be with us all evermore.
> Amen.

215

The mourners waited beside the grave. The preacher turned away. He hesitated, waiting for Mrs Darren, but she remained by the fresh-dug pit, staring into it. He mumbled something to her then walked away. As the others began to step back from the graveside, Mrs Darren and Joe Morgan remained motionless. Leyton was sure by now that Morgan had registered him, but the blond man stood with his arms folded across his front, as if waiting for Darren's widow to make a move.

Approaching Leyton came two hard men bulging out of charcoal suits, shoes crunching gravel as they drew near. Leyton stood in the centre of the path with feet apart, watching them. They were new to him. Like nightclub bouncers the two men stopped abreast of him, one at each shoulder, looking beyond him, ready to link their arms in his and bustle him away.

'Whatcher doing here?' Knox didn't answer. 'I'm talking to yer.'

When the man thrust his arm through his, Leyton turned to him. 'Don't do that.'

'You want trouble?'

Leyton moved his foot and placed it on the other's shoe. 'The last man who asked me that, I broke his fingers.'

They were face to face. Leyton pressed his knee against the man's inner thigh to show him where he was vulnerable, and watched as three more men led by Mrs Darren came along the path. As she walked, she held herself erect. When she reached Leyton she stood almost touching, chest to chest.

'I suppose you came up here to gloat?'

He smelt the whisky on her breath. 'Your husband's death was nothing to do with me.'

'Is that a fact?' As if rolling her neck to ease a headache, Mrs Darren tilted her head and spat into Leyton's face.

He said, 'Missed.'

Her eyes narrowed.

'Wrong target, lassie. It wasnae me who killed your husband.'

Leyton shook his right arm from the bouncer's grip and plunged his hand deep inside his pocket. When the man grabbed his forearm Leyton asked, 'D'ye want a Glasgae greeting?'

She said, 'Leave him.'

Leyton pulled out a handkerchief to dab his face. He could still smell those whisky fumes.

'If *you* didn't kill him, mister, d'you know who did?'

Leyton knew the value of his information: he had known that before he came. 'No,' he answered carefully. 'But I know a man who does.'

Someone sniggered. Mrs Darren turned to the man almost lazily and he stopped. She turned back to Knox. 'That's why you're here?'

Leyton took his time. Before replying, he glanced at the surrounding bunch of men, nodding slightly as if to acknowledge greetings. For one further moment he held the gaze of Joe Morgan, distant at the graveside, waiting alone. Then he returned his attention to Darren's white-faced widow. He said, 'I came to offer my . . .'

'Condolences?'

'Was that the word?'

21

On the morning of November 5th, Hawk woke and lay staring at the ceiling, wondering why he felt uneasy. Reality drifted back. Nearly two days had passed since he and Knox had been at Pritchett's – a day and a half since Pritchett's wife had told the police; a little less since the police had taken her husband. Since then, nothing had happened. Just as nothing had happened about Harry. It had been a news item – not big – with no mention of the planted rifle, no link to Darren's death. Had the police not found it, or were they staying schtumm? What did they think was going on? Hawk had a picture in his mind of Harry's blue Volvo standing in the police yard, put aside. Inside would be traces of white dust from when the Law had fingerprinted it – but was his gun still lying beneath the squab? Could the stupid, thick, pig police really not have found it? Was that possible? Maybe he had hidden the gun too well – maybe they hadn't been over the car from top to toe. Damn police, he thought, you can't rely on them.

Hawk found he was totally awake now, as if he had just this moment lain on the bed to think. He had had a night of unbroken sleep. He hadn't dreamed, hadn't woken, had not been disturbed.

He sat up, listening to the silence, then climbed out of bed, padded across the room, and stared from his window. The glass was damp with condensation; during the night the temperature had dropped. Outside, the Thames was the colour of dull pewter, and the grey sky was brushed with cloud. Dirt-coloured gulls swooped aimlessly. Hawk walked to the radio, checked the clock, chose the television instead – without sound. TV news repeated each fifteen minutes: he could keep an eye on it.

On his way to make coffee he pressed the button on his CD and, while the kettle boiled, he listened to the *Ode To Saint Cecilia*. Peaceful morning music, while people mouthed silently on TV. As he poured that first essential coffee, the disk reached its climactic track:

> The trumpet's loud clangour
> Excites us to arms!

Hawk grinned – it was hardly suitable. There was no clangour, nothing was happening. Time seemed to be suspended, as in soldiers' tents on the morning of battle. Nearly a week since Harry's murder; a day and a half since the Law took Pritchett – who would not hold out. Why should he?

> With shrill notes of anger
> And mortal alarms!

As Hawk gloomily considered the next link in the chain of consequence, it seemed odd that no one had called. By now, Pritchett would have spilt the names of both Hawk and Knox, would have said they were from Kazan. He'd have named the Morgan boys as well, because his wife would have told the police there were four men. Those Morgan boys, maybe they were in hospital, maybe not. Maybe they had been identified, maybe not. It didn't matter.

> The double double double beat
> Of the thundering drum . . .

What would happen now? The Law didn't have Hawk's address, but Al Kazan could be taken either at home or in the office. Probably the office, best for evidence. No, the Bill wouldn't wait for Kazan there – he might not come. The obvious place to snatch him was at his house.

Hawk glanced toward his phone. It would be easy to find out, though if the cops were at Kazan's house now, it was not a sensible time to phone. He would wait. Hawk tried to imagine Al being grilled. Where – in that front room? Al wouldn't crack. Hawk imagined Irena fluttering in the hall outside, like a trapped butterfly inside a jamjar. He brushed the thought aside.

> The double double double beat
> Of the thundering drum
> Cries Hark! Hark!
> Cries Hark, the foes come.

Hawk checked the television. It was reverting to politics: men in suits bouncing out of cars, men on podiums giving speeches. The ones in power laughed dismissively, the ones without clenched their fists. With half an eye on the screen, Hawk let the chain of consequence unfold. By now, Pritchett should have spilled Hawk's name, along with Kazan's and Leyton's. At Kazan's name the police would pause: here was a known gang boss whose cousin's husband had been shot. And here was Kazan now, involved in a squabble with another gang boss over the Isle of Dogs, which lay temptingly between their two territories. Yes, the police should be interested, all right – once Philip Pritchett started talking, they would be very interested. The Old Bill might not be bright, as Al often jeered, and they might not be able to find a planted rifle when it was handed to them, but even they would be able to work out who had a motive to bump dear old Harry. So why had the Bill not put the squeeze on the Morgan gang?

The inescapable fact was that they didn't seem to be buying this well-constructed story at all. Maybe they hadn't found the gun. Maybe some blade had fingered Hawk for Darren's death. Yes, that was possible – could explain a lot. And by now the wretched Pritchett would also have blabbed his name. Which meant that now the damn police would be most anxious to have a word with this fellow called Tim Hawk.

They could be looking for him at this moment.

Hawk glanced again at that irritating TV screen, went through

220

his chain of circumstances again, tried to find a gap he could squeeze through. He couldn't see one.

The TV screen showed a reporter outside an anonymous block of flats with, behind him, a policeman on guard outside the door. When the picture changed to a poor quality still of Terri, some years before, the reporter informed the world that the murdered woman had been identified as Miss Terri Law, a prostitute who had been shot in an untenanted apartment. But it didn't matter what he said: Hawk had the sound off.

> 'Tis too late,
> 'Tis too late
> 'Tis too late to retreat.

Hawk gazed glumly around his flat, wondering if this might be the last time that he saw it. The place looked the same as always. He crossed to the misted window and stared out of it, hoping that out there he might find one symbolic chink of sunlight. But he didn't. He picked up the phone and dialled Kazan's number. The phone was answered by Cecille.

He said, 'Hi, what's happening?'

'Hawk, is that you?'

Used my name, he thought, that's good. 'Yeah. Anything I should know?'

'Why are you calling before breakfast?'

'I said is everything all right there at the house?'

She hesitated. 'As far as I know, man. What's worrying you?'

'You haven't had the Bill around for breakfast?'

'What you think this is, man – pig heaven?'

'I'm serious.'

Her voice deepened. 'You think I'm stringing you? It's cool, man, no one's here. What's going down?'

'Is Al in the house?'

'Sure.'

'And Irena?'

'Lying right beside him, as far as I know – but then, I don't take in their morning tea.'

'You could be about to get a visit.'

'With a search warrant?'

'I guess.'

'Should I wake up Mr K?'

'He already knows.'

'Is this about Harry?'

'No, it's about a man called Pritchett – a civilian. The Bill have had him in two nights.'

'Two nights – a civilian? The only man whose breath holds out that long is a deep-sea diver.'

'Could be a bad day, Cecille.'

'For all of us?'

'You've done nothing wrong.'

'Let me put you right about that some day.'

'Hope we get the chance. 'Bye, babe.'

'Hey, Hawk.'

'What?'

'Take care.'

Either this is a gigantic game of bluff or Philip Pritchett should make deep-sea diving his career. Eleven in the morning, no one has heard a thing. At 8.30 Leyton Knox answers his phone, says he's none the wiser, then disappears from the scene. Or maybe he just stops answering his phone. Kazan comes through at 8.45, then at 9.15, then a little after 10. Still nothing. The first time Hawk rings into the office he gets no reply. At 10.15 he gets Calvin, who gives the same story – which is no story. Calvin asks if he can go home.

At 10.30 Hawk takes a walk. He carries his radio-phone in his pocket and makes his usual circuit via St Anne's. This is the one where he leaves Narrow Street for Three Colt Street at Dunbar Wharf. At the Housing Centre, he turns left below the railway viaduct into Newell Street, which, being an original Georgian terrace among modern flats should have been a highspot of the area – but the Georgian houses have become shabby, the paint-work is old, plaster mouldings are crumbling away. At the corner of St Anne's Passage huddles a small group of tourists. 'This house that you see here,' the thin guide is saying, 'was often visited by Charles Dickens. His godfather, Christopher Huffam, lived in this very house.' The guide looks sceptically at his audience. 'Charles Dickens, the famous author.'

Hawk grins as he pushes by. Maybe one day he should bring Irena here: the way she goes on about Dickens she'll certainly be more impressed by the little house than by the huge white church tower looming ahead. Someone once told Hawk that St Anne's clock is the second highest in the country, second only to Big Ben. The tower is one of those wedding-cake affairs where each stage reaches a natural height, then has a narrower piece on top. At the very peak above the clockface is a final set of dainty pointed towerlets, reaching further into the sky. As he peers up at them, Hawk finds that his eyes have begun to water – but it's only that the sun has broken through, that's all, perched up between those little towers. Alone in the empty churchyard, Hawk wipes his eyes and looks at the neglected gravestones. At least he won't be tempted to slip inside the church for a quiet prayer: in this neighbourhood it is always locked.

The bunch of tourists has started to trail towards him along the cobbles of St Anne's Passage, so Hawk leaves the churchyard at the other side. The pub in the alley outside the gate – The Five Bells and Bladebone – seldom gets much local custom. It has a small, dark, one-room interior, and is run by a blonde overflowing Scotswoman and an easy-going Irish brunette. Hawk feels that he can hide there. He is hiding now. Perhaps for the last time.

He is halfway through his drink when the tourists crowd through the tiny door, jostling awkwardly in the cramped saloon. They look at the dockland nicknacks on the wall. They look at Hawk. Today it seems he cannot be alone.

Once he has left the pub, the sense of departure stays with him. He strolls past the well-kept, unused-looking Church Institute, and continues along Trinidad Street beside the arches of the Docklands Light Railway. Each arch houses a small business – a car repairers, an Asian grocery, the Docklands Handwash Car Company, a day nursery for the kids. From these tiny premises beneath the railway, proprietors look across to megalomaniacal office blocks, to the so-called proper businesses, but they hardly give the smart-suit brigade a glance. They concentrate on their own lives, on the here and now.

Hawk thinks he should do the same.

At a few minutes before twelve, Hawk and Al Kazan face each other in Kazan's office. Still no move from the police, no word about Philip Pritchett, what he said. Hawk watches Al as he stands sorting through his files, scanning the contents, replacing papers in cardboard folders. So far, only three documents have been burned. Hawk didn't ask what they were.

'Did you ever box?' Hawk asked suddenly.

'You mean in the ring – me?' Al shook his head, perhaps pleased that he'd been asked.

Hawk continued: 'It must feel like this on the day of the big fight – hanging around until it's time. Nothing to do but wait.'

Al nodded, flicking through a sheaf of invoices, concentrating on what they revealed. Then he broke the silence: 'I saw a film once – *The Day The Earth Caught Fire*. You ever see it? No, black and white, before your time. Anyway, the Earth's gone off its orbit or something, heading for oblivion –'

'Is going to crash into the sun.'

'That's right. Did you see that movie?'

'No, just guessed.'

'But listen. The world goes crazy: earthquakes, heatwaves, storms and drought. Riots. In the end, the only way they can save the planet is to set off these two massive nuclear explosions – simultaneously – that are so big they'll jolt the Earth off its collision course.'

'Oh, very reasonable.'

'That's the point, idiot, it ain't reasonable. It's one big risk. Very likely it will fail. So anyway, these explosions are timed for – I don't know – twelve o'clock, let's say. They have a countdown. Once the boffins have set them off –'

224

'Boffins? How old is this movie?'

'I told you – black and white. Now listen: the explosion is not the climax – the Earth will survive that. The climax is immediately afterwards, when the computers calculate whether the experiment has worked, whether the Earth has been jolted off its course, whether everyone will live or die.'

'I'll never guess what happens.'

'Yeah? What does happen, smart-arse?'

Hawk grinned. 'You tell me.'

'This is the point of the film, right? See, at the end, everybody's waiting – just like you and me are waiting for these cops – only everyone is waiting for this announcement. The world carries on spinning but every person on it has come to a halt, and is waiting by their radios. Just waiting, right?'

'What happens?'

'Oh, you're interested now, are you? Right. A lot of this film has been shot in the offices of a newspaper, and at the end of the film there is complete silence on screen – no music – and the camera is prowling slowly through the empty machine-rooms where they put the newspaper together.'

'Compositors' room.'

'Very likely. Slowly – in absolute silence, remember, we don't know whether this experiment has worked or failed, don't even know if anyone's alive – slowly the camera reaches the printing press where the latest edition of the paper has been set and is ready to roll. The camera starts to track slowly across the front page – complete silence – and we get to read what the headline says. You ready? It says "World Saved!" '

Hawk chuckled.

'But wait a minute,' Al said. 'The camera continues to track along *past* the paper. Now we see a second version also set to print. It says "World Doomed!" See? They've got both results set up, and once they know what happened, they'll set off one of these machines to print. But which one? That's the question. The film ends, and they don't tell us. What d'you think – good ending, eh? Spooky. I tell you, in the cinema that was spooky.'

225

'Yeah,' Hawk muttered. 'Black and white.'

'Yeah.'

They stared at each other for several seconds till Hawk dredged up a weary grin. Al nodded. They stood silently in the office while a clock ticked. Then the phone rang.

Al took it. 'Who is this?' His eyes widened and he frowned at Hawk. 'A moment,' he said, and coughed. He switched from earphone to loudspeaker. 'Mr Pritchett,' he said wonderingly.

'Are you alone?' Pritchett sounded nervous on the little speaker.

'Sure.' Eyes never leaving Hawk's face. Christ, *Pritchett* sounded nervous? How the hell did he think *they* felt? The police must be listening to this.

'Why am I on loudspeaker?'

'I'm eating lunch,' Al lied. 'Hands full of greasy chips. It bother you?'

'Not me,' said Pritchett. 'You're the one who has to worry, Kazan. I don't know how much you've heard about it, but I have been questioned by the police.'

'Is that right?' Here it comes. Here comes the killer-punch.

'After you sent your men round to my house, my wife was upset − understandably. She went straight down to the police station.'

Al silently watched Hawk across the office. He realised that Pritchett was silent too. 'Go on.'

'The police *collected* me from work, took me in for questioning.'

Another pause. The bastard was dragging this out − or someone was prompting him. Al said, 'And?'

'They questioned me for several hours, then let me sleep, then questioned me again. They were persistent.'

'Yeah, they do go on, don't they? What did you tell them?'

'I tried to ring you twice this morning, Kazan, but the man on your phone said that you weren't in.'

Al frowned. 'I wasn't. You leave your name?'

'Yes. Did you get the message?'

'No.' He and Hawk glared at the office door. If Calvin were

226

listening out there, he'd know it was time he left for home. Al repeated his earlier question: 'What have you told them, Mr Pritchett?'

'That's why I'm phoning you, Kazan. I've had enough.'

'Enough?'

'I can't live with this. You and I – we're from different worlds.'

Al closed his eyes. 'Look, we've done all that before. What lies have you told the damn police?'

'Nothing.'

Al's eyes opened.

'I refused to talk.'

Al blinked. 'You're in there with the police for two whole days and you've said nothing?'

'I told them I had decided not to press charges. They tried to make me, but I refused.'

'Not to . . .' Al breathed out. '*You* wouldn't press charges?'

'For forcible entry, issuing threats. Of course, the police knew there must be a reason –'

'And they bought it? Where are you?'

'I had to resign my job. That'll be of no importance to you, of course, Kazan – just the end of my professional life. But once I had resigned, you see, there was nothing criminal I could be charged with.'

Al screwed his face up in bafflement. What the hell was happening? 'Nothing criminal? You accepted bribes. You took that weekend in Hamburg.'

'But I didn't give anything in return. A bribe is a payment for services, and I haven't given . . . services yet. That makes me clean with the police, Kazan – out of work, without prospects, but clean. You understand that? Now I want to be clean with you.'

'Christ.' Al tried to concentrate, not sure if he'd heard this right. 'You mean you're free?'

'Yes, but I know what you are, Kazan, I know how you deal with people. What I want you to appreciate is that I did not implicate you in any way. I did not reveal your name. You were not mentioned at all.'

Al took it slowly. 'I see, you didn't finger us. But we've lost that Piazza contract, am I right?'

'Well, naturally. That's the price we have to pay. But you still have the rest of the island.'

Al almost chuckled with disbelief. 'It was a lot of money, Mr Pritchett.'

'But you are not in jail. Look, I did my best for you, Kazan. I didn't cause this catastrophe in the first place, but I didn't . . . rat on you, if that's the word.'

'It'll do.'

'In return, I'm asking you not to come after me – not to come after my wife. You wouldn't gain anything by doing that.'

'No.'

'And – I have to say this – if you do come after us, Kazan, as I hope you won't, and if anything does happen to my wife or to myself – an accident, anything at all – then I have to warn you that my solicitor holds an envelope –'

'Who *is* your solicitor?'

'Mr – I can't tell you that.'

'Nearly got you there, didn't I?' Al laughed, he actually laughed. 'Well, don't worry, I get the picture. Solicitor, huh? Hey, Pritchett, you know something?'

'What?'

'You've seen too many movies.'

Al switched off the phone. He shook his head, grinned delightedly at Hawk. 'Well, Christ,' he said. 'Who'd have thought it? That goddam Pritchett – *he* will not press charges! The cheek of it.'

'You believe that story about an envelope at his solicitor's?'

'Who knows. He nearly coughed me up a name. But I think he said it because, like I said, it's what people always say in the movies. I mean, can you imagine waltzing into your solicitor, handing him an envelope which says, "To be opened only in the event of my death" – can you imagine doing that?'

'I don't have a solicitor.'

Al chuckled again. 'Well, *you* don't rightly exist, do you,

Hawk? Hey, that Pritchett, he surprised me – impressed me, almost. Tell you what: if he's out of work, maybe I should offer him a job!'

He squinted across the room at Hawk: 'Hey cheer up, boy – we're out of it. We don't have a single thing to worry about – am I right?'

22

'Limehouse Piazza – A Prestigious New Development . . .'
Hawk ignored the rest of it. The huge cream and green
hoarding, elegantly set in Univers typeface, expounded on the
gracious features, airy accommodation, the sympathetic blend of
assorted units. 'Creating jobs in Docklands' it claimed. There
was little sign of that. Behind the temporary board fencing the
site was waste-land – flattened mud, oily puddles, scattered rub-
ble. Every wind from the river seemed to detour and linger there.
Loose balls of paper rolled across the ground looking for puddles
they could drown in. In one corner of the site stood an ancient
portacabin, in another the blackened scar of an old bonfire.

The door of the portacabin swung open.

Leyton Knox emerged on to the step and called Hawk to
come across. Hawk shook his head. 'You come over.'

'What's the matter, Timmy?'

'Clean shoes.'

Leyton closed the door and set out across the mud. Hawk
watched beyond him to the cabin windows. He could see no
movement behind the glass, no one else. No one showing. When
Leyton arrived he crossed to the kerb to scrape slime from his
canvas shoes. He said, 'I'm here to say goodbye, Timmy.'

'Is that all?' Hawk had taken the call while in his van.

Leyton frowned at his shoes, decided they were as clean as
they would get. 'Well, Timmy, where do we go from here?'

There was no expression on Hawk's face. He said, 'You
haven't asked the latest news, Leyton. Or have you heard?'

230

'About Pritchett's resignation?'

'Who told you?'

Leyton looked him in the eye. 'Who d'ye think, Timmy?'

'Morgan.'

'Mrs Darren.'

Hawk frowned at him, and Leyton said, 'Keep it in the family, eh? It's chilly out here.'

'Let's move. The Piazza pisses me off.'

Leyton turned to walk. 'Hey Timmy, you weren't afraid to come inside the portacabin, were ye?'

'Should I have been?'

'You have to trust *somebody*, son.'

They were passing the front of the site. Mud had oozed beneath the shabby wooden boards. Hawk said, 'Mrs Darren.'

'Aye.'

They walked on a little. Hawk asked, 'What did you come to say?'

'That sounds like you're still on Ally's side.'

Hawk continued walking.

'Well, here it is, Timmy. Kazan has played the game wrong – lost his grip. It's Mrs Darren who runs things now.' Knox glanced at him. 'Funny, isn't it? – If you feel like laughing. See these boards here, Timmy, whose lads d'ye think erected them?' Hawk didn't answer. 'Ah well, it doesnae matter any more.'

They crossed a road.

Knox said, 'Well?'

'Well what?'

'Are ye interested?'

Hawk kicked a loose stone. 'I haven't heard the offer.'

'And you owe it to yourself, don't you?' Leyton sniffed. 'You're a useful man, Timmy. She and Joe could use you on their side, but it's up to you.'

'I have a choice?'

'Aye, them or Kazan. Win or lose.'

'You're sure Kazan will lose?'

Leyton screwed his eyes against the light. The two men were

231

at the waterside of West India Dock, where massive cranes reached into the sky. 'I cannae honestly see him winning.' He turned to Hawk. 'Can you?'

Hawk held his gaze. 'You'll fight against us, then?'

'Us?'

'Kazan.'

Knox continued watching him, then said, 'No, as a matter of fact, I will not. They don't expect me to fight against old friends. You credit that?'

'Don't trust you to, more likely.' Hawk stood with his hands in his pockets, looking out across the rectangle of brown water. 'They wouldn't want me to fight Al either?'

'No.'

'What *would* I do?'

'For the moment, nothing. That's the point, Timmy. All they want is for you to do absolutely nothing.'

Hawk watched a straggly flock of gulls skim the surface of the water. 'How long have I got to make up my mind?'

'Can you not do that now?'

Hawk's voice was low. 'It isn't easy to betray your friends. Didn't *you* find that?'

Leyton didn't answer. Hawk asked, 'How long?'

'Oh, some time today.'

'You mean now.'

Knox punched him playfully on the shoulder, and Hawk rocked. 'But you're no quite ready *now*, are ye? How about I call ye this evening?'

Hawk nodded. 'Firm decision?'

'Aye. Yes or no.'

Hawk watched the flock of gulls across the dock. Something must have been floating on the water – perhaps fish-heads from nearby Billingsgate. The gulls were whirling in the air, flapping their wings, shrieking at each other, diving at the water to peck the surface.

He turned to Knox and said, 'Yes, ring me tonight.'

* * *

Hawk sits alone in his spartan flat. He lays a sheet of newspaper on his coffee table and a second sheet on the floor. On to that second sheet he places his .38 revolver, and from a leather case he takes out his tools: the little mop and brush, some oil, a jag and bronze.

He picks up the pistol, opens the chamber, holds the barrel against his cheek. He nuzzles the butt. When he uses the rods to clean the barrel, his hand pumps like a piston, nice and slow. He tries the mechanism, a solid click.

While Hawk cleans the handgun he weighs in his mind the strengths of the two sides. The outcome seems as certain as the action on this gun. Squeeze the trigger, the hammer fires. Every time, the hammer fires. Chambers empty, chambers full, the hammer fires every time.

Unless the gun jams. But could it? The way Knox explains it, Mrs Darren has more men, is in the ascendant, while Kazan slides. And she has a powerful motive. Add to that the fact that Leyton – and who knows who else? – has changed sides, and the odds seem overwhelming against Kazan. Hawk feels as he did this morning when it seemed equally inevitable that Pritchett would bring them down. Perhaps that was the time Hawk should have quit, but he waited, stared down his fate. Now once more the sensible tactic must be to run from Kazan's side. But Hawk cannot do it. He knows he will wait a second time, will stare fate down again. He defeated it this morning.

The bleakest moment was when Pritchett called – while Al was sorting through his files, burning occasional papers, preparing for the end. They shared that time together. Hawk cannot leave now and betray his friend. Because Kazan, in some intangible but real way, *is* his friend. When Al told Irena that Hawk owed him everything, it was true. He had plucked Hawk from the streets when he had no identity, little money, was just a runaway from the Home. Al gave him work, found a roof for him, and now Hawk works to repay the debt. It is their agreement, and it still stands.

Hawk phones the office. Al isn't there. He tries the house. Cecille replies, saying that Al has taken Irena shopping.

'Pity you aren't with them, Cecille.'

'He told me the scare was off – said the Law couldn't touch him.'

'It's Mrs Darren who wants him now.'

'Mrs – you serious?'

'Endgame.'

'Oh, shit. It's started?'

'Yeah. This could be when you and I earn our wages.'

'Hell, you know me, Hawk. I do it for love, not money.'

'Makes you the perfect woman, Cecille.'

23

Leyton Knox sat in the unlit train, looking out of the grimy window. Five minutes they had been stopped: no reason. The intercom was silent, the guard invisible. Grey afternoon light congealed on the thick glass of the train window. Through it was a view of blackened backs of houses, domestic yards. Across cramped balconies and in the deep well-like gardens drooped overloaded strings of dismal washing. Knox preferred Glasgow, it was less forlorn. This London journey was monotonous: train then tube then train again – each one shabbier than the one before. South Londoners might whinge about their inadequate transport system, but north of the river there were parts just as isolated – other forgotten lands.

Generally, the different character of London ghettoes seemed petty to Leyton Knox. Like London accents, he found their variations insignificant: minute tribal borderlines, minute tribal wars. In the warm unmoving train, the tribal analogy amused him. He cast himself as a roving mercenary, hired by natives to toughen up their armies. Knox was the cool professional – unlike Hawk. In neutral battlegrounds, as in the Pritchett business, he and Hawk worked well together, but the closer Hawk got to Kazan the less professional he became. He let emotions rule his head.

In the empty carriage, Knox smiled. Of course, Hawk was a boy emotionally, saw Kazan as a stand-in father. He hadn't understood, as Knox had, how little a father could be worth. A kid, maybe, would look up to his father, think of him as the champion in a race. He seemed powerful, far ahead, but as the

235

boy began to gain on him, he realised the man could be caught. The boy drew level, moved free of him, and once his father had slipped behind, once the boy could no longer see him strong in front, he no longer mattered. This was a lesson Hawk had not yet learnt, because he had found his father late.

Leyton shrugged, gazed again through the train window. The houses were beginning to look familiar. He would grow used to this drab journey; the slow, jolting carriages that never seemed to admit fresh air; the monochromatic view of crowded buildings; these sudden halts, silent and unexplained. His dusty carriage seemed disconnected from the engine, to be slowly sinking into the rails. Beyond those dingy houses must be a busy road: a faint drone of lorries filtered through the window, the only sound in the waiting train.

Then like an old man waking from his nap, the train jerked, gasped, stirred itself and crept creakily on its way.

Cecille chuckled down the phone: 'You want to speak to his missus instead? She's still home.'

'You told him it was important?'

'That man don't listen to me, Hawk. He's got something on his mind.'

'Good or bad?'

'I ain't a mind-reader.'

'How did he seem?'

'Like always – in a hurry.'

'No idea where he went?'

'The day Mr K talks to me, Hawk, is the day I lock my bedroom door.'

Hawk spent another five minutes wandering restlessly round his flat. He adjusted the position of a lightweight armchair, turned the CD player off and on, stood frowning out of the window. He walked back across the room, picked up his radio-phone, wondered where else he might reach Al. He had left messages at the house and office: there was nowhere else he could call – except the car-phone. Hawk punched the number,

236

heard it ring. No answer. He frowned again. Not only was Al uncontactable but Louis wasn't in the Daimler. Hawk exhaled. Pacing round his flat only emphasised how cut off he was from the world. He thrust the phone in his jacket pocket and headed for the door. His hand was on the catch when he hesitated, turned, came back inside. From the drawer of his bedside cabinet he took out his .38 revolver, weighed it in his hand. Almost the only time it left the flat was for weekly shooting practice. Hawk didn't wear a gun for decoration – it was a tool of his profession, a weapon of attack. So why did he need it? According to Knox, Morgan wanted him on his side. All Hawk had to do was step aside a while, do nothing. The last thing he needed was a gun.

But he had started down a path where the gate had slammed behind him. He would keep the gun.

'One lump or two?'

Irena was pleased she could use her china tea service. With Al away it had not seemed right to bring it out just for Cecille and herself. And it being almost 6 o'clock, she was concerned it might be late for tea, but Hawk and Cecille had said no, don't worry, tea would help to pass the time.

'Shall I pour your milk first? That is correct, yes?'

They agreed it was.

'In my country we drink tea without milk. Alexei says that it doesn't matter whether I put tea in the cup first or the milk, but I have read that it does matter. Is that right?'

Milk should go first, they said, in south east London. They balanced the bone china cups and the pinging, high-rimmed saucers warily on their knees. These delicate constraints were unfamiliar to them.

'A biscuit?'

Hawk decided it would be more correct to take just one, but Cecille winked and helped herself to three – she was used to Irena's teas. Irena hastily put down the plate and scrambled to her feet. 'The scones!' she cried, rushing to the kitchen.

'Scones?' Hawk murmured.

'With cream, if you're lucky,' Cecille said. 'And I *love* cream.' She licked a fat pink tongue slowly round her lips. 'I bet Irena loves it too.'

'What would I like?' Irena had reappeared, carrying Al's cake-stand heaped with fresh warm scones. As if sharing a secret, she added, 'That little microwave is wonderful. Do you have one, Tim?'

'Mhm.'

'Hey, you should see Hawk's kitchen,' Cecille cut in, eyes fixed on his face. 'Get him to invite you round to see it.'

'Oh, yes – would you, Tim?' Her eyes were as wide and innocent as Cecille's.

'Nothing to see.'

Cecille chuckled. Irena smiled too. 'Have you seen it, Cecille?'

'His kitchen?'

'Of course.' Irena held Cecille's eyes a moment, then both girls chuckled. 'So,' said Irena archly, 'you have been inside Tim's kitchen?'

'Well –'

'You cannot remember?'

Hawk felt he was being used as an audience.

Cecille said, 'I ain't seen inside this one. The man keeps changing his address.'

'Oh, so you are his *old* girlfriend – not recent?'

'I'm not his girlfriend –'

'You are blushing, Cecille.'

'How would you tell?' The phone rang. 'Anyway, I'm not.'

It was Hawk's radio-phone. He took it from his pocket. 'Excuse me.'

Glad of an excuse to leave the settee, Hawk took the phone nearer the front window. 'Hello?'

It was Leyton Knox. 'Evening Timmy. You alone?'

With hardly a pause, Hawk said that he was.

'Just wondered if you had reached a decision?'

Hawk had forgotten that Knox would call. 'Sorry, I was thinking of other things.'

'Oh, come on, laddie. You have to make up your mind.'

Hawk wished Al had not been uncontactable all afternoon. 'I'll give you an answer in the morning.'

'I cannae wait till then.'

'Why not?' Hawk was aware of the two women watching him. Though they didn't seem to be listening, they did not talk while he used the phone. He pressed it hard against his ear to reduce sound leakage.

'Listen, Timmy, remember I told you not to do anything?'

'Yeah. Do nothing, you said.'

'That's right. Are you in your flat?'

'Yes.'

'All alone?'

'That's what I said.'

'Why don't you just stay there for a quiet evening in front of the television? Cook yourself a nice slow meal.'

'And play some music,' Hawk said.

'Yes, one of your four-hour operas! That'd be grand.'

'Anything to keep me indoors. Just for tonight?'

Leyton laughed. 'Don't you bother your wee head about that, Timmy. Och, nothing will happen tonight – don't worry. Just enjoy your opera.'

'I'll try.'

'That's my boy. Don't worry.'

Hawk put the phone back in his pocket. As he approached the women his face stayed neutral. Cecille looked guarded: '*What's* just for tonight?'

'Hm?'

Her eyes drilled into him. 'Something happening tonight?'

Irena said, 'Of course! It is the night of Guy Fawkes.'

'That's it.' Hawk gave Cecille a pointed look.

'Tonight,' Cecille said.

'Yes.'

Irena had not noticed their hidden message. 'I hope Alexei comes soon. He will take me to the fireworks.'

Hawk turned to her. 'Didn't he give some idea when he'd be back?'

239

'I told you – about eight.'

Hawk glanced at his watch. Cecille said calmly, 'I think it's time to clear the decks. Excuse me, all.' She began to pile crockery on a tray.

'Tim, you are looking worried. Is it something about Alexei?'

'It'll pass.' He lifted a teacup and carried it to the tray.

Irena watched him. 'Did you and he have an argument?'

'Argument?' Hawk smiled as he dropped the crumbs on Cecille's tray. 'No, no. That was a lovely tea.'

'But you will wait for Alexei?'

'Yes.'

As Cecille picked up the loaded tray, Irena pressed him, 'You are still friends with him?'

He stared at her. 'Of course. Why?'

Cecille began to cross the room. Irena asked, 'You would not harm him?' Cecille paused.

Hawk asked, 'What makes you think I might?'

'Well.' Irena shrugged. 'I saw the gun inside your jacket.'

Cecille turned round. Hawk took his time before replying. 'I'm here to help him.'

'We all trust you, Tim.'

Cecille said, 'Excuse me, but I really *must* slip upstairs.' She turned a pair of dead eyes on Hawk and disappeared with the tray.

There was a pause while Irena studied him. He said, 'I'm sorry about the gun.'

'That I saw – or that you are wearing it?'

He didn't know how to reply, so he wandered across the room. Irena followed, keeping a pace or two behind. 'I am not afraid of guns, you know. We are used to them in Ukraine.'

He nodded.

She said, 'At home, many men carry guns.'

She took an extra pace to stand close by him. 'You know, the first time I saw you was when you had killed a man. You brought his coffin – do you remember?'

'Yes.'

'You made a gift of him to Alex.'

'Stupid idea.'

Her hand brushed against his sleeve. 'It was a wonderful idea. – so . . . theatrical. As if Alexei were an emperor.'

'It didn't work.'

She held his arm. 'It was magical. I thought, in a way, that it was a gift for me as well: your emperor's new bride. What did you think when you first saw me?'

Hawk mumbled something.

'Oh, you hardly noticed me. Tim, isn't it? You only paid attention to that coffin.'

'I noticed you.'

'Later, yes.' She had drifted closer. He kept his arms down by his side. 'Do you remember, Tim, before you left us? You took a flower from your breast – a red carnation – and you gave it to me. As a token, you said.' Now she touched him again. 'You did not say what kind of token, Tim.'

He closed his eyes a second, but found he could still see her. She was standing so close that her face remained fixed in his mind. 'I suppose the flower was a kind of wedding-present.'

'I kept it in a vase and it lasted several days. But before you came to see us again, Tim, I am afraid your flower died.'

'I can wait,' Cecille said.

They spoke in low voices while Irena changed her clothes upstairs.

'When he gets back,' Hawk said, 'tell him not to stay in the house –'

'You've said all that.'

Hawk looked at her. 'You're sure you don't know where Al went?'

'I told you –'

'To meet someone?'

'I don't know.'

Hawk glanced round the room as if someone might be listening. 'What do you think he should do?'

241

Cecille looked at Hawk askance. 'He's the boss, ain't he? He decides that himself.'

'It isn't easy,' Hawk muttered.

'It ain't easy for us either, Hawk. I mean, listen to me, man, is this wise? What the hell are we hanging round Kazan for?'

He stared at her. 'I owe him.'

Quietly, she said, 'I don't.' She held his gaze. 'I'm only doing this for you and her.'

'Thanks, Cecille.'

'But you listen to me, man, I ain't laying down my life for him. I'll deliver your message, but –' She shook her head. 'I can't promise nothing more.'

He nodded. 'You carrying iron?'

She shrugged. 'I don't want to use it, Hawk.'

'But you're carrying?'

'Do birds fly? Hey, Irena's coming down. Listen now, don't you bring her back here afterwards. Take her away.'

'She may not come.'

'She will with you. Hiya, honey!'

Irena appeared, wearing a bright red pullover and new jeans. She carried a black coat across her arm and wore boots. She looked excited. 'I am ready now.'

'You look good enough to eat,' Cecille said. 'Little Red Riding Hood. Well, you enjoy yourself, you hear?'

'Of course – I love fireworks. Are you ready, Tim – don't you have a coat?'

'In the van.'

Irena moved toward Cecille. 'I wish you could come with us. It will be such fun.' She leant forward and kissed Cecille on the cheek.

It seemed to embarrass her, because she laughed uncomfortably and said, 'I must wait for Mr K.'

Irena smiled. 'I suppose *someone* must look after the house.'

This suddenly reminded Hawk of when he arrived. 'Who's on your gate tonight?'

'Oh, no one is. The man is sick. He asked if he could have the evening off.'

'Sick?'

'Perhaps he wanted to take his children to the fireworks.' Irena shrugged, unaware of the reaction from the other two. No one at the gate. Louis not on duty in the car. Leyton Knox switched to the other side.

'A girl could feel lonely,' Cecille said.

'Then come with us.'

'I better wait for Mr K.'

Normally it would be ten minutes' walk. But as they approached the park they found themselves slowed by a thickening crowd – young couples, families, kids in groups. Everyone headed for the same venue. One or two children clutched lighted sparklers, reminding Hawk of the sparklers at the riverside by the Festival Hall. As he and Irena walked with the crowd he recalled that over-restrained music, those over-restrained concert-goers, that unexpected meeting with Peter Raggs. Hawk found he was still brooding about that meeting. Just as they had begun to ease into the rhythms of their old friendship, Raggs had introduced him to Derek Cardew. Hawk didn't understand why he had felt betrayed when he saw them together. Was he jealous? Of course not: Hawk shook his head vehemently as they walked along. Both men had in their own way tried to seduce him. So what? It wasn't because of *that* that he felt hurt. So why?

Hawk sneaked a look at Irena, striding by his side, as if afraid she could read his thoughts. She seemed as happy as the surging crowd, was almost panting in the dark. Her bright red jumper flashed beneath her coat. Hawk opened his mouth to speak, but found there was nothing he wanted to say. Memories dominated his thoughts. It was not as if Cardew had stolen Peter Raggs from him – though he had stolen . . . something. Hawk tried to brush the idea aside. He remembered that terrible evening years ago, when Cardew tried to kiss him in his room. Hawk had had no idea what was in Cardew's mind. He really had thought of Derek as a friend. But the illusion had been destroyed. Years later at the concert, Cardew had managed it again; another illusion de-

243

stroyed. It wasn't important, Hawk told himself, that Raggs was gay; a surprise, nothing more. What did it matter? Anyway, Hawk never could picture any of his friends – anyone he knew – engaged, actually engaged in the extraordinary act of sex. Not physically *doing* it. Hawk found it impossible to imagine *any* coupled entwined naked, performing that grotesque act.

He glanced suddenly at Irena – tried to visualise her with her husband . . . He could not picture it. No image came. He could not imagine Irena making love with Al Kazan – nor with anyone. With himself? He shook his head. He was continually shaking it, he realised, shaking off the thoughts he did not like. If Irena had been watching him, instead of watching all these people converging on the park, she might have thought him pestered by mosquitoes. But she wasn't looking at him. She had him by the hand, that was enough.

No, he couldn't imagine Irena . . . Yet somehow it *was* possible to imagine Cardew – almost as if he and Hawk, or . . . Hawk realised that he was shaking his head again, because when he imagined Cardew coupled with Raggs, literally *coupled* with him, Raggs became lost to him. The boy he remembered did not exist. Memory was false, it had betrayed him all these years.

Hawk dragged his mind back from that unsettling meeting by the river. Tonight would be different. Those polite, tepid celebrations outside the Festival Hall bore no resemblance to this laughing throng, this smell of hot dogs and onions, these shrieking children scampering among the crowd. Arriving at the park, everyone shuffled cheerfully forward with admission money in their fists. Irena, warmly wrapped, bright-eyed, squeezed Tim Hawk's hand – like any other girl with her young man. Hawk and Irena, young and blond, camouflaged in the crowd.

At the barrier, Hawk paid to let them in.

With a great cheer from the crowd the fireworks begin: a burst of crackers, and a barrage of rockets into the sky, then Roman Candles and coloured smoke. Flittering through the fluorescent glow, dark shadows unleash more displays: whizzing Catherine

Wheels, fizzing rockets, whirling windmills of spitting fire. As each starburst explodes, the crowd gives a ragged cheer. They clap the shimmering tableaux, the ship of light firing balls of phosphorous, the fiery train on glowing wheels, the cartoon face in flickering flame. All the ground-based fireworks are seen through mists of pastel-coloured smoke. Only the high rockets flare fantastically against clear night sky. Yet in the few pauses between set-pieces the crowd grows instantly restless, shuffling their feet on the cold hard ground until another dazzling cannonade has them cheering again in the dark.

Irena is more excited than the children − who, like gleeful goblins, dash between stolid adults, clutching legs, pulling faces, pausing only for fresh bright lights and deafening bangs. Irena watches everything − her upturned face washed in coloured light. She clings to Hawk's arm, she chatters in his ear. After a while she asks if, below that dry, sharp scent of detonated fireworks, he can detect the sweeter smell of baked potato. Can they have one? Soon, he says, when the display has reached its climax. It will not be long.

Al Kazan barged into the front hall of his house, shouting for those who were not there. Cecille waited till he subsided − till he accepted they were alone.

'Goddam fireworks! *I* was taking her.'

'They've started.'

'It ain't even eight o'clock.'

'It was seven for seven thirty. Fireworks are for kiddies, you know? They go to bed early.'

'I've had a *pig* of a day.'

'Tell me about it.'

He caught a breath − glared at her. 'Watcher mean − tell *you* about it? Why would I tell you?'

She threw her hands wide. 'Have it your way. If you want to yell at someone −'

'Yell? Listen − Shit, I come home, what happens? You tell me my wife's out gallivanting with Tim Hawk.'

'You have worse problems.'

'The pair of them at the goddam fireworks – which *I* was gonna take her to –'

'You listening to me, Kazan?'

Al stopped, his mouth still open. 'What you say?'

'Hawk took her away so she'd be safe.'

'Safe? Safe! What is this?'

'Darren's gunning for you.'

'Darren? Darren's dead.'

'Mrs Darren.'

He gaped at her. 'Mrs Darren? I should give a shit.'

'I guess you should.'

'Get outta here,' Al almost smiled.

Cecille said, 'And the Darren gang.'

Al paused, Cecille said, 'While Hawk looks after Irena, I have to look after *you*.'

Kazan hesitated. 'Wait a minute. It's *your* job to look after my wife. Why the hell is she with Hawk?'

'She wanted to see the fireworks.'

'She don't need Hawk for that.'

Cecille shrugged. 'He thinks this is where they'll hit.'

'Here? You're joking.'

'Who'll stop them?'

He paused. She could see him thinking. He muttered, 'There was no one on the gate.'

She nodded. 'Man told your wife he was sick.'

'And goddam Louis has disappeared.'

'Yeah? And Leyton Knox has changed sides.'

Al's mouth dropped.

She said, 'Pig of a day, right?'

He glanced around the hall. 'Who else is here?'

'No one.' Which confirmed what he had guessed.

'So what am I supposed to do – leave the house empty?'

'You're the boss. You decide.'

'You trying to be clever?'

'I just do what I am told.'

He jabbed a finger at her. 'I didn't like you from the start. How do I know this ain't a set-up?'

'You think I'm going to kill you?'

He shrugged. 'Whatever.'

'I'd have killed you already.' She stared at him.

He found it hard to hold her gaze. 'I ain't no ordinary man – don't you forget that.'

'I ain't no ordinary woman.'

He paused. She might be right. For the first time since he came in, Al did not speak to her aggressively. He sounded almost plaintive. 'I'm supposed to just walk away from my house – leave it open and unguarded?'

She spoke quietly too. 'You have a choice?'

Whatever he was about to say, he thought better of it. 'Anyone could come in.'

'Not anyone. No burglar will touch *your* house.'

'But these Darren guys . . .'

'Yeah?'

'I let them walk in my empty house and wreck it? I do not believe this shit. Where's my wife?'

'In safe hands.'

'That goddam Hawk?' He whirled round on her. 'She's *my* wife, ain't she? If she needs a man's safe hands, she turns to me!'

The last blazing tableau lit the words 'Thank You For Coming' in coloured fireworks. As they began to fade, a bank of whirling Catherine Wheels began, and a last fusillade of rockets shot high into the sky. When the audience started to applaud, a pack of wolf-cubs marched into the arena with flaming torches in their hands. They approached the mountainous dark bonfire and surrounded it. Their flaming torches shed pools of light. The boys stepped closer, dipped their torches, lit the base of prepared tinder. Flames whooshed, ran up the sides. Timber crackled. The entire twenty-feet stack came alive with petrol-assisted fire. The sound in the arena was as if people in the crowd had simultaneously let out a breath. Darkness melted in the glare. A million

247

fragments of blackened paper floated up to dance crazily in orange smoke.

'There he is,' Irena breathed.

On the peak of the flaming pile, Guy Fawkes sat precariously on a broken kitchen chair. Flames rushed towards him, surrounded him, seemed to leave him there unsinged. A moment later, the timber shifted, his chair tilted, he slipped sideways at a drunken angle, then collapsed. A shower of sparks sprayed above what was now his funeral pyre. For one final moment, the shape of the dummy hovered above the bonfire – then it vanished, became a part of it, was discarded rubbish to be burned.

Once, in a distant land, a boy named Sergei had set light to three haystacks. On the anniversary of independence, he lit beacons. But his fellow villagers did not rejoice: food was scarce and the Russians had not moved away. The farmer whose ricks were burned knew who it was had set them burning. He saw the crop he had tended in summer reduced to blackened ash. He knelt in the acrid embers and the smoke made tears trickle down his cheeks.

Most farmers in the neighbourhood might have called on the boy's father for retribution: a thrashing for the boy, money for the corn. But Sergei had neither money nor a father, and the angry farmer knew that the winter would be long and cold. He suffered from sciatica. The boy, although studious, was strong.

Perhaps the farmer did not realise what would happen. Perhaps he thought that the soldiers would punish the boy in the way that a father might have done. But when he reported it, the Russians saw Sergei's wilful arson as an act of treason; they knew the anniversary and its significance; they guessed how the boy might boast of what he'd done.

To punish him would not be enough, the whole village had to understand. The Russians held a brief trial in the village hall, then led the boy to the dusty square. It was a sultry day.

The village school overlooked the square and the three teachers inside tried to keep the students at their books. But when orders rapped out in the morning air, the teachers could not stop the children quitting their desks and crowding by the windows, jostling for a view. Irena did not watch. Later, when she did look out, she saw the young body in the silent square. One or two people hovered in shadows at the edge, but most had left for home. Because Sergei was an orphan, no one considered it their duty to care for him, and when Irena walked alone into that empty square, she half-expected the crack of rifle fire again. But not a sound was heard, not a single sound. In that heavy late summer season, even the birds no longer sang. Irena knelt in silence over Sergei. He had been a clever boy – quick, ambitious – such hopes there had been for him. But he lay in the yellow dust as lifeless as the hard-packed ground. She closed his eyes and wept for him.

Now on the night of November the fifth in England, Irena felt the heat of a bonfire on her face, and smelt the smoke. As the blaze began to settle, she snuggled close and squeezed Tim's hand. She waited for an answering squeeze.

Al didn't walk. Though it wasn't a mile down to the park he took the Daimler. Because everyone was inside the ground, the roads were relatively empty. But there was nowhere he could park. Cars were solid along the kerb. Beside the park were No Parking cones. Al couldn't see the sense of it. Here was the best place for parking and the cops had coned it off. Too close to the park. Too convenient. Too goddam easy for the motorist.

Al drove to the entrance gates. The hell with it, let the idiots stick a ticket on his car. Half the time they ignored the Daimler anyway – thought it belonged to some celebrity or civic bigshot, such as that one: at the park gateway a big black Rolls stood gleaming in the darkness, the chauffeur ignoring traffic cones. Al drew up immediately behind it, leapt out, made for the gate. From a handful of police around the entrance, two moved to intercept. But he brushed them aside, saying, 'Goddam mayor's behind his schedule.'

One of the cops made as if to grab him, but his colleague touched his arm, 'I know that face.'

'Yeah – who is it?'

249

'Trying to place him. Must be all right.'

'You think?'

'Well, it *is* a Daimler.'

Irena wanted her baked potato. She and Tim queued at a stand in the fragrant darkness, another young couple holding hands. Here, the smell of potato was overwhelming – burnt and buttery, spiced with smoke. The queue of people chattered to their neighbours, stamped their cold feet in the dark. Accents varied from middle-class Greenwich – which Irena considered standard English – to the hard, back-of-the-mouth Deptford, which she found quaint. To her, these were the two accents of Dickensian London – the accent of teachers, lawyers and gentleman's families contrasted with the warm slang of urchins, street-gangs and fantabulous low characters.

While she clutched Tim's hand, Irena watched the animated faces, listened to their chatter. This was the England she had looked forward to. Her usual evening indoors – pleasant, quiet, unexciting – were like scenes Dickens set in middle-class Victorian homes. Life and vigour in the great man's novels were found outside those solid doors. Yet the odd thing, she thought, queuing patiently with Tim Hawk, was that Alexei and Tim and all their people ought to resemble the low characters he described – ought to have been bouncing with outrageous life. But they seemed as respectable as the Chuzzlewits, as Mr Brownlow, as John Jarndyce in *Bleak House*. What had happened to life's tang?

Kazan pushes through the crowd, one eye watering from smoke, his swarthy skin like a gypsy in the night. He is not the only person searching through the throng; anxious mothers and fed-up fathers wander around the bonfire, looking for their lost ones. But most gaze at the fire itself, have its orange warmth roast their faces, study the patterns in the flames. Above their heads, distant rockets burst in the sky from smaller celebrations elsewhere.

'I even missed the goddam fireworks,' Kazan mutters. His eye is still watering.

250

A group of small children rushes towards him, blind to un-known adults in the dark. They scamper round his legs, surround him, run off laughing toward the fire. Kazan pauses briefly, curses, stands his ground. Slowly he turns full circle, peering into the grey mass of people, strangers everyone.

With his back to the settling bonfire, his collar raised against the chill, he calls softly, 'Where are you, Princess?'

They were holding potatoes, piping hot.

'These are like the bonfire,' she said. 'See how they smoke.'

'Steam.'

'I know the word, silly. But a potato is – oh, now I *have* lost the word – you make me forget, Tim – it is a *furnace* in our hands. It is so hot it may hurt my tongue.'

'You'd better be careful.'

They had moved away from the potato stall to stroll among the crowds in the dark trampled field. Occasional rockets flared overhead like silent shooting stars in the night. The bonfire had subsided further – it was still burning, was still a comforting warm glow, but was watched now by only pockets of spectators. The smell of smoke had faded beneath more pungent aromas of sausages, onions, baked potatoes, and the bonfire's heat was barely noticeable – there was more heat from the hot food stands, islands in the swirling currents of drifting people.

'Now I *have* burnt my tongue. Oh, I always eat too fast.'

'I warned you.'

She laughed at him, plunged her face again in the steaming flesh. 'I eat the edges where it is not so hot.'

'You'll be sorry.'

'I am never sorry.' She watched Hawk curiously as he picked at the potato with his fingers. 'You are a fussy eater, aren't you, Tim?'

'No.'

'You are. I remember watching you eating scones. What is the word? Dainty.'

He frowned and glanced away. She nudged his arm. 'You

should *enjoy* your food – like this.' Again she plunged her face in the hot potato, only to spring back, crying, 'Hot – it is still so hot!'

Specks of white clung to her lips, and her eyes streamed as Irena laughed. 'My poor tongue,' she spluttered. 'I have burnt a hole in it.'

One hand clung to Tim's arm. 'Oh, look at me. Has my tongue turned fiery red? Do I look ridiculous?'

'No.' He smiled as if she were a child.

'Please look to see. Examine me please, doctor.' She squeezed his arm, tossed away the remains of her potato, came closer, put out her tongue.

Tim glanced at it. 'Looks fine to me.'

'You did not look properly. Oh, throw away that potato!' She took his wrist, shook it to make him release the food. She kept hold of both his arms, swayed closer so their bodies touched. 'Now look again.' She opened her mouth, showing her pink moist tongue.

He had to move his head back so he could focus. 'Nothing there.'

'But it hurts so, Tim. I need medicine, I think.'

'Medicine?'

She gripped his arms and she pouted at him. 'Don't you *want* to kiss me, Tim?'

He hesitated, nonplussed. When he moved to kiss her cheek, she forestalled him. Her mouth fastened on his lips. He felt the surprising wet warmth of it, her tongue thrusting between his teeth, the sudden flush right through his body. He smelt her perfume, felt her hair. He felt the way she slipped one hand behind his back, ran her fingers into his hair. His eyes were wide with astonishment. So he closed them.

When they broke apart – and it was she who broke, because Tim had never had the initiative – she said, 'There. That was not so bad, was it?'

'No.'

'Did I surprise you, Tim?'

'Yes.'

252

She pulled a face. 'I don't think you like me, Tim.'

'Of course I like you. I think . . .'

Her eyes were fixed on him. She could have been twenty years older than him – an experienced woman initiating a young boy. 'You think what? You must tell me, Tim.'

He smiled uncertainly.

She asked, 'Have you noticed how often I say your name? Tim: I like the sound it makes. I like the way that the name Tim makes me press my tongue against my teeth – oh, my poor tongue, it needs more medicine, Tim.' She gave a devastating glance. 'And you hardly ever use my name.' She stroked his arm.

'Yes I –'

'What the hell you at?'

Al Kazan erupted at their side, glaring like a bull escaped its pen. 'What's going on?'

Hawk gaped at him. Irena said, 'Alexei! You have come home.'

'Yeah, and the damn place was empty.'

'You were too late for the fireworks. I asked Tim to keep me safe.'

'Safe?'

Hawk stared at him intently. How much had Kazan seen? He had arrived – what? – ten seconds after their kiss: he must have seen it.

'Goddam safe from what?'

No, it was more than ten seconds, twenty. Perhaps he had come too late.

Al turned to him. 'Everyone's run out on me. Is that right?'

Hawk shrugged.

'What's the matter with you, Hawk?'

Hawk asked, 'You've been to the house?'

'Yeah. The goddam black chick gave some crap about Leyton Knox was gonna raid it.'

Irena interrupted. 'Are we in danger?'

Kazan answered her: 'No danger, Princess. Just a little trouble with my business.'

She was not persuaded. 'What is this trouble, Tim?'

Al exploded. 'Since when the fuck is *he* running things?'

'Alexei! Such language.'

He waved a hand at her and continued after Hawk. 'You got this black chick working for you – tries to get me out the house?'

'It's where they'll come for you.'

'Where'd you get this shit?'

'Alexei!'

'From Leyton Knox.'

'Knox – that shit-arse?'

'Alexei!'

'He tried to buy me.'

'You believe what that punk says? That black bastard is on *their* side.'

'I still believe him.'

Al's eyes glittered in the dark. 'Yeah, you never could tell your mouth from your arse, boy, that's been your trouble.'

'Alexei!'

He spun round on her. 'Keep your trap shut, understand?' His gaze flickered. 'It's for you own good, Princess.'

Hawk hovered in the entrance to the park. Scores of homebound spectators streamed past the patch of shadow where he stood into the road. In it, Al Kazan was arguing furiously with two policemen and a light-haired giant in a T-shirt and anorak. Behind Kazan's Daimler at the kerb stood an unmarked van with engine running. A man stepped out of it carrying a heavy yellow clamp. He grinned eagerly, showing prominent teeth, like a squirrel cracking nuts. By this time, Kazan had ripped the ticket from behind his wiper and was trying to remove a notice gummed across his windscreen. It warned him, as if he didn't know, that not only was his Daimler parked illegally but that it was shortly to be clamped and towed away. He would have none of it. 'That goddam junk stuck on, I can't see to drive.'

'It's parked illegally –'

'I don't give a shit about that shit!' Kazan glared at the T-

254

shirted giant as if the man had not been twice his size, as if he could crumple him like the parking ticket. But the two policemen shouldered their way between them and eased the big man aside. So Kazan started on them. 'How'm I suppose to drive it? This is goddam vandalism here.'

Hawk tried to merge into the shadow. Beneath his jacket he felt the weight of his handgun. He must avoid the Law, yet if he walked away, Kazan was bound to call after him, to summon him to help. From his anonymous vantage point, Hawk watched Irena insinuate herself with the policemen, smiling at them, soothing, cooing about stress. Meanwhile the smaller, grinning, squirrel-faced man muttered in T-shirt's ear, stepped forward with his clamp. Al whirled at him. A policeman touched his shoulder and Al spun back.

Hawk closed his eyes and opened them, as if by doing that he could change channels, get a better picture. He saw Irena slide between the policeman and her husband, saw the grinning clamper kneel by the car, saw the way the crowd lingered.

A separate argument now started between the clamper and a cop as to whether a clamp could be fitted after the car-owner had arrived to drive away. Squirrel maintained that once the vehicle had been ticketed, he was obliged to apply the clamp. No, said the policeman, not if the driver had reappeared. T-shirt supported Squirrel, declaring that once an operation had been started . . .

There was still nobody on the gate. Unchallenged, Hawk walked into Kazan's garden and approached the house. The front door opened. 'I saw you coming,' Cecille said.

'Glad you're awake.'

'You think I was gonna settle down and watch TV? Where's Irena?'

'Trying to save Al from being arrested. They want to clamp his Daimler.'

'That should make his night. You coming in?'

In the hall, she said, 'I'll ask this only once, Hawk.' She paused. 'Why are we doing this for Kazan?'

255

Hawk chewed his lip. 'This is where I have to be. And you?'

Her eyes gave nothing away. 'It's what I'm paid to do.'

Hawk grimaced. 'Maybe you ought to get out while you can.'

'Yeah, I'd sleep easy if I left you in the shit.'

She was still staring at him. Then she stomped into the sitting-room, calling him to follow. Inside the room the lamps were already off. She said, 'Choose a window, Hawk.'

After three minutes they saw Kazan's Daimler swing through the gate. Half the sticky notice had been scratched off the glass. When the car stopped, Al bounced out, ran for the steps, before he stopped. He turned, saw Irena was stepping out, then turned back, clumped up the little steps, rammed his key in the front door.

'Man ain't happy,' Cecille whispered.

While she slipped across the darkened room, Hawk waited at the window. Cecille flicked on the room light and opened the door into the hall. 'Hi there, Mr K.'

He did not reply. Hawk waited alone in the sitting-room while she went out to fetch Irena. Here they are, Hawk thought, could both get killed, and the Kazans decide it's time to have a spat. He felt depressed. He felt flat. He had none of the nervous tension that he needed. He felt tired.

He heard Irena chatting to Cecille, and their voices echoed in the hall. The door opened. Al stared at him. 'What you doing here?'

Hawk felt too tired to reply.

'Where the hell did you disappear?'

Hawk's voice was almost slurred. 'I didn't want to mix with the police.'

Al stared at him. Hawk stared back. After a while, Hawk said, 'I see you've still got your car.'

Irena entered from the hall. Without turning, Al said, 'Stay outside.'

She said, 'It's me, Alexei, not Cecille.'

'I said outside.'

256

Irena frowned at Hawk across Kazan's shoulder, but he was past reacting. She shook her head and left the room.

Silence hung suspended till Al said, 'Spit it out.'

'Spit what out?'

'Don't fuck about.'

With a shrug, Hawk said. 'Ask the questions and I'll answer.'

Kazan glared at him: Hawk could not be bothered to wonder why. His mind turned slowly, like an old engine winding down. Perhaps Al *had* seen him kiss Irena, perhaps he didn't trust him about Mrs Darren, perhaps he was still fuming about the car. Hawk waited.

Kazan said, 'I asked you once. What the fuck are you doing here?'

Hawk inhaled. The air was stuffy. 'I told you. The Darren boys are coming after you.'

'You should've killed the cow.'

Hawk shrugged.

Al said, 'You think the old man's lost his grip, don't you? You think that now I'm married I got a hard cock and a soft brain. Am I right? Yeah, you think you can take over, push the old man out the way. The only difference between you and those other shit-heads, Hawk, is that you got the nerve to come and face me. I don't know if that means you got more guts or that you're just more stupid.'

'Finished?'

Al jabbed a finger, arm extended. 'Don't try talking back to me. D'you think I ain't had it to *here* with your prissy lectures? What can you tell *me*? I raised you, boy, I taught you how to think. Now I'll teach you one last thing, I am the boss round here, you ain't. I call the tricks, you don't. Got that?'

Hawk nodded slowly.

'So sod off outta here.'

Hawk shrugged, made for the door. He said, 'When you need me, give me a call.'

257

24

Outside in the dark, Hawk sat brooding in his van. Al refused to understand the trouble he was in; he would not accept it. With his men deserting all around him, he rejected Hawk to stand alone. Kazan's instructions were quite clear, he had ordered Hawk from the house, expected him to drive away. Then what would happen? If tonight was the night, he would be hit. Most nights he stayed home, so this was where the Darren gang would come to find him. Simple, wasn't it?

Hawk stopped. He raised his head to listen. When he rolled the van window down he heard voices in the darkness. Someone laughed, someone else called out a question. Though Hawk's eyes were now acclimatised to the dark, he could see no one in the garden. Quietly, he opened the van door, and when he walked across the unlit lawn his steps fell soft as shadows on the grass.

Now he began to make it out. In one of the other houses – what, two gardens along? – the family was outside. Each of these six big houses had large gardens. Two doors along was forty yards. Across the fence, between the trees, Hawk saw a sudden flare of flame. He heard a cheer. The family had come out for a bonfire party. Presumably they had made a pile of branches and garden refuse and that was what now blazed like an incendiary flare. In the flickering light across garden walls Hawk saw their heads and shoulders, the mushroom cloud of smoke, the family fireworks. Unlike during tonight's earlier civic festival, these went off one by one: two Catherine Wheels, a Roman Candle, several bangs. He heard a kid laugh at the explosions.

Hawk stood in Kazan's garden, hands deep in his trouser pockets, and exhaled a single breath. He didn't know what to do. Something whizzed in the other garden – another Catherine Wheel, he guessed. A child shrieked. It kept shrieking. Then Hawk realised it was not a child. The sound came from Kazan's house.

Hawk started towards it. He saw the front door jerk open, a shaft of light flood down the steps: Irena silhouetted. He saw her turn to yell angrily indoors. Kazan, beyond her, was yelling back. He raised his arm to hit her. Hawk found himself running towards them across the lawn. The door slammed and, as the light cut out, she disappeared. When Hawk reached the foot of the stone steps she reappeared in the gloom above. She had not seen him. She had her back to him, was staring at the door. When Hawk called her name she turned round.

For two seconds, neither moved. Then she rushed down the steps and flung herself at him. 'He has beaten me,' she said. 'It is your fault.'

On the dark doorstep they wrapped around each other like teenage lovers outside her home. Hawk could not have said anything if he had wanted to because she stopped him with a kiss. He stared across her shoulder, expecting that at any moment the front door would open, would pick them out in a shaft of light. He shook free, began to hurry the girl away. When she saw where his van stood waiting, she ran towards it, pulling him after her in the dark.

Hawk wanted to ask what had happened, but he heard an explosion from behind. A thunderflash at the bonfire party. She stared wide-eyed as he explained. 'A family fireworks party. Don't worry about it.'

'Take me away.'

In the kitchen, Cecille confronted Al Kazan. 'What the hell have you gone and done?'

'Get the fuck out.' Kazan opened the fridge, grabbed a vodka bottle.

259

'What did you do to Irena?'

'She's a bitch, and you knew it.' He pointed the bottle at Cecille before raising it to his lips. One fiery slug. He replaced the cap. 'That goddam Hawk.' When he smacked the bottle down on the table it was part of the single continuous movement that brought him round to face Cecille. 'Think I don't know?'

'Know what?'

'Your part in this.'

'I'm her bodyguard.'

Kazan snarled, raised his hand. The black bitch did not flinch, just stood there staring at him. He slammed his fist at her woolly head. Then he gagged. In one move Cecille had blocked his blow, stepped inside, gripped his throat with an iron hand. Her teeth were at his ear. 'Don't try that again.'

He tried to claw her hand free. She squeezed tighter, said, 'I wouldn't struggle.'

Trembling, eyes bulging, he dropped his hands. She relaxed her grip. 'Now listen,' she said, her hand still on his throat. Al stood shocked into stillness, her voice again at his ear. 'You get this straight. You listen. I'm here to protect you both. Hawk is the same. We do it because we get paid. You hear me?'

Kazan nodded. His face rubbed against her hair. For some stupid reason he was wondering whether this was what every black woman smelt like.

She said, 'You're wrong about Irena. She looks up to you. The girl is grateful because you pulled her out of the shit.'

But does she love me? he could not ask.

Cecille stepped away from him, left him alone. She said, 'Now I'm going to fetch your wife.'

The garden was alive with strange noises. Two houses along, the fireworks party was at its height, flames leaping in the air, kids shouting, fireworks popping and hissing, flickering light from the roaring flames, smoke drifting through the gardens.

Cecille glanced around Kazan's front lawns, saw the gate was hanging wide. She approached the unlit gateway from the side, stepped through to peep outside. No Irena. The dark private lane curved away among the trees. Where was the girl? Where the hell was Hawk?

Cecille quietly closed the gate, ran quickly round the far side of the house to the rear gardens. It was darker – still with the smell of smoke. She could hear the bonfire crackling, people laughing unaware. Cecille ran lightly through the gardens, calling Irena's name.

Hawk stared through the van windscreen, eyes fixed on the road ahead. Twice he had asked Irena to stop leaning on him – she prevented him changing gear. When they left Shooters Hill she started crying. It only lasted a few moments, as if she had suddenly been alone, but he was glad she did not continue. Tears made Hawk uncomfortable.

She asked, 'Where are we, Tim?'

'Blackheath.'

'Will you take me to your house?'

'It's a flat.'

Those were the last words the two exchanged till they had left Deptford for Rotherhithe. Only then, as the van sank into the tunnel, did she clutch his arm again. 'What is going to happen?'

Ahead of them in the tunnel, baleful white lights stretched overhead. Hawk wished there were some way he could avoid her question. He didn't know what Kazan would do, though at least if he came chasing for his wife he would escape that other confrontation at the house. Kazan could either wait for confrontation or chase after it, while Hawk, in turn, was doing what Knox had told him to, staying out of it, avoiding it, doing absolutely nothing.

'What d'you mean – she's disappeared?'

Cecille shrugged. 'Vanished. Not out there.'

'If she's with Hawk –'

Al did not want to talk to the black bitch. How come she was the only one that he had left? He turned away. Cecille said, 'Maybe she's out wandering the streets. I'll go look.'

'She can go to hell.'

Cecille looked at him. 'You too, mister.' She went out.

Irena thought Hawk looked as if he needed help. His face was grim, distracted, like a young boy on his first date. When he led her into his flat he headed immediately for the kitchen. 'I'll make coffee,' he said.

'Tim!'

He hesitated, his back towards her. For a moment Irena waited, her gaze concentrated between his shoulders as if she could *will* him towards her, could draw him in on an invisible cord. Then she ran to him. 'Hold me.' She flung herself at him, wrapped her arms about his neck, wet his face with tears and kisses. 'You must take that off,' she said.

It pressed hard against his body and, when they embraced, it stood between them like a rock.

'Your gun.' She placed her hand on it. 'You don't need to protect yourself from me.'

The trace of a smile dawned on his face. She said, 'Please take it off.'

He slipped out of his jacket, hesitated, hung it neatly across a chair. She smiled at the boy's fastidiousness. Then he removed the shoulder holster, hung it from a second chair. She said, 'It looks like a cowboy film in here.'

He removed the jacket from its chair and draped it across the other to hide the gun. 'I'm no cowboy,' he said.

'I am glad. They must have made rotten lovers, always in a hurry, travelling on. We are not in a hurry, are we, Tim?' He smiled uncertainly. 'Oh, it is warm,' she said. Suddenly she pulled the red sweater up to reveal her white shirt beneath. Just before her head disappeared inside the sweater, she grinned at him, and while her head stayed inside, Tim watched her breasts move in the cotton fabric. She flung the sweater on a chair, shook out her luxuriant blonde hair.

When she approached him, he said, 'This is the first place he'll come and look.'

'I don't think so,' she said firmly, though she feared it might be true. 'Does Alexei know that you live here?'

'He owns the place – gave it me.'

'He won't come. He doesn't want me any more.'

'Because he hit you? He loves you, Irena, he won't give you up.'

'Then we must run away.'

Tim smiled; she could be so naïve at times. 'That's not the answer.'

'But Tim –'

The phone rang, his little radio-phone. He looked hard in her eyes, then crossed to pick it up. They both guessed who it would be. Kazan said, 'OK, Hawk, where are you?'

'Why?'

'I need you here.'

'Didn't you just kick me out?'

'Cut it. Are you in the flat?'

Hawk couldn't avoid a slight hesitation. With his eyes on Irena, he said, 'Not yet. I'm still in the van.'

'Oh yeah? I can't hear the engine.'

'What do you want?'

'A straight answer: have you got Irena?'

'Isn't she with you?'

'Answer the goddam question.'

'No.' Hawk said it clearly, eyes still fixed on Kazan's wife. 'I have not got Irena. What happened?'

'She ran out. Women, you know? I need you here, Hawk.'

Tim paused. 'It's late.'

'Just get here.'

'Why?'

'What's with all these questions? If you're so sure they're gonna hit me, well, I need protection.'

'You didn't believe me.'

'Just get over here.'

Cecille jogs from the wooded lane into the road, peering into darkness. Up on Shooters Hill there are few side roads. Irena is

263

unlikely to have ventured onto the lonely golf course or to have strayed deeper into Oxleas Wood. She will not be in a neighbour's house.

Taking the run allows Cecille time to clear her head. She spits a gob of sweet phlegm into the gutter. Somehow she has got herself stuck on the wrong side of the argument. She is meant to be with Irena. She is paid to provide protection, like a police escort, but, like the Law, domestic disputes are not her responsibility. She has to stay out of stuff like that.

Now there is another battle, more serious. Hawk says that tonight Kazan will get hit. Already Kazan has lost a driver, he has no guard now on his gate and Leyton Knox has left him. But if Hawk is convinced this will be the night, he won't run away from it. If he's got Irena, he'll stash her and come back. That's right. Cecille and Hawk are both paid guns for Mr K. Hawk belongs here. When the chips are down, Cecille decides, she can rely on Hawk.

That's the theory. Yeah, the theory, Cecille mutters as she jogs along the road, but you really are stuck on the wrong side, defending this baboon. Why do it? You ought to keep on running, honey, run back to Bermondsey, find yourself a friend. Get your head down out of sight. Though you will be running out on your duty. Duty! She spits another gob of phlegm. The only duty she has now is to make sure Irena is out the way. She can't leave the kid up here if bullets are going to fly. Yes, that's the reason Cecille is searching, to make sure Irena has really gone.

Kazan was grinning, actually grinning, his teeth bared like a zealot whipped into righteous pain. He relished every lash. After that call to Hawk he tried four different employees: three weren't in, one pretended a wrong number. He dialled Hawk again, still grinning furiously. No answer – what, Hawk as well? Each time Al hit the phone, it bounced about on the hall table. He stabbed so hard he jammed a key. Al scooped up the flimsy handset, shook it, forced himself not to smash it down against the table. By now, Al was shouting random words. He was like a wino in the street, almost incoherent. If he did manage to get through, Hawk would struggle to understand his words. He hit a number, got the whine sound – unobtainable, had keyed it wrong. Holding the handset in the flat of his square palm, Al Kazan jabbed each key slowly and forcefully as if he were squashing a squad of ants. Once again he punched Hawk's number. Once again he heard it ring. Heard the number keep on ringing. Why didn't he goddam answer? Why wasn't he goddam there?

'Ignore it, Tim, don't answer.'

'But –'

'It is not a camera, you know. They cannot see that you are here.'

'You *know* who that is.'

'No.' She stood unmoving in his arms. 'I am not a camera either.' She forced her eyes to show amusement, tried to transfer the mood to him. She had not expected him to be tiresome. Each time she kissed him, he seemed distracted, removed from her. He responded, but nothing more. He was waiting for that phone to ring. Irena was determined he should not disappoint her. She pressed her bosom softly against his young chest, tried to create an atmosphere of intimacy, just the two of them, cut off, alone. She had made him turn the lights down, had said, 'Some music, Tim, play your special music.'

The phone stopped. 'Take it off the hook, then find your music. This is our private world.'

'He's gonna come for you.'

'Don't be silly, Tim.'

Hawk knew she wanted him to make love to her, but he also feared that once they started, Al would walk in through the door. Perhaps some men could cope with that. Hawk remembered Louis once telling him how he'd screwed a woman against the kitchen door, while all the time her husband had sat in the lounge playing poker with his friends. Louis had claimed it added to the excitement.

When she was a teacher, Irena had learned to deal with little boys. She took Hawk's hand. 'First the phone,' she said. He turned it off. 'Now the music.'

Cecille came in the front door, saw Al sitting on the stairs, the telephone in pieces at his feet. He looked up like a man bereaved. Neither of them asked their question: they saw the answer in each other's eyes. Cecille said, 'There's a Guy Fawkes party two doors along. You know the people?'

Kazan shrugged.

'She might be there,' Cecille said, and left.

As she slipped back into the night, she heard him say, 'Yeah, my wife likes fireworks.'

Cecille didn't believe Irena would be out there, but anything was better than staying indoors with Al Kazan. Besides, she was hot from jogging – inside was stuffy and warm, the air all used up. Cecille took a lungful of November darkness. She raised her head and saw no stars. High cloud cover. If she cared to wait for it, someone would surely send up a rocket, a brief spray of pretty stars. But she couldn't wait.

Silently, she ran to the side wall and climbed over. The intervening garden was empty. Cecille slipped across their lawn to the far wall where she could stand beneath an overhanging, broad spreading tree. The stone wall here was barely shoulder height, giving a clear view of the garden beyond. Cecille watched from deep shadow.

Their bonfire had died down, the party with it. Two white boys, about ten and twelve, poked the embers with sticks, raising sparks and occasional spurts of flame. Their father was fiddling with a last firework, while his wife waited with a younger child wrapped in a blanket in her arms. Both the child and its mother had tired faces. The child sucked its thumb. Beneath the tree, Cecille withdrew deeper as the father lit the fuse. 'Watch this last one,' he cried. 'Silver Rain.'

A bright fountain of white sparks gushed in the darkness, thousands of fizzing white specks surging upwards, arcing over, falling in cascades to the ground. It seemed to illuminate the whole

266

garden. Cecille ducked behind the wall, watched the flaring light bouncing among the branches of her tree. She held the memory of those faces, tired, bleached, unused to pagan celebrations in the night. The smoky fire's warmth had dried their voices. When the Silver Rain went out, she heard the family trundling back indoors. She heard the mother call to the son who stayed behind. She heard the french windows close.

Silence. Cecille decided she would wait there until Hawk came back.

She stood up again in the darkness, stretched, leant on the wall to gaze at the bonfire embers. The night was peaceful. Though the glowing fire transmitted no heat to her, she heard the sighs and crackles as it continued to burn. She smelled the smoke. For the next hour perhaps, that glow would gradually grow fainter until its light finally disappeared and there was nothing left but cooling ashes.

'I shall be honest with you,' Irena said. 'I will not go back to him until he begs me to. I will not let a husband beat me, never! So, there you are, I have left him. If you would like me to, Tim Hawk, I will stay with you. Do you want me to? Be honest.'

'Of course, but –'

'Ah.' She cut him off crisply, as if closing the lid of her school desk. 'You do not like me enough. Say no more about it.'

She raised her hand to silence him, turned to walk across the room. Perhaps that dismissal steadied him, because it was with a firmer voice that he said, 'I do like you, want you, I mean.'

She paused, kept her back to him.

'I know I didn't grab you, I didn't bundle you into bed, but that doesn't mean I . . . wasn't going to.'

She turned to face him, still silent.

'You see, Al is not just my boss . . .'

Hawk produced a weak smile. He and Irena stood ten feet apart in his starkly furnished room, the gentle baroque music turned down low. 'I couldn't steal his wife, just like that.'

'Ste-al?' she repeated, stretching the word out long.

267

'That's how I felt.'

'How you felt, or how you feel?' The schoolteacher again.

Tim paused. 'How I felt.'

Her expression did not change, except somewhere deep behind her eyes. Hawk continued, 'I'm the sort of man who finds it difficult to change.'

'No excuses, Tim Hawk.'

'No.'

They remained like statues, the baroque music pulsing quietly, until she said, 'Come to bed with me.'

He shook his head. 'Not tonight.'

'Why? Do you have a period?'

Hawk smiled, but still made no move. She stepped towards him. 'You are very difficult, you know.'

'So they say.'

'We will play a game,' Irena said. 'First is my turn, then yours.' She opened the collar of her shirt. 'One button at a time, you understand? Try it. It will not be difficult.'

Cecille was almost asleep. She had been watching the dying embers for so long that she could almost believe the feeble heat really did warm her face. Her eyes stung from smoke. Drowsy, she had not noticed the new sound from the wooded lane in front of the houses. She had not registered the sound of a car slowing to a halt. It was only the low voices that made her jump.

There were men at Kazan's gate. They rattled it gently, found it locked. As Cecille emerged from beneath the trees she saw movement. Her view was uninterrupted across the intervening garden through Kazan's to his outside front wall. A man was climbing over it from the lane. Cecille knew that if she dashed forward now, he could see her as easily as she saw him. She had to wait until he dropped inside the wall. Then she must wait while the others entered the same way. So she waited. Once all three were inside, once they had begun creeping towards the house, Cecille could begin her crouching run.

* * *

268

First they took off their boots, then they each undid shirt-buttons one by one. Irena, having fewer buttons, dropped her shirt first. She stood before him, erect and proud in a low-cut brassière, then undid the top button to her jeans. Hawk undid a shirt-button at his navel – the loose material gaping to reveal his chest. Irena tugged at the zip on her jeans. 'Wait,' she said. A slight shake, her body trembled, the heavy denim fell to the floor. She stepped out of them. Now she was dressed only in bra and panties. Tim undid the last of his shirt-buttons, but she raised a brow at him, and stood waiting. Casually, as if he were not really participating in the game, Tim slipped the shirt from off his shoulders, let if float away. She moved her hands behind her back to the hook on her brassière. The movement pulled her shoulders back, pushed her breasts forwards and upwards. She held that teasing moment, watching him, absorbing the shape and strength of his naked torso. The creamy white skin. The lean hardness of him. When Hawk's gaze flicked to her face, she let her tongue peep out and she licked her upper lip. Still she held her fingers on the hook. Then she unclipped it. Instantly, the bra lost its tautness, leaving its two cups draped like crumpled pennants across her breasts. She brought her hands slowly forwards, holding the soft material in place. In a tantalisingly slow movement she unpeeled the brassière from her breasts, pausing a moment before dropping it. She saw his eyes drawn to her nipples, pink on her flesh. He started forward. 'No,' she said. 'It is your turn now, your trousers.'

That nervous grin, she thought, was because the boy was shy with her. She watched him fumble with the fastening at the top of his dark trousers. He smiled at her and said, 'Button and zip – that's two separate goes. Your turn again.'

She placed her hands upon her panties, the only garment that she wore. 'Then I would finish before you. So you must catch up.'

He chuckled, a short gasp, and undid his zip. Why does a man always need two hands, she wondered, to undo a zip? He let the trousers fall, stepped out of them. She studied him, amused at

269

the way his tight black underpants struggled to contain his size. 'Excited?' she asked.

Once more it seemed to Irena that Tim Hawk seemed nonplussed, thrown by her teasing words. Or was it because she had command in this seduction? Was he inexperienced? She would soon find out. Irena stepped forward to end the first stage in their game.

Cecille waited behind the garden wall, peeping over its smooth stone top. She watched the men fan out: one for the front door, the two others round the side of the house, out of sight. Damn. But she guessed what they would do. The front door man leant his back against the house wall, did not make a sound, just checked his watch. He would be counting seconds. Cecille wanted to get closer. But the man was looking out across the front garden, he would notice a sudden movement. While he waited he slipped his hand inside his coat, brought out a pistol. She couldn't see the make, but it was a big boy. When the man had counted long enough, he turned to ring the front doorbell. He moved away from the door frame, and he kept his back to her. Cecille vaulted the stone wall. She plopped into the garden, soft as a bird. Then she crept silently toward him.

Irena astride Tim, leaning forward, breasts dangling in his face. Tim on the floor gazing up at her, hands creeping from her strong back to stroke her upper ribs. Irena shivering.

Tim's hands move onwards, along the sides of her soft breasts. Now he too is shivering. When he touches her firm nipples, she stretches upwards, sitting back from him, taking his eager hands and moving them in slow circles, letting him press her pliant breasts gently against her chest. Now she drops her hands, brings her body down against him. She squirms along his trunk, stroking, kissing his smooth pale skin. She has her hand on those tight underpants, she strokes him from outside. His back arches. She sits across his knees. Her fingers grip his elastic waistband. She unpeels the black material. She releases him.

* * *

270

Kazan's voice, tinny, sibilant, squawks brusquely from the entryphone, carries out across the garden. As the gunman leans to speak to him, Cecille begins her silent run. She holds a gun in her right hand, her little Browning 38. It has been tucked inside her top. Her eyes are trained on the whispering gunman. Through the wall-speaker Kazan squawks again, suspicion in his tone. While he is engaged with the unseen caller, Cecille guesses that the two others will force an entry round the side. He may not hear them. The man with his back towards her concentrates on Kazan. He never hears Cecille's soft footfall across the silent dark damp lawn. She doesn't let the man turn round: she doesn't want a sideways target. Thump. She fires a single savage bullet. It lands between his shoulderblades, one inch beside his spine. Without breaking her stride, Cecille runs lightly up the front steps, leans over the fallen body, shouts into the entryphone: 'Kazan, you better take cover! Two hit men are in the back.'

Tim and Irena roll naked across the carpet, taking turns to crawl on top. They wrestle. They laugh in each other's faces. While a counter tenor sings encouragement, Irena delays the moment Tim will enter her for their first time. Whenever he tries to pin her down, she tickles, she squirms away from him, she slithers across the floor. He cannot deal with her. If he tries to make her yield, she finds a new way to defeat him. He is prey to every trick of her mischievous femininity. He is growing mad for her. Which is what she wants. He cannot wait. Which is what she wants. He starts to use his young strength. Which is what she wants.

Kazan's hall is empty. The house seems to quiver with unnatural silence, a grenade without its pin. Cecille squats against a wall, watching internal doors. She knows the hitmen are inside. They'll have come in the house on the ground floor, and will be behind one of those doors.
Which one?
It has to be on the right, unless they came in through the back. Which is possible. Very possible. More likely, in fact. The *least*

likely room must be that one opposite at the front. They have to be somewhere at the back. Cecille inches towards the stairs so she will be out of their line of sight.

Where is Kazan?

Last time she heard his voice was on the entryphone. Cecille thinks about it. There are three mikes: one here, which he did not use; one in the kitchen, which seems unlikely; one upstairs. Kazan is hiding upstairs, the hitmen down here.

She should join Kazan upstairs, then he and she will have the high ground. If they can cover the stairs, the house is sealed. Yes, she should join the boss up there.

Cecille leans sideways to peer into the upstairs hall. Nothing. But if she slips silently up those stairs, and if Kazan's finger is waiting on the trigger, she could stop a bullet. If he sees a movement, he will fire. But if she calls up that she is coming, everyone else will hear. So far, the other two spiders don't know she's in the house.

It isn't safe to go upstairs. It isn't safe to stay in the hall. Where can she go? She can't risk the right side of the house, or the back, or upstairs. She could slip into Kazan's study. She could keep the door slightly open, and wait like a cat outside a mousehole – patient as a cat as well. It is now obvious to Cecille that they are *all* playing cat and mouse. Each player has found a secure spot to wait till someone else makes a move. Even if she slips into the study behind, there is a risk that in doing so she will make the only movement in the house. Cecille studies the two doors opposite: neither is open, not a crack.

So far, Cecille has been able to move freely in the hall. So far she has been careful. Keeping her eyes peeled for movement, Cecille inches along the wall to the study door. She puts her hand on the doorknobs, hopes the damn thing does not squeak. She turns it. Throughout the entire manoeuvre Cecille holds her Browning chin-high, pointing out across the hallway. Now she leans against the door, eases inside the darkened room.

The barrel of a gun rams against her cheek.

* * *

It is a triumph for both of them. Tim kneels above Irena like a jousting knight upon his charger. She, the white steed, nostrils flaring, waits for the charge. Finally she has captured this elusive blond-haired boy – this virginal young man who fascinated her from the start. Hawk bears down upon her, lies a moment on her breast, penetrates with a sigh. She feels a shudder through his body – fears for just one moment that he might have ejaculated instantly – but then knows from the strong thrusting stroke that their climax is yet to come.

Cecille is pulled into the room, the gun barrel at her head. She swivels. The man glaring at her through the gloom is Al Kazan. He says, 'Give.'

'Three of them: one at the front, two at the back. Two got inside.'

'How'd *you* get in?'

'Stopped the front man.' Her gun hand has dropped to her side, the pistol hidden behind her thigh. But Kazan nods at it. 'With that?'

'Yeah.'

'I heard. So it's you and me?'

'It's what I'm paid for. Not for talking.'

Before he moves his gun away, he hesitates, and when he does move it he seems unsure. Trusting her will be a risk. But Cecille whispers, 'Keep the door slightly open while we wait.'

Suddenly Hawk has lost every part of his reserve. He is ablaze with joy. For such a long time he has held himself tight-reined, has controlled how he behaves. Now he pounds wildly into Irena – this beautiful blonde, Irena – ecstatic, lost to everything, crying out with happiness. And Irena, adoring his sudden wildness, knows how uncontrolled he has become. Though she could lie back and let him storm into her, she wraps her legs around his back, she crushes him within; she keeps hold of him, restrains him, won't let this fairy-tale boy-lover leave her incomplete again.

* * *

273

Crash! The window shatters behind them. An explosion rocks the room. Cecille and Al Kazan leap apart, dive for the floor. A second explosion. Deafening. The floor shudders, as if a rock has smacked beside their heads. Cecille aims her Browning at the window, ensures her aim and fires. She fires a second time. She lies on her belly, feet apart, left hand against right wrist, elbows hard against the floor. She fires again, Something moves. She fires a fourth and final time. Kazan is firing too. He stops. A ringing silence. A thousand tiny echoes inside her head. Blackness outside the windows.

After a moment, Cecille asks what he can see.

'Nothing. But I got one bastard — I know I did.'

'Me too.'

'That's both then.'

'Maybe. Here's what we do: we dash for the window. You cover while I look outside.'

'OK.'

'Let's go.'

They reach the shattered window. Broken glass and cold night air. Cecille crouches, gun poised, below the corner of the window frame, while Al stoops at the other side. 'Take a peep,' he says.

'After you.'

'I'm paying.'

They stare at each other, master and employee. Al smiles faintly in the gloom. 'Here.' He lays his pistol on the floor, slips off his jacket, bundles and throws it low across the floor.

'Thanks.'

Cecille calmly counts to three: any more, she could lose her nerve. Then she tosses his crumpled jacket outside through the gaping window frame.

Nothing happens. No one fires at it. Either there is no one out there, or no one has fallen for her trick. Cecille tenses: now she has to put her head up above the parapet, take a peep, see and be seen. From her crouched position below the window, she suddenly bobs up, glances into darkness, bobs down again. Kazan waits beside her. She says, 'Couldn't see. Need a longer look.'

'Well, when you're ready.'

She nods grimly. She is about to move when the door bursts open. Gunfire crashes through the room. As she rolls sideways she sees the man framed for an instant, automatic rifle spitting fire. Cecille shoots. Kazan also. A brief crescendo of unsilenced guns.

The sudden quiet is filled with echo, like a rush of air. The man in the doorway hits the floor with a thud and sigh. He doesn't move. Cecille knows he's dead: she does not miss.

Al says, 'I got the bastard.'

'Yeah.'

'I'll need the decorators after this.'

Cecille wonders about the hit outside – is he dead or is he waiting? She does not allow herself time to think, simply vaults across the windowsill to land crouching on the ground. She glances about her, gun erect. Feels her shoulders slowly relax. Says, 'You can come out, Mr K.'

On the cold dark ground close beside Cecille the man lies as lifeless as Kazan's jacket. He lies on his back in a curiously twisted pose, as if he has fallen from a height. He looks as if he has been dead for quite a time.

Hawk could have been crying in his sleep. His breath was a series of broken gasps, as if a second, more languid climax convulsed his body. He and Irena had not moved from the carpet. Their clothes were in little heaps where they had been discarded. Music played.

Irena shifted on her side, rested her hand on his blond head. He smiled but did not open his eyes. She watched him, stroked his face, buried her fingers in his soft hair. She needed to touch some part of him to assuage the emptiness now he had gone. He stirred.

'You were falling asleep,' she said. 'That is hardly polite.'

'I was not.'

'Yes, you were.'

He smiled, reached out for her. Her irresistible white breasts lay inches from his face, and he cupped one in his hand, saw the nipple harden. It looked tender, vulnerable, as if his touch might bring it pain. To Hawk, Irena's dark pink nipples seemed the most intimate area of her body. He leant forward and kissed one, licked it, took it delicately in his mouth. His face burrowed in her soft white flesh. Irena's fingers were in his hair and her other hand stroked his spine. He began to harden. As he shifted on the floor he brushed against her, and he gasped. She slipped her hand from behind his back, entrapped him, and asked, 'Don't you have a bed here in this flat?'

Cecille trotted up the drive from the front gate. The night seemed darker now, and the air held a lingering smell of smoke. She came to where Kazan stood beside the body on the grass, and said, 'Car's empty. There were just the three.'

'We better lose them.'

'We can use their Cavalier.' Their tone was matter of fact, as if they had stepped out after dinner for a breath of air.

'They leave the keys in the dash?'

'No, I'll search their pockets. Got any gloves?'

'Gloves?' A faint breeze stirred.

'Sure. You touch his wallet, you leave a dab. Wool are best – let your fingers flex.'

'I don't wear *wool* gloves, for Chrissake. Maybe Irena . . .' Kazan stopped. He looked as if he suddenly felt cold in his dark garden.

Cecille nodded. 'Maybe she has. I'll go look.'

Irena lay beside Tim in his bed, thoughts racing through her head. This beautiful boy was so sweet, quite inexperienced, it seemed to her, but so eager, so young. She smiled. She must stop thinking like an older woman – she was only slightly older than Tim, yet he had such innocence in bed. Compared with Alexei, of course, he *was* innocent, was as innocent as little Sergei. Irena sighed. She had been aware from the start that sex with Alexei was the price she would have to pay for marriage and escape –

not an ordeal, not unpleasant, simply something that a wife did. At least this was not the time of Dickens, when young virgins often married older men. Louisa in *Hard Times* was just nineteen when she married Mr Bounderby – fifty-two years old: she married him without love. What must it have been like for such a frigid little virgin the first time she climbed into bed with her crude husband? Did he bring her pain or only disappointment? And what must it have been like for Bounderby, to have a beautiful unresponsive doll lying inert beneath his flesh, someone he had lusted after for years, but who now waited for him to stop so she could go to sleep? At least Irena had not behaved that way with Alexei. She had been fond of him, she still was; he was still her husband. So he had tried to beat her once – what of that? She was dependent on him. Without him as her husband she could not remain in England; she might be sent back to Ukraine.

Of course, she had always assumed that eventually she would be unfaithful to him – no, not unfaithful: the romantic dalliances she had anticipated with handsome Englishmen would not really be betrayals of her husband: merely games. She did honestly intend to stay with Alexei, to tend his body and his house, to repay her debt in full. Realistic faithfulness. Yet Alex had thrown her out. For what? For nothing. It was only afterwards that she gave him cause, by making love with sweet Tim Hawk. So it served foolish Alex right. Surely he would take her back? Of course he would. He had to, he loved her, he wanted her at his side. She needed *him* also, and was quite happy to be a wife to him at night and to appear daily at his side.

Alex must realise that she was much younger, that she would need occasional release. She ought to be allowed to spend a little time with people her own age. She would tell him that, he would understand. Of course, if Alexei persisted in imagining her jumping into bed with other men, it would be unfortunate. He would be wrong. She needed the *company* of her own age-group, that was all. One day Alexei would be dead, and what did he suppose she would do then if she had spent her life isolated with the old? She must explain this to him. Alexei would have to see that they had a bargain, one they could both enjoy. He did not need to be Mr Bounderby to her Louisa; he could be a proud husband to a young wife, in every way, not just for show. It was not as if Alex believed she was a virgin when he married her, he surely did not think that? Irena raised a hand to stifle an illicit smile, and the movement made Tim stir.

'This time you *were* asleep,' she said. He did not deny it, which was nice. Men always dozed after making love, and they always denied it.

'I was listening to your music,' she said. 'It is very elegant.'

Tim propped himself on his crumpled pillow and smiled. 'I like the trumpets best.' It was *Acis and Galatea*:

> Love sounds the alarm
> And fear is flying.

'Sorry I've nothing more romantic – pop, or strings or something.'

'*This* is romantic.' The tenor repeated his message, decorating that same phrase:

> Love sounds the alarm
> And fear is flying.

'Anyway,' she said, 'I do not like pop music much.'

'No?'

'The happy tunes are not about anything, they just jump up and down like a little girl in the playground. And the unhappy tunes are . . . bored, uninterested in life.'

> When beauty's the prize
> What mortal fears dying?

'I do like sad music – we have much sad music in Ukraine. We can cry with it, let it clean our hearts. Those pop tunes have no real emotion.'

> When beauty's the prize
> What mortal fears dying?

Tim said, 'It's beautiful, isn't it?'

'Yes, though it too has no emotion. It is just beautifully composed.'

'Well —'

'You have to admit, Tim, that this music does not stir your heart.'

He thought for a moment, but didn't know how to answer her. 'To me it's beautiful,' he said. 'It's everything I want.'

> Love sounds the alarm
> And fear is flying.
> When beauty's the prize
> What mortal fears dying?

Cecille parked the Cavalier in a quiet stretch on Maze Hill beside Greenwich Park. An expanse of flat grass disappeared in the night. At its northern horizon gleamed the lights of London across the Thames. Tower blocks above moving traffic. The warning beacons on Canary Wharf Tower pricked out its profile like a laser lighthouse.

Stored in the back of the Cavalier were two dead men. The third would not squeeze in. He lay on the floor behind her seat, covered with a rug.

Cecille stepped into the road, sniffed the damp night air, locked the car. As she walked away she changed her mind. She went back to the car, opened it, replaced the keys in the ignition. She made sure that all the little door-poppers were standing up. Then she closed the door and walked away. With any luck, some kids would come by and think the car looked easy. The kids would joy-ride a mile or two, leave lots of dabs, then stop somewhere quiet to see what was in the car. Bit of a shock. Dead funny. They'd hightail it good and sharp, leaving the Cavalier where they had dumped it, somewhere well away from Cecille. The idea grew on her. Maybe she should have left the car somewhere more populous.

A hundred yards back along Maze Hill, Kazan was waiting in

his Rover. She got in. 'Right,' Cecille said. 'Where now – back to the house?'

'No,' Kazan replied. 'Not just yet.'

He had gone silent on her again. Driving through the north of Deptford, parallel to the river, it would have been easy to believe he was mad at *her*. Kazan hunched over the padded steering-wheel as if they were in a dodgem at the fair. Fortunately, the roads were empty. Evelyn Street cut a swathe through the run-down district. The rain-dampened tarmac glistened dully in the street-lights and the few cars around seemed to be cruising on half power. The only bus looked empty.

As Kazan drove into the Rotherhithe Tunnel, Cecille closed her eyes. She hated this long, bent passage beneath the Thames – the continuous white neon strip overhead, the grimy white tiles, the oxygenless air. It was like being wheeled through an underground corridor in a hospital. There were no detours off the route, nothing to look forward to at the end. If Kazan were heading north, Cecille decided, he must be aiming for Mrs Darren and Joe Morgan up in Tottenham, to give back a sample of their medicine. But Kazan wouldn't tell her what was in his mind. Oh, no. Just sit in your seat, girl, and let the man drive.

At the tunnel exit he surprised her by not heading west. From Shoreditch they could have gone straight up to Tottenham via Dalston. But the man went east for the Isle of Dogs. What did he want there?

Kazan stopped suddenly at the kerbside. Double yellow line. 'Take it round the block,' he said. 'Come back and get me in five minutes.'

He stepped out into the road. Because the front cockpit of the Rover was too cramped for Cecille to slide across the gear knob, she climbed out as well. Across the roof of his car she asked if he might need a hand.

He paused, seemed to sneer at her. 'Oh, you wanna come along? Yeah, I bet. Guess you recognise the place?'

'No,' she said wearily. 'Not my manor, Mr K.'

It was true, though Kazan did not believe her. 'What – you ain't been here before?'

'That's right.'

'Go drive the car.'

Cecille walked round the front, slipped in behind the steering-wheel. Man's still paranoid, she thought. Who does he think I know round here? She had hardly cruised ten yards before she realised. She slammed the brakes. Tim Hawk. Cecille watched her boss in the rear-view mirror, saw the door that he ap-proached. Was that a bunch of keys in his hand or a gun? Cecille had the Rover halted. She saw Kazan glance along the street at her. Saw his dark frown. Saw him insert a key in the door then disappear.

Cecille leapt from the car, pelted back along the street. The door was shut, unmovable. On a panel to the right was a bank of buzzers for the entryphone. She read the names. There it was. She pressed the bell. Hawk. She pressed again, Hawk. She kept pressing, Hawk. Hawk. Hawk.

'What the hell –?'

'Do you think that you should answer?'

'Oh, it's just kids. It often happens.'

The buzzer stops. They breathe out. But it starts again.

Hawk sits up, swings his feet out of the bed. 'Trouble is,' he says lazily, 'kids think it's fun. They think anyone they don't recognise is stinking rich.' He has to talk above the buzzer.

Hawk walks naked from the bed, but he does not get far. As he reaches the bedroom door it crashes open in his face. He reels backwards. Al Kazan is in the door space and he holds a pistol in his hand. He points it at Hawk. Irena screams.

'Shuddup,' snarls Kazan. The buzzer is continuous.

'No!' Irena shouts, scrambling from the bed. 'Please, Alexei!'

She is naked, his wife. 'Get some clothes on.' Because his attention is on Hawk, Irena ignores what Kazan says. She runs forward. Kazan screams at her, face contorted, 'Stay still or I'll fucking kill you!'

She hesitates, aghast. Her husband's gun is aimed at *her*. From the incensed hatred in his face, he could at any moment start firing the gun convulsively. One shot won't be enough, he'll have to discharge every one.

Kazan glares furiously at Hawk. The buzzer changes from continuous to single bleeps – a distress signal. 'You are not gonna live,' Kazan declares. He moves to fire.

'One favour,' Hawk bursts in.

'Fucking favour do I owe you?'

'Don't do it in front of her.'

'Why not?' The buzzer's loud clangour seems to excite Kazan's fury. 'Let the bitch see what it means.'

'Let me put my trousers on.'

Kazan roars – a dragon's laugh. 'You're so fucking finnicky, ain't you, Hawk? Like a goddam pansy. You know what –'

'Please,' continues Hawk, reaching for the clothes draped on the chair. The buzzer stops.

'I thought once you *were* a pansy, you know that? Now I find you with my wife –'

Hawk fumbles with the clothes. He moves his jacket.

'No, you can die naked, boy. She can goddam –'

Hawk reaches his holster beneath the jacket. Kazan sees it. Hawk pulls his pistol from the chair and he spins across the floor. Kazan fires. He fires again.

Two jagged holes stab into Hawk's chest. Irena screams, begins to run. For a moment, as Hawk crumples against the wall, it is as if two blood-red carnations have flowered on his pale skin. But when Irena arrives, those little holes have become craters, pumping red larva from his core. Irena leans naked across his body. When she turns to face Kazan he wavers with his gun. 'I can't do it, you little bitch. Oh, Christ.' He aims the gun away from her in case his trigger finger starts to twitch. He cannot look at her. Gazing towards the ceiling, Kazan cries, 'How could you betray me, Princess? After what you meant? I always –'

The sudden shot from Hawk's pistol veers high. It catches him in the throat. Kazan does not fall. He reels backwards away from her, hands clutching in the air. Using both hands to hold Hawk's gun steady, Irena fires again.

The last Alexander Kazan saw of his young wife was as she knelt naked beside her lover, arms extended to aim the gun. Perhaps he never saw her. Perhaps he never saw the floor rush up to meet him. Perhaps he never felt the pain.

Irena placed the gun on the bedroom carpet, and calmly she stood up. She did not look at either man. From the pile of clothes on the upturned chair she found blouse, jeans and panties, and she began to put them on. She heard the buzzer restart but continued to dress. When she had finished, Irena walked into the living-room and collected her handbag and red sweater. At the main door leading from the flat she saw the entryphone. Its buzzing had become sporadic, as if whoever was calling had abandoned hope. Irena studied the unfamiliar device and pressed the grey button that protruded. She heard a voice. She pressed again. Almost to herself, she said, 'Cecille?'

'Jesus H Christ,' Cecille muttered. 'Who did what?'

Irena told her. She told the whole story in three short sentences. She would have elaborated, but Cecille grabbed hold of her and drew her against her breast. 'You poor kid,' Cecille said, stroking her tangled hair. 'Which gun did you use?'

Irena nodded to the pistol by Hawk's side. Cecille bent to pick it up, then paused. She leant closer against Hawk's face, as if to catch something he had said. She touched him and he sighed.

Irena instantly dropped to the floor beside Hawk's head. When she touched his cheek, he opened his blue eyes. Hawk made a further faint sound, as if he wanted to speak. But although his gaze moved between the women leaning over him, his eyes seemed unfocused, like a new-born babe.

Cecille pressed gently on his shoulder. 'Ssh, take it easy, honey. You ain't in heaven yet.'

283

She glanced across at Irena, looking stunned. 'Stay with him,' Cecille said. 'I'll call an ambulance.'

When Cecille returned, Hawk was no longer conscious. She thought he was probably not alive. 'Leave him now,' Cecille said. 'I want to help you get things straight.'

'Straight?' Irena looked dazed.

Cecille helped her to her feet, placed her hands firmly on her shoulders. 'Listen, Irena, you didn't kill no one, understand?'

'*Any*one,' Irena murmured.

Cecille frowned. 'Your husband shot Tim Hawk, but he didn't kill him, understand? That's why Hawk is still alive. Now, after your husband shot him, Hawk managed to get him back. Yes?'

Irena nodded. Cecille hoped it meant she understood. Cecille continued: 'If we're lucky, Hawk will live at least until the ambulance arrives. If not . . . well, maybe the autopsy will show that he didn't die straight away – that he did have time to shoot.'

Cecille was holding Hawk's pistol now, and was using her handkerchief to clean off the prints. Irena mumbled, 'Oh, I don't know.'

'Yes, you do know, honey. Yes, you do. Listen, this is what you and I saw happen, right? You and I. We were both here all the time.'

'They will not believe us.'

'Who'll tell them different?'

Irena stared into Cecille's face, then began to cry. 'Don't worry,' Irena said, dabbing at her eyes. 'These tears will soon be over, Cecille. I will be strong.'

'Good girl.' Cecille squeezed her shoulder. 'Good girl. It'll be all right. They will believe us, mark my words.'

'Perhaps it looks better if I do not dry my tears?'

'Right! That's my baby.' Cecille grinned. 'Listen, you're Al Kazan's widow – his only heir. You realise what that means? All you've got to do is play it the way I told you. D'you remember what I said?'

Irena nodded. 'I am good at lessons.'

284

Cecille smiled, reaching out to squeeze her once again. Irena moved forward, huddled into Cecille's arms. Cecille soothed her, saying, 'There, there, don't worry. I'll support you, babe. OK?'

Irena leant back, tried to smile at her through tears. 'OK.'

Cecille nodded. 'Just you and me, babe.' She reached down for Tim Hawk's hand and wrapped it round the gun. She was empty, dispassionate as a nurse as she fitted the gun butt into his palm.

Suddenly, Irena bent down towards him. 'He is still alive.'

His face was an astonishing grey-white, and his chest was a mess of blood. He stirred slightly, as if shifting in his sleep. He made a gargling sound, then stopped. The girls knelt beside him and Cecille removed the gun from his limp fingers. She said, 'Don't try to talk.'

Hawk moved his hand about an inch, and Irena seized it. He opened his eyes as if to look at her, and made that gargling sound again.

'Sergei,' Irena cried.

He made a slight movement of his head, coughed, lay still for another moment. Again he tried to speak. Irena stared into his face, but while she did so, Cecille saw fresh blood flow from his chest. The two women heard Hawk inhale like a draught in a rusty pipe. They saw his head jerk. They heard him whisper, 'Peter . . . listen . . . trumpets . . .' Then his head flopped suddenly forward and Hawk gave up trying to speak. He gave up trying to do anything.

Cecille reached to take the blonde girl's hand. Neither said a word. They sat on the floor beside Tim Hawk, waiting for the ambulance. It no longer mattered how long they had to wait.